Stone Junction

Stone Junction

AN ALCHEMICAL POTBOILER

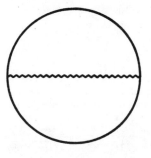

Jim Dodge

GROVE PRESS
NEW YORK

Published simultaneously in Canada
Printed in the United States of America

FIRST PAPERBACK EDITION

Library of Congress Cataloging-in-Publication Data
Dodge, Jim.
    Stone junction: an alchemical potboiler/Jim Dodge.
    ISBN 0-8021-3585-4
    I. Title.
    PS3554.0335S7   1990   813'.54—dc20   89-35587

Design by Laura Hammond Hough

Grove Press
841 Broadway
New York, NY 10003

98 99 00 01 10 9 8 7 6 5 4 3 2 1

To my brother, Bob,
whose courage and humor are a constant inspiration,
even if he catches fish like he catches cards.

My gratitude to the following people for their help, encouragement, and forbearance:

Victoria Stockley (first, foremost, and more), Patricia Sinclair, Leonard Charles, Lynn Millman, Richard Cortez Day, Jeremiah Gorsline, Gary Snyder, Freeman House, Jacoba, Jack Hitt, Melanie Jackson, Robert Funt, Jack Gilbert, T. J. Mullen, Jenny Berry, Morris Graves, Gary Fisketjon, and Anne Rumsey (tune and tone).

INTRODUCTION

Thomas Pynchon

IF WE ACCEPT THE NOTION THAT USING POWER AGAINST THE powerless is wrong, a clear enough set of corollaries begins to emerge. We become able to distinguish, as populations (though not always their rulers) have usually been able to do, between outlaws and evil-doers, between outlawry and sin. Not much analysis is needed, because it is something we can sense in all its dead-serious immediacy. "But all they are are bandits," the rulers whine indignantly, "motivated only by greed." Sure. Except that, having long known the difference between theft and restoration, we understand the terms of the deal whereby outlaws, as agents of the poor, being more skilled and knowledgeable in the arts of karmic readjustment, may charge no worse than an agent's fee, small enough to be acceptable to their clients, ample enough to cover the risks they have to take, and we always end up loving these folks, we cheer for Rob Roy, Jesse James, John Dillinger, at a level of passion usually reserved for sports affiliation.

Stone Junction is an outlaw epic for our own late era of corrupted romance and defective honor, with its own set of sleazy usurpers and Jacobitoid persistences—though the reader who's expecting eighties nostalgia or, have mercy, some even earlier-type romp through the pleasures of drugs, sex, and rock and roll, should be warned that lurking herein, representing the bleaker interests of that consensus ever throbbing along despite and apart from all the fun and pleased to call itself "Reality," are to be found some mighty evil contract personnel, who produce some disagreeably mortal plot developments. One of the book's manifold graces is its author's choice never to dance away into wistful gobbledygook, remaining, rather, conscientiously grounded in our world as given, where, as Pam Tillis, in a slightly different context, reminds us, Destiny turns on a dime.

The other day in the street I heard a city policeman in a police car, requesting over his loudspeaker that a civilian car blocking his way move aside and let him past, all the while addressing the driver of the car *personally, by name.* I was amazed at this, though people I tried to share it with only shrugged, assuming that of course the driver's name (along with height, weight and date of birth) had been obtained from the Motor Vehicle Department via satellite, as soon as the offending car's license number had been tapped into the terminal—so what?

Stone Junction was first published in 1989, toward the end of an era still innocent, in its way, of the cyberworld just ahead about to exponentially explode upon it. To be sure, there were already plenty of computers around then, but they were not quite so connected together as they were shortly to become. Data available these days to anybody were accessible then only to the Authorized, who didn't always know what they had or what to do with it. There was still room to wiggle—the Web was primitive country, inhabited only by a few rugged pioneers, half loco and wise to the smallest details of their terrain. Honor prevailed, laws were unwritten, outlaws, as yet undefinable, were few. The question had only begun to arise of how to avoid, or, preferably, escape altogether, the threat, indeed promise, of control without mercy that lay in wait down the comely vistas of freedom that computer-folk were imagining then—a question we are still asking. Where can you jump in the rig and head for any more—who's out there to grant us asylum? If we stay put, what is left to us that is not in some way tainted, coopted, and colonized, by the forces of Control, usually digital in nature? Does anybody know the way to William Gibson's "Republic of Desire?" Would they tell if they knew? So forth.

You will notice in *Stone Junction,* along with its gifts of prophecy, a consistent celebration of those areas of life that tend to remain cash-propelled and thus mostly beyond the reach of the digital. It may be nearly the only example of a *consciously* analog Novel. Writers since have been obliged to acknowledge and deal with the ubiquitous cyber-realities that come more and more to set, and at quite a finely chopped-up scale too, the terms of our lives, not to mention calling into question the very traditions of a single author and a story that proceeds one piece after another—a situation Jim Dodge back then must have seen coming down the freeway, because the novel, ever contrarian, keeps its faith in the persistence of at least a niche market—who knows, maybe even a deep human need—for modalities of life whose value lies in their having resisted and gone the other way, against the digital storm—that are likely, therefore, to include pursuits more honorable than otherwise.

One popular method of resistance was always just to keep moving—seeking, not a place to hide out, secure and fixed, but a state of dynamic ambiguity about where one might be at any given moment, along the lines of Heisenberg's uncertainty principle. Modern digital machines, however, managed quickly enough to focus the blurred ellipsoid of human freedom even more narrowly than Planck's Constant allows.

Equally difficult for those who might wish to proceed through life anonymously and without trace has been the continuing assault against the once-reliable refuge of the cash or non-plastic economy. There was a time not so long ago you could stroll down any major American avenue, collecting anonymous bank checks, get on some post office line, and send amounts in the range "hefty to whopping" anywhere, even overseas, no problem. Now it's down to $750 a pop, and shrinking. All to catch those Drug Dealers of course, nothing to do with the grim, simplex desire for more information, more control, lying at the heart of most exertions of power, whether governmental or corporate (if that's a distinction you believe in).

You look at Windows 95 blooming on to the screen, and you think, Magic. But for those who understand the system down to molecular level, nothing magical remains—all is revealed as simple repetitive drudgery, what we might even denounce as a squandering of precious operating time, were it not for Technology's discovery of how to tap into the velocity situation prevailing down at the smaller scales—*Nnggyyyyow-w-w*! like the Interstate down there!—and leave all the kazillions of brainless petty chores to their speedy new little devices.

Stone Junction's allegiance, however, is to the other kind of magic, the real stuff—long-practiced, all-out, contrary-to-fact, capital M Magic, not as adventitious spectacle, but as a pursued enterprise, in this very world we're stuck with, continuing to give off readings—analog indications—of being abroad and at work, somewhere out in it.

The fatal temptation for a fiction writer who must accept the presence, often a necessity, of magic in his own work, is to solve difficulties of plot, character and—more often than is generally suspected—taste, by conveniently flourishing some prop, some *ad hoc* amulet or drug, that will just take care of each problem as it arises. Fortunately for us here, Jim Dodge, by the terms of his calling, cannot indulge in that particular luxury. Magic is in fact hard and honorable work, and cannot be deployed at whim, nor without consequences. A good deal of Daniel Pearce's character growth comes by way of learning the business and earning the powers—making *Stone Junction* a sort of magician's *Bildungsroman*—in which teachers, more or less unorthodox in their methods, appear to Daniel one by one, each with particular skills to pass along, all linked in an organization known as AMO, the Alliance of Magicians and Outlaws, a proto-Web that tends to connect more by way of pay phones, mail drops and ESP than linked terminals, and overseen by the enigmatic, not quite all-powerful Volta.

Through all this meanwhile runs a second plotline—a whodunit, in which Daniel must solve the uncompromisingly earthly question of who murdered his mother, Annalee Pearce, in an alleyway in Livermore, California when he was fourteen, complete with multiple suspects, false trails, the identity of the killer not revealed till the final pages. The story traverses a map of some moral intricacy, sure-footed as Chandler, providing twists as elegant as Agatha Christie, as all the while Daniel's education proceeds.

Wild Bill Weber teaches meditation, fishing, waiting. Mott Stocker teaches Dope, its production and enjoyment. Ace safecracker Willie Clinton (yep) instructs the boy in how to get past all kinds of locks and alarms, rendering him thus semipermeable to certain protected parts of the world, setting him on his path to total dematerialization. For a while Daniel teams up with poker wizard Bad Bobby Sloane, roving the American highways in search of opportunities to risk capital in ways that cannot be officially controlled, climaxing in a legendary Lo-ball confrontation with the cheerfully louche Guido Caramba, in a literary poker passage as classic as it is funny, and in its appreciative devotion to a game where the moral stakes are so high, ranking up there with comparable parts of Kawabata's *The Master of Go*.

The shape-shifting genius Jean Bluer teaches Daniel the arts of disguise—another illicit skill, given that it's already forbidden to impersonate policemen, doctors, lawyers, financial advisors, and who knows what all besides, as if someday all varieties of disguise will be statutory offences, including Impersonating an Ordinary Citizen. At last Daniel comes circling back to Volta, by now also one of his prime suspects in Annalee's death, who teaches him the final secret of Invisibility. None of your secular Wellsian tricks with refractive indices and blood pigmentation here, but rather the well-known and time-honored arts of ceasing to be material.

At last Daniel is ready to set off on the metaphysical Quest all these teachers have been preparing him for, which now swiftly unfolds as an elaborate techno-caper, with a mysterious and otherworldly six-pound Diamond as its target. Too early in those days for keyboard dramas, emergency downloads, and cyber-fugues to relentless countdowns at the corner of the screen, the technology Daniel goes up against is mostly of the analog sort—optical surveillance, strain-gauge sensor grids and thermostatic alarms—his nondigital responses to which include nerve gas, plastique, and invisibility.

He takes the Diamond, and then the Diamond takes him. For it turns out to be a gateway to elsewhere, and Daniel's life's tale an account of the incarnation of a god, not the usual sort that ends up bringing aid and comfort to earthly powers, but that favorite of writers, the incorruptible wiseguy known to anthropologists as the Trickster, to working alchemists as Hermes, to card-players everywhere as the Joker. We don't learn this till the end of the story, by which point, knowing Daniel as we've come to, we are free to take it literally as a real transfiguration, or as a metaphor of spiritual enlightenment, or as a description of Daniel's unusually exalted state of mind as he prepares to cross, forever, the stone junction between Above and Below—by this point, all of these possibilities have become equally true, for we have been along on one of those indispensible literary journeys, taken nearly as far as Daniel—though it is for him to slip along across the last borderline, into what Wittgenstein once supposed cannot be spoken of, and upon which, as Eliphaz Levi advised us—after "To know, to will, to dare" as the last and greatest of the rules of Magic—we must keep silent.

Thomas Pynchon, 1997

One: AIR

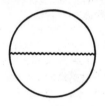

Unam est vas.
—Maria Prophetissa

DANIEL PEARSE WAS BORN ON THE RAINY DAWN OF March 15, 1966. He didn't receive a middle name because his mother, Annalee Faro Pearse, was exhausted from coming up with a first and last—especially the last. As near as she could figure, Daniel's father might have been any of seven men. Annalee decided on Daniel because it sounded strong, and she knew he'd need to be strong.

At Daniel's birth, Annalee was a sixteen-year-old ward of the Greenfield Home for Girls, an Iowa custodial institution administered by the Sisters of the Blessed Virgin. She had been placed there by court order after attempting to steal an ounce bar of silver from a jewelry-shop display case. She told the arresting officer she was an orphan of the moon, and told the judge that she didn't recognize the court's authority to make decisions about her life. She refused to cooperate beyond giving her name as Annalee Faro Pearse. The judge sentenced her to Greenfield till she was eighteen.

Her second month at Greenfield, Annalee confided her suspected pregnancy to one of her roommates. The next day she was called before Sister Bernadette, a small, severe woman of fifty with an office as meticulously spare as her heart, though not nearly as dour.

"Sit down," Sister Bernadette said. It was a command, not an offer.

Annalee sat down in the straight-back wooden chair in front of the desk.

Sister Bernadette stared at Annalee's face for half a minute, then shifted the gaze to her belly. A muscle twitched in the Sister's flaccid cheek. "I understand you are pregnant," she said evenly.

Annalee shifted her weight on the hard chair. "I think so."

"You were raped," Sister Bernadette almost whispered. "The child will be put up for adoption."

Annalee shook her head. "I wasn't raped. I was fucked by a man I loved. I liked it. I want the baby."

"And *who* is this *loving* father?"

"I don't know."

"You don't know." Sister Bernadette blinked slowly, folding her hands on the desk. "Is that because you never got his name, or because there's too many names to remember?"

Annalee hesitated a moment, then said firmly, "Both."

"So," Sister Bernadette nodded curtly, "you're a slut as well as a thief."

Blue eyes flashing, Annalee stood up.

"Sit down, slut," Sister Bernadette screamed, slamming the desk top with her open hands as she jumped to her feet. "I said *sit down!*"

Annalee, just under six feet tall and a little over 130 pounds, broke Sister Bernadette's jaw with her first punch, a roundhouse right with every bit of herself behind it.

Annalee spent three months alone in what the girls called "the blocks"—a row of tiny cinderblock sheds that had been used for smokehouses when Greenfield was a pig farm. Except for the series of ventilation slits high along the roofline, Annalee's room was windowless. Nor, with just a saggy cot and a toilet prone to clogging, were her quarters particularly well appointed. She received two meals a day, invariably thin soup, stale bread, and a withered apple. Once a week she was allowed a shower, and once monthly a visit to Greenfield's doctor, a retired physician deep in his dotage whose main diagnostic technique was having patients do jumping-jacks naked in his office.

For the first time in her life Annalee began a program of daily exercise, which did not include naked jumping-jacks for the doddering doctor. The exercise helped burn off the rancidity of confinement and answered some faint maternal intuition that she needed to be strong for this birth.

Annalee's regimen occupied about two hours a day. The rest of her time she daydreamed, long spiraling reveries. A week later she felt the baby move inside her for the first time, and her entire attention began a slow pivot inward. Using the spoon that came with her meals, working in the few minutes available between eating and the retrieval of her tray, she scratched what she'd learned into the cinderblock wall: "Life goes on."

When she returned to her dorm, she was welcomed as a heroine. Sister Bernadette was still eating through a straw, and it was rumored she was being transferred. Annalee didn't particularly care about Sister Bernadette's fate. She was worried about her own and her baby's. The new Mother Superior—Sister Christine, who the girls said was "cool"—told her that Sister Bernadette had decided not to press charges for assault.

"Why not?" Annalee demanded.

Surprised by Annalee's aggressive tone, Sister Christine sat up straighter at her desk. "Perhaps Sister Bernadette found some compassion in her heart."

"Only if you could find some in a mustard seed. And if there is any, it's not much."

Sister Christine said softly, "It saddens me to hear you say that. I've given my life to Christ because I believe in His Divinity and His Wisdom. Central to both, in the heart's quick, is the power of forgiveness."

Annalee leaned forward, conscious of her swelling girth. Just as softly, she said, "Sister, I've devoted half my life to survival because I've found life mean. Forgiveness is a waste of spirit because there's nothing to forgive. I believe in the wisdom of *what is* and the power of *right now*. I'm pregnant. I intend to keep the baby. It's my life and the only real power I have is taking responsibility for it. If you deny me that power, we go to war, hopefully on front pages and the six o'clock news. 'Pregnant Waif Sues Catholic Prison.' 'Little girl orphaned by murder/suicide of parents prays every night in tears: Please God, don't let them take my baby, she's all I have left.' Forgive me, Sister, but that's how it is."

Sister Christine, eyes bright with tears, reached across the desk and gently squeezed Annalee's shoulders. "Oh, I wish they were all like you. There are so many who must seek God; only a few whom God must find. I'll do what I can, but beyond Greenfield my influence is minimal. And I do think you should consider adoption, because you have no way to support the baby once you leave here—assuming by some miracle you're allowed to keep it here—no skills, no home, no family. If you think life is mean so far, try it with a kid. You'll end up a thirty-year-old waitress with hemorrhoids and a third husband, so depressed that drugs don't help, and a kid who hates your guts."

"How would you know?" Annalee said sharply.

"Because I've seen it so many times I can't even feel the heartbreak any more—or not until I meet someone like you, so strong, so real."

Annalee covered Sister Christine's hands with her own. "I'll make you a vow of my own: If you don't break my ass, I won't break your heart."

At the beginning of her last trimester, Annalee radiated a powerful and vital tranquility. Her roommates held her in awe. Their attitudes and touches softened. They made sure she had extra pillows and any food she desired. They asked her excitedly what it felt like. Annalee told them it felt like she was becoming someone else, and that it was the most amazing thing she could imagine.

The birth was without complications. Nineteen hours later, after the nurse had brought Daniel for his third feeding, Annalee swung out of bed, dressed quickly, and left the hospital with Daniel bundled in her arms.

It was drizzling outside, cold but not quite freezing. Annalee turned left and started down the street, looking for keys in ignitions. The drizzle thickened. She pulled the blanket closer around the child. "Okay, kid," she said, "here we go."

* * *

Letting the road rock the baby against her breast, Annalee sang along with Smiling Jack Ebbetts, the Singing Truck Driver, as they roared down I-80 West in the tuck-and-roll cab of his '49 Kenworth. Annalee had stolen a car five blocks from the hospital, but, deciding it was too risky to stay with for long, had ditched it near the Interstate and put out her thumb. In less than a minute Smiling Jack pulled over, and they were fifty miles gone before the engine had cooled on the stolen Ford.

Smiling Jack Ebbetts didn't haul freight. He made his living singing at truckstops and bars across the country, performing as it pleased him or finances required. He lived in the long-box trailer the Kenworth hauled. The trailer had a small kitchen, cozy living room, cramped shower and toilet, and two tiny bedrooms in the rear. The rig, Smiling Jack explained, represented a compromise between his homebody heart and his vagabond soul.

As good-humored as his name implied, Smiling Jack was in his late thirties. He had a faded IWW button on his Stetson's band and a pair of rolling dice on his belt buckle. Annalee liked him immediately. When he asked what she was doing on the road with such a young baby—"looks like he's barely dried off"—Annalee told her story. He sounded two long blasts on the airhorn when she recounted breaking Sister Bernadette's jaw.

"Well *all right!*" he crowed admiringly when she'd finished. "You got it straight as far as I'm concerned." He reached over and patted her shoulder. "You'll do fine. You got heart, you got brains, and you got the spirit to keep 'em glued together." He turned his attention back to the road. "You got any idea where you and this newborn fellow here are going?"

"California, I guess. I want to be warm."

"Got people there?"

"No."

"Any money?"

"No."

"I'm a mite depleted myself at the moment," Smiling Jack said, "but when we hit Lincoln I want to buy li'l Daniel here some duds for his birthday. Shirt and jeans and stuff. And some diapers."

"That's kind," Annalee told him, "but please don't spend what you can't afford."

Smiling Jack smiled. "If I don't spend it, how do I know what I can afford?"

Smiling Jack taught her some of the songs in his bottomless repertoire, and they practiced them together as they crossed Wyoming, down through Evans and Salt Lake City. They worked out harmonies as the big diesel hauled

6

them across the salt flats into Nevada, Daniel asleep between them on the seat, or nursing.

Annalee and Smiling Jack sang together three nights at a bar in Win- nemucca, followed by a weekend gig at a small club in Reno. Smiling Jack gave Annalee forty percent of the take and paid all expenses. When they crossed Donner Pass and dropped into California, Annalee had a used bassinet, an old stroller with bad wheel bearings, and seventy-five dollars in the pocket of her Salvation Army jeans.

They stopped that afternoon east of Sacramento, Annalee washing dia- pers at the laundromat while Smiling Jack changed the oil in the truck. Back on the road, Smiling Jack said, "I was thinking back there, all scrunched up under the rig and watching oil drip in the pan, that I might have a proposition for you and the boy. You see, I got this half-ass ranch way the hell and gone out Spring Ridge, which is about a hundred and fifty crow-miles north of 'Frisco, couple of miles inland from the coast. My uncle won it in a card game back in the thirties—four deuces against aces full. Not the dead mortal nuts, but like Uncle Dave said, good enough to take it all. Uncle Dave willed it to me when he cashed out five years ago. It's about two hundred acres, big ol' redwood cabin, clean air, good spring water. Nearest neighbor is seven miles of dirt road, so it's bound to cramp your social life, but it might be just the place to hunker down a spell till the wind drops, if you know what I mean. I can't stand the ranch because it's always in the same place and the taxes come right out my tank, so if you're interested, I'm in the mood to deal. Rent would be taxes and caretaking; stay as long as you want. The taxes are $297 a year, and they're already paid till next January. If you want to give it a shot, country life is great for kids. And if you're still there next time I come through, I might have a job that'll make you a little money. Till then, you'd be on your own. What do you say?"

"Thank you."

Smiling Jack laughed. "Hell's bells, you deserve it, sweetheart. Don't feel obliged."

Smiling Jack's Kenworth was too much for the narrow rutted road, so they walked the last mile to the ranch, taking turns carrying Daniel. Four spread deuces were nailed to the cabin door, the cards so sun-bleached they appeared blank. The cabin was festooned with spider webs and littered with woodrat droppings, but nothing a broom and scrub brush couldn't fix. The woodshed roof sagged under the weight of a thick limb a storm had torn from a nearby apple tree, but the shed itself contained three cords of seasoned oak. Smiling Jack showed her where the kerosene was stored and how to fill and trim the lamps, instructed her on using the woodstove and propane refrigera- tor, produced bedding from an old seaman's chest, and generally squared her away. Out on the back porch, in the warm sunlight, they shared a lunch of sourdough bread and cheese they'd purchased the previous evening in San Francisco. After lunch, Smiling Jack waved farewell and headed up the road toward his truck.

Daniel started to cry. Annalee unbuttoned her blouse and offered a breast. Daniel pushed it away and cried louder. Annalee was sixteen; Daniel, barely two weeks. It was April Fools' Day. She was somewhere in California, in a drafty, shake-roof cabin built by some shepherd in 1911, with nothing to eat but some bread, cheese, and a few rusty cans of pork and beans in the cupboard. She had sixty-seven dollars in her pocket. "You're right," she blurted to the bawling Daniel, and started crying, too. Then she got to work.

The cabin caulked and spotless, water hooked up, Annalee hitched to San Francisco with Daniel in her arms ten days later. It took them three rides and twelve hours. They spent the night in a Haight Street crash pad where a woman in her early twenties, who called herself Isis Parker, offered her a joint and the use of her father's American Express Card.

The next morning Annalee checked the *Chronicle* Want Ads under baby-sitters, made a few calls, settled on a woman with a sweet voice, caught the bus and delivered Daniel, then headed downtown to abuse Isis's father's credit card. She bought Daniel a whole shopping bag full of clothes. For herself, she chose a stylish tweed suit, matching bag and shoes, three pairs of hose, and a gray silk blouse.

That afternoon a middle-aged broker coming out of Bullock & Jones was stopped by a tall, lovely young woman—a girl, really—wearing an impeccably tailored suit. The young woman was clearly distraught. "Ex-excuse me," she stammered, "but . . . but my purse was just stolen and . . .," she faltered, blushing, then continued bravely, "I have to buy some sanitary napkins."

Bam. A hundred dollars an afternoon. She generally worked the financial district, taking care to choose well-dressed men in their fifties because they tended to cover their embarrassment with generosity. A few declined, usually just walking away without a word. One fainted. She never tried it on other women. They were too smart.

In all, it was the perfect nick, so good that even its clearest failure proved its greatest success. One crisp October afternoon she approached a tall, dapper man with graying hair as he left the Clift Hotel. He listened attentively to her plight, immediately reached for his wallet, and handed her a hundred-dollar bill. Annalee had never seen one before. She counted the zeros twice. "I'll bring you the change," she managed to say, thinking somehow she would.

"Nonsense." The man grinned. "You keep what's left after the Kotex—which I imagine will be a hundred dollars. It's an excellent hustle. Talent's rare these days, and deserves encouragement. Besides, I just won eight grand in a poker game and I like to keep the money moving."

"Well, go get 'em, cowboy," Annalee laughed. She was still laughing when she picked up Daniel.

She usually worked the city once a month. At first she just worked an afternoon, but after Daniel was weaned she'd leave him with a sitter for two or three days while she hit Montgomery Street and spent the evenings and nights with the young artists and revolutionaries in the Haight, smoking weed and drinking wine. She was attracted to poets and saxophone players, but hardly confined herself to their company. She never took any of them home.

Annalee and Daniel spent the rest of each month at the ranch. She'd bought a single-shot .22 with her earnings, and she occasionally killed a deer or wild pig, freezing what she could cram in the refrigerator's tiny box, drying or canning the rest. There was a large garden and a dozen chickens and ducks. The old orchard still produced, and nearby Cray Creek held small trout year-round, with salmon and steelhead arriving in the fall. She worked hard, but they lived well, buying the few things the land didn't provide.

Annalee spent the evenings reading library books her poet friends had recommended or playing the old guitar she'd found under the bed, making up songs for Daniel's amusement. *Song*, in fact, was his first word. But he was talking well enough to rush in excitedly and announce, "Mom, someone's coming," when Smiling Jack, three years late, finally returned.

Annalee and Jack greeted each other with whoops and hugs on the front porch. Smiling Jack had hardly changed—a touch more gray in his hair, the smile-wrinkles around his eyes perhaps more pronounced. But Annalee had changed immeasurably: At nineteen she looked strong, solid, and wild. Her movements carried a sense of ease and grace, and her eyes looked right at you. Smiling Jack was impressed. He held her at arm's length, declaring, "Sweet Lord o' God, girl, but if you ain't lookin' about nine hundred forty-seven percent better than the last time I seen you. You must take to this country living."

Annalee laughed, tossing her hair. She said to Daniel, who was standing in the doorway, "This is Smiling Jack Ebbetts, the man who let us stay here."

"Hi," Daniel said.

"It's a pleasure, Daniel." Smiling Jack offered his hand, which Daniel eyed hesitantly before shaking. "Doubt if you remember this crazy ol' double-clutcher, 'cause you hadn't made a month o' life when I swept you and your momma off the cold shoulder of I-80 right outside Des Moines and hauled you on out here to look after the Four Deuces, but I sure remember you and our long, sweet ride to the coast."

"I don't remember you," Daniel said.

"Not many folks remember very much from when they were babies."

"Yeah," Annalee said, "but when most people say they'll be back in a few months, they aren't three years late."

"Had to see if you were serious about making a go of it here."

Annalee folded her arms across her breasts. "We're still here."

"Naw," Smiling Jack waved dismissively, "I was joshing on that—never had a doubt. What happened was I got involved in all sorts of family stuff back in Florida, and then on my way back out here, I found a monster three-card monte game in Waco. Lost my truck seven times."

Annalee nodded. "And how many times did you win it back?"

"Eight or nine," Jack smiled hugely, "plus enough money to burn a wet mule."

"Well come on in," Annalee said, gesturing toward the door. "I'll help you count it."

Smiling Jack broached another proposition to Annalee when they'd finished lunch. "Me and some friends have a notion to use this place as a safe house, and—"

"What's a safe house?" Annalee interrupted.

"Just a fancy term for a hideout, I guess. A safe place."

"Running from the law?"

"Generally," Jack nodded. "Not always, though. Sometimes just resting."

"And the proposition?"

"I want you to run it. Take care of the people."

"Do you have eight or nine trucks really?" Daniel cut in, tugging at Smiling Jack's sleeve.

"No, pardner, just one. A '49 Kenworth diesel."

"I'd like to ride in it," Daniel said.

"You're on, but you're gonna have to wait a little bit. Right now your momma and me are doing some business negotiation."

"Okay," Daniel said. He went outside.

Smiling Jack turned back to Annalee. "You'd get a thousand dollars a month, plus free rent, whether the place is used or not—and most often it won't be."

"What sort of people will I be dealing with?"

"The very best." His voice promised it.

"What happens if somebody finds these people they're looking for? I don't want Daniel at any risk."

"I can't guarantee that. All I can tell you is that they won't be coming here till they're very cool. This will sort of be the next to last move, a staging stop while the final move is being set up."

"How much am I supposed to know about these people?"

Smiling Jack shrugged. "Whatever they tell you."

"And 'take care of them.' What exactly does that mean?"

"Shop, cook, keep 'em company if you feel like it."

"Mostly men?"

"I don't know."

"What about children?"

"Possibly. I really don't know."

"I couldn't do it for long. Daniel should start school in a few years."

Smiling Jack quit smiling. "You ain't gonna send him to school? There's nothing he's gonna learn there but how to get along with other kids under completely weird conditions. Right out that door is the best education in the world. But hell, you do what you think's best—don't listen to me. I'm a tar-ass reactionary on the subject. Had my way, no kid would learn an abstract word till they was ten years old. Wouldn't get their minds so gummed up."

"I'll think about school, but I can't promise we'll be staying. I'll do it for a thousand a month, two years for sure—but after that we're free to go."

Smiling Jack's smile returned. "Or free to stay. We can work out the details later. Just needed to know if you were interested. Wasn't presuming you would be, but I brought a load of lumber to build a little guest room down the hill. Three in here is a tad close."

"What would you have done if I'd said no?"

"Leave you be and find another place."

"And what makes you think I wouldn't betray these people in a cold second for two thousand bucks?"

"If I thought you'd sell 'em out for *two million*, I wouldn't be talking to you."

"Jack, if your criminal friends are half as sweet as you, I'll give you back the grand a month and call it even."

"*Outlaws*," Smiling Jack said. "Not criminals: *outlaws*. My friend Volta says there's an important difference. Outlaws only do wrong when they feel it's right; criminals only feel right when they're doing wrong."

That night, after Jack had left to sleep in his truck, Daniel asked Annalee, "Can we still live here?"

"Sure, and as long as we want. But we'll be having some company occasionally, friends of Jack's who'll be stopping by."

"He said they would be hiding."

"Well, *resting* really, waiting to move on."

"Why are they hiding?"

"Because they're outlaws."

"Are we outlaws?"

Annalee thought about it for a moment. "I suppose *I* am. As for you, that's something for you to decide when the time comes."

"When does the time come?"

Annalee slipped her tanned arm around Daniel's slender shoulders and hugged him against her hip. "You're a good kid, Daniel, but you've got to stop beating on me with all these questions that I can hardly answer for myself, much less you. There's all kinds of things you just have to figure out for yourself. That's half the fun of being alive."

"What's the rest?"

"Changing your mind."

"Is it as much fun as riding in Smiling Jack's truck?"

"Hey," Annalee said, tightening her grip, "fun's fun."

Four months after its completion, the guest cabin remained unused. Annalee, as promised, received a one-thousand-dollar check at the beginning of each month, drawn on the account of Orr Associates Trust Fund in Nashville. She cashed the checks in San Francisco and always stayed a few days to party. Such leaves from the post were permissible, Smiling Jack had assured her, providing she left a time and number where she could be reached. Smiling Jack gave her a "location line" to call when she planned to be away and a confirmation code for their calls.

Annalee used the kitchen phone at an all-night coffee shop on Grant, paying the cooks twenty dollars a month for the service. She happened to be there dunking doughnuts and discussing Japanese tea ceremonies with Japhy Ryder, a young poet of considerable charm, when Louie stuck his head out of the kitchen and called her to the phone.

"Hello," Annalee answered.

"Mrs. Ethelred?"

She recognized Smiling Jack's voice. The married name was the beginning of the confirmation code. "Yes, this is Mrs. Ethelred. And Daniel."

"Where did we buy the diapers?"

"Lincoln."

"Was I late getting back to you?"

"Thirty-two months."

"That's actually pretty quick for me. But I hope you can make it home a helluva lot faster than that. There's a duck on the pond. Sorry to do you like this the first time out, but things got screwy somewhere else and we had to make a hot switch. Your friend may be there waiting, or already gone."

Annalee had a vehicle now, an oil-guzzling '50 Ford flatbed, and she immediately picked up Daniel from the sitter's and drove back to the Four

had said when they reached the top of the knoll. He'd tilted his head back and groaned out, "Oh, blowing up dams is a *tremendous* responsibility, an *important* responsibility, a *grave* responsibility. . . ." And then he'd laughed like a loon, the sound echoing distantly across the flat and then lost in the hush of rain. He squeezed Daniel's hand and grinned at Annalee. "It's only at moments like this that I'm glad we're all going to die."

Seven Moons stayed seven months that first time, and visited for a week or two about four times a year after that. When eight months had passed since his last visit, Daniel began to worry.

When Smiling Jack showed up a month late for Christmas, Daniel asked if Seven Moons was back in prison. Smiling Jack didn't know, but promised he'd check on Seven Moons' whereabouts as soon as he had the chance. He cautioned Daniel it might take a while since Seven Moons wandered as he pleased—no phone, no address. Since Smiling Jack's colossal tardiness was the result of a similar temperament, Daniel didn't expect a speedy reply. A week after Jack's departure, there was a letter in the P.O. box when they went into town for supplies. Smiling Jack said Seven Moons was staying near Gaulala taking care of his mother, who'd been very sick but was getting better, yet he probably wouldn't get away until the fall. Without reason, Daniel was convinced he would never see Seven Moons again. When Annalee, concerned by his sudden and uncharacteristic moping, finally coaxed out his secret conviction, she suggested that he go visit Seven Moons in the spring.

Annalee was glad to help Daniel arrange the visit, which she hoped would last through the summer. If it could be worked out, then she'd ask Smiling Jack for a three-month vacation. She needed some unclaimed time. Running the safe house, while never unpleasant, had become increasingly boring. Daniel, with his sweet hunger for information and action, was inspiring, but he was also exhausting, and the random appearance of guests made it even more difficult for her to find and sustain a psychic rhythm of her own, an undistracted sense of herself. Annalee was particularly troubled by the recent onset of sexual desire for her son. She wasn't sure if the desire was simply a convenient focus for the heightened eroticism that had begun with the walk in the rain or whether it was something specific between them, or between all mothers and sons at Daniel's age, whirling in that prepubescent blur between boy and man. It didn't help that he was tall, lanky, blue-eyed and fine-spirited. Lately, the sight of him naked unsettled and confused her. Not that she would ever act on the desire. So it wasn't the fear of succumbing to temptation that bothered her so much as the distraction of dealing with it, and that's why she was so eager to send Daniel off to Seven Moons' summer camp that she used the location phone to leave Smiling Jack a message to get in touch as soon as possible.

She shouldn't have bothered. When she and Daniel returned from San

Francisco that night, Smiling Jack smiled at them from the kitchen table when they walked in. With him was a new guest, the first Jack had ever delivered, a striking man in his mid-thirties named Shamus Malloy. And everything changed.

Shamus Malloy was a professional smuggler, an alchemical metallurgist, a revolutionary thief, and—my goodness—a poet of more than modest accomplishment. At a trim six feet two he was slightly taller than Annalee, and, at thirty-six, ten years older. He had unruly hair the color of sandstone, intense blue eyes that hid nothing, and a resonant baritone voice that caressed long vowels and lightly rolled the *r*. What made his handsome presence unusual was the black glove he wore on his left hand.

Annalee was smitten.

Daniel was impressed and somewhat intimidated by Shamus's magnetic quality, but not enough to squelch his curiosity about the black glove. Annalee had always told him that if you want to know something, don't be afraid to ask, but Daniel knew by the way she was behaving—which was goofy—that she would get upset if he pressed Shamus about the glove. He had to be clever. He waited till Smiling Jack had departed and Annalee, who was sure tossing her hair out of her eyes a lot, was in the kitchen making tea, which she never drank. Then he casually inquired of Shamus, "How many falcons do you hunt?"

He was immediately sorry. Shamus fixed him with those direct, uncompromising blue eyes. The teakettle began a low banshee whistle in the kitchen, mounting toward a shriek before Annalee lifted it off the stove.

In the sudden silence Shamus said, "Daniel, what are we talking about?" His tone was pleasant, but tinged with both irritation and challenge.

Daniel could feel his mother listening. "Falcons," he said. "Mom and I spent a whole year studying birds of prey. Raptors is what that class of birds is called. Raptors. Isn't that an amazing word? Like rapture."

It didn't work. "Indeed—a lovely word. Directly from the Latin *raptor*, meaning snatcher, derived from the root *rapere*, to seize, which is also the source of both rapt and rape, seizures of two different kinds, since in one the recipient is transported into joy and in the other is violated and demeaned. But tell me, Daniel, how is this etymological exploration germane to your question about the number of falcons I hunt?"

Annalee came in from the kitchen then with the tea. The cups were on saucers. He was sunk. "Well," he began, trying for a tone of bewildered innocence, "that's a falconer's glove, isn't it?"

"No, Daniel, it isn't," Shamus said, his voice as cold and level as a frozen lake. "I wear it because my hand is disfigured, scarred from a burn."

"How did it happen?"

"I accidently spilled a vessel of molten silver."

"Do you always wear a glove?"

"Yes. Otherwise it attracts morbid attention, or revulsion, and a pity I find far more hideous than my hand."

"Do you take it off when—"

"Daniel!" Annalee lashed. "That's enough. You've gone from a tactless question to being plain rude."

He used bewildered innocence again, appealing to Shamus with dismay and a hint of contrition. "Was I being rude?"

"You were," Shamus said, then, added, "but I ascribed it more to cunning curiosity than thoughtlessness."

"Daniel wants to know everything," Annalee explained, her tone, Daniel noted with relief, fond and forgiving.

"I'm sorry," Daniel said to Shamus. "Seven Moons told me it's hard to know when to put yourself first."

Shamus smiled, blue eyes glittering in the lamplight. "Your gracious and elegant apology is warmly accepted." He leaned forward, opening his glove hand palm up in front of Daniel. "I want you to understand this, Daniel. My hand is horribly disfigured. The black glove is mysterious. I would rather inspire mystery than horror in the beholder's eye, and heart, and soul. That is my choice. If you don't respect it, you are not a friend."

"But maybe it would be better to just see it instead of imagining what it looks like."

"Maybe so. I clearly don't agree, given my choice."

"All right," Daniel said, leaving no doubt he meant it.

They stayed up late that first night, listening raptly as Shamus talked about precious metals, how and where they were mined, the processes of refinement, their colors, textures, properties, malleability and melting point, their importance in the parallel refinements and applications of human consciousness, their irreducible and essential purity—literally elemental. Both Daniel and Annalee were taken by his passion and eloquence, both excited and vaguely disturbed by the power of his appreciation, which seemed to vibrate between reverence and obsession.

After Shamus had gone down to the guest house, Daniel said to Annalee as she brushed her teeth, "You like him, don't you?"

Annalee rinsed and spit. "Yes," she said. "Extremely attracted."

"I thought so."

"And what made you think that?"

"The black glove."

Annalee laughed. "More likely the blue eyes."

"Yeah, but the black glove too."

"Good-looking, spirited, intelligent, emotionally alive, surrounded by an aura of mystery and danger—yes, I'm attracted."

Daniel thought for a moment. "Well, don't get too strange or he'll quit liking you."

"It shows, huh?"

"To me," Daniel said, "but I know how you really are."

Suddenly serious, Annalee said, "I wish I knew how I really was. That's something I really need to know, that I've gotten hungry to know this last year. I need some mystery and danger and dark, handsome strangers. Do you understand what I'm messing up saying?"

"I'm not sure. But it doesn't matter; it's your choice."

Annalee hugged him. "Daniel," she solemnly swore, "you are a joy to my soul."

The next evening, after explaining to Daniel that Shamus had invited her down to the guest house to discuss the alchemical properties of silver and gold, and that she hoped to be out quite late, Annalee waltzed out the door. Daniel was cooking some oatmeal when she floated back in the next morning.

"Oh no!" she declaimed, throwing a wrist to her forehead, "what a derelict mother, her lonely child starving as she frolics the night away."

"Boy," Daniel said, "you look happy. You must have really frolicked."

"We did. We built a castle and then we burned it down."

"Does that mean you made love?"

"For real and for sure. Tenderly and wildly. Sweet and scalding. Eye to eye and breath to breath."

Daniel nodded, not exactly sure what she meant but knowing she was pleased. When she paused, he said quickly, "Can I ask you something?"

"Sure," Annalee said, but it was a nervous permission.

"Did he take off his glove?"

"Nope."

Daniel nodded thoughtfully. "I didn't think so. Can I ask another question that may be rude?"

"Shoot," Annalee said, less nervous now than resigned.

"Did you *ask* him to take off his glove?"

"No."

"You like him a lot, don't you?"

"More every day," Annalee grinned.

More every night, too. She and Shamus began leaving as soon as the dinner dishes were done and not returning to the cabin till mid-morning. Daniel didn't mind the shift in her attention—he was honestly pleased to see her so happy. Though he still felt slightly overwhelmed by Shamus and his black glove, and wasn't sure if his respect was based on admiration or fear, he did like Shamus, and more so when Annalee elicited a playfulness that Daniel hadn't suspected. Annalee, however, worried that Daniel was feeling neglected, and after the fifth night of sexual rampage suggested to Shamus that they should spend an evening with Daniel.

"We'd better," Shamus had replied, nuzzling her shoulder, "or I will not survive what was supposed to be a time of contemplative rest."

The next evening after dinner Shamus joined their study of their temporarily abandoned subject for the year, which was, loosely, American history and culture—or "how it was in the old days," as Daniel put it. The current text, barely begun, was *The Adventures of Huckleberry Finn*. They took turns reading aloud, stopping at the end of each scene to ask questions or offer comments. Shamus even took notes in a red notebook he kept in his briefcase. His briefcase, like his black glove, was always there.

When Shamus finished his stint as reader, he wondered aloud if school ever recessed so that he might catch up on his notes.

"Good idea," Annalee said. "I'm hungry. You guys want some popcorn?"

"Two batches," Daniel said. "I'll melt the butter."

"Let's do it," Annalee said, squeezing Shamus's thigh as she got up from the couch.

"I have to pee first," Daniel said.

"Go," Annalee said. "Never resist the call of nature. It strains the organs."

"She's a wise woman, your mother," Shamus said to Daniel, looking at Annalee.

Daniel came back in almost immediately. "Hey, I hear a helicopter coming."

"Fuck!" Shamus hissed. He shoved his notebook into the briefcase, extracting, as if by some magical exchange, a Colt 9 mm. automatic. "Let's go," he said calmly. "Right now or we're dead."

Daniel grabbed his coat from the rack. As he hustled to put it on, a sleeve whipped the kerosene lamp off the end table. The lamp shattered, instantly bursting into flame.

"Now!" Shamus commanded, flinging him toward the door. Annalee grabbed Daniel and they sprinted toward the flat, Shamus right behind them, the helicopter suddenly louder as it came over the ridge. They plunged downhill at the flat's edge, following a runoff ravine, the water shallow but numbingly cold. They could hear the helicopter swing over, the pulsing mechanical chop like the heartbeat of a frenzied locust. Annalee in the lead, Daniel between her and Shamus, they headed downhill toward the South Fork, battling a passage through the ferns and gooseberries and redwood suckers.

They rested a moment at the creek. Shamus panted "Coast?" Annalee nodded, and they each took one of Daniel's hands and forded the creek, the water shallow but swift, the rocks slippery. In moments they were gasping up the steep eastern slope of Seaview Ridge. Daniel felt like he was burning and freezing at the same time. Mindless, breathless, falling down and getting back up, he scrambled for the top.

They collapsed at the crest, huddling against the trunk of an ancient bay laurel, heaving for breath. Across the canyon, flames from their cabin paled the stars. At the edge of the flames they could make out six or seven vehicles, red lights blinking. With a strangled sob, Annalee began weeping. Shamus put his arm around her and pulled her close. "Just as well. Leave them ashes. You could have never gone back anyway."

Annalee tried to slug him, all her fear and rage and grief gathered into the blow. She was in too close and Shamus, feeling her weight shift as she drew back her fist, caught it with his forearm. He grabbed her wrist and held it for a second before pulling it toward his chest, bringing Annalee's face to his. "I'm sorry, Annalee. Even though it's the truth, it was a crass and thoughtless remark. I forgot it was your life. I'll try never to let it happen again. Your life—and Daniel's—matter to me."

Annalee sighed raggedly, then wiped her face. "Do I have time to cry?"

"Survival says no; love says forever."

"Mom," Daniel said, "do you think you can still love someone when you're dead?"

Annalee wasn't sure if it was an innocent question or not. "I don't know."

"We want the nearest bar or café or motel from here," Shamus said. "Without being seen."

"Three miles south," Annalee said. "Tough ones."

Shamus asked Daniel, "You got three miles left?"

"I think I do."

"Let's vanish then," Shamus said.

They followed the ridge line for almost a mile, then angled downhill until they saw the occasional flash of headlights on the highway. They traveled parallel to the road for another half mile, keeping to the trees, then descended abruptly into the Shell Cove Inn parking lot. Shamus hotwired a '59 Impala and they took off for San Francisco, heater on full blast.

Shamus stopped at a gas station in Santa Rosa and made a call from a pay phone, then drove them south to a wrecking yard on the outskirts of San Rafael. There he introduced them to José and Maria Concepción. Maria loaded them into an old Chevy panel truck while José wheeled the Impala into the wrecking yard for some fast midnight dismantling. Maria whipped them across the Golden Gate and into her warm Mission District apartment, replaced their wet clothes with luxurious terrycloth robes from the hotel where she worked part-time as a maid, and filled their bellies with a spicy menudo.

When they woke the next morning, José was there with with a suitcase full of clothes for each of them. When they had dressed, he drove them to an airstrip near Sacramento and turned them over to a pilot who flew them to Salt Lake City in his battered old Beechcraft while regaling Daniel with tales of World War II dogfights in the clouds over France.

A thin, hawk-faced man was waiting for them at the landing strip near the Great Salt Lake with new driver's licenses for Shamus and Annalee (now James and Maybelline Wyatt), credit cards in the same name, four thousand dollars in cash, and a '71 Buick registered to Mrs. Wyatt. He told them to drive to Dubuque, Iowa, and make a phone call to the number he provided. It wasn't until the three of them were alone in the Buick and moving east that they finally caught up with themselves. Shamus tried to explain what he thought was going on.

, Three weeks earlier, after eighteen months of meticulous planning, Shamus had attempted to steal some uranium-235 from a Tennessee refinery. When Shamus slithered through the hole he'd cut in the cyclone fence, a guard who wasn't supposed to be there called halt, but Shamus clubbed him with his flashlight just as the guard pulled his gun. It went off harmlessly, but the shot brought security at full alarm. A searchlight pinned him to the ground. He kicked the guard's gun away, pulling his own when they started shooting. He took a wild shot at the searchlight, missed, instantly understood he didn't have a chance in a gunfight, rolled to his left as a burst of automatic rifle fire geysered dust behind him, rolled again, and came up running. Using the dust cloud for cover, he sprinted for the nearest building.

He got lucky twice in a row. The first piece of good fortune was a bullet that grazed his lower lip, so close it raised a blister but didn't break the skin. The second break was a rumpled old man walking toward the parking lot, oblivious to the probing searchlight and bursts of gunfire, so lost to the moment that when Shamus pressed the gun barrel to the back of the old man's head and told him, "Get in the car and go," he'd turned around and said, puzzled, "Escargot?"

Finding a hostage, however obtuse, wasn't the end of Shamus's luck, for the old man who drove him through the front gate with a gun at his head was Gerhard von Trakl, Father of Fission and the ranking nuclear scientist in America. Shamus intended to keep von Trakl only until they reached the getaway car, the first of three switches he'd already set up.

But to Shamus's wild surprise, von Trakl begged to go along. He told Shamus that he was a virtual prisoner of the U.S. government and was no longer interested in the work they wanted done. He wanted to explore the other side of the equation, the conversion of energy into mass, and ultimately, he supposed, the obliteration of the distinction. He confided to Shamus that he'd made a fundamental scientific error in his career—he'd viewed the universe as a machine instead of a thought.

While Shamus was delighted to discover that the most brilliant physicist in the country was a fellow alchemist at heart, he knew that von Trakl's employers would never stop looking for him till the old man was returned. But von Trakl refused to be freed, and for reasons Shamus honored.

Shamus compromised. He kept von Trakl through the first car switch, but a mile from the second switch Shamus pulled over and forced von Trakl out on the empty country road. He promised von Trakl he'd leave the car a mile up the road, wished him luck with his new research, and thanked him for his company, then fried rubber as von Trakl started to reply.

A mile down the road he exchanged the car for the dirt bike he'd stashed the day before. He gunned the dirt bike up the hill. He cut the engine at the crest and coasted down the long, gradual slope into Coon Creek Valley. He abandoned the bike in a dense stand of hickory, covering it with the camo netting he'd pulled off the battered Gimmy pickup he'd hidden there earlier in the week. But when he reached to open the truck's door, a laconic voice behind him said, "Ain't none of my business, friend, but less'n my scanner done fucked *all up,* they'll have a roadblock at the end of the valley 'fore you can fart the first bar o' 'Dixie.' Be my suggestion to ride with ol' Silas Goldean here, seeing as how me and most of the local law grew up together and get on fine, and they know I got a fondness for going over to the res'vor this time of night and soaking a doughball for them catfish. Got a good place for ya to ride, too."

And so Shamus went through the roadblock curled up in a cramped compartment under the backseat of Silas's dusty Packard sedan while Silas jawed with a sheriff's deputy about a turkey shoot early next month to raise money for the local Grange. Silas's second cousin was waiting at the reservoir in a funky johnboat to ferry him over to another cousin who locked him in a camper and drove all night to an airstrip south of Nashville. A cross-country flight punctuated with what seemed like twenty refueling stops eventually ended on Cummins Flat, two miles down the ridge from the Four Deuces, where Smiling Jack had picked him up.

Though Shamus found it difficult to believe, Gerhard von Trakl had evidently made his own escape, a fact that pleased Shamus immensely even though it meant personal grief. The Feds unfortunately assumed the daffy old bastard was still his captive and had poured on the heat—or as much as they could without causing undue media attention. They didn't seem to want *any,* in fact, since there hadn't been a hint in the press or on screen that the country's foremost nuclear physicist had been kidnapped inside the nation's largest facility for the production of fissionable materials—an understandable silence, as such information would not inspire the citizens' confidence or advance any political careers.

"But," Shamus said, bringing his story up to date, "somebody wasn't silent. Somebody had to tell them where to find me, because they did. When they turn up the heat, somebody burns, and then it all starts burning, collapsing as it's consumed. I can't tell you how sorry I am about your losses—your possessions, your home, the labor and heart you put into it."

"It's not the first time," Annalee assured him. "That's how we got to the Four Deuces, even though Daniel might not remember." She was driving, so had to prompt him with a quick glance over her shoulder, "Not that you *should.*"

But Daniel, who'd listened intently from the backseat, didn't want to talk about what he didn't remember. "How many people knew you were staying with us?"

Shamus responded without hesitation, obviously having given it some thought himself. "You, your mother, Smiling Jack, and the pilot, a young black guy named Everly Cleveland, Bro for short. Those are the ones I know for certain; there were probably others."

"The pilot betrayed you," Daniel said.

"Said with great certainty," Shamus noted. "Your evidence?"

"Mom and me wouldn't do it and neither would Smiling Jack. And besides, the pilot flew over two thousand miles with a bunch of stops, so the plane almost had to be noticed. See, that would be smart—to check the little airstrips."

"Yeah," Shamus sighed, "that's the most likely case, but who knows? If it was the pilot, though, I hope he turned me cold. Went straight to a pay phone and snitched me off."

"Why?" Daniel said, puzzled.

Shamus, who had turned around to face Daniel, shifted his gaze past Daniel and out the rear window, following the white line back to the horizon. Daniel didn't think Shamus was going to answer but Shamus suddenly snapped back to attention, his eyes boring into Daniel's as he said, "Because if he didn't turn me cold, they beat it out of him, and that puts his blood on my hands."

On a hand and a glove, Daniel thought. He didn't say it because something in Shamus's voice and eyes frightened him, something feverish and weak, something that fed on its own corruption, drew nourishment from its self-loathing and suffering, and Daniel wanted to leap away from Shamus's intimate guilt. He prefaced his question with a vague reassurance. "But you've got friends, too. Besides Mom and me, I mean. Somebody is helping you. Helping *us,* really. Who is it?"

Shamus glanced at Annalee, then back to Daniel. "You're sharp, Daniel. What one of my teachers called 'a good sense of what's going on inside what's going on.'"

Daniel shrugged off the praise. "It's pretty obvious that somebody is flying us around and giving us cars and money. And instructions."

"AMO," Shamus said.

Daniel didn't understand. "You mean like ammo for guns? Ammunition?"

"No, though the pun is suggestive. *Amo* as in the Latin *I love.*" Shamus reached backhanded along the front seat and lightly touched Annalee's neck with his right hand.

Annalee wanted to pull over and hold him in her arms and let him touch her just like that anywhere he wanted, the warmth of his bare fingertips at the base of her neck, the brush of soft leather on thigh, belly, nipples, throat.

She listened distractedly as he continued. "AMO is the acronym for Alliance of Magicians and Outlaws—or, as some members claim, Alchemists, Magicians, and Outlaws, which they contend was the original name. Another faction, small but vocal, insists AMO has always stood for Artists, Mythsingers, and Outriders. As you might sense, there is constant and long-standing contention about AMO's origins and development, a situation encouraged by the fact that the Alliance does not keep a private account of itself—all records must be public. Since AMO forbids nearly all direct reference to its principles and practices, the public accounts—books and music being the most available—are extremely oblique, hidden in images and the arc of metaphor.

"But whatever the true derivation of its name, AMO is a secret society—though more on the order of an open secret, in fact. Basically, AMO is a historical alliance of the mildly felonious, misfits, anarchists, shamans, earth mystics, gypsies, magicians, mad scientists, dreamers, and other socially marginal souls. I'm told it was originally organized to resist the pernicious influences of monotheism, especially Christianity, which attacked alchemy as pagan and drove it underground. From what I gather (I'm not a scholar on the subject), AMO has survived as an *extremely* loose international alliance of self-described moral outlaws and wild spirits. And though the alliance is so loose it's nebulous, the center is tight."

"What do you mean?" Daniel said.

"In each country or region, there's a seven-member council called the Star. Council members can serve up to forty years or resign at any point. Star members nominate potential successors, who must be approved by the other council members. I've never been sure exactly what the Star's job is beyond administration and special projects. Each Star member has a small field staff to assist her—and I use *her* because four of the seven Star members, by tradition, must be women."

"That's wise," Annalee nodded, glancing at Shamus long enough to flash a smile.

"Can *more* than four be women?" Daniel said.

"Yes—but not any fewer. That make sense?"

"I suppose," Daniel said, not so much lacking conviction as withholding judgment.

Without taking her eyes off the road, Annalee said, "I have a feeling that we were keeping house for AMO, right? That's who we've been working for?"

"Smiling Jack is a field assistant for Volta, one of the Star members, so I think that's a safe assumption. But they dislike the phrase *working for*. They prefer thinking of it as a natural alignment of mutual interests, and therefore an extension of the alliance."

"Well shit," Annalee said, "why not tell us? Or ask us to join?"

Shamus raised his hands in mock defense. "Don't ask me why they do what they do. The only policy I know about recruitment is that you're not supposed to approach people till they're ready, and then to tell them the truth. I would suspect in your case that there's some legal concern about Daniel, since you might be nailed for conspiracy if membership could be proven, and that's a harder fall. Also, members are supposed to donate five percent of their net income to the cause, so maybe they didn't want to lean on a single woman's purse. Besides, you spent enough time on the street to understand the wisdom of knowing no more than you need to."

Before Annalee could reply, Daniel leaned forward intently and said, "You keep saying *they*. Aren't you a member?"

"I was," Shamus said. "I quit."

"But they're still helping you."

Shamus sighed. "It's complicated. I started out as a smuggler. Cigarettes and watches at first, then drugs, then gold. Gold was the first thing I'd ever moved that moved *me*. The first bar I ever saw, it was like the sun rose in my blood. I was working out of Florida at the time, very young, ambitious, imaginative, with a talent for safely transporting contraband from point A to point B. I was reliable, I was discreet, and I was making lots of money. And unlike most smugglers, I didn't fling it away on drugs, racing boats, and high-flying women. I had fun, but at a level less extravagant than my income, because no matter how good you are, you can get unlucky.

"I'd got to the point where I had plenty of money and lots of doubt that my luck could hold, so I was thinking about getting out of the business when Red Lubbuck paid me a visit. Red was the main mover on the Gulf side, so naturally I assumed he wanted to talk business; I was surprised when he told me about AMO instead. It was, like Red himself, very straightforward: I could enjoy the benefits of alliance in return for the annual dues, five percent of my net, paid on my honor—no collectors, no audits, no questions asked. The benefits of alliance, according to Red—he went into detail, but I'll just mention them—were technical and legal assistance; a network of skilled and reliable people; the use of various facilities, from safe houses to machine shops; access to intelligence services, which Red claimed, correctly, were exceptional; and the possibility of using communal knowledge and educational opportunities to expand one's own talents.

"Red was persuasive without applying pressure, but I'd always worked independently and was thinking about retiring anyway, so there was no sense in joining an organization of strangers on vague promises of unusual opportunities and collective strength. I told Red I was flattered, but my answer was a friendly no thanks.

"My Boston Irish can't accommodate Red's Cracker twang, but I can quote his reply from memory: 'Hell son, we ain't interested in your smuggling. That's just an occupation, prone to go belly-up any time. What we'd like you to do is go study precious metals with Jacob Hind, who you probably never heard of, being young and unawares, but we think he's one helluva teacher, a flat-out *master*—forgotten more shit about precious metals than you'll ever learn. But Jacob Hind is pushing ninety. You'd be his last student.'

"That snared me. As mentioned, I was becoming increasingly taken with precious metals and nervous about smuggling. Smuggling, after all, is a job, and no matter the danger or reward, a job gets boring. So I joined AMO, and three months later I was on an island in Puget Sound, the lone and bewildered pupil of Jacob Hind."

"Was this like regular school?" Daniel wanted to know.

"Not like today's, no. If anything, it was plain old-fashioned master-apprentice."

Daniel poked Annalee's shoulder. "We just were reading about that a month ago, huh Mom?"

"We sure were," Annalee said. "But let Shamus finish his story."

"Was Jacob Hind a good teacher?" Daniel said to Shamus. Annalee wasn't sure if the question was meant to defy her or encourage Shamus to continue.

"A *good* teacher?" Shamus repeated thoughtfully. "It's a *good* question, even if I can't answer it. At first I thought he was completely loony, this daft old Dutch-English fool who lost control of his bladder when he was excited, which was often. Half the time he babbled in Latin and when he did speak English it was almost entirely in metaphor. 'The most precious stone is the river in flames.' 'One who has a man's wings and a woman's also is the womb of matter.' The Latin may have been all metaphor, too. Anyway, I had difficulty grasping his lessons.

"However, he had a great metallurgical laboratory and a better library—even though, again, half of it was in Latin or Greek. I was just beginning to understand his methods, and with them a sense of his substance, when he died suddenly of a heart attack."

Shamus paused, taking a deep breath. "That's how I burned my hand. When Jacob's heart gave out, he staggered against the lab table. We were in the middle of an exercise involving the transformation of silver, and when he flailed his hand out to catch himself he hit the crucible of molten silver, spilling it on my hand. In that instant of shock before the pain consumed me, Jacob grabbed me by the shoulders and, with such power it seemed effortless, pulled me to him in a fierce embrace, shuddering as he gathered breath to whisper in my ear: 'Make them return to ninety-two.'"

Annalee said, "What did he mean, 'return to ninety-two'?" Daniel was glad she asked.

"I'm not sure what he meant," Shamus said. "In the Periodic Chart of Elements, ninety-two is uranium, a precious metal, the last natural element—last by being the heaviest in terms of atomic weight—before the fifteen created by man. If I'd understood him correctly in our brief time together, he despised man-made elements because they were dangerous, corrupting, confusing, and unnecessary."

"But how could you make them return to ninety-two?" Annalee said.

"I wish I knew. I wonder about it every day."

Daniel said, "Now I understand."

"What?"

"Why you quit, and why they keep helping you: They owe it to you for hurting your hand."

"But I *didn't* quit then. In fact, when I recovered I took over Jacob's lab and continued my studies. AMO not only approved, they provided me with a Latin teacher. In six months of demon study I could read most of the old texts. Out of the emerging connections, I became fascinated by the radioactive elements, and, not surprisingly, uranium in particular. Old ninety-two itself, Jacob's point of return, the end of the natural line before the man-made mutants of linear accelerators and nuclear reactors. I had uranium samples, of course, but it was uranium-235, the fissionable isotope, that interested me. But since 235 is used in nuclear bombs, the government has it all. And if nothing else in my studies was clear, it was overwhelmingly obvious that we cannot comprehend elemental powers and processes without direct communion.

"At any rate, I decided to steal some U-235, and I asked AMO for help. They sent a member of the Star to see me, a man named Volta, and he not only turned down my request, he tried to persuade me not to attempt it on my own. He said he sympathized, but—I'm quoting—'Personal fascinations aren't sufficient reason to commit AMO to a course of action where success would be more dangerous than failure.' Which was Volta's elegant way of saying that the theft of nuclear material would bring down the heat so hard and hot that other projects and many people would be jeopardized.

"I was pissed, so I said something like 'Since I *am* going to steal the uranium for my own selfish reasons, the only honorable thing I can do is quit AMO.' And Volta said, 'As you choose. Not that it'll make much difference— the scrutiny will still be severe and disruptive. And not that your honorable gesture is pointless; honor never is. By all means, do as you will.'

"And I did," Shamus smiled ruefully. "And it fucked up. And the heat came down. And here we are." The smile had disappeared.

Annalee reached over with her right hand and squeezed his thigh. "I can think of worse places to be."

"Now what will happen?" Daniel said. Annalee could have strangled him. The future would come fast enough.

"Who knows?" Shamus answered Daniel. "They'll probably split us up in Dubuque and get me out of the country."

"Suppose we don't want to split up?" Annalee said.

Shamus turned to her and said softly, "But we do. So far I've got you burned to the ground, uprooted, and on the run. I'd love to stick with you, but that'd be an indulgence I don't deserve and a risk I won't take right now."

Annalee started to say something, then changed her mind. She reached over and snapped on the radio, looking for some rock 'n' roll she could crank up loud. Her brain told her splitting up was the most sensible move, but her heart reminded her she didn't have to like it.

Transcription:
Denis Joyner, AMO Mobile Radio

Oooooowwweeee! You got me when you weren't looking, the ol' DJ hisself, the Duke of Juice, coming at you live as I can handle on KOOOOL mow-beel radio, where you find it is where you get it, but don't look on the dial, baby, 'cause we're not there. We're OTD, OD, and O Sweet Leaping Jesus could this possibly be real! It is—heh-heh—it is indeed: The Blue Man in the Silver Van come to seed your dreams and feed your lonely little monkey.

What we're talking here is HIGH Kulture. Towering! The

Immensely Outasight! Magnificent Spirit-Shots into the Void! Direct Brain-Bang Transmission Leaps! Solid-State Astral Sex-Launch! That's right, you got it! Welcome to the Cloud-Walker Kulture Klub.

Now just between you, me, and the cave walls, kids, tonight we've got a bodacious show. If it don't get you off, you must be chained down.

Think I jive? Well, brothers and sisters, check it out. We're gonna hear Karl Marxxx doing his Number One single, "Undistributed Surplus Income and What It Means for Working Stiffs Like You and Me," featuring Peter Kropotkin on dobro and Leon Trotsky on violin. We got Jean-Paul Sartre from that new Essays-on-Tape series, in this case his neglected disquisition on postindustrial anxiety called "Incipient Arousal and Feelings of Doom." You digging it so far? Want more? Well, write this one down: out-takes from a rare Walt Disney interview where he holds forth at length between pipes of opium on Electromythology and the Tinkerbell Fetish (and hey you guys, 'fess up—don't you remember wishing little ol' Tinkerbell was about five feet taller?).

And why stop there? Hell, why stop at all? We're also gonna have *live,* in the here and right now, the *entire* Mormon Tabernacle Choir doing the dirty version of "Staggerlee." Fuck me if we ain't! Plus—*mercy,* mama!—the recently discovered Bach violin partitas as performed by the Tap City Strutters, Demerol Jones conducting. And if that don't leave you squealing, heap on our regular features—like Carl Jung on astrology, Consumer Hot-Line with Attila the Hun, Corliss Lime's ultrabitchy book reviews, and me, the Duke of Juice, on drums.

So hang in there and I'll hang it in your ear.

When they reached Dubuque later that day they stopped at a Conoco station. Shamus called a number from the pay phone. It was a short conversation, and he came back to the car looking thoughtful.

Annalee studied his face. "So, where to?"

"The *City of Baton Rouge.*"

"Louisiana?" Daniel said from the backseat. "That doesn't make sense."

Shamus smiled. "The *City of Baton Rouge* is a boat, an honest-to-god old Mississippi stern-wheeler docked just out of town."

"Of course," Annalee nodded absently, "the Mississippi River. And down the mighty Mississippi to the Gulf at New Orleans. From there, I suppose, to Cuba by submarine."

Shamus tousled her hair. "That's the spirit. From Cuba to Brazil by glider. At night. No moon."

"Just starlight on the water and the rush of wings."

"You got it," Shamus said.

Annalee started the car. "First let's find this riverboat."

"They'd never find us in the jungle," Daniel said with excited conviction.

Annalee said to Shamus, "Truth time—do you know where we're going or are you just jacking us up?"

"Take the last exit before the bridge, then north along the river. Elmo Cutter, one of Volta's field men, is going to meet us there. Beyond our immediate destination of the *City of Baton Rouge*, I have no idea where we're going. But I'm sure Elmo will have some suggestions."

Elmo Cutter was short, swarthy, and squat. A thick, black cigar—which he never lit—wagged under the grimy bill of a Chicago Cubs cap. He greeted them on the dock with an assortment of gruff monosyllables, then led them aboard.

The *City of Baton Rouge* was the last of its class, a steam-driven stern-wheeler riverboat of sleek and majestic line. Before the turn of the century it had carried an elegant trade of businessmen, gamblers, and high-stepping women; and even now, though stripped and abandoned in 1950, it still had an aura of green felt, soft conversation, a waltz drifting from the ballroom. You could smell the fragrant mix of sourmash whiskey, country ham, and fresh magnolias in the serving girls' hair; almost hear the soft clicking of chips as a pot was raked in the gaming room. But not even a fulgent imagination could blur its present state of weathered, empty decay.

Elmo led them to the dining room. Once two hundred had sat down at long tables sagging with fried chicken, ham, mashed potatoes, slaw, hot biscuits, butter-slathered corn, baked quail, greens, gravy, and thick slices of pumpkin pie. Now there was only a beat-up card table and four folding chairs.

Elmo went straight to the point: "You split up here."

Annalee flinched.

"Shamus, you're gone tonight. It's not all set, but it's pretty solid." He turned to Annalee. "You and the boy have a choice. You probably already know it, but you were keeping house for AMO—affiliates, so to speak. Some of the folks that stayed with you weren't even AMO members—Dolly, for instance, we sprung just because we like her on the loose. Now she's joined. And we're inviting you to join if you want."

Annalee, as blunt as Elmo, said, "Why weren't we asked before? Or at least informed?"

Elmo shrugged. "Got me, Miss Pearse. I wasn't there. But I'd guess there probably wasn't much reason, seeing as how you were already sort of allied, just not official. We don't stand on formality."

"What happens if we don't want to join? Maybe we know too much."

Elmo made a sound somewhere between a grunt and a chuckle. "No ma'am, you don't know too much. Cause some inconvenience maybe, but nothing major. AMO is like mercury. That's how we've survived for centuries. So if you don't want to join forces, you get the car, the four grand, and our fond farewell. And we'd probably try to help you out if you took a hard tumble—but that ain't a promise, just our likely inclination."

"And if we join?"

"Interesting work if it's available, fair pay, good people, expanded opportunities, and the shared benefits of alliance."

"Do you have school?" Daniel said with an intensity that made both Annalee and Shamus glance at him. He didn't notice; his attention was locked on Elmo.

"No schools," Elmo told him. "We got teachers, though, that'll take you on if you're serious about learning. And we have sort of a loose network of doctors, too—some of them fairly primitive by AMA standards, but that don't mean the medicine don't work. So I guess you could say there's some educational and medical benefits. Legal as well, come to think of it—some real sack-ripping lawyers. And that's it for my sales pitch. Don't mean to lean on ya, but we best move it along."

"What do you think, Shamus," Annalee asked. Feeling she might have slighted Daniel, she added "Daniel and I would appreciate your advice because we're the two who have to decide."

"I told you my story," Shamus said. "They're good friends and fair adversaries."

"We should join," Daniel said. "It's practical. And some day I'll need a teacher."

Annalee shut her eyes and opened them almost immediately. "Sign us up," she told Elmo.

"Done," he nodded. "And now if you'd like to check out the boat, I've got a few things to discuss with Mr. Malloy. I'm sure you understand that ignorance is often the best protection."

"But that's really knowledge, isn't it?" Daniel said.

"Same difference," Elmo grunted, then added as an afterthought, "Our teachers will love you."

Flustered by Elmo's comment, Daniel turned and followed his mother out on the main deck.

When they'd gone, Elmo told Shamus, "Detroit by train tonight, then a tour bus across the border and cold storage in Montreal. We got us a boiling case of bad heat. That wacky scientist you latched still hasn't turned up. Car you left him never moved. He could be stone dead in a runoff ditch or wandering around talking to rocks for all we know, and we pride ourselves on knowing those kinds of things."

"That you do," Shamus said.

"If they find him, dead or alive, things would cool considerably."

"I understand. I left him off exactly as I said."

Elmo chewed on his cigar. "No idea which way he might have drifted?"

"Up. Lost in thought."

"Yeah." Elmo spit a piece of tobacco. "All right, we got a fucking UFO on our hands. Figures he'd be a space cadet."

Shamus folded his hands on the card table, bare hand over the gloved. "So where are we?"

"Volta would like some consideration for the time and money it's gonna take to keep helping you."

"I have money. I'll gladly pay you back, with interest, when I can get to it."

"That'd be the right thing to do, but there's no press. What Volta would like is your cooperation. He said to think of it as a couple of years of honorable protective custody. What that means to me is he wants your word you won't run amok for a while. Otherwise, we cut you loose right here—a car and two grand, same as we offered the girl."

"You offered her four," Shamus corrected him.

"She's got a kid."

"Good point," Shamus said. "Guess friends don't come cheap."

"Nope—especially when you screw the heat to 'em."

"If I didn't feel for sure that that guard off smoking a joint was an accident, a random twist, I'd have to believe Volta would have found a way to make sure I didn't pull it off."

"I couldn't say. Seems you did fine fucking it up by yourself. That's what we got to deal with."

"Put me on the train, then, and somewhere down the line I'll try to make it right."

"Another thing," Elmo said, pointing with his cigar stub. "The glove's got to go."

"It doesn't come off. How about a cast?"

"Whatever."

Shamus held up his gloved hand. "We could cut the arm off at the elbow."

"Whatever," Elmo repeated.

"Speaking of fuck-ups," Shamus said, "any idea how they turned the ranch?"

"Yeah."

"The pilot?"

"You got it. They just missed your ass at the Nashville airport. Got the plane's ID and somebody saw the switch in Denver. Took 'em a few days, but they finally run the pilot down in Portland. Pounded it out of him."

"I'm sorry about that," Shamus said.

"Not as much as he is. He loved to fly, but he was fond of walking too."

Shamus slammed his gloved hand down on the card table. "Goddammit, whipping on me isn't going to change it. If you didn't like my judgment, why did you people recruit me? Why did you send me to Jacob Hind? Why did you encourage me to study radioactivity?"

"Hey," Elmo spread his arms, "why the fuck are we helping you? Huh? I'll tell you why: because we all make mistakes."

"Trying to steal that uranium *wasn't* a mistake. It just went wrong."

"Shamus, you're talking to the wrong man—do I look like a debate team? My job's to get you clear. You get to Montreal, you'll have tons of time to sort the fly shit from the pepper. Right now, we're moving on the quick."

"Fine," Shamus said. "Let's move."

They found Annalee and Daniel admiring the wooden drive wheel.

"Ready?" Annalee said. Shamus didn't look happy.

"Yep, ready," Elmo said.

"Where to?"

"You and Daniel, right here."

"Dubuque?"

"Here," Elmo said, pointing at the deck. "We want you to restore the *Baton Rouge* to her previous glory. The drydock stuff's all done; she just needs the finish work. Use the four grand to get started. When you run out, call Dave Jaspars and mention the Historical Restoration account—he's in the book. He's your contact here. Any emergency, let him know."

"Whoa," Annalee said, head cocked. "How do you want it done? Shit, *how* do we do it? We've pounded nails and cut boards, but that was ranch-style construction—we're hardly skilled. And what about colors and stuff? I mean—"

Elmo cut her off. "Listen, you figure it out. We don't let dummies in AMO."

"Can we live on the boat?" Daniel was enthralled by the prospect.

"Sort of assumed you would, but you don't have to. Us, we have to make some tracks."

Annalee and Shamus kissed farewell with feeling. "Gold doesn't rust," he whispered in her ear. "I'll see you again."

"Promises, promises," Annalee murmured, then held him fiercely as she fought tears.

Shamus shook hands with Daniel, and accompanied Elmo down the boarding ramp and up the dock. Annalee watched till they disappeared across the landing. When she finally turned to look for Daniel, he was leaning against the railing behind her, watching the gray Mississippi slide by. She went over beside him at the rail and put her arm around him. "Well," she sighed, "what do you think?"

Still gazing at the river, Daniel said, "It's just like Mark Twain described it. Beautiful and ugly at the same time."

It took Annalee and Daniel nearly two years and $52,000 to refinish the *City of Baton Rouge.* For Daniel, the time passed quickly. When he wasn't sanding the walnut stairs or painting one of the forty staterooms, his nose was buried in any book he could find on the subject of riverboats—especially their construction, appointments, and history. The old, grainy photos of the *Natchez,* the *Grand Republic,* the *Robert E. Lee,* and the *Mary Powell* moved him with their power and grace. He read about the great races, disastrous wrecks, and other river legends; the courageous captains and slick gamblers and the wily, drunken roustabouts. In the late evening, checking his set-line at the end of the dock for catfish, he imagined the whistles and bells of ghost riverboats passing in the mist. Each bit of knowledge, each feeling, brought a deeper and more passionate respect to his daily work on the *City of Baton Rouge.*

For Annalee, though, time moved as slowly and sluggishly as the Mississippi itself. The sense of accomplishment that animated Daniel didn't move her as solidly. The work was interesting, challenging, and rewarding, but it didn't thrill her—not the way the run from the Four Deuces had, not like the touch of Shamus's glove at the base of her spine.

She phoned Dave Jaspars whenever they needed money for material or tools. The first time she'd called, he'd told her there was an account at the local First National Bank under her paper name of Maybelline Wyatt. She was now the widowed daughter of J. C. Allsop, a Louisiana sugarcane tycoon and original owner of the *City of Baton Rouge,* its landing facilities, and forty acres of adjoining riverfront property—all of which she'd recently inherited upon his untimely death in a New Orleans brothel. In a rather feminine voice, Dave

Jaspars explained that the boat would be used as a communications center and occasionally for large meetings. To Daniel's sharp disappointment, however, the steam engine would not be replaced, nor would any other means of locomotion be installed. The *City of Baton Rouge* would remain moored.

As the work progressed, there was never a quibble over expenses or style. Every call requesting money was answered with a prompt deposit in her account, and no issue of taste or method was raised. They never met Dave Jaspars. No one from AMO came to inspect their work. The only visitors were occasional riverboat nuts (whom Daniel always invited to dinner and pillaged for lore) and the workmen they hired for special tasks. Daniel, who favored wood heat and the original oil-lamp chandeliers, was disgusted by the power lines and the backup generators in the engine room.

Annalee had hoped they would finish by Daniel's twelfth birthday, but they'd just started painting the dining room when March arrived. Annalee had given him his major birthday present—an excellent telescope—that morning, so when they'd finished his birthday dinner, they took the telescope up to the top deck and looked at the winter constellations. The chilly, wind-whipped evening soon sent them inside to the captain's dining room, which they'd made their own. Daniel waited at the head of the table while Annalee ducked into the galley and immediately reappeared with his birthday cake, twelve candles blazing, and set it in front of him as she sang happy birthday. Daniel's eyes glistened in the candlelight.

"Don't forget to make a wish before you blow them out," she reminded him.

Daniel thought for a moment, took a deep breath and blew out all the candles except the one in the center. Annalee quickly reached over and pinched it out.

"I guess I don't get my wish," Daniel said. Annalee seldom heard self-pity in his voice. She didn't know how to respond to his sudden shift in mood. "You know what I wished?" Daniel said, then continued before she could answer. "I wished I knew who my father was."

She grasped the connection with his birthday, but she was still stunned. She sat down across from him, feeling suddenly old and helpless. "I've told you before, Daniel—I don't know. I was young and crazy and lost. I was sleeping with anyone who'd hold me warm all night. It could have been a number of men. I wish I could tell you."

"Tell me," Daniel cried. "Tell me! You *have* to know!"

"I can't, Daniel. I honestly don't know."

"Liar!" He exploded from his seat. *"Tell me!"* He raised his right arm and smashed his fist down on the cake.

Annalee slapped him so hard it numbed her hand. Daniel staggered, barely catching himself against his chair. He brought his frosting-smeared hand to his cheek, blinking rapidly at the tears.

"Goddammit, you little shit," Annalee yelled, "it *hurts*. Do you think it doesn't hurt me too?"

Crying, Daniel nodded mechanically.

"Where is this coming from? Why are you doing this?"

Daniel kept nodding.

"Talk to me, Daniel. You can't do that to me and go hide. What is it?"

Daniel sobbed. "I just want to have something. Something I can imagine."

Annalee understood now what he wanted. She sat down, suddenly calm. "I first saw your father," she began, "when I was hiding out at a resort in Anchor Bay, about fifty miles down the coast from the Four Deuces. There'd been a bad drought for almost two years; nearly everyone was out of water. I woke up one summer dawn and looked out the window. Thin fog was swirling outside, milky in the first light. I saw a man out in the pasture, a tall, bearded man wearing a top hat and a flowing black cape. He was witching for water with a forked stick, holding it in front of him. I could feel his attention as he worked the field. I walked out in the pasture and stood in front of him. He spread his cape on the ground. Without a word, we made love. When we were done, he covered my shoulders with the cape. Before he left, he pointed out into the field and said, 'There's a deep spring near the center, but there's no need to dig. It's going to rain soon.' And the next morning I woke to a soft, soaking rain."

Daniel nodded solemnly.

"Your father," Annalee said, "was a riverboat captain. His boat was the *Delta Queen*. I was a serving girl, a young Cajun from the bayou. I remember how strong his arms were from handling the wheel. You were conceived on the pilot house floor while the wheel twirled slowly and the boat ran free. The next night there was an earthquake. I couldn't feel it on the water at first, but you could hear people screaming on shore and see the treetops lashing in the moonlight. The river just seemed to roll over everything and you could hear the boat's timbers snap loud as gunshots and glass shattering in the salon. I was on my way up to the wheelhouse with a bottle of brandy and was knocked back down the stairs. People were screaming and jumping overboard. Suddenly your father was there, lifting me in his arms and carrying me down to the main deck. There was a small dinghy lashed to the bow. He cut it loose with his knife, then lifted me inside. He kissed me, said he loved me, then lowered it. He went back to help the others. As I drifted away, still holding the bottle of brandy in my hands, I saw him run into the salon just before it burst into flames."

Daniel shut his eyes, absently touching his cheek where Annalee had slapped him.

"Your father was a bandit," she continued. "I was working as a cocktail waitress in this horrible Chicago bar. We'd closed up and the bartender and I were washing the last few glasses when he stepped out of the bathroom with a pistol in his hand. He tied up the bartender and locked him in the storeroom, then emptied the till. He skidded a roll of dimes down the bar toward me, where he'd told me to sit and not move. 'Put some music on the jukebox,' he said. I asked him what he wanted to hear. 'Whatever puts you in the mood,' he laughed. It was the sweetest, loosest laugh I ever heard. I ended up driving the getaway car to his apartment. No. Wait. I'm lying to you."

Daniel glanced at her sharply.

"We didn't go to his place. We made love right there, on the long mahogany bar."

"Mom!" Daniel blushed. "Geez."

"You want to know your father and I don't know who he is. So I'm going to tell you everything that moved me in the men I've known, what I've admired and enjoyed and dreamed and desired. And when I'm done, you still won't have a father, still won't know who your father is, but you're going to have a much better idea who *I* am, and that you're my son, and that I love you.

"Your father was a mountain climber who disappeared on the peak. I met him in a Katmandu café just before he started the ascent. I remember . . ."

The smashed cake between them untouched, Annalee went on for nearly two hours, every man of flesh or dream she could remember or invent, heroes, poets, outlaws, fools. Daniel listened intently, and when she finished he did something that brought tears to her eyes: He broke a piece of the mangled cake and offered it to her.

To their mutual amusement, they finished the boat on April Fools' Day. Their work, they agreed, was excellent. The forlorn queen had been restored to magnificence—from the Belgian carpet to the chandeliers, she possessed a muted elegance and luxurious dignity.

Annalee phoned Dave Jaspars that evening and told him the work was complete.

"Fantastic!" He sounded genuinely pleased. "Take a vacation for a few weeks or just hang out and enjoy the fruits of your labor. Elmo's supposed to pass through toward the end of the month and he'll tell you what's next."

"I don't suppose you'd have any idea what that might be," Annalee prodded. Dave Jaspars loved to gossip, and was always dropping hints he knew far more than he could tell.

"Well . . ." he began, letting it trail off. "You know I shouldn't tell you this—but you're going to Indianapolis to join the Sisters of Blessed Mercy convent and Daniel is going to Paraguay to study hallucinogenic medicine with a Yatati shaman."

Annalee was stunned. She could hear herself producing a strange nasal whining sound, but until she actually blurted "No!" she had no idea she was trying to speak.

"April Fool!" Dave Jaspars yelped with glee. "Got you!"

"You miserable fucker," Annalee said coldly, "it's a good thing I don't know what you look like or I'd hunt you down and show you some serious foolishness."

"My goodness, Mrs. Wyatt," he said, "I had no idea you thought of me like that. Didn't you know that April Fools' is the only religious holiday we celebrate?"

"No," Annalee said, smiling, "but it figures."

When Elmo Cutter entered the main salon, he took the cigar out of his mouth and whistled softly. "Holy shit."

Daniel thought it was a good moment to press his case for complete restoration. "It would be really beautiful on the river, but that'd mean getting the engine rebuilt, or maybe putting in a new one."

"Nope, Daniel, it ain't gonna happen. It's gonna serve as a stationary communication center. She'd attract way too much attention on the water."

Exasperated, Daniel flung his arms out to indicate the salon. "Then why bother doing this? *Any* of this? Why not just make it cheap, practical, functional?"

"Because it wouldn't be doing it right," Elmo said. You could have broken a fist on his voice.

"Is doing it *halfway* doing it right?"

"In this case, yes. Shit, son, we couldn't really afford to do this much right, and a power plant would double up the budget and make it worthless for what we have in mind."

Daniel muttered, "It just makes our work seem pointless."

Elmo dropped a meaty hand on Daniel's shoulder. "Now *that's* up to you, whether it's pointless or not. Far as I'm concerned, you two did one helluva job, and before you go on bulldogging my ass about this engine and get me feeling mean, let me say thanks, okay? Now you can keep chomping if you want, or we can sit down at this fine table here and talk." He lifted his hand from Daniel's shoulder and touched the polished tabletop. "What kinda wood is this anyhow?"

"Walnut," Daniel said.

Elmo caressed it with his thick fingers. "That's just plain fine."

Annalee said, "A long way from that scabby old card table, isn't it?"

"A million miles." He glanced at Daniel. "You done chewing?"

"If it makes any difference," Annalee said, "I agree with Daniel."

"It makes a difference, but it doesn't change nothing."

Annalee sat down. "Then let's talk about something else, like the million miles between here and there and where we're going next."

"That's up to you," Elmo said, sitting down across from her. "Next month the boat here'll be fitted out with radio equipment. There'll be a permanent crew of about a dozen, and occasionally a full house. You're welcome to stay on and learn some communication engineering, which is a good skill to have these days, or there's an opening in our Waco language school if you want to learn Spanish while making sure our borders stay open to certain goods and people. There's a communal salmon boat in Washington that could always use some extra hands; it's got an engine, too, at least most of the time, and a crew that would have been pirates a hundred years ago. Or, if you want to learn the fine arts of printing and photography, there's a paper house about to start production—"

"Paper house?" Daniel interrupted.

"Documents. Licenses. Stuff like that."

"Forgeries." Daniel nodded.

Elmo shrugged. "Well, we have a lot of official seals; we just don't have a lot of official authorization to use them."

"Where is this paper house," Annalee asked.

"Berkeley. In California."

"Berkeley, California," Annalee repeated with a dreamy joy. "Credentials of identity, certificates of accomplishment. Perfect. We'll take it." She looked at Daniel. "Assuming it's acceptable to you."

"I'd like to live in a city," Daniel said.

"For how long?" she said to Elmo.

"Till you get tired of it or it burns up—paper houses tend to do that. But the better the papers, the lower the heat."

Annalee nodded. "When?"

"Now, if you want. It'll be another month before all the tools and materials are delivered, but the house is ready."

"It doesn't need an engine, does it?" Daniel said, but he was smiling.

Elmo grinned in return. "You know what they call a bulldog that knows when to let go?"

Daniel shook his head.

"Smart."

"Do you know what they call a boat without an engine?" Daniel said.

Elmo sighed. "Let me guess. Dumb?"

"No. They call it a communications center."

"You know, I'm gonna start packing a spoon with me."

Daniel didn't bite.

Elmo explained anyway. "All the shit I have to eat on this job, I could use one."

Annalee said, "As long as we're asking questions, and since you trust us enough to run a print shop, there's something I want to know. Where's Shamus Malloy these days?"

"Out at sea with a small crew of treasure hunters. That batty scientist still hasn't showed."

"What sort of treasure," Daniel asked.

"Silver and gold."

Annalee smiled. "I bet he's happy."

"Jesus," Elmo said, "let's hope so."

The house in Berkeley was on McKinley Street, not far from the high school. When the Helmsbro Movers ("If we can't truck it, fuck it," their typically Berkeleyan card proclaimed) delivered some ostensible furniture a month later, Annalee and Daniel found reams of blank birth certificates, drivers' licenses from every state, draft cards, passports, and various official seals of sundry state governments and federal agencies. The small darkroom in the second-floor bathroom had been completed before their arrival, and the Multilith and platen press, flanked by a battery of typewriters, were set up in an adjoining room. After the friendly tutelage of Jason Wisk, their nominal real estate agent, they could document a new identity in half a day. Since Annalee enjoyed the camera work and embossing while Daniel was particularly fond of the printing, the labor divided itself along lines of natural interest. Jason coordinated the job orders, which were steady enough to keep them busy but not enough to be a burden. No customers came to the house; if photos were required, Annalee either worked from negatives shot elsewhere or shot them herself at Jason's real estate office.

Because Daniel was often hassled for not being in school, he seldom left the house before 3:00 on weekdays. He usually printed till noon and read after lunch for at least a couple of hours before going out to explore Berkeley's street life.

By mutual agreement, the nights belonged to Annalee. She was particularly taken with Dr. Jamm's Get-Down Club out on Shattuck. She quickly made friends with the musicians and artists who hung out there. Soon she was a singer and lead kazoo in a perpetually ripped aggregation known as the Random Canyon Raiders, whose repertoire included traditional, if obscure, favorites, as well as spontaneous and raucously pornographic sociopolitical polemics. The Random Canyon Raiders were devoted to high times and low art, and Annalee rediscovered a social life. She began to cut loose.

But some trajectories are immune to change: A year later, early in May, looking for a book of poems recommended by one of her Random Canyon friends, she saw Shamus Malloy standing by the chemistry section in the Berkeley Public Library. His hair was black, he was clean-shaven, and, to judge by the pinned sleeve on his jacket, he'd lost his left arm. But she was so sure it was Shamus that she browsed over beside him and tugged his empty sleeve.

Shamus closed the book he was examining and slipped it back on the shelf without acknowledging her. "I've loved you and missed you every minute for the last two years," he whispered, staring at the stacks, "and I'm afraid to look at you, afraid it won't be you, that'll it be some desperate hallucination, some hungry dream."

"Is it cool to hug you in here?" Annalee said, her open hand pressing against the small of his back.

"Probably not," Shamus grinned, "but please, please do it anyway." When he turned to look at her there were tears in his eyes.

She felt his arm under his jacket when they embraced.

"What are we doing inside on a lovely spring day?" Annalee murmured. "Let's stroll, if that's permitted."

"Everything's permitted," Shamus said, "as long as we're careful." He looked in her eyes when he said it, then glanced over her shoulder. "After you, milady."

They walked two blocks to Swensen's Burger Palace, ordered coffee, and took a table near the back.

"All right," Annalee said, "what's going on. The only news I heard was that you were off treasure-hunting."

"True. I holed up by sailing away. We were diving wrecks off Colombia. It was work, but it certainly had its moments. It has to be one of the most astonishing sensations in the universe to stand on deck with a bar of gold, still dripping sea water, raised in your hand. It's not as wonderful as holding you, of course, but one takes what's available."

"Talk that talk," Annalee said. "Daniel was asking me the other day why I liked you poets so much; I told him because they talked good."

"And how is Daniel?"

"Thirteen going on thirty, and working hard to cut the apron strings."

"That shouldn't prove difficult—you're not the smothering type."

"You never gave me a chance."

"If there's no other men in your life right now, maybe I will."

"Just Daniel, and it's not clear whether he's a young man or an old boy. But how about you? Can you come out and play?" She idly ran a finger around the rim of her coffee mug.

"My deal with Volta was that I'd be a good boy for two years. *Cooperative* was the term. I guess you didn't hear that Gerhard von Trakl wandered back to work last week mumbling about sequential centers and the inextricable dance of particle and wave. He claimed he'd been out in the desert thinking things over. Probably true, according to AMO's information— dressed in tatters with wild long hair and beard. No info on the debriefing, but evidently he told it like it happened, that I let him off and drove away in the night. It's hard to believe they could cover his absence so long, but the old geezer doesn't have any family, and the official word was that he was on special assignment."

"So now you're cool?"

"Well, not completely. They're still looking, but the urgency has faded."

With a thin smile and a definite weariness, Annalee said, "So you're ready to try for the uranium again?"

"No," Shamus said. "Plutonium—the dark, decadent queen herself. And this time for ransom: the dismantling of *all* nuclear facilities in the country. Not to mention the political embarrassment of having it stolen, the admission of vulnerability." He leaned forward across the table. "Nuclear weapons are madness. It has to be stopped. The knowledge and the technologies are always there before our ability to understand the consequences. Linear accelerators, breeder reactors—what do they do except speed everything up beyond comprehension while accumulating deadly materials in kinds and quantities nature never intended? It's a sickness of greed and power, like amassing gold, and that much power in the hands of so few rots the heart. We've got to stop, stop and think hard about the consequences of possessing so much energy and what unleashing it might mean. I said the ransom would be the dismantling of all nuclear facilities, but that really isn't it. The ransom is time. Time to consider, evaluate, judge. Time is the heart of tragedy. I reread Sophocles on the boat: 'All understood too late.' It takes time to come to understanding, and pride and ignorance and fear just grease the chute. We're running out of time. It's almost too late. That's what my guts tell me: We have to buy time. And the only currency I can think of is plutonium."

"Gold doesn't rust," Annalee reminded him, "but plutonium decays."

"Exactly. And it's a deadly decay. Plutonium is man-made, the first transuranium creation. She is the real bride of Frankenstein: magical, entrancing, powerful—but without a soul. We don't need her. I think that's what Jacob Hind meant with his last breath: 'Return to ninety-two.' If you steal fire, you'll be burned."

"But isn't that what *you* want to do?"

"Yes, but with a crucial difference. I'm going to steal it *from* man and give it *back* to the gods. Or at least demand we give up our literal firepower until we're wise enough not to use it."

Annalee smiled sweetly. "I'd love to discuss the philosophical implications of firepower with you when we're done fucking."

For a moment she thought she had made a mistake, that she'd committed the female sacrilege of not taking men and their power seriously, of questioning their heroic passions, but the flash of anger in his eyes faded immediately and she felt his gloved hand on her thigh under the table.

"I missed you, too," he said. "I have a place in Richmond, and I assume your print shop is busy."

"I wondered why I had the feeling our meeting in the library wasn't mere coincidence. How did you know where to find me?"

"I'm not without resources. And AMO, fittingly, is full of romantic souls who like to see young people get together even if it's bad for security."

"I bet it wasn't Elmo."

"Elmo wouldn't tell me if I had an arrow in my back."

As they stood to leave, Annalee said, "Do you think AMO will try to stop you?"

"I think they'll do what they think is right, just like I will. But first they have to find out what I'm going to do, which is unlikely, but not impossible. AMO has a genius for procuring high-quality information; it's their real strength."

"Mine, too," Annalee said, slipping her arm around his waist, hooking a thumb in a belt loop. "Face to face, skin to skin, breath to breath."

Annalee didn't return to McKinley Street until late that evening. Daniel and Jason Wisk were at the kitchen table playing chess.

"Hi Mom," Daniel greeted her, but his attention stayed on the board.

"I used to be pretty good at this game," Jason said, "but Daniel is introducing me to reality."

Daniel moved a rook behind his queen.

Jason dourly regarded the move. "Three more moves and only an act of God could save me. I concede." With elaborate formality, he toppled his king, nodding to Daniel. "You play well."

Annalee, standing behind Daniel, ran her hand through his long brown hair as she said to Jason, "When I play him, he has to spot me a rook, two pawns, and three oversies. And he still beats me like a dumb dog."

" 'Oversies,' " Daniel repeated with disgust. "She says that's girls' rules. Do girls really have different rules?"

"So they claim," Jason sighed.

"Are they written down?"

Annalee gently pushed Daniel's head down toward the board, answering, "Never. That's the first rule."

Jason laughed. He was bright, sweet, considerate, good-looking, and self-effacing without being wimpy. He treated Daniel like a real person instead of a kid. She liked him, had initially been attracted to him, but the fact that he had a solid marriage and three children at home had kept things comfortably uncomplicated. But it was unusual for him to be out so late, so she said, "Did Millie finally throw you out or do we have a rush order on the board?"

Jason cleared his throat. "None of the above. Millie and the kids are visiting her folks in Santa Monica so I'm allowed on the streets after dark, and other than the traveling papers for Mr. Elwood the board is clean, and there's no hurry on those. I only stopped by to learn some humility at Daniel's hand and to relay some information that may or may not interest you—since it makes no particular sense to me, I wouldn't presume to know. The message is that the wandering scientist has returned and you might expect a visit from an old friend named Malloy. I have a number for you to call if you want more information. Or have any." He handed her a folded slip of paper from his jacket pocket. " 'Gone Fishing' is the access code."

Daniel rolled his eyes. "That's pretty corny."

"But discreet," Annalee said. She put the number in her purse without looking at it.

As soon as the door closed behind Jason, Daniel turned to Annalee and said, "I'll bet you a hundred nights of doing dishes against that old piece of celery in the fridge that you were with Shamus today."

"You shouldn't try to take advantage of your mother when she's in a weakened condition. No bet, kiddo. But I must say you're either very perceptive or I'm really transparent."

"Well, it was easy for *me* to tell because you got a look just like you had that morning after the first time you spent the night with him."

"What sort of look? Glowing? Transported? Stupid?"

"Yeah. Except I would say it was more like shining and happy and a little bit worried. No, not worried—sad."

"That about covers it," Annalee said. Shamus had specifically asked her not to tell Daniel about the plutonium theft he was plotting, but he didn't know Daniel like she did. She'd agreed not to tell him. But she trusted Daniel more than she could ever trust Shamus. The powerful combination of girls' rules and mothers' rules provided an exception. She told Daniel everything except the target. When she finished, he had his usual barrage of questions. The first one twisted her heart.

"Do you think he can pull it off?"

"Arrggh," Annalee groaned. "The only trouble with you men is that you're males! What difference does it make if he pulls it off? If he doesn't he's dead or in prison for a billion years, and if he does he's hunted into the ground. There's no fucking *difference*, don't you see? When I'm with Shamus, there's something between us that I need. It's not Shamus and it's not me; it's what we are together. A connection. A circuit. And if we're not together there's no connection and the circuit's broken and the juice doesn't flow. And whether he steals the plutonium or not we won't be together."

"You're in love?"

"I'd like the chance to find out."

Daniel thought for a moment. "Maybe you better call that number Jason gave you and get more information."

"I can't. It would be a betrayal. They'd try to stop him."

"No, I meant get some information on love. You wouldn't have to mention the plutonium."

"Daniel, I *would* have to. Besides, I've got more information on love than I need."

"Well, maybe you could talk Shamus out of it."

"Maybe I could talk a bird out of the sky."

Daniel started putting away the chess pieces. "I don't see any good endings."

"Me either."

"What are you going to do?"

"Enjoy it while I can and cry when it's over."

Daniel gave her a puzzled look but said nothing. He folded the chessboard and put it back in its box. "I thought of a good ending."

"Tell me."

"If Shamus steals the plutonium and gets them to close all the nuclear plants, maybe he'll be a hero. Maybe they'll give him a medal instead of putting him in prison, and you could get married."

"You want to bet a hundred nights of dishes on it?"

"No."

"How about one night for you against a thousand for me?"

"Sure. I'll always bet that *anything* can happen. I love longshots."

"Oh yeah? Well I love *you.*" She put an arm around his shoulder and squeezed him to her side. "Thanks for the moral support." She giggled. "*Moral* support. Can you give *moral* support to an unwed mother forger who has her head up her heart over some crazy poet planning a plutonium heist? Jesus, Daniel, I have no idea what I'm doing."

Daniel gave her a little hug, but he didn't say anything.

Annalee saw Shamus once a week for the first month, running checks on each other to be sure they weren't followed. When things seemed secure, they began meeting more often, but always at his apartment on the edge of Richmond. Daniel went with her sometimes, but on those occasions they'd meet Shamus at a prearranged location and go to a movie or an A's game or drive up the coast in Annalee's old Toyota. Daniel didn't accompany them often. He felt that he disturbed some current between them. Shamus also seemed to be trying too hard to impress him. And it bothered him that Shamus never mentioned that he was planning to steal some plutonium.

When Shamus and Annalee had been lovers again for almost half a year, he asked if she would help him with the theft.

Annalee sat up in bed, an unseasonably warm October breeze from the open window billowing her hair. "Doing what?"

"I'd rather not tell you until it's all set up. That's for your protection, you understand. In fact, I'll be the only one to know you're involved. But the task itself is safe and simple, and it requires someone I absolutely trust."

Annalee said softly, "I don't want you to do it, you know. Which doesn't mean I won't help you with everything I've got."

"Sweetie, I'm going to try whether you help me or not. And I'll love you whether I succeed or not. But I can't love you if we're nuked into oblivion. There are things more important than us."

"Well, go make love to them." Annalee tossed her hair. "Go make love to the world."

Shamus touched her bare shoulder with his black-gloved hand, then ran it gently down her spine. "I am," he said.

Trembling, Annalee slid down beside him and put her hand on his chest. "I'll help you."

As Christmas approached, Shamus became increasingly moody and intensely preoccupied. He explained to Annalee that he'd hoped to steal the plutonium on Christmas Eve but that the plan wasn't coming together. Some of the people he needed wouldn't be available till late January. It was the first she'd heard that others would be involved. She knew better than to ask who they were or how many were included, but she was worried to learn of accomplices—the more who knew, the greater the risk. Shamus assured her they didn't know each other and, with two exceptions, would never meet—and the two who would meet would be together less than ten minutes, and that would be after the job. He still wouldn't tell Annalee her role in the heist. When she argued that she'd like to be prepared, he promised he'd tell her in plenty of time.

For Christmas Shamus gave Daniel a beautifully framed copy of the Periodic Table of the Elements from which he'd carefully excised what he called "the transuranium abominations." He gave Annalee a lovely gold chain necklace, each delicate link intricately connected to the next in a different way. As she examined it again later in her bedroom mirror, she was taken with the terrifying understanding that she was all he had left of reality. She felt a wild impulse to rip the necklace off and tear it apart, but instead she flung herself on the bed and wept. She wished it would happen, be over, end—even though she still didn't see a good ending. But her and Daniel's present to Shamus at least kept the faith of a happy conclusion. When he opened their package, he found seventeen separate identities to choose from. He laughed at the Harvard diploma certifying his doctorate in chemistry. It was the only time he laughed all day.

January was worse. He talked obsessively about plutonium, citing its connection in myth with the underworld, that in fact it took its name from Pluto, god of the dead, and that its namesake planet was absent from the ancient astrological charts—because, he speculated, it was meant to remain unknown, forbidden knowledge, the perilous edge. Nor did it escape his notice that the American political system, despite its democratic façade, was clearly a plutocracy, a government by wealth, whether rich individuals or corporate monopolies. The signs, he repeated incessantly, made it overwhelmingly plain that human consciousness was hurtling toward a plutonic apocalypse, a reign of shadow. The only hope of stopping it was a leap of wisdom, and wisdom took time. He would kidnap death and ransom it for time.

Annalee was wondering how much more she could stand when she knocked on his apartment door the night of February 3. She'd decided that if he mentioned plutonium or Greek mythology or any other associative notion she would turn around and leave. Instead she found a bottle of Mumm's on ice, glasses ready on the candlelit table, and a happy, relaxed Shamus. "It's set for the evening of the fifteenth," he greeted her. "The Livermore Lab. I want you to place a diversionary device—a small bomb—in an alley in the industrial area. It runs between two warehouses and no one should be around—there's not even a watchman. When you've placed it, I want you to call me from a pay phone. I'll give you the number and the exact locations that morning. Until then, let's not talk about it, think about it, worry about it. Just you and me in the here and now, every night till then."

"Pour the champagne," Annalee said.

Annalee didn't get home until noon the next day. She knew by the way Daniel looked at her that he knew something was up. She consulted each of her mixed emotions as she worked in the darkroom, debating whether she should tell him or not, and reached no decision. After dinner he said, without preamble, "You weren't supposed to tell me about the plutonium theft to start with. Since you did, you might as well tell me the rest."

So she did and was immediately sorry.

"I want to go with you," he said. "I want to help."

"No. Absolutely, finally, unalterably *no*. No you can't go, and no discussion. You're not riding around with a bomb in a car."

"You are. And you told me Shamus said it's safe."

"I'm not going to risk you. No. End of discussion."

"I won't risk you, either. Suppose somebody happens along and sees you between the time you leave the car and go in the alley and come back? You need someone in the car, a lookout, to warn you if a cop or somebody shows up—that's the point of greatest vulnerability. Besides, I'm great cover—if you get stopped, who'd suspect a bomb with a kid in the car?"

"Exactly. Not a mother on this planet would be that stupid. Including me."

"Algerian mothers took their kids along when they planted bombs."

"Oh yeah, how do you know that?"

"I read books."

"No. *No.* Forget it."

"I want to ask Shamus."

"Goddammit, Daniel, you *can't* ask Shamus: You're not supposed to *know*, remember?"

"But I do."

"What does that mean?" Annalee said, ice in her tone. "That you'd betray me out of childish spite?"

"No. It means I'm implicated, but that I can't share in the responsibility. That's a betrayal, too. Mom, we share a lot between us—not everything, but a lot. I'm willing to share the risk of delivering the bomb because I share the risk of knowing about it. You have to quit feeling responsible for me. I'm almost fourteen. I need to be responsible for myself."

"I don't like it," Annalee shook her head. "It doesn't feel right."

"Besides, you need a lookout and moral support. And cover. And I need to do it. Let me go."

Annalee put her head down on the table. When she lifted it, she said with weary resignation, "All right. You can go. Not because you're my son—that defies my maternal instincts—but because you're *you.*"

The next night with Shamus she told him that she was sure Daniel knew something was going on.

"Shit!" Shamus exploded, jumping from the bed and pacing the room naked.

Stung by his vehemence, Annalee said nothing.

"Okay," Shamus said, more in control, "what does he know, or think he knows? And how?"

"How? Jesus, Shamus, he's a piece of my heart! He can feel it from me, that's how. And that's probably *what* he knows—nothing specific, just something in the air, a tension, an edge."

"Has he *said* anything specific?"

"A couple of times he asked me if I was okay. Yesterday he asked me if there was anything going on that he should know about."

"What did you tell him?"

"I told him we were going through a tense time in our relationship."

"Do you think he's talked to anyone else?"

"Never happen."

Shamus paced for a moment, then came over and sat down on the edge of the bed. "Daniel's bright, he's got heart, he's loyal, but he's a kid. I don't know about kids. You do, and you know him in particular. Any suggestions how to handle this? Or is that why you brought it up?"

"If you're absolutely sure about the bomb being safe to transport, I think he should go with me."

Shamus stared at her. "Annalee, if that bomb wasn't safe, *you* wouldn't be carrying it. Do you understand that?"

"Yes. And I know I can trust Daniel as much as I trust you."

"Fine. You work it out with him. But absolutely don't tell him *when* it's going to happen or *where* until you're on your way in the car. And don't tell him what's involved. Just that we're going to need his help."

"Shamus, he's been an outlaw his whole life. He forges papers every day. He understands how it is. When the theft hits the news, you think he won't know who did it, what went down? And be hurt and pissed off he wasn't trusted enough to be included—especially when he might have to suffer the consequences? You don't think there's going to be a shit-rain of heat?"

"Obviously. But don't forget, the plutonium is our umbrella. That's why I *have* to pull it off. Because without the plutonium, there's no leverage. They're gutless, Annalee, not stupid. They won't fire if they know we can fire back. And they'll have the whole world watching, because I'm going to make sure it's on every front page and television set in the world, and the first demand will be amnesty for everyone involved."

"And if they call the bluff? Won't negotiate?"

"I lose. I'll surrender myself and the plutonium on the condition that everyone else involved, who I'd duped or forced into doing their tiny, innocent, unconnected parts, be granted amnesty. But even if it comes to that, it will be a success, because I'll have held up a mirror to their madness, ripped off their masks."

"And they'll lock you up forever as an example, maybe even execute you, and I'll never see you again."

"Annalee," Shamus pleaded, "it's beyond us. It cries to be done."

"I'll cry, too," Annalee said.

Shamus took her in his arms and embraced her, rocking her as he said, "Do you think I won't?"

When Annalee left for Shamus's apartment the evening of the fourteenth, she hugged Daniel and said, "I'll bring you a bomb for breakfast."

"Are you nervous?" Daniel asked her.

"About to fall to pieces. Are you?"

"Yes. But excited, too."

"Right. Which is why you should go to bed early and get plenty of sleep so you'll be rested and sharp, because tomorrow's going to take the very best we've got. And remember to lock the doors."

"I will."

He didn't.

Daniel was undressed and in bed when he remembered the back door. He'd locked it earlier, but then, deciding to gather all the equipment together and have it ready for tomorrow, he'd gone out to the garage for the tent and couldn't recall if he'd relocked it. He was reaching for his nightstand light when a woman's voice said from the doorway, "I'll look for you in the shadows."

Carefully, Daniel reached for his pants beside the bed and took out his pocket knife, opened it, and slipped it under the covers. When he set his pants back down on the floor some change in the pockets jingled.

"I seek you in the dark by the jingle of silver and the sound of your breath." He could hear her hand patting along the wall and then the overhead light switched on. The woman standing in the doorway was young, pretty, and, as Daniel quickly judged from her eyes, very stoned.

She peered at him intently. "Ha. I found you." She smiled at him. "But who have I found?"

"My name's Daniel," he said, too surprised not to answer.

She giggled, "Then this must be the lion's den." She walked into the room.

"Not really. It's my bedroom. Who are you?"

But she was staring at the poster of the Horsehead Nebula on the wall over the bed. "What's this?"

"The Horsehead Nebula. It's what's called a dark nebula, because it doesn't contain any bright stars. The dark nebulae block the light of the stars beyond them, so from here they look like dark patches in the sky. They're like huge interstellar dust clouds. Some astronomers think they'll eventually collapse into themselves and form new stars."

She stared at it intently for half a minute. "It's beautiful," she said, and began to cry.

"I feel the same way sometimes," Daniel said.

Sniffling, she sat down on the edge of the bed and, head cocked quizzically, looked at him. Though it was a cold night, she wore only a thin blouse, blue jeans, and sandals. "Nebula, nebulae; nebula, nebulae," she intoned. "You're too young to be a scientist, aren't you?"

"Are you too young to be a burglar?"

"Hey," she said sharply. "I'm not a burglar."

"Then why are you here in our house, late at night, without knocking?"

"I lost the party," she said. "When you lose the party, you have to find something else. You have to look for an open door."

"Did you take something at the party?"

She sniffled, shaking her head. "I don't know."

"What's your name?"

"Tonight it's Brigit Bardo. Like that old French actress."

"Are you an actress?"

She peered at him closely. "I'm not anything."

"Do you need some help?"

"No," she laughed suddenly, "it's easy."

Daniel started to say something but she reached out and put a finger to his lips. "No more questions for awhile." She pressed harder with her finger. "All right?"

Daniel barely nodded.

She trailed her finger over his chin and throat and down his chest to the edge of the blanket that covered him.

"What are you doing," Daniel asked uneasily.

"Something you'll never forget." She pushed the blankets down slowly. When she saw the knife, she reached over and folded the blade closed. Leaning down, she bit him lightly just below the ribs, then lifted back the blankets. When she took his cock in her mouth, Daniel shuddered and shut his eyes.

Her mouth was unbearably warm, infinitely slow. As Daniel passed through the Horsehead Nebula he learned there are things beyond imagining that exist anyway.

She left an hour later, locking the door behind her.

When Annalee returned home in the late afternoon, Daniel was waiting to open the door. They looked at each other and asked, "Are you all right?" and then laughed.

"You look like you didn't get much sleep," Annalee told him.

"And you look jumpy and exhausted," Daniel said.

"You'd be jumpy, too, driving around with a bomb." Noticing the camping equipment piled on the living room floor, she pointed. "What's this? We taking to the hills?"

"That's our cover. We're going camping in Yosemite."

"There's a small flaw, isn't there? Like the fact that it's February?"

Daniel reached into the pile and produced two pairs of snowshoes. "We're going *snow* camping. I rented these at REI this morning. Out in the parking lot, a short, bearded man asked me where I was headed . . ."

Annalee listened distractedly to the elaborate cover story Daniel had concocted in case they were pulled over with the bomb in the car. How the bearded man had given him a package to deliver to his sister in Livermore, some sort of illegal cancer treatment from Mexico. The story was well conceived, but wouldn't make any difference if they were busted on the way, which she was sure Daniel understood. When she finally saw the point, she shook her head.

"Daniel, bless you, but there's no way you can protect me if we get popped."

"I'm a juvenile. I wouldn't go to jail."

"You're a sweetheart. And I'd go to jail for contributing to your delinquency on top of possession of an explosive device."

"We could try it."

Annalee didn't want to argue. "Sure," she said, "but let's hope we don't have to."

Daniel pointed at the ceiling. "Something else. The paper upstairs. I put the blanks and seals in the safe, but if anything happens and they search here, they'll find them."

"Yeah, well, AMO will just have to eat it."

"I was thinking we could drop the incriminating stuff off at Jason's. Tell him we decided to go camping and didn't want to leave it around."

"But we've taken off before and just stashed it. He'll know something's weird. And we don't have time."

Daniel considered this a moment, then shrugged. "Do you know where we're going?"

"Las Postas Avenue in Livermore. An alley between a machine shop that just went out of business and an empty warehouse."

"I can't cover both ends of an alley."

"You don't have to—it's a blind alley, T-shaped. Just for deliveries and garbage pickup."

"What's the bomb look like?"

"A sealed black metal cube about a foot on each side. It's in a paper shopping bag."

"What sort of bomb?"

"I didn't ask."

"I mean does it have a timer? Fuse? Remote control?"

"I don't know. I don't care, either. What difference does it make?"

"I just wondered if it was armed."

"No. I have to do that in the alley. There's a button I push. A red light should come on. Whether it lights up or not, we leave immediately and call a number from a pay phone a half mile away."

"Probably a timer," Daniel said to himself.

"Right, I guess it is. Shamus said it had a Mickey Mouse clock inside. He said the guy that put it together was in the avant garde of demolition."

"How is Shamus?"

"Gone. Not there. Electric with purpose. The damn bomb was under the bed all night, if you can believe that."

"Yeah," Daniel said noncommitally. "How's our time?"

"Too much, not enough, and running out." She felt tears welling in her eyes and turned for the bathroom.

Daniel caught her by the hand as she passed him and held her at arms' length. "You sure you're okay? We have to concentrate."

"If I concentrate any harder I'll disappear." She took a deep breath to gather herself, slumping as she let it out. "This whole thing is stupid and impossible and pointless."

"We've got outs," Daniel said gently. "Call the number Shamus gave you and tell him the car broke down. I can dump some sugar in the tank."

Annalee hugged him fiercely. "I know, I know." She buried her face on his shoulder and squeezed him again. After a moment, she pushed herself away and gave him a weak smile. "I'm all right. I got shaky there for a minute, but I'll make it."

"Then let's go." Daniel smiled back. "You'll be fine. You always are."

A light rain was falling when they left Berkeley. As Shamus had planned, Daniel and Annalee were just in front of the heavy rush hour traffic on 580 through Castro Valley. It was almost dark as they left Dublin Canyon. Annalee glanced at her watch when they saw the Las Postas exit.

"We doing good?" Daniel asked. They'd hardly spoken since they'd left, but the silence was solid and comfortable.

"We're doing fine," Annalee said.

When they passed a Texaco station she pointed out the rain-blurred window and told him, "That's the pay phone we want, so we're close now. Look for 4800."

When Daniel spotted it moments later, she turned right and circled the block. There were few cars on the wet streets, fewer pedestrians.

"The rain's a blessing," Daniel said. "It's hard to see out the side windows, makes people concentrate on the road."

Annalee said absently, "Small blessings."

She stopped at the mouth of the alley. As she reached to switch off the ignition her hand stopped. She giggled, "Help! Do I turn it off or leave it running?"

"Off," Daniel said. "Along with the headlights. And pull up the hood on your coat."

"Thanks." She smiled at him as she killed the engine. She glanced in the rearview mirror and then up the street.

"Looks fine," Daniel said.

"Well," she said, reaching over into the backseat for the shopping bag, "here we are."

"I'll give two short honks if anything looks like trouble."

Annalee opened the door and slid out, pausing to tell him, "You're special, Daniel." She shut the door with her knee, adjusted the bag in her arms, and walked briskly down the alley.

Daniel could barely see her through the rain-smeared glass so he cranked the window down halfway. He caught a flash of headlights in the rearview mirror and turned to watch as a car hissed past. The rain came down harder. He turned back to the alley just as Annalee disappeared around the left corner. He checked the streets quickly for pedestrians. Not a soul. He was just turning to check the alley when he heard Annalee scream, "Daniel! Run!" and the bomb exploded, blowing the car fifteen feet sideways and hurling a shard of metal through his right temple. He staggered from the car, swayed, collapsed on the wet pavement. Shaking his head, he pushed himself up on his hands and knees, crawled toward the alley, and collapsed again. He lay still, blood and rain in his eyes. When he tried to blink them clear, they stayed closed.

Far below, he saw a tiny point of light. He began sliding toward it, helplessly gathering momentum. As he plunged, the light slowly enlarged, gleaming so brilliantly he was blinded. Daniel was falling into the sun. Just as he was about to be consumed, he realized the light was being reflected from a mirror. He tried to raise his hands to protect his eyes but his hands wouldn't move.

They were lifting him into the ambulance when his heart stopped. The two attendants clamped a defibrillator to his chest, each jolt shooting a thin stream of blood from Daniel's temple, flecking their white uniforms. Daniel's heart fluttered briefly, faded, then weakly started beating again.

Daniel was in a coma when Annalee was buried five days later. Only a few stunned friends from the Random Canyon Raiders attended the brief service. They were photographed from an unmarked car as they left the cemetery.

That night, weeping, Shamus dug far down in the still-loose earth of the grave. He left his black glove, a large gold nugget nestled in its palm gleaming in the moonlight before he covered it over.

Jessal Voltrano was a prodigy of the air. At fourteen, critics were hailing him as a master of the aerial arts, and perhaps the best trapezist who ever lived. For the next five years, he dazzled crowds from Paris to Budapest. He refused to perform or practice with a net. As he explained to one reporter, "Nets discourage concentration."

But two weeks before his twentieth birthday, during a solo performance in Prague, the empty concentration essential to exquisite timing failed him for an instant. He would never forget that disembodied moment when he saw himself open from the plummeting whirl of somersaults, never forget how softly the bar brushed his fingertips as he continued to fall.

One of the clowns reached him first. Jessal was still conscious. "I can feel my skeleton," he whispered in amazement. "I can *feel* it."

No doubt. Except for his hands, he'd broken nearly every bone in his body. During his grueling convalescence, Chester Kane, an American intern, introduced him to sleight-of-hand magic. Jessal practiced the tricks with the same diligence he'd brought to the trapeze, absorbing the nuances of each grip, shuffle, slide, and turn. His therapy became his passion, and when he left the hospital nine months later, he was teaching Dr. Kane.

Jessal returned to the trapeze, but it wasn't the same. His brilliant grace was lost forever to damaged nerves, knotted bone. He left the circus and never looked back.

Changing his name to The Great Volta, he wandered through Europe, Africa, and Indonesia, walking by day, sleeping where night found him, performing his magic wherever people would gather to watch, surviving on the coins they tossed in his hat. As opportunity offered, he watched other magicians work, consulted with them, taught and learned; in every town, he scoured the library for useful texts. At the end of four devoted years, he was an accomplished practitioner of sleight-of-hand magic. However, he began to feel an increasing dissatisfaction, as if his craft and knowledge had become a trap.

One afternoon in Athens, as he performed for a crowd of pensioners and street urchins, Volta muffed a simple card trick, turning the queen of hearts instead of the ace. As the audience hooted at his blunder, Volta realized his magic was hollow, a magic of distraction and mechanical deceit, a manipulation of appearances that could never produce the substance he sought. Volta tossed the deck high in the air, laughing with the crowd as the cards fluttered down. He would remember that moment as his first great escape.

His second occurred a month later, summer solstice 1955. He was sailing to America on a Greek freighter, watching the moon rise from the top deck, when a leaky fuel tank exploded, hurling him into the sea. Watching the moon rise saved his life, for another tank detonated a minute later, engulfing the ship in flames and screams. Volta saw a life raft hit the water and swam for it.

Volta found only one other survivor, and he was badly burned. After attending to him as best he could from the meager first-aid kit, Volta propped him in the bow. He checked the raft's provisions: a week of canned rations, five gallons of water, compass, flare gun, and a steel signal mirror. He set a westerly course and began to row.

When the burned man died five days later, calling deliriously for his mother as Volta held him in his arms, Volta barely had the strength to slip him overboard. A day later he was too exhausted to row. Caught between the punishing sun and the icy moon, he let the raft drift.

The food ran out first. The next night, his throat still aching with the last swallow of water, Volta fired the three flares in quick succession, blooding the sea. He dropped the compass over the side, the first-aid kit, then the flare gun. But when he picked up the signal mirror, he caught an image in the mirror. It wasn't him. The face was swollen and peeled. In his exhausted delirium, he thought that to see his real face he would have to put his mind within the image in the mirror, look at himself through its burned eyes. With his last speck of concentration, he sent himself into the mirror, surrendered himself. When he opened his eyes, there was no one in the raft. He looked into the mirror. It was empty. As he started to fall, he could hear, distantly, a terrified scream wrenched from his lungs. Just as he returned to his body, Volta dropped the mirror into the sea. He was still following its sliver of light when he heard a woman singing. He listened, then opened his eyes.

Her name was Ravana Dremier, the twenty-six-year-old daughter of a French smuggler and Jamaican shamaness. By general consensus, Ravana was the most gifted healer in AMO. She explained to Volta that they'd found him unconscious in the raft four days earlier. They were on the *Pinga del Ray,* one of the few boats in AMO's Caribbean fleet. When he asked her if she'd been singing, she said, "Only if it was your song."

In their four years of travel as allies and lovers, Ravana led him deeper into the magical arts. Ravana's mother had, like Volta, "entered the mirror," a practice, according to Ravana, she'd abandoned almost immediately, warning it was solitary magic, a sensational power not worth the risk. She'd told Ravana, "Entering the mirror requires a unique combination of gift and circumstance. But entering the mirror is simple compared to escaping it. To escape, you must swim the river of stone or fly into the sun."

"Yes," Volta said. Near death on the ocean, he'd found his magic—the art of escape.

Having affiliated himself with AMO before the *Pinga del Ray* reached Haiti—Ravana possessed an eye for talent and persuasive ways—Volta availed himself of Alliance resources, particularly the LUC, its Library of Uncollected Collections, a wildly decentralized network of personal libraries. With a phone call and an access code, a book was mailed the next day. Even better, Volta discovered, was picking the book up in person, because the librarians were scholars of their keep, repositories of distilled information. When they didn't know the answer, they knew the best place to look. They saved Volta time by keeping his focus precise. Volta supplied the passion and discipline. Less than two years later, he performed his first magical escape.

While each of Volta's seventeen escapes are renowned, and each culminated in that moment of dramatic astonishment at the heart of magic, his final escape is a legend of the art. It was performed in St. Louis, on a barge towed to the center of the Mississippi River. Dressed only in tights, Volta was bound in a straightjacket and then shackled in twenty-gauge chain. Assistants helped place him in a cramped steel cube, each side drilled with a series of one-inch holes. When the cover plate was bolted down, a gas-driving crane swung the shining cube over the side and dropped it into the river. People thronged to the rails. Fifteen minutes later, as their anxious babble faded into a numbed silence, Volta, attired in a tuxedo, his hair dry, stepped from his makeshift dressing room. "Forgive my tardiness," he said, adjusting the rose in his lapel, "but I wanted to change into something more comfortable."

The crowd went crazy.

So did Volta.

When all explanations but the impossible were eliminated, the secret to all of Volta's escapes was simple: He dematerialized his body; disintegrated; vanished into air. The steel cube was empty before it touched the river. But as Ravana's mother had warned, with each disappearance, returning became more difficult. He almost hadn't returned the last time, had barely escaped the escape. With a cellular certainty that both terrified and compelled, Volta knew if he ever entered the mirror again, he would not return. The next day he announced his retirement.

But though he'd returned to his flesh, his spirit had snagged on the threshold—he was physically intact, but not quite coherent; dull to sensation; emotionally hollow. He couldn't find a material essence powerful enough to silence the siren-song beyond the mirror, its promise of ecstatic oblivion, final surcease. He couldn't find that binding essence in Ravana's flashing eyes, couldn't feel it in the wind or sense it in the shimmer of salmon moving upstream in the moonlight, couldn't touch it in petals or flesh. Ravana brought her powers to bear but she couldn't reach him. As his desperation drained into depression, Volta realized he could no longer love her as she needed and deserved; to honor Ravana, he forced himself to leave.

AMO provided him with a new identity, a small apartment in New York, and a job as a *sensori*, the Alliance designation for freelance investigators who identified and assessed useful information. The only information Volta wanted was a way to wrest his spirit from the mirror. He found it in a New York museum displaying the Treyton collection of precious stones. Saw it in the brilliant center and irreducibly dense reality of the Faith Diamond, fourth largest on Earth. Needed to touch it, hold it, feel its clarity. He smashed the display case glass with his forearm and was gently lifting the diamond in his cupped hands when a guard clubbed him from behind.

Released from the hospital three days later, Volta was taken directly to jail and booked on grand theft. A squat, pug-faced sergeant with a child's pink skin uncuffed Volta in front of an open cell, punched him in the kidneys, and shoved him inside. Volta grabbed the rust-stained wash basin to keep from falling. When he looked up, he saw himself in the steel mirror bolted above the basin and instantly spun away from the glittering hunger in the mirror's eyes. He used a washcloth to cover the mirror.

Volta was dreaming of sensuously interlocked loops of diamonds when he was slammed awake by a long shuddering wail: "Nooooooo!" As two guards wrestled the new prisoner past Volta's cell, he glimpsed a skinny, pimpled kid, not more than eighteen, throw his head back like a coyote and howl again—"Noooooooooo," a cry at once a denial and a plea.

For an hour after he was locked up and the guards had left, the kid continued wailing, at ten-second intervals, that single, anguished "Nooooooo!" oblivious to the other prisoners' curses to shut up.

The double metal doors at the end of the cellblock banged open and the pug-faced sergeant, his pink skin florid with rage, shambled down the corridor, lightly slapping a blackjack against his pudgy thigh. The cellblock fell instantly silent; then the kid, as if understanding what that silence meant, screamed "Nooooooooo!"

As he unlocked the kid's cell, the sergeant said thickly, "You know what your problem is, son? You need something to plug that little pussy mouth of yours. Now you get down on your knees here for me."

"Nooo," the kid moaned, but his cry had lost its haunting denial. He was begging.

Volta screamed, *"Noooooooo!"* He heard the two quick blows from the blackjack and the kid's sharp cry slurring into a whimper.

The sergeant panted, "I said, on your knees, fuck-face."

When Volta heard the kid gag, he tore the face cloth off the mirror. If he vanished and reappeared quickly in the kid's cell, he might be able to stop it—but only if he could reappear. The eyes looking into his own—wild, inviting—urged him to try. Volta looked through them into the mirror. "No," he said. And he stood there watching himself weep until the kid's choked sobs and the sergeant's thin, rapid wheezing finally ceased.

Stood facing himself as the sergeant, humming, swaggered out, leaving the kid lying on his cell floor, vomiting.

Stood looking at his own haggard, mortal face, his tears, the spittle on his chin. Stood listening through the long desolate silence suddenly broken by three quick sounds: the tiny shriek of springs as the kid leaped from the top bunk; a strangled gasp as the noosed belt cinched; the soft, moist pop of the neck bone breaking.

Volta closed his eyes, leaned back, and, drawing every shred of power from nerve, meat, and bone, howled, *"Noooooooooooooo!"* And when he looked in the mirror again he saw a large spherical diamond—perfect, radiant, real. He was looking for the light in the diamond's center when the sergeant bellowed, "Which motherfucker was it?"

Volta turned from the mirror and walked slowly to the barred cell door. He could hear the faint rhythmic tap of the blackjack against the sergeant's leg.

The sergeant, his voice dropped to a cold murmur, warned, "Last time, scum-buckets: Who screamed?"

"Me," Volta said.

"Well pucker up, fuck-face, 'cause you're next."

"No. You're next," Volta promised. "That boy just hung himself."

"Good," the sergeant said. "S'posed to cull the weak." He yelled over his shoulder to the other guards, "Bring a mop" then turned back to Volta. *"One, fucking, peep* . . . and you're going to die trying to escape."

"You don't understand," Volta said, starting to laugh, "I've already escaped."

"Yeah, sure looks like it t' me, you loony fuck."

Volta gathered enough breath to explain, "Appearances are deceiving," and then surrendered to the comic beauty of his last escape, finding freedom in jail. He wanted to share his delight with the diamond in the mirror, but the diamond had vanished.

Hours later, Volta was released on bail supplied by AMO. The Alliance also provided lawyers from their in-house "firm"—warmly referred to as Sachs, Pilledge, and Berne—and the charge was quietly dismissed on the court-directed stipulation that Volta receive mental health care. His psychiatrist was Dr. Isaac Langmann, a member of AMO's Star, who agreed with his patient that the best course of treatment was advanced training in the Raven's arts.

Shortly after Volta completed his training, Dr. Langmann offered Volta a job as his field representative on the Pacific coast.

Volta loved the work. Since a field representative functions as a nerve to the Star—mediator, messenger, field general, fixer, and roving trouble-shooter—each day brought new people, places, and problems. The people he worked with were impressed with the clarity of his understanding and the fairness of his judgments. When Isaac Langmann retired from the Star in 1963, he nominated Volta to replace him. Fulfilling its most important function, the appropriate integration of talent and task, the Star unanimously approved Volta on the first poll. At the time of the Livermore explosion, Volta had served with distinction for seventeen years.

Volta was standing at the foot of the bed when Daniel, after nine weeks in a coma, opened his eyes. Daniel looked dully around the hospital room and then, squinting, focused on Volta.

Volta nodded slightly. "Welcome back, Daniel."

Daniel trembled as he tried to speak. Volta waited. When Daniel failed again, Volta said softly, "Your mother is dead."

Daniel lifted his hands as if he were going to cover his face but they collapsed weakly across his chest. He shut his eyes tightly, but couldn't stop the tears.

"I share your sorrow," Volta said. "I appreciate the poverty of condolence at such a loss, but I offer it nonetheless."

Daniel moaned, arching against the bed as if trying to sit up.

Volta said, "I know I'm presuming on the intimacy of your grief and have clearly violated your privacy, but I'm afraid I must."

Nodding distractedly, Daniel brought his hands to his face, fingertips pressed hard against his closed eyes.

"My name is Volta. You've met two of my most trusted friends, Smiling Jack and Elmo Cutter. I serve AMO as a member of the Star, the Alliance's facilitating council. I'm here to offer our heartfelt regrets and, if you want it, our wholehearted help.

"Your situation is complicated, Daniel. You were injured in the explosion; a sliver of metal from the clock's hand pierced your temple, traveled upward at approximately a forty-degree angle through the edge of the right hemisphere of your brain, and lodged against the skull. Although the EEG and other tests indicate 'normal' brain function—whatever that might be— you have been in a coma for nine weeks. There may be damage the tests haven't revealed, but other than the coma, all indications are excellent.

"You are nominally under police guard, no visitors allowed, but since the posted guards were withdrawn a month ago, the restrictions are merely formal. When they find you've regained consciousness, you'll likely be arrested. If so, you can expect to be interrogated by people who know how. My advice is to say you don't remember anything from at least a month before the blast; conditional amnesia is medically consistent with trauma. So is selective recall. It would probably be best if you had no idea that your mother was planting a bomb. All she told you was that she was delivering something for a friend— better yet, a stranger."

Daniel uncovered his eyes, looked up at the ceiling for a moment, then back at Volta. He wet his lips. "How did you know? The bomb? That it wasn't already there?"

Patiently, Volta explained, "I know because Shamus called and told me everything. He was extremely distraught. He blames himself."

"They were in love!" Daniel sobbed. He shook his head helplessly. "Oh Mom, Mom, Mom."

"Yes," Volta said, "I know they were in love. I know it hurts."

Daniel lashed, "Tell me who killed her!"

"Nobody," Volta said calmly. "By all evidence, it was a faulty bomb."

"Nobody? Then why were her last words 'Daniel! Run!' "

Volta looked at him sharply. "She called to you?"

"She *screamed!"* Daniel sobbed.

"And then?"

Daniel struggled for composure. "The bomb exploded before I could even turn to look. Like her scream set it off. That fast."

Volta considered the information.

"She was *warning* me," Daniel said.

"Clearly. But about what? Did you notice any people or activity immediately prior to her shout?"

"No. And I was looking."

As much to himself as Daniel, Volta murmured, "She may have sensed something go wrong with the bomb."

Daniel didn't respond.

Volta asked, "Did she arm the bomb before entering the alley?"

"No."

"Did she have time to do it before it detonated?"

"She must have. It blew up."

"The pavement was wet. Maybe she slipped and dropped it. Heard a connection sputtering."

"I don't know," Daniel said weakly. "I don't know. She screamed and it exploded."

"If you want, we'll look into it. It will take time, no doubt, but perhaps less if you know who built the bomb."

"I don't," Daniel said. "Shamus should, though—ask him."

"I'd like to. However, I've been trying to locate him for over a month now to discuss your situation, but he seems to have vanished. Any ideas where he might be?"

"No. But I want to know anything you find about my mother. I want to know what went wrong."

"Naturally. You will be kept completely informed—on that you have my word. Which leads to other matters we have to discuss. For instance, your future, and how we might help you."

"Help me do what?"

"First, to escape the thirteen or so charges that will be filed against you. They only have inklings that the bomb was connected to a plutonium theft, so be very careful about what you say."

"They haven't linked her with Shamus?"

Volta lowered his eyes, then looked back up, straight at Daniel. "Your mother didn't leave any fingerprints, Daniel. Everything they know is from paper. They think she was Mrs. Wyatt. We've cleaned the *Baton Rouge* connections, the bank account and land titles, and would be grateful if you forgot Dubuque completely." Volta kept talking to distract Daniel's imagination from what the blast must have done to his mother. "However, from the snowshoe rental receipt in your pocket—the homemade driver's license in your wallet had a phony name but the right address—the McKinley Street house was raided before we could cover it, so you also face some forgery and illegal possession charges. You'd be well advised to have an exceptional attorney, and we'd be glad to provide one free if you so choose."

"I'd appreciate that," Daniel said.

"You're fourteen, so you'll be tried as a juvenile—actually, if things go well it'll probably end up as a hearing, not a trial. It would help things go well if your amnesia proves intractable. Follow your lawyer's instructions. We'll try to get all charges dismissed and have you placed in your aunt's custody."

"I don't have an aunt."

Volta cocked his head. "Aunt Matilda and Uncle Owen? The Wyatt Ranch up in Mendocino County?"

"All right," Daniel said.

Volta crossed his arms. "Now, your future. Many people have spoken highly of you, people whose judgment I esteem—Smiling Jack, for one; Dolly Varden, Johnny Seven Moons, Elmo, and others. They think you have special qualities which should be developed and refined. AMO has some uniquely talented teachers who might help you transform potential into ability."

"Can I accept the legal help and not the teachers?"

"There's no negotiation necessary. These are unconditional offers of assistance. Avail yourself as you please."

"I want the lawyer. The rest I need to think about."

Volta said, "I'll contact an attorney the moment I leave, which must be soon. But first I want you to know that I facilitated your return to consciousness by using simple, but suppressed, techniques that were taught to me by a woman named Ravana Dremier. Basically I joined your mind through the powers of empathy, and then I reminded you of life. I assure you I implanted no ideas or suggestions; I merely summoned your attention. I'm telling you this because you may remember my voice calling you—if you don't at present, you may in the future, particularly in states of dream or reverie. It was your decision to return. I'm sorry about Annalee, Daniel. Heal quickly."

Volta was at the door when Daniel called, "Thank you."

Volta turned and said, "Yes. You're welcome," and closed the door behind him.

Two: EARTH

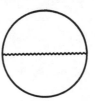

*The earth, being eager to generate, always produces something; you
will imagine you see birds or beasts or reptiles in the glass.*
—Philalethes

VOLTA: Bill, it's Volta. I need a decision about Daniel.

WILD B.: You're *sure* he's never been to any school?

VOLTA: As perfectly sure as the last time we discussed it.

WILD B.: Well, what about *organic* brain damage. Anything show up?

VOLTA: They've run every test they have. No evidence of impairment.

WILD B.: So why was he in a coma for nine weeks?

VOLTA: It's what the *Corpus Hermeticum* calls "hiding on the threshold."

WILD B.: Still pounding them dusty tomes, huh?

VOLTA: Still curious.

WILD B.: And curiouser and curiouser, I bet. Personally, I'm partial to Westerns.

VOLTA: If you keep tweaking me, I'll let it be known that when we first met, you were still a Jesuit priest—*and* a rather sensational young Latin scholar.

WILD B.: Just more proof them books get you in trouble.

VOLTA: That's like blaming your legs for taking you to the whorehouse.

WILD B.: (laughing) "Silence is golden."

VOLTA: Indeed. And decision is of the essence. That's why I need yours on Daniel. And I do understand that you have some personal work planned, that you're tired of teaching, that you're old and cranky and have lost your edge, but Daniel may be the student you've been looking for.

WILD B.: Didn't know I was looking. But all right, you've met him. How do you feel?

VOLTA: He's got a ferocious mind, and, for one so young, not completely at the expense of subtlety. He strikes to the meat, but he's impulsive, of course—youth again—yet remarkably self-possessed. He's held himself together through some hideous blows, and I think—

WILD B.: (cutting him off) *Feel.* How do you *feel* about him?

VOLTA: (after a long pause) Powerfully attracted; powerfully repelled.

WILD B.: Ah, so that's what got your attention.

VOLTA: On further consideration, you may be the worst choice imaginable.

WILD B.: Are you appealing to my pride or perversity now?

VOLTA: I wasn't aware you made the distinction.

WILD B.: (laughing) Sold. I'll take him. But no more than eighteen months, and I get to go off to the desert in peace. Plus you owe me a serious favor.

VOLTA: What's that now? About three hundred and seven?

WILD B.: At least.

VOLTA: The Wyatt Ranch? Two weeks?

WILD B.: I'll be there.

*DANIEL WAS ARRESTED AN HOUR AFTER HE OFFI-*cially regained consciousness. Alexander Kreef, an attorney specializing in juvenile law, arrived a few minutes later with a handful of writs and injunctions. He was accompanied by Daniel's physician, furious his patient had been disturbed without his approval.

The dour lieutenant attempting to question Daniel was not impressed.

"Excuse me all to shit," he bowed to Dr. Tobin, then turned to Alexander Kreef and said with nasty delight, "The kid ain't retained attorney yet—just come to."

Alexander Kreef smiled pleasantly. "I was hired by Mr. and Mrs. Wyatt, his aunt and uncle, and am entered as attorney of record." He handed an eight-pound pile of papers to the lieutenant, who looked at them and dropped them on the floor.

Alexander Kreef kept smiling: "You ask my client one more question and I'll bust your ass so hard you'll shit through your ears. No, on second thought, ask away; we get more dismissals on procedural errors than airtight alibis."

"Fuck you." The lieutenant glared at Alexander Kreef, then Daniel, but put his microcassette recorder away.

"Un-uh," Alexander chided, motioning for the recorder. "Inadmissible without due counsel."

"Wow. Gee, no, really? Not that it matters, Counselor—seems he don't remember shit. I mean it's pretty fucking hard to remember something as quiet as an explosion that blew your momma into memories and bone chips."

"You cold prick," Alexander hissed, but it was lost in Dr. Tobin's outraged howl: "Good God, Lieutenant! This young man has suffered profound cerebral trauma, been in a coma for nine weeks, and you expect him to answer questions? Did it ever enter your feeble mind that the boy might have some form of amnesia common to severe head injuries—total, partial, or conditional?"

"I'm not a physician," Alexander said, "but total seems likely in this case."

"Yeah, I bet. Probably won't even remember if he was the alleged Mrs. Wyatt's son, or who his alleged father might be. 'Course with that paper factory they were running, probably hard to keep all the identities straight. Yeah, fucking hard to remember anything." The lieutenant looked at Daniel. "Ain't that right, kid?"

"I don't remember you," Daniel said, then shut his eyes.

Daniel's hearing was held on December 7. The serious charges were dropped in exchange for his mitigated *nolo contendere* to the lesser counts. He was placed in the guardianship of his aunt and uncle until he was seventeen, at which time, assuming no further arrests, his record would be sealed. Some red tape remained, but Alexander Kreef turned it into Christmas ribbon, and on December 21 Daniel was released. He left that afternoon with Matilda and Owen Wyatt for a cattle ranch in the coastal hills, roughly fifty miles north of the Four Deuces.

The Wyatts were in their mid-fifties, a happy, vigorous couple who took great pleasure in their life on the ranch. The Wyatts owned 1400 acres, but had always run fewer cattle than the carrying capacity allowed. While a struggle at first, their operation was now considered a model of ecological intelligence.

Riding north with the Wyatts Daniel felt tentative and vaguely numb, though they were easy company. He learned that they'd known Volta for fifteen years, from the time he'd helped end a serious rustling problem that had plagued them.

"So you're repaying a favor?" Daniel inquired, curious why they'd gotten involved.

"Hell no," Owen told him, "we're members of the Alliance."

Daniel found that difficult to believe. "So the cattle are a front?"

"Daniel," Tilly explained, "you don't have to be illegal to be an outlaw."

"But you stood up in court and said I was a relative—perjury is illegal."

"The cops couldn't prove otherwise," Tilly said, "so how do *you* know you're not kin? We got big families on both sides, and both share the same motto: One Hand Washes the Other. Besides, we got tired of being so *straight.*"

As they pulled into the ranch just after dark, Owen pointed to his left. "You'll be staying in that cabin down there past the feed barn. You see it there, got the light on?"

"I see two lights," Daniel said.

"The little cabin's Wild Bill's, your teacher—he pulled in a few days ago. Tilly and I'll get the house warm and some chow on the table while you go down and say hello."

"If you want to," Tilly added.

"You see who runs this outfit," Owen groused, but it was plain he wouldn't have had it any other way.

Nobody answered Daniel's knock. He knocked louder, and when there was still no answer he opened the door and called, "Hello?"

When a voice squawked "What?" he went in. Wild Bill Weber was sitting cross-legged and naked on the floor, slowly and methodically hitting himself between the eyes with a large rubber mallet. "Pleased to meet you, Daniel," Wild Bill said, continuing the rhythmic mallet blows. "I'm Bill Weber. We'll be working together."

"You're my teacher?" Daniel said, not so much incredulous as nervously perplexed.

Wild Bill threw the mallet at Daniel's head.

Ducking, Daniel heard the mallet whiz by his ear and hit the wall with a dull *thock,* the wooden handle clattering as it rebounded across the floor. He started to pick it up and hurl it back, but instead turned on Wild Bill and demanded, *"Why* did you do that? What are you doing?"

Wild Bill was watching carefully. After a moment he said, "Daniel, let's get it clear right from the jump: *I'm* the teacher. *I* work on the questions; *you* work on the answers. So *you* tell *me* why I chucked my brain-tuner at you."

"I don't know," Daniel said. "No idea."

"Good," Wild Bill nodded. "That's the right answer. But from now on there are no right or wrong answers."

"I'm not following this at all," Daniel admitted.

"You probably won't for about a year, so just relax and do what I tell you and maybe we can both get through without much damage."

The year passed quickly for Daniel, the time greased by routine. He woke at 4:00; did his dawn meditation; joined Tilly, Owen, and Wild Bill in the main house for breakfast at 5:00; worked until 4:00 in the afternoon; did his evening meditation; ate dinner at 6:00; did the dishes if it was his turn; had free time from then till 9:45; received formal instruction from Wild Bill between 9:45 and 9:50; and then did his dream meditation and went to bed at 10:30. The diversity of the routine saved Daniel from boredom.

The day's work was anything from branding cattle to scrubbing the kitchen floor. Daniel fixed fence, fed stock, and cut wood. They planted and cut hay and did special projects, like building a smokehouse. He usually worked with Owen or Tilly, for Wild Bill flatly refused any direct contact with the cattle, dismissing them as "twisted critters and dumb insults to wild spirit." Tilly and Owen argued otherwise—persuasively, Daniel thought—and the subject caused some strain. But one winter night some lightning-spooked steers broke down the corral. Wild Bill saddled up and rode out with the rest of them in the storm to herd the cattle home, bringing the last strays in well after breakfast.

Owen grinned hugely as Wild Bill rode in, enjoying the sight of Bill working cattle as much as the return of the steers. "Well, well," Owen had greeted him, "git along li'l dogies."

Wild Bill reined up sharply, barking, "Don't be getting no goddamn notions now. I might be a fanatic, but I'm no purist. As long as I'm living here, I'll lend a hand when you're truly pressed. Don't mean I'm joining the fucking Grange."

Daniel's three daily meditations, like the ranch work, shared only a structural formality. Wild Bill's instructions had been brief: "Morning meditation is to fill your mind; evening meditation is to see what it's filled *with,* and dream meditation is to empty it. You'll figure out right away that filling it, seeing it, and emptying it are the same, but keep in mind that they couldn't be the same unless they were different. So it's not so much concentrating *on* the purpose, as concentrating *through* it. This first week we'll sit together and I'll show you the postures and breathing and such, but after that you'll do them alone in your cabin. I'll check on you whenever I want. The first time I find you not doing your meditations, I'm through as your teacher. So if you ever want to quit and don't have the guts to tell me so, all you have to do is let me catch you fucking off when you should be sitting."

After showing Daniel the postures and appropriate breathing for each meditation, he'd explained, "Now the most important thing is to get your mind dialed in on Top Dead Center, focus down for depth, and put the needle right through the zero. I'll show you what works for me."

Wild Bill went to the closet, explaining over his shoulder, "I'm going to my audiovisual department. Can't hardly call yourself a teacher these days without some audiovisuals." And had stunned Daniel by reaching in the closet and pulling out a human skeleton.

Daniel, though he flinched, didn't say a word.

"Okay," Wild Bill said, holding the skeleton by the spine, "before every meditation you do this little exercise called 'Counting the Bones.' Probably the oldest psychic woo-woo practice in the world—goes all the way back to the Paleolithic shamans as far as I can follow. What you do is simple: You imagine your skeleton, and then, starting with the toes, count your bones. And I don't mean that 'one, two,' shit—just see each bone clear in your mind and move on. You go *up* the body from the toes, both legs at once, join at the pelvis, shoot up the spine, swoop across the ribs, run out the arms, sail back to the shoulders, up the neck to the skull, and then right to the center of your brain."

"The brain isn't a bone," Daniel said.

"Neither is your dick," Wild Bill explained.

If Daniel found such explanations baffling, he was even more bewildered by the five-minute daily segment that constituted his formal study. Wild Bill asked one question and Daniel had five minutes to answer. Wild Bill never indicated if an answer was right, wrong, faulty, inspired, weak, provocative, or ill-considered. And the questions were such that the answers couldn't be checked.

"Where did you set your fork when you finished your waffles this morning?"

"That bird we saw in the orchard—what color was its throat?"

"What did Tilly say about the cornbread recipe Owen claims he learned from his Grandma?"

"When the wind shifted along Fern Creek this afternoon, which direction did it blow?"

During his dream meditation, supposedly emptying his mind, Daniel thought about the questions and his doubtful answers. Slowly he became aware of himself in the world, seeing what he saw, doing what he did: laying the posthole digger next to the picket maul; the shapes of clouds; the curved black plume of a cock valley quail on the fencepost; the phase of the moon.

But no matter how much he concentrated in the physical moment or focused through meditation, he kept hearing his mother scream, "Daniel! Run!" And as his numbness gave way to grief, and grief to the buried rage of depression, the only question he really wanted answered was what had happened in that alley.

He told Wild Bill, "Volta said he would investigate my mother's death and let me know what he learned—he gave me his word. And in ten months I've heard from him *once*, to say there was no progress. I guess I better do it myself, which means I've got to quit here and go back to Berkeley. It's nothing personal. I mean, it's nothing between you and me; it's with Volta."

"Then take it up with him." Wild Bill shrugged. "But I'll tell you this: If Volta gave you his word, I can stone guarantee two things—he's working on it, and he'll let you know. Volta may be the most honorable man I ever met. To a fault, perhaps. And besides, AMO has an extraordinary intelligence network. You won't do any better on your own. And you do understand that if you just take off, Tilly and Owen might catch some shit. My suggestion is to talk to Volta. Give him a call in the morning. And sleep in if you want, since I guess we're done with school."

"Let me talk to Volta first," Daniel said. "I would have before, but I don't have a number for him."

"I got about twenty," Wild Bill said.

But Daniel didn't need them. Volta arrived the next morning with a letter from Shamus. They went to Daniel's cabin.

"Before you read it," Volta said, "let me supply some context. Shamus is hiding. When the bomb exploded, it aborted the plutonium heist; therefore, there was no overt connection. But there were suspicions—"

"I know," Daniel interrupted. "They asked me about him specifically. I couldn't remember."

"It's these damn computers. They probably pulled anybody who'd made a try, came up with him fleeing the Four Deuces with a woman and child—an idiot could see the connection. We've got to recruit more people with computer knowledge so we can either eliminate the information they want to retrieve or replace it with what we'd like them to have."

Daniel said pointedly, "But *nobody* knows where Shamus is, right? Not the cops, not you?"

"That's correct." Volta smiled. "Forgive the digression on the skills the Alliance lacks. But while we didn't know where he is, we did let it be known that we'd like to talk to him about the other people involved in the plutonium job."

"How did you do that? Let him know?"

"We went looking for the others hard enough that the pressure was felt. Thus, the letter. It was sent from Topeka, Kansas, for what that's worth." Daniel read the letter carefully.

> Volta—
>
> There were three people involved besides myself, Annalee, and Daniel (who was included at Annalee's discretion, against my advice). Of the other three, two did not know about the diversionary bomb nor who would deliver it. The third, who constructed the bomb, did not know what it was for, when it would be used, or who would deliver it. It was evidently a faulty bomb, though the maker insists that given the nature of the device, accidental detonation was virtually impossible.
>
> Leave it alone. I accept the blame. You have my word I will never make another attempt. Let me be.
>
> S.M.

Daniel read it again. It looked like Shamus's handwriting, but he wasn't sure.

Volta said, "I want your permission to put out word that your mom yelled for you to run before the bomb exploded. Perhaps we can draw Shamus out—we need more information about those involved."

"Of course," Daniel agreed, then added with clear annoyance, "I figured you would have already done that. I mean, Shamus deserves to know. He's blaming himself."

"He should," Volta said.

"What do you mean? Do you think he messed with the bomb?"

"No. I have no evidence he tampered with the bomb; none at all. I only meant that he was the agent for the occasion. He enlisted her help in a patently dangerous undertaking."

"She *wanted* to help him."

"Did you?"

"Yes."

"Why?"

Daniel paused before answering. "It's complicated. I wanted to help my mom, once she was involved. And I wanted to help Shamus because I thought he felt I was jealous that Mom liked him. I wasn't. I just wanted her to be happy. And he made her happy, I guess. And also because I believed in what Shamus was doing, and because of the excitement, too, I suppose. Like I said, it's complicated."

"It's *all* complicated, Daniel. That's why it's taking time to sort it out."

"So why didn't you tell him that it wasn't an accident?"

Volta said, "First of all, because we don't know it wasn't an accident. Secondly, because Shamus might already know it wasn't."

"How?"

"Maybe Shamus didn't intend to leave any implicating witnesses." Volta cocked his head slightly. "You do understand that possibility?"

"I don't believe it," Daniel said flatly.

"Do you want to proceed on the basis of belief, Daniel, or should we seek some concrete information?"

"Just proceed is good enough. You're wrong about Shamus, though—but I guess that's something you'll have to find out for yourself."

"I intend to. I'd also intended to stay through tomorrow and enjoy the good company here at the ranch, but something urgent has developed in L.A., and I must be there this evening. But I can't leave without asking how you're doing with Wild Bill and his odd pedagogy."

"You'd have to ask him. I have no idea."

Volta smiled faintly. "Well, just remember that from Wild Bill 'maybe' is high praise."

After Volta left, Wild Bill walked over to Daniel's cabin, feigning surprise when he saw Daniel sitting on the porch. "Still with us?"

"Still here," Daniel said absently.

"What is it now?"

"I don't know. Volta . . . I don't quite ever believe him."

"He's done right by you, near as I can tell. He is a tad slippery, but that's because he doesn't leap to conclusions. Likes to get a grasp of what's going on, the big picture, before he starts mucking around."

Daniel said, "Is that why you called him last night?"

"Wrong," Wild Bill chuckled.

"Just a coincidence he shows up this morning?"

"Hasn't it ever occurred to you that coincidence is the natural state of affairs? 'As above, so below.' Only time I worry about coincidence is when it *quits* happening. That's when your ass goes up for grabs. But for now, why

81

don't you get your little cracker ass up off itself and go fetch the shotguns and a couple o' boxes of number eights—I told Tilly we'd stroll up the creek and see if we could find us some quail for dinner."

"What about lunch? Should I pack some sandwiches?"

"Probably a coincidence, but I already did it while you were jawing with Volta."

The routine held through April without significant change. Daniel was restless and increasingly impatient with Wild Bill. The lovely spring weather didn't help. Then, on the last night of April, during formal instruction, Wild Bill surprised Daniel with a question that had an answer, albeit an answer Daniel was reluctant to provide.

"You know that skeleton I gave you out of my audiovisual department to help you counting bones?"

"Yes."

"What do you call it? I mean its secret name."

"Well," Daniel stalled, "it's sort of ridiculous."

"Let me judge that. I'm an expert."

"I call him 'Mudflaps.' "

Wild Bill laughed helplessly, catching his breath only long enough to shriek in delight, *"Mudflaps! Mud . . . Flaps."*

"I'm glad you find me so amusing," Daniel said.

Collapsing to his knees, Wild Bill managed to gasp, "Me too."

Daniel turned and walked out the door.

The next day Daniel ignored Wild Bill. He did his meditations and his work, but with an air of bored efficiency and chilly indifference. That night Wild Bill surprised him again.

"Three holy men were traveling together. One was an Indian yoga, one a Sufi dervish, one a Zen monk. In the course of their journey, they came to a small river. There had been a bridge, but it had washed out in the winter flood. 'Let me show you two how to cross a river,' the yogi said—and damned if he didn't walk across it, right on top of the water. 'No, no, that's not the way,' the dervish said. 'Let me show you guys.' He starts whirling in a circle, faster and faster until he's a blur of concentrated energy and all of sudden—*bam!*—he leaps across to the other side. The Zen monk stood there shaking his head. 'You fools,' he said, 'this is how to cross the river.' And with that, he hiked up his robes and, feeling his way carefully, waded across."

Daniel waited.

"Now the night's question is this: What's the point of that story?"

Daniel said without hesitation, "The river."

Wild Bill looked startled. "Maybe," he said. He considered a moment and then repeated, "Maybe."

Daniel said, "Volta claims that's high praise from you."

"He does, huh?" Wild Bill said distractedly. "You know, I should piss you off more often." He smiled. "Mudflaps. It's all I could do to keep from laughing all day."

Daniel smiled with him.

The next morning Wild Bill surprised Daniel yet again, announcing, "It's my turn to quit. Actually, I'm going on vacation for awhile, which means you're on vacation too—free to do whatever you want as long as you pull your weight on the ranch."

"I must have done really well or horribly poor last night," Daniel said, finding himself unsettled by the sudden changes.

"Naw, you're just ready for other angles, and we're both tired and need to unbend. Like it says in the book, 'Take care, from time to time, to unbend your mind from its sterner employments with some convenient recreation, otherwise your spirits may be weighed down, and you might lose heart for the continuation of the work.' "

"What book is that from?"

"The Ordinal of Alchemy."

Playfully, Daniel said, "I didn't even know you could read."

"Used to all the time, but I started losing heart so bad I almost destroyed myself on the 'convenient recreations.' "

"Are you going to see Volta?"

"I hope not," Wild Bill said. "Jenny Sue is more like it."

An hour later Wild Bill set out down the dirt road, his banged-up rucksack on his back, humming a marching song for the occasion, a lyric that made up in heartfelt emotion what it lacked in scansion:

Jenny Sue, ooooooo Jenny Sue,
Ain't nothing in this whole gloriously sweet and delightful world
That little gal won't do . . .

In Wild Bill's absence, Daniel, like most students, screwed off. He converted the morning and dream meditations into sleep, and the evening meditation was reformed into fishing. In his free time he tied trout flies, read among his promiscuous selections from the library, or played cribbage with Owen. May warmed into June and June drowsed into July without word from Wild Bill. Then, on the fourth of August, what was left of him returned.

Daniel grimaced when he opened his cabin door and saw Wild Bill sagging against the frame. Both eyes were black, his left ear hideously swollen, a front tooth was chipped, and there was a neat row of stitches above his left eye.

"Holy shit," Daniel blurted. "What happened?"

"Aww," Wild Bill mumbled, "bunch of guys stomped the piss outa me."

"Why?"

" 'Cause that's what I was trying to do to them."

"What about Jenny Sue or whatever her name is—your girlfriend?"

"Last time I looked, she was helping them."

"Do you want me to take you in to the hospital?"

Wild Bill touched the stitches on his forehead. "I just got out."

"You want to come in and lay down? You look like you could use some rest."

"Kid, any more rest would fucking kill me. Pack up whatever you plan to live on till next spring. We're going to the mountains." He reached into his shirt pocket with a scab-knuckled hand. "Here's a list of stuff you'll probably need. Another thing—we ain't comin' back for visits, so you're not gonna be hearing from Volta or anyone else. You can call Volta tomorrow to see if there's any news. You'll be wasting your dime, 'cause you'd of heard if anything was happening. If you don't want to go, I'll go without you and we'll call the teaching done. If you want to go, be ready in the morning."

"What about Owen and Tilly? They need a hand around here."

"There'll be folks along to take care of that."

"Why the mountains? Are we hiding out?"

Wild Bill snapped, "No. We're getting serious."

His vehemence startled Daniel. He didn't reply.

"You want Volta's numbers or not?"

"No," Daniel said, "it's okay."

"Get shaggin' then. I want to get the fuck out of here."

"Not till you tell me what happened. What the fight was about."

"No secret. I said the bottle never ran dry. The bartender and his buddies said it did."

"I guess it did, huh?"

"No shit," Wild Bill said. "Always."

Tilly drove them north the next morning to the Huta Point trailhead at the edge of the Yolla Bolly Wilderness. Along the way she and Wild Bill figured out the resupply plans, deciding on a monthly interval, with the food and equipment to be cached in two metal footlockers near the old crossing on Balm of Gilead Creek. She hugged them briefly in farewell. Tilly was the last human being Wild Bill and Daniel would see for six months—besides each other, of course. They would see plenty of each other.

Daniel followed Wild Bill down and then up dark slopes of old-growth Douglas fir. He refused to ask where they were headed. Wild Bill didn't offer a destination. He remained uncommonly silent, applying his breath to the trek, maintaining a steady pace.

They camped that night on the Middle Fork of the Eel. Each had brought his own tent. Wild Bill had explained, "I hired on to teach you, not sleep with you. And anyway, I've been known to do some late-night meditating that your snoring wouldn't encourage."

They finished pitching their tents as the last light faded. Daniel, ravenous, was eager for dinner, but Wild Bill told him that they hadn't done their sunset meditation, which they were now adding to the other three. Its purpose was simply to sit and let the river roll. While he was on the subject, he informed Daniel that meditations, by ancient tradition, were doubled in duration while in the mountains.

"That's six hours a day!"

"Eight for me. I normally do a half-hour at midnight and another at two. You probably should be doing eight hours yourself, but I'm easy."

"Does the question-time get doubled to ten minutes?"

Wild Bill ignored the sarcasm. "No. Five minutes is already too much work."

Daniel had tried not to anticipate the question, but he had assumed it would be perceptual, not personal, and was caught slightly off guard when Wild Bill poked the fire and said, "Why haven't you asked where we're going?"

"Because it makes no difference," Daniel replied.

Wild Bill rolled his eyes. "Oh, bullshit. When has that ever stopped you? I think it's adolescent perversity myself. It's wasted on the mountains. Just be real, that's all it takes. And since you haven't asked where we're going, I'll tell you."

Their destination was a geomorphological anomaly called Blacktail Basin. In the center of the basin was a twenty-acre lake. Wild Bill claimed he'd never seen the lake on any map, thus giving credence to the local Indian legend that a Nomlaki shaman had cast a spell of invisibility on it after his first encounter with a white man. Since the lake was spring-fed—"filled from within," as the Nomlaki described it—they considered it a place of great power, and thus a place to be protected. Although Wild Bill had discovered it independently some fifteen years earlier, he contacted the Nomlaki elders whenever he planned to go there. They always let him. In their view, he had "seen through" the spell, which could only mean the place had chosen to reveal itself to him. Who were they to grant a permission that was already so clearly given?

Since the lake was under the spell of invisibility and therefore didn't exist, it couldn't have a name—a referential problem the Nomlaki had neatly solved by calling it Nameless Lake.

Wild Bill spoke highly of Nomlaki culture. "The Nomlaki were known out to the coast and up to the Klamath for their shamanistic powers, healing and sorcery in particular, which are two of the tougher arts. And you've got to like a culture where the most precious thing you can own or trade is a black bear hide to be buried in."

They crested the lower rim of Blacktail Basin late the next afternoon and headed down toward what Wild Bill assured Daniel was the lake, though it wasn't visible. Daniel had expected the basin would be dramatic, but in fact it was quite shallow, with less than a four-hundred-foot elevation drop from the low southern rim to the center. The basin was heavily forested along its upper slopes. As they made their way downhill, the trees grew farther apart, and the fern and gooseberry understory gradually thinned away. Despite the change in density, the flora seemed arranged in such a way that while you had a feeling of open forest, you couldn't see more than ten feet in front of yourself. Daniel almost walked into the lake before he saw it.

Daniel followed Wild Bill around the lake to a terracelike meadow. Sheltered by the steeper northern rim, nicely oriented to the sun, with an unobstructed view of the lake, the meadow was a perfect campsite.

Wild Bill slung off his pack. "Goddamn! It's a pleasure to get out from under this load."

"How high is this lake?"

"High as you wanna get."

"I meant elevation."

"Close to three thousand feet," said Wild Bill.

"We'll probably get some snow then, right?"

"Just enough to occasionally change the view."

Stretching, Daniel looked around. "I can see why the Indians think it's under some spell—the trees are a natural screen."

"What you don't see," Wild Bill told him, "is that the shaman moved the trees."

With a playfulness that both allowed and protected his mild disrespect, Daniel said, "Whatever you say, Teach."

"You're learning. And I say we set up camp and then jump on the chores."

When camp was squared away, Wild Bill announced, "All right, we're home. Now to the chores. There's only two: fishing for dinner and gathering firewood. Take your choice."

Daniel said, "I'll fish."

"That's my choice, too," Wild Bill told him.

"So I lose, right?"

"Well . . . given my experience and all, I *should* fish—I'm a fish-catching fool—but don't ever say Wild Bill ran you over by abusing his natural authority on almost anything that matters. Tell you what: I'll fish for about an hour while you collect wood, and then you fish for an hour while I sit there and laugh. Whoever catches the most fish, he's the Official Camp Fisherman for a month—the loser can practice when the rod ain't required by the champ for survival protein production."

"You're on," Daniel said.

Wild Bill winked. "That's just what I tell them fish when I set the hook."

Wild Bill caught two.

Daniel didn't catch any. He couldn't understand it—he was fishing off the same overhanging boulder where Wild Bill had caught his, and he could see the surface swirls of feeding fish. He was concentrating so deeply that he was startled to hear Wild Bill at his shoulder. "Count your catch, the hour's up."

"Okay," Daniel sighed, "what's the secret?"

"Give me the pole and I'll show you how it's done."

Daniel reluctantly surrendered the rod.

"Now pay close attention," Wild Bill said.

When Daniel turned slightly to watch, Wild Bill put a hand on his chest and pushed him backward off the boulder into the lake. The shock of cold water brought him gasping to the surface.

Wild Bill was pointing down into the water. "See them rocks there in the shallows? Now see them black dots? Those are the stick-and-stone houses of caddis fly larvae, which is what the fish are feeding on today."

Teeth chattering, Daniel waded to shore. He was furious, but he had to know. "Okay, what kind of fly were you using to imitate them?"

"Well shit," Wild Bill said, putting his arm around Daniel's wet shoulders, "I took my pocketknife and sliced that goony looking batch of feathers off the hook and put on some of those real caddis fly larvae. That's what the fish are eating—not a bunch of feathers and tinsel and such."

Daniel shivered. "That's cheating."

"You got to fish 'em *real slow,*" Wild Bill explained. "Sort of let 'em swirl up easy from the bottom. I tell ya, takes tons of patience and a pretty good sense of humor to get it right."

The regimen was much like that at the ranch: meditation, daily work, nightly question. The only significant change was the addition of what Wild Bill called teaching, which amounted to Daniel listening to him tell stories around the campfire.

"My dad saw something over on the Middle Fork that I doubt either of us ever will. He saw two full-grown male bears fighting over a she-bear. *That* ain't so unusual, of course, but the thing of it was, one of the bears was a black bear and the other was a grizzly bear. Quite a tussle."

"Who won?"

"Well, like daddy always said"—Wild Bill paused to spit emphatically in the fire—" 'Son, if you're gonna be a bear, be a grizzly.' "

"What kind of bear was the female?" Daniel said.

"You know what, Daniel? You could fuck up a steel ball."

Daniel bristled. "What do you mean?"

"I mean it ain't easy to fuck up a steel ball."

Although the regimen was basically the same, the quality of the days was different. They existed quite easily. Along with the food they'd packed in—heavy on rice and beans—there were fish, edible plants and fungi in season, and birds, small game, and an occasional deer that fell to the .222/.410 they'd brought. To preserve ammo, they only took one shell in each chamber while hunting, a practice, Daniel soon discovered, that greatly increased his accuracy. On average, they spent less than an hour a day on food.

Daniel used his free time to explore the basin, day-dream, or work on various projects, most of which failed. He could hardly hit the hillside with the bow and arrows he made. His hand-carved duck call hastened mallards on their way. His fish traps didn't.

Wild Bill was no help and less solace. "You can usually trace failure back to one of two things: design or execution. Looks to me like both of 'em got you."

At the end of each month they hiked back to the Balm of Gilead crossing and picked up their month's supplies from the two hidden footlockers. Tilly or Owen always left a note with any important news. There had been one message from Volta to say there was nothing to report. It took them ten hours to walk down with empty packs, and a tough sixteen going back. Twice during the winter they had to use ropes to cross the rain-swollen Eel. At first Daniel despised the overnight treks, but by winter he was actually beginning to enjoy the grueling all-day push back to the lake; the sheer physical exertion seemed to cleanse him of a rancid congestion that he could feel but not locate.

January was a terrible month for Daniel. It rained or snowed nearly every day. He stayed in his tent as much as he could. He discovered, as many others had before him, that the mountains impose you on yourself. He came to some realizations he didn't like. The first was that he hadn't recovered from his mother's death. The raging, wrenching grief, once so palpably present, had faded into a haunting emptiness.

Daniel's second unpleasant realization was that he hadn't dreamed since the bomb explosion. Worried that this might indicate brain damage, he became so aware of his dreamlessness he could hardly sleep. He woke exhausted and eye-sore, as if he were a pilot who'd spent the night fruitlessly searching the ocean for a raft or signs of wreckage. He didn't mention his dreamlessness to Wild Bill. If it meant something was wrong, he didn't want to go back to the hospital, and if it didn't mean anything other than that he wasn't dreaming or couldn't remember them, then it didn't matter.

His third realization was that obsessive carnal desire and almost daily masturbation was preferable to gloomy contemplations of his heartache and dreamlessness. He remembered Brigit Bardo's face a hundred times a day, and her mouth a thousand, each accompanied by a pure genital urge for release. An early spring poured fuel on his fires. He couldn't meditate for five minutes without an image of breasts or tautly curved buttocks or silken thighs affecting his concentration much like a boulder hitting a mud puddle.

Wild Bill noticed. One mid-February morning, clear and warm, right in the middle of their meditation, Wild Bill jumped to his feet and glared down at Daniel, demanding, "Just *what* in the holy-fucking-hell is *bothering* you?"

Daniel wanted to run for his tent. "I don't know if I know," he stammered, "except I haven't been dreaming, not since I was hurt."

"Goddammit, worry about your dreams when you're asleep. Worry about getting wet when it's raining. When you're sitting, just *sit*. Don't wiggle. Don't wobble." Wild Bill started to resume sitting when he thought better of it. "Actually, I'm tired of fighting your hormones for attention, and I'm tired of looking at you. Go."

"What?" Daniel said, both crushed and strangely relieved.

Wild Bill pointed north. *"Go.* That old fir snag there—go dead uphill from that and about a hundred yards over the crest you'll find a little spring, and if you follow it down beneath the rock outcrop, there's a cave. You can stay in the cave or wander around—I don't care. But if you get lost and I have to find you, you'll wish you'd *stayed* lost."

"Is this personal, or some sort of teaching?"

"Both."

"So what am I supposed to do?"

"First," Wild Bill said with exaggerated patience, "you go. Then you have dreams and visions. If you can't dream, just have visions. Explore the visions for value. Examine yourself for value. Try to figure out what's valuable and what ain't. In seventeen days you can come back."

"Fine," Daniel said with a touch of petulance, "but I'm taking half of everything. Since you're staying by the lake, it makes the most sense that I take the gun and leave you the pole."

"Nope," Wild Bill said with finality. "I'm over sixty and you're pushing sixteen. You take a knife and your sleeping bag; I keep everything else."

Daniel yelped, "Forget it! That's not fair."

"Bye." Wild Bill fluttered his fingers in farewell.

"Fuck you," Daniel muttered.

"Way your hormones are flooding, that's kinda what I'm afraid of."

"It'd probably be better than getting beat up." Daniel immediately regretted saying it.

But Wild Bill laughed, and waved again. "Adios."

Daniel stalked to his tent, stuffed his sleeping bag in its sack, and left without another word.

He spent the first week at the cave, eating from the thin smorgasbord of early spring plants. When he wasn't foraging, sleeping, or meditating—he continued to sit, but half-heartedly—Daniel was absorbed in erotic fantasies of such sensual detail and endless possibility that he lay on his sleeping bag and masturbated till his forearm cramped.

To break the siege of desire, he decided to walk north to the headwaters of Cottonwood Creek. The weather was clear but cold. He ate whatever was available, mainly wild onions and some early miner's lettuce, supplemented occasionally with frog legs. The nourishment kept him going, but wasn't enough to fuel his usual pace. He tired easily and had difficulty concentrating for more than a few minutes. However, he experienced a lightness that wasn't confined to his head, a sort of metabolic austerity, and with it came a profound sense of objectivity—uncluttered by judgments or combustible desires. He quit meditating and masturbating. He didn't have any dreams or visions. After eight days of wandering in a slow loop, he reached the cave just hours before a storm.

The storm proved the last gasp of winter, but winter died hard that year: blinding lightning strikes; thunder so loud it raised dust on the cave floor; winds that sent widow-makers spinning out of the lashing firs, snapped off snags that splintered as they crashed; and then torrential rain. As he sat snug in the cave, a good fire with plenty of dry limbs stacked against the walls, watching the wind suck smoke out the cave mouth in a ropy braid, Daniel decided he would fast and meditate for his last three days. He wanted dreams and visions.

As Wild Bill would later rule, Daniel had two near-visions and one for sure, but Wild Bill was a hanging judge.

One near-vision began with the color pink. At first Daniel felt it was some sort of overture to an erotic fantasy, but as he watched, the color constricted slowly into the terror-brightened pink of a lab rat's eye. And then he was inside the rat, running a maze, turning left, right, right again, running until he caught the scent of his own fear still hanging on the air and realized he'd tried that passage before. Daniel rose out of the rat's body like mist lifting from a field. He could see the maze below him, a perfect square, infinitely intricate, no entrance or exit. The maze exploded when he screamed.

The other near-vision began with him floating just under the surface of Nameless Lake. He wasn't dead, but had barely enough strength to lift his left hand out of the water. He knew no one would see, but it was all he could do. He floated, gathering the energy and will to lift his hand again. When he did, his hand was seized by another, powerful and sure. As it lifted him from the water, he saw a woman he didn't know, tall and lovely and smiling, and he wanted her to lift him into her arms and hold him tightly, but in the same motion of pulling him free of the lake, she hurled him into the heavens. He fell through the galaxy, his hand still outstretched, but it didn't matter—he would fall forever. He might as well have been waving good-bye. When he laughed, the wind-lashed rain was hurtling past the cave.

The real vision occurred on his last night. The storm had passed, trailing a thin fog in its wake. Feeling faint and dislocated, Daniel was sitting at the cave mouth watching the wisps of fog tatter and swirl in the moonlight when he heard his mother clearly call in the distance *"Alie-alie-outs-in-free,"* just as she had so many evenings playing Hide-and-Seek at the Four Deuces when he was a child. *"Alie-alie-outs-in-free,"* she called again, her voice more distant; and then once more, barely audible. She didn't call again. Rocking back and forth, arms around himself, Daniel wept.

As he worked his way carefully downslope toward camp the next morning, Daniel felt simultaneously serene and raw.

Wild Bill was cooking pancakes when Daniel walked into camp.

"Those smell wonderful," Daniel greeted him. "If there's extra batter, drop one on for me. I've been fasting for almost a week."

"Yeah?" Wild Bill tried to flip the pancake on the griddle, then had to pause and unfold it with the spatula. "What were you fasting for?"

"Dreams and visions, as instructed."

"I don't remember any instructions about fasting. Fasting is tricky. It can put an odd twist on things."

"It worked. I had visions."

"Just a second." Wild Bill slid the creased pancake onto a tin plate and handed it to Daniel. "So. What'd you see."

"I saw . . . " Daniel started, then hesitated. "Well, actually I didn't *see* anything."

Wild Bill grunted. "Good start."

Daniel couldn't tell if the grunt was playful or cutting or both. He could feel the warmth of the pancake through the tin plate against his palm. "Do you want to listen or not?"

Wild Bill looked up. "Is it important to you?"

"I *cried*," Daniel said, feeling like he was going to again.

Wild Bill said softly, "Then I'd be honored." He gave the pancake batter a quick stir and poured it sizzling onto the griddle.

"It was something I *heard*," Daniel explained. "I heard my mother calling *'Alie-alie-outs-in-free.'* That's what you yell at the end of Hide-and-Seek when you give up the search. That's how the other players know—"

"I've played the game. When did you hear her?"

"Last night."

Wild Bill watched the bubbles burst thickly on the pancake's surface, then slipped the spatula under the crusted bottom, hefted it a moment, flipped. The pancake turned over two-and-a-half times, splatting down perfectly. But Wild Bill looked glum. "Goddamn, Daniel, I don't want to crap on your parade, but you deserve the truth. That wasn't your mom you heard last night. It was me. Yodeling."

Daniel stopped his pancake halfway to his mouth. "Yodeling?"

"Yodeling," Wild Bill affirmed. He lifted the pancake and slipped it on Daniel's plate. "Eat. You're delirious with hunger."

"You weren't yodeling," Daniel said.

Wild Bill turned solemnly and faced the lake. He tilted his head back, exhaled slowly, took a slow deep breath, then another, and then astonished Daniel. With a power and bell-note clarity completely unlike his habitual grunts and mumbles, Wild Bill blended and blurred long open vowels and gliding consonants into an undulant song that shifted between rejoicing and keening, delight and lament. Daniel heard it clearly toward the end: *"Allleee-allleee-ah-sen-freeee."* Wild Bill repeated the phrase, then whirled it through itself in tight variations, winding it inward, suddenly leaping an octave, then slowly letting it slide into the last haunting note.

Wild Bill stood listening to his voice echo across the basin until it was absorbed into the air. He turned to Daniel. "Yodeling. I learned it from Lao Ling Chi, my teacher when I was doing work on breath and breathing."

Daniel said, "That was lovely, it was close, but it wasn't *your* voice I heard—it was my mother's."

"Whatever," Wild Bill shrugged. "You heard it, so it's yours to understand. Me, I'm going to go look for mushrooms for tonight's rabbit stew. If you feel ambitious, I got a stack of fir saplings I thinned that need to be trimmed up and hauled back to camp. They're piled at the base of that big maple on the west side. Take the hand-ax."

"Fine," Daniel nodded, wolfing down a pancake. "See you." He wondered what Wild Bill wanted with the fir poles but refused to give him the satisfaction of asking.

Swinging the horribly lopsided basket he'd woven from split reeds and grasses, Wild Bill made his way around the lake and then up the south slope to the rim. As he went over the crest, he stopped and gave a short yodel: *"Oodell-a-eee-ooooo."* It resounded in the basin.

"Jerk," Daniel muttered. Wild Bill—always watching for mistakes, and taking a malicious glee in pointing them out. What kind of teacher was that? Daniel was beginning to suspect Wild Bill's eccentricities were merely a screen for incompetence, and with a mean satisfaction he realized how much he'd enjoyed the seventeen days by himself—no scrutiny, no picking and prodding and little put-downs.

Daniel did the dishes, then took the hand-ax and headed around the lake. The saplings were stacked on a small bench about a hundred yards upslope from the lake's edge. As Daniel hauled the first one off the pile he caught a flicker of color in the corner of his eye, thin bright red, thinking *snake* at first flash, then, with a bolt of terror, realized it was a wire.

A voice screamed from the sky. "Daniel! Run!"

He swung the ax at the wire but he was a moment too late. The explosion rocked him and he staggered backward, hands covering his temples, staring blankly as the blast-showered confetti of soggy leaves settled around him. He looked at his hands: no blood. He picked up the ax and spun around. When he saw a wisp of smoke from the small crater fifty yards uphill, he let the ax drop to his side and started looking for the wire.

With the piercing cry of an osprey, Wild Bill dropped on him from the overhanging limb of an ancient fir, driving Daniel to the ground. Wild Bill picked up the ax and tossed it away as Daniel rolled and came up quickly. He hit Wild Bill in the chest with a round-house right, following with a glancing left off his cheek. Wild Bill rolled his heavy shoulders and brought his fists up to cover his face, elbows tucked to protect his solar plexus. Daniel hit him a solid right to the stomach. Wild Bill grunted but kept his hands up.

"Fight!" Daniel yelled, and hit him hard in the stomach again. When Wild Bill's hands dropped for an instant, Daniel followed with a left to the head. Wild Bill yelped, staggering sideways a moment before catching his balance. He shook his head to clear it, blinking against the blood running from a cut above his eye.

"Fight, you fucker!" Daniel screamed again.

"She's dead, Daniel. Dead."

Daniel threw a left uppercut that hit squarely on the point of Wild Bill's elbows, sending a jolt of pain up Daniel's arm to his shoulder.

"Come on," Wild Bill said wearily, "get it all."

Daniel hit him with a right hook above the ear but Wild Bill rolled with the blow. Daniel threw a left but there was no strength in that arm so he threw a right that Wild Bill easily blocked with a shoulder. Daniel threw another, another, another, and then he had nothing left, all the rage and fear and loss emptying in a rush, and he fell into Wild Bill's arms.

Back in camp, Wild Bill held an improvised compress to his cut eye and Daniel soaked his swollen hands in the cold water. They didn't speak for a long time. Daniel was exhausted and Wild Bill had nothing to say. Finally, Daniel stood shakily and worked his hands. "When are we leaving?"

"I'm heading out in the morning," Wild Bill said. "You're welcome to go with me or you can stay if you want. Owen'll be there around dark if you want a ride."

"What then?"

"I'm going to Arizona and put some desert between my ears. All this lushness sort of depresses me. Makes the eye sloppy."

"What about me?"

"You go on with your training. Up to you."

"My *training*? I didn't know I was being trained. What for?"

"Depends on what you learn."

"Uh-huh, right. Well, one thing I've learned is not to expect a straight answer."

"I take teaching seriously, Daniel. I won't tell you what I don't know."

"Then tell me what you do know."

"There's sort of three levels of association with AMO. The first is friends and kindred souls. That association is a loose system of mutual aid and moral support. They don't pay dues. The second is allies, actual members of AMO who pay their yearly five percent, and who receive and provide direct benefits of the Alliance. And then there are adepts. They are people with particular gifts and understanding who sustain and expand the Alliance's traditional arts and practices."

"Is that what you're trying not to tell me, that I'm being trained as an adept?"

"No one is trained as an adept. An adept is one who has mastered a particular art, who has achieved a certain understanding. You can't teach mastery. You can only teach certain skills of awareness, which in turn lead to the recognition of possibilities and opportunities for further development—as well as the dangers involved. Beyond that, you're on your own. But as Synesius noted as early as the fourth century, 'There is always guidance available if you're available.'"

Daniel considered this a moment, flexing his hands. "Do you think I have potential as an adept?"

"I don't give grades, Daniel. But yes, clearly, you have potential. Most everyone does. But you see, it's like this: The brain processes information, and information can be an endless ride. With the addition of the heart, some information becomes knowledge. The spirit, or soul, transforms it into understanding. But that's the problem with abstraction—it misleads by separation."

"What sort of potential do I have? I mean, what direction should I take? I'm not asking you to make the decision for me, understand—it's just that I'd value your opinion."

"I don't know. But I have a strong *hunch* that you'd make one helluva a thief. Actually, what AMO calls a Raven, which goes way beyond stealing. 'Agents of exchange and restitution' is what Volta calls them. Ravens are the only adepts that AMO allows to kill other human beings, and they can only use their imaginations as the weapon."

"You mean by imagining them dead? Or like shooting them from a hot-air balloon drifting by their window?"

"I mean by writing them a note saying 'I'm going to kill you tonight.' And the next day, one that reads 'I was detained; it's tonight,' and the next day, 'Prepare yourself,' and do it day after day for a couple of weeks and then catch him asleep one night and fire a bullet just above his head and when he screams awake say, 'Oops, shit, I missed—oh well, there's always tomorrow.' And ten days later the guy runs his sports car into a concrete abutment."

"Jesus, what had he done?"

"Daniel," Wild Bill scolded, "silence is golden."

"It's still murder, though, in a way. Right?"

"If you want to split moral hairs, talk to Volta. The use of violence has always been hotly debated in AMO, and over the centuries there's been about a hundred different 'official' policies—I'm relying on Volta's scholarship here. The current policy is what Volta calls 'compassionate condemnation.' That means you shouldn't use lethal violence except in the most extreme circumstances—like self-defense—but that people, out of fear and ignorance and rage, make mistakes. And there *is* a meanness in the world that must be dealt with."

"How's your eye?" Daniel said.

Wild Bill chuckled. "It'll heal if you don't keep hitting it."

"That was dangerous what you did, setting off that explosion. You couldn't know for sure how I'd react."

"Not for sure, no, but life's full of hazards. Despite the boom, it was a piddley charge, plus it was fifty yards from us, buried, and I had the det-switch in my hand. 'Course I was tired from having to haul ass back down the hill to get up in the tree, and then you spotted the wire."

"So while I was out starving and having visions, you were setting me up."

"Nope. As a matter of fact, for about the first two weeks I was in sunny Florida visiting my sister, and then I hustled back here to be with you. Had to hump it in two nights ago during that storm. I tell you, crossing the Eel cinched me up—I was going hand-over-hand on that rope we rigged, and that water had me *horizontal.* Don't think my feet touched bottom once. Only way I made it was telling myself that I didn't care how much Volta sweet-talked me, if I got across I was a retired teacher, finished and gone, just watch those desert sunsets and yodel with the lizards."

"That's something I have to ask you," Daniel said, "something I really need to know. *Were* you yodeling last night?"

"I was. But given the acoustics of the basin, I doubt you could hear me. Besides, you heard what *you* heard. I was just trying to help you understand it, that's all."

"Why didn't you say so this morning?"

"Because I wanted you thinking. That way I could take you by surprise."

"I had two other visions if you want to hear them."

"Always interested in visions. But let's talk over lunch, because not only did I dare the raging river with explosives in my pack, but also four thick filet mignons from Tilly and Owen, plus lettuce, broccoli, sourdough bread, and a twenty-buck bottle of Cabernet. Not to mention a small personal gift for you that must wait for the proper moment."

They feasted and talked till late in the afternoon. Daniel recounted his visions, listened to Wild Bill explain why they weren't quite truly visions, and then listened as Wild Bill gave him some history of AMO—*his* version, he stressed, since certain AMO lore was only transmitted orally, which invited revision and invention, and thus kept the facts straight. Wild Bill was relaxed, direct, and far more articulate than Daniel had ever seen him, but whether it was the wine, the morning's events, or his last day as a teacher that allowed the mask to slip, Daniel didn't know nor particularly care.

As the sun dipped toward the basin rim, Bill, a bit wobbly, stood and announced, "All right, Daniel, it's the proper moment. Follow me."

They walked down to the lake's edge and faced the setting sun. After a long silence, Wild Bill took something from his pocket and turned to Daniel. "I want to give you a gift. I give one to each of my students—not like a damn diploma or a token of passage, understand, but an expression of gratitude for all they made me learn in order to teach them anything." He gently placed

96

a hand-worked, solid-gold turtle the size of a quarter in Daniel's palm. The turtle's eyes were tiny, brilliant diamonds.

"It's beautiful," Daniel murmured, enthralled by its weight, its luster, the crystalline eyes.

"Most of my students think the turtle is a symbol of balance between earth wisdom and water wisdom, but what I have in mind is slow learners."

Daniel closed his hand around the turtle and looked at Wild Bill. "You know what I don't understand?"

"No," Wild Bill smiled, "but there's a lot to choose from."

Daniel ignored the charm. "I don't understand why you're so afraid of your tenderness."

"That's another reason it's a turtle," Wild Bill said. "Why do you think they have shells?"

Daniel laughed. He curled his index finger around the gold turtle, cocked his sore wrist, and threw it as far as he could toward the center of the lake.

The turtle hit the water with a silent splash, concentric ripples languidly spreading from the point of impact.

Stunned by Daniel's act, Wild Bill watched the ripples, tried to feel their calm, inevitable dissipation within himself. He turned to Daniel then, nodded, and said, "Good. *Very* good. In fact, Daniel, that was *excellent.*"

"I had an excellent teacher."

They stood watching as the sun slipped below the rim of the basin. For a moment, as if the turtle in its depths was surrendering its light to the sun, the whole lake turned golden.

*Transcription: Telephone Recording Between
Volta and Wild Bill Weber*

WILD B.: *"Lapidem esse aquam fontis vivi."*

VOLTA: Indeed. And how are you, Bill?

WILD B.: Headed for the desert.

VOLTA: You have a choice, Bill. I will give you one million dollars, or I will get down on my knees naked and beg you, if you'll consent to teach another five years.

WILD B.: I'm done. Bye.

VOLTA: (laughing) All right, school's out. How was your last student?

WILD B.: He's paying attention.

VOLTA: No doubt. What do you think of him?

WILD B.: No limit. He slows himself down with questions, but some of them are the right ones. Even more, I think he's capable of understanding some answers.

VOLTA: How did he react to the explosion?

WILD B.: As expected.

VOLTA: By the way, I was honored you consulted me. Or were you just trying to spread the responsibility in case it went awry?

WILD B.: Even the bold and brilliant get nervous.

VOLTA: True. But as long as they're not *too* bold, they also grow wiser.

WILD B.: He knew to let it go, that he had to. He even had a powerful premonition the night before. He heard his mother calling *Alllee-alllee-outs-in-free*.

VOLTA: I told you he might be the student you were looking for.

WILD B.: You wouldn't happen to know who his father is, would you? Daniel said not even his mother knew, but since you know everything, I thought I might ask.

VOLTA: Your flattery is wasted on my failure—I have no idea. His mother, Annalee, as I believe I mentioned, was a woman of well-founded pride and immense courage. There's evidently much of her in Daniel.

WILD B.: No argument, but let's not get carried away. He's young. The young make some hideous mistakes.

VOLTA: They're supposed to.

WILD B.: And there may be a problem. He hasn't dreamed since his injury, or at least he doesn't remember his dreams.

VOLTA: That's dangerous.

WILD B.: So is remembering them.

VOLTA: Let's not pursue it, Bill. Let's honor our friendship by respecting our disagreements. You might also honor it by telling me what the problem really is, since you would never consider the lack of dreams anything but a blessing.

WILD B.: Daniel likes the edge. He's a little too dazzled by oblivion.

VOLTA: Adolescence encourages ecstatic mistakes.

WILD B.: *Too* dazzled. But that's just a sense I have, nothing else.

VOLTA: Is there a possibility your own fears or desires amplify your perception of his?

WILD B.: Of course.

VOLTA: I'm not challenging you. I sense the same thing in Daniel. You know, Bill, we ride the same wave so often, if it weren't for your hard-headed foolishness, we'd have no disagreements at all.

WILD B.: Praise life for the saving graces.

VOLTA: That's a bit like praising time for tomorrow.

WILD B.: Speaking of tomorrows, Daniel wants to know what's next.

VOLTA: I wouldn't attempt to consider it without consulting you. You've been with him eighteen months.

WILD B.: And about the last three he's been cooking in his own juices.

VOLTA: Ah, hormones. Kiss the brain farewell. Any specific recommendations?

WILD B.: Sex, drugs, and rock 'n' roll. Daniel's had a solid dose of the alchemical salts; an infusion of outlaw spirit might be timely—though it would be wise to have a tempering influence near at hand.

VOLTA: The Stocker operation. Mott and Aunt Charmaine.

WILD B.: Bingo.

Through more of Alexander Kreef's legal wizardry, Daniel was released from custodial probation and, after passing a high school equivalency exam, allowed to seek gainful employment. Alexander Kreef had heard that Ariba Farm and Ranch Company was hiring, and happened to have one of their cards in his pocket. Daniel was hired over the telephone and told to report to the Rocking On Experimental Range Station, a three-thousand-acre ranch in southern Oregon. Mott Stocker, the ranch foreman, would be expecting him.

When they met at the horse barn a week later, Daniel was glad Mott had expected him and not been taken by surprise. Mott was six foot eight and a solid 260, his powerful physical presence strengthened by the thunderbolt-shaped scar on his forehead, his long black tangled hair and beard, and what proved to be his usual attire: an Australian bush hat with a band of sharks' teeth strung on a thin, gold wire; a long-tailed buckskin shirt, grease-stained and grungy, belted with a snap-holstered Colt .45 automatic and sashed with a bandolier of extra ammunition; a jockstrap (buckskin pants when he went to town); and a pair of motorcycle boots. The only thing fragile about Mott Stocker was the pale blue of his eyes, a color that seemed almost too delicate to exist, that hovered on the threshold of perishing back into light.

Daniel liked Mott's eyes and worried about the rest. As they saddled up, Daniel wondered how Mott's mule, Pissgums, could survive his rider, not to mention the weight of the bulging saddlebags and twin scabbards, one holding a sawed-off twelve-gauge pump, the other a marine-issue M-16.

Daniel, with an attempt at lightheartedness, nodded toward the arsenal and said, "Are we expecting trouble?"

With a deep and thoughtful drawl, Mott said, "Better to have 'em and not need 'em than to need 'em and not have 'em."

"What's in the saddlebags?"

"Grenades, small mortar, extra rounds and clips, some other stuff."

"Well, you have 'em, that's for sure."

"Yeah. But what I'd really like is a bazooka—one of those World War Two jobs. Awful hard to come by, though."

A little nervously, Daniel asked, "Just where are we headed."

"Gonna ride up on Grouse Prairie and meet Lucille."

"Who's she?"

"Dan, they told me you were coming here to learn the ropes. Some of the rope can tie us up, some of it can hang our ass. It's an important part of the business to never ask more questions than you need answers for."

"I thought this was a cattle ranch."

"Moo," Mott drawled.

They reached the log bridge on Crawdad Creek right after sunrise. Halfway across, Mott jerked back hard on his mule's reins, bellowing "Whoa, Pissgums, you sum'bitch!" Daniel, following, pulled up his horse. Mott dismounted and reached under the bridge timbers for a quart jar of clear liquid.

He unscrewed the cap and lifted it toward Daniel. "Breakfast." He drank a third of the bottle. *"Wahhh!"* he roared, offering the bottle to Daniel.

Daniel took it, his eyes watering at the fumes. "What's this?"

"Warmth in a cold world," Mott wheezed. "Whiskey. Homemade."

Daniel took a cautious sip. "Whew," he said huskily, "it burns."

"Don't be shy. Best have another slash—long ride to the top."

Daniel took an even smaller sip and handed the bottle back to Mott, who offered it to the mule. Pissgums sniffed the bottle, snorted, shied slightly, then lipped the rim. Mott poured slowly till Pissgums tossed his head and backed away.

"Goddamn, you're getting particular," Mott said to the mule, then turned to explain. "He don't like it if it hasn't been aged at least a month."

"Hee-ee-yaw-yaw-yaw," Pissgums brayed, and bolted suddenly across the bridge.

Mott pulled his .45, cupping it as he swung on the fleeing mule.

Daniel yelled, "Hey! Don't shoot!"

Mott fired, the bullet kicking up dust twenty yards in front of the mule. Pissgums stopped in his tracks and began browsing innocently.

Mott looked at Daniel. "Don't worry, Dan. I always give him a warning shot 'fore I cut loose for serious."

"Maybe you shouldn't give him the whiskey," Daniel said.

"Naw. The whiskey's *good* for him. Gets him perky. Don't *ever* give him any dope, though. Can't handle it at all. Gets the *bad* paranoia."

"Don't worry," Daniel promised.

A half hour later they dismounted in a grove of white oaks. "Coffee break," Mott said, pulling a stainless-steel thermos from a saddlebag. "Hope you like it strong." He poured a black ropy goo the consistency of hot asphalt into one of the cups. "I mix it equal parts coffee and hashish. The hash thickens it up."

Daniel hesitantly took the steaming cup. "I thought you were supposed to *smoke* hashish."

"Ruin your lungs," Mott told him, pouring a cup for himself.

"Do you take a lot of drugs?"

Mott drained his cup, wiping his mustache with a buckskin sleeve. "Yup. You?"

"I tried some in Berkeley."

"What'd ya do? Give 'er up?"

"Not really. Things just changed."

"Ya see," Mott said slowly, "that's *exactly* the reason I take 'em. The drugs never change, but you do, so that way you have something to measure your changes against—sorta like a boulder in the river tells you the water level."

"I'm not sure I follow that," Daniel said, taking a sip of the resinous brew.

Patiently, Mott said, "Look at it this way, Dan: How can you know you're changing less'n something else isn't?"

"Suppose it's all changing together?" Daniel countered.

"Then you'd need drugs just to keep up."

"Or something," Daniel said. He was having difficulty just keeping up with the conversation.

"Besides," Mott grinned, "I like it when the colors all run together."

There were three more stops before lunch: a fire-hollowed fir stump that held a tank of nitrous oxide which Daniel politely sampled and Mott nearly drained; a buried stash of black opium the consistency of taffy—Daniel declining, Mott biting off a piece the size of a walnut; and taped in the crotch of a young maple, a waterproof canister of LSD microdots, Daniel trying one, Mott several.

They ate lunch at the Palmer Ridge line shack. The cupboards were stocked with quart jars of chili and the propane refrigerator was full of beer. Mott dumped the contents of several jars into a large, cast-iron kettle. "Seeing as how we just met today," Mott said as he lit the stove, "I'm gonna cook you up my Special Mott Stocker Seven-Course Mountain-Man Shitkicker Lunch: a bowl o' red and a six-pack. I make a whole bathtub full o' chili the end o' every month and stash it around wherever I might find myself working. Let me warn ya right now, Dan: It's pretty damn tasty fare."

The first bite left flesh hanging from the roof of Daniel's mouth. He sucked air to cool it.

"Spicy, huh?" Mott said, shoveling another spoonful.

"Yaaa," Daniel gasped.

"You bet. Secret's in the chiles. I grow my own, out o' my own stock—been perfecting it for about ten years now. You mighta noticed that little hothouse out in back of the barn? That's all chiles. And I go in there every chance I get and insult 'em. Call 'em stupid-ass, low-down, dipshit heaps of worthlessness. I pinch 'em, piss on 'em, slice off a branch here and there. Water 'em just enough to keep 'em alive. No water—that's what makes 'em hot, but the abuse is what makes 'em *mean.*"

Daniel, popping his second can of beer, was still unable to speak, but he nodded in understanding.

Mott shoveled down more chili, sweat coursing off his forehead. "This is venison chili. Where's the beef? Hey: Fuck the beef. And fuck all them fancy chili cookoff winner recipes. This stuff is deer meat, chiles, spring water, little bit of wild pig blood, and three tablespoons of gunpowder. Sometimes I throw in a handful of them psilocybin mushrooms if there's any around, though personally I think they weaken it."

"So would sulfuric acid," Daniel mumbled, his lips numb. At the mention of acid he noticed the cabin walls seemed to be melting.

"Eat up," Mott urged. "Lucille's due in an hour and we still got ground to ride."

"I don't want to insult your hospitality, but the chili's a little hot for me. Makes my ears ache."

"Supposed to. Good bowl o' mountain red should just kick the dog piss outa ya and make your dick grow an inch. But don't worry, you'll work up a taste for it. Only thing that'd be insulting is if you brought a sack lunch with a cheese-and-sprouts sandwich or some such stuff. Tuna. Shit like that."

"I'll wash the bowls," Daniel volunteered.

Mott drained another beer. "I'll twist us up a coupla joints for the trail."

"What should I do with the leftovers?"

"Dump it back in the kettle for Pissgums. He deserves a treat. Hasn't tried to kick me in the nuts since last Tuesday."

Daniel watched with fascination as the mule slurped the chili from the pot, alternating each bite with a mouthful of damp moss from the trunk of his hitching tree. Daniel tried a handful. It helped.

"You're really pretty smart," he said appreciatively, patting the mule's neck.

Pissgums snaked his head sideways and bit Daniel savagely just below the ribs.

Daniel's yowl brought Mott rolling through the cabin door, his .45 in one hand and a large knife in the other.

"No! No!" Daniel yelled, waving his arms. "It's just Pissgums. The son of a bitch bit me." Daniel hiked his shirt and showed Mott the egg-shaped bruise.

"You fucking with him or did he get outa line?"

Daniel wasn't sure if Mott was asking him or the mule, but he answered anyway. "I wasn't doing a damn thing except feeding him and giving him a friendly pat on the neck."

"Shit. *Never* do that. Pissgums *hates* affection." Mott holstered his pistol and slipped the knife back in his boot.

"You know," Daniel said, rubbing the bite, "I've spent a lot of time in the hills. I know the hills. I feel safe there. When I woke up this morning I was looking forward to a pleasant day gathering cattle, and here I am six hours later, reeling from drugs, my ears still humming from lunch, with some whiskey-drinking sadomasochist mule who almost ate my rib cage, on my way to see a mysterious woman for even more mysterious reasons that—you were right—I really *don't* want to know, and I'm beginning to believe that things are seriously out of control."

"Always," Mott agreed. "But it's like the Rock Island Line: You gotta ride it like you find it."

"Fine," Daniel said. "Fine with me."

"We're gonna get on real good, Dan," Mott grinned, a wild twinkle in his faded blue eyes. "All aboard." He slapped Pissgums on the nose and swung into the saddle. "Let's go meet Lucille."

Daniel and Mott heard her coming. They'd stopped in the trees at the edge of the ridgetop and waited a few minutes when Daniel caught the sound. Startled, he glanced at Mott. "What's that?"

Mott, holding in a lungful from the cigar-sized joint he was smoking, answered in a strangled wheeze, "Lucille."

"No," Daniel said, listening intently. "No, it's a machine—hear it?" He imitated the sound: "Chwop:chwop:chwop:chwop . . . " When his drug-soaked brain finally realized the sound was familiar, he whirled on Mott: "Fuck! It's a helicopter!"

"Yuuuup," Mott exhaled. "That's what we're waiting for." Behind the dense cloud of smoke, Mott's voice seemed disembodied.

Daniel felt relieved, then irked. "Jesus, you might have said something. I've had some bad experiences with helicopters—they make me jumpy."

"Like turpentine on a sanded asshole, I'd say," Mott said.

"So why is Lucille coming in on a helicopter?"

"She isn't. Lucille *is* the helicopter."

"Right. That makes as much sense as anything. And I suppose she's bringing in your daily drug supply."

"You're close, Dan. But it's the *weekly* drug delivery and pickup. Pilot's name is Low-Riding Eddie. He's pretty good people for a flatlander, but I wouldn't bad-mouth Lucille or you might find yourself in a knife fight."

The helicopter roared in above the treetops, banked sharply, circled once, then settled, its rotor-wash flattening the grass. It was an old Sikorsky, Korean War surplus, but it had been altered dramatically. The body was chopped and channeled, all visible metal chromed, and the fuselage gleamed with hand-rubbed coats of metal-flake Midnight Blue. Ornate gold script on the rear panel spelled out *Lucille.* A large pair of pink foam dice dangled from a roll-bar in the cockpit.

"That's the Low-Rider," Mott said, lifting off a saddlebag. "Leave our beasts here and we'll go give him a howdy."

As they walked toward the chopper, Low-Riding Eddie clambered out of the cockpit with a battered suitcase in one hand, the other covering his head as he ran, crouched, from under the rotor.

On that high, Oregon mountain prairie, Daniel witnessed a sight few mortals can claim to share: A half-naked mountain man buying thirty pounds of Afghani hash from a thin, sallow-faced youth dressed in the highest late-fifties fashion cool: scuffed white bucks, black chinos held up by a skinny belt so pink it probably glowed in the dark, and a scarlet silk shirt, the back of the collar rolled up to the well-pomaded point of Eddie's DA 'do.

Mott and Daniel met him at the tree line.

"New cat in the band?" Eddie asked Mott, indicating Daniel with an almost imperceptible shift of his sullen brown eyes.

"This here's Daniel the Nooky Spaniel, gets more ass than a toilet seat in a sorority house. Sent him here to learn a useful trade and eat some o' my chili to grow back what he's wore off his pecker."

Eddie nodded, regarding Daniel under hooded eyes.

"It's a pleasure to meet you," Daniel said. "And it's a real joy to behold that beautiful machine you're flying. She's a work of art."

"I busted a knuckle or two," Eddie replied with a studied indifference. "She'll turn two and a half in calm air. Blow the fucking doors off any chop the sky fuzz can put up, that's for sure."

"That must be comforting," Daniel said.

"Fuckin' A," Eddie mumbled. "Peace of mind's almost as good as a piece of tail."

"Low-Rider, goddammit, don't remind me," Mott said. "I'm so horny I could fuck the crack o' dawn."

Eddie said, "Just so you don't go fucking with Lucille."

"Naw," Mott assured him, "the only machines I like are guns."

"Man, you *got* to cut back on the drug abuse—your eyes look like . . . what do you call them fuckers anyway?"

"Pinwheels?" Daniel offered.

Eddie snapped his fingers. "That's the one. Can't tell if they're whirling in or whirling out."

"I know," Mott sighed. "But unless I can get Dan here to pull some weight, I'm stuck with all the product evaluation. It's a tremendous responsibility, but I'm built for the *load*, if you get my drift. If you're interested, just happen to have a joint in my pocket off'n a plant I grew myself and high-graded into stash. Cross between some Trinity Trainwreck and Humboldt Polio. Get ya so high your nose'll bleed."

"Thanks anyway, man, but I can't fly two planes at the same time, and I don't have the time to start with. They added a drop in Cave Junction. Let's jump on business. I gotta split soon."

"So whatta we got?"

Eddie lifted the suitcase. "Black 'Ghani, gold-stamped bars from the heart of the Hindu Kush. Last big load out before the Russians. Twenty pounds."

"Tell me in money." Mott reached into his shirt. Daniel, recalling the knife he'd produced from his boot, tensed.

"Sixteen of the big ones."

Daniel relaxed when Mott produced a large elkskin pouch.

"Sixteen?" Mott repeated with a touch of doubt. "That seems *awful* cheap."

"Don't rumble it with me, man; I'm on salary."

Mott took a huge roll of hundred-dollar-bills from the pouch and started counting. "I could turn it for twelve a pound and have 'em lined up at my door."

"We got a good buy, and you know the rule: Can't tack on more than a hundred a pound if the Alliance fronts it."

Mott grunted and kept counting.

"Why that rule?" Daniel said to Low-Riding Eddie.

"Cools the greed."

Mott finished flicking through the bills and handed a wad to Eddie. "That's four grand. Squares us on last week's peyote buttons."

Eddie peeled off a single bill and stuffed the rest in his back pocket. "You make your nut?"

"No problem."

"How's the biz?"

"Smooth and quiet. Any rattles down your way?"

"Nothing shaking." Eddie took out his Zippo and held it under the hundred dollar bill. "Ready?"

"Always," Mott said. "Fire away."

Shielding it in front of himself against the light breeze, Eddie lit a corner of the bill.

Daniel, peaking on acid, was too stunned to say anything. He watched enthralled as the flames spread along the bill, leaving a flutter of ashes in their wake. When they reached the oval face of Ben Franklin engraved on the bill, Mott chortled, "Fuck-oh-dear, but I do like to see old Benny Franklin burn. Hated that motherfucker ever since they tried to convince me what a great thinker and citizen he was when I was back in first grade, back before I took warping my brain into my own hands. I'll bet you a mink coat against a cornflake that the only time Benny Franklin ever got off was when that lightning zapped his kite."

Daniel watched raptly as the flames burned closer to Eddie's fingers.

Eddie didn't let go. Instead, he dropped the bill in the palm of his left hand, slapped it almost simultaneously with his right, then brushed the ashes on the ground.

Pale eyes glittering, Mott enthusiastically suggested, "Let's burn another one."

"Ain't happening," Eddie mumbled. "They're already pissed off about one. Wanna know why we can't use a twenty."

Mott erupted, "We can't use a fucking *twenty* because Ben Franklin's on the *hundred!*" He took a breath. "And you see *right there* how that Puritan killjoy tight-ass Ben Franklin has infected the American mind." He minced in a searing falsetto, "'A penny saved is a penny earned,'" then boomed, "Well, *fuck* that shit. A penny blown is a penny *enjoyed.*"

"They're squares, man, what can I tell ya?" Eddie said. "Volta's pretty cool, though; he digs it. He was the only vote in favor of burning more. Told me he'd ride up sometime and we could burn a grand of his personal income."

"Aw, piss on 'em," Mott said with sudden resignation. He picked up the suitcase and stuffed it in the saddlebag. "Let's move."

"Later," Eddie waved.

As they walked back into the trees, Daniel said, "Shouldn't you check the suitcase to see if it actually does contain hashish?"

"Shouldn't Eddie have counted the money?"

"So you're saying you trust him, right?"

"We trust each other. It's the backbone of the trade and the heart of the Alliance."

"What was burning that bill all about?"

"For the hell of it."

"I can understand how you enjoy it, hating Benjamin Franklin, but what about Eddie?"

"I have the feeling it just gets the Low-Rider off. A little kink in the wiring. I mean, look how he dresses. And every time I mention being horny he gets nervous about Lucille. I know I can get a tad rambunctious, but hey, I ain't gonna fuck no helicopter."

Daniel said, "It felt like a ceremonial purification."

"Better safe than sorry," Mott replied. He stopped in his tracks, groaning "Did Benny Franklin say that?"

"I think so," Daniel said gravely. He didn't know, actually, but he'd never seen Mott look scared before.

Mott had the knife in his hand before Daniel saw him move. He tossed the knife up, caught it by the back of the blade, and extended it to Daniel, handle first. As Daniel took it, pearls of sunlight shattered on its edge.

Mott dropped to his knees in front of Daniel. "Cut out my tongue."

Mott closed his eyes and stuck out his tongue. His abject vulnerability suddenly frightened Daniel. "Cud da fugger od!" Mott demanded, sticking his tongue out farther.

Daniel realized then that Mott was as stoned as he was. He shifted logic. "You won't ever be able to taste your chili again," he reminded him.

Mott opened one eye thoughtfully, then the other. "Couldn't eat pussy either, could I? Kinda the clincher, huh?" He got to his feet. "Well, even assholes like Ben Franklin get it right once in a while, I guess."

Daniel handed the knife back to Mott.

"You're a clear thinker, Dan. I like that. We'll make good pardners. I'll keep you loaded, you keep me sane."

They arrived back at the barn shortly after dark, taking a different route: cocaine, vodka, demerol, and, the last miles, a few Dexamyl spansules.

Daily life at the Rocking On was remarkably like that at the Four Deuces and the Wyatt Ranch, except the work involved the production and transfer of drugs. Mott assigned Daniel seven marijuana patches to plant and tend—each with thirty holes—and it took a long day's ride to complete the circuit. Later he only had to check twice a week through the summer to make sure the drip-irrigation systems hadn't clogged and the fences hadn't been breached. Low-Riding Eddie usually delivered some illegal substance for sale once a week, and there were always general chores. Mott worked the same basic schedule, so he and Daniel seldom rode together except to meet Lucille. Mott claimed a seven-day work week on the grounds that drug use constituted research and testing, not recreation. After that first obliterating trip with Mott, Daniel kept his drug intake down. He declined so often that Mott finally told him, "Tell me when you want something," and quit offering.

The ranch house and numerous outbuildings occupied a thirty-acre alluvial plain above Dooley Creek. Many of the outbuildings had been built by Mott when he was taken by the notion that American carpentry as an art form had never gone through a period of surrealism. Mott had set out, with gargantuan energy, to rectify this. Daniel's "cabin," for instance, looked like a head-on collision between a Maidu sweat lodge and a Swiss chalet, while the guest cottage might have been the bastard offspring of a Mongol yurt and a Texarkana motel. The only structures spared the influence of Mott's surrealist period were the original ranch house and barn, and the forty-foot-square cinder-block bunker with a single iron door, which served as Aunt Charmaine's laboratory.

Aunt Charmaine was a moderately tall woman in her early forties, thin, hazel-eyed. Daniel enjoyed just watching her move—each gesture was economical and precise, imbued with an elegant certainty. She wasn't Mott's aunt as he'd first assumed, nor anybody's as near as he could tell. She was often absent from the ranch, sometimes for weeks at a stretch, but when she was there she spent most of her time in her lab. Daniel was curious what she did in there, but the extent of her explanation was that she was a research chemist. She gracefully deflected further questions until he understood her research was not a topic of discussion. She was friendly but distant. Daniel was fascinated by her, and not the least because Mott treated her with almost intimidated deference, actually calling her "ma'am."

When Daniel questioned him, Mott said, "I don't hardly know a thing about her, and she's been here for three years. I don't have a clue what she works on in that lab. I've never been invited inside, and you mighta noticed she don't exactly jabber. Tell you the truth, that woman's a little spooky. You get the sense she knows exactly what is going on and just what to do about it if anything needs doing. Like, one time we were having a little harvest party in the house and she came up to have a polite glass of wine before she trucked on back to the lab. When she was there, this big ol' fly got in a jug of wine. People were all trying to figure how the fuck to get it out when Charmaine calmly gets a chopstick outa a drawer, pokes it down the bottle, and that wine-soaked fly hops right on the chopstick and she takes it outside where it buzzes away. People are going, you know, 'Wow, that was slick,' and she sort of looked puzzled and said, 'Nothing wants to die.' And I got this really *weird* feeling that the fly had told her what to do. It's your call, Dan, but I know in my bones that if you got outa line with her, she'd line you right back up, and maybe line your ass right *out,* if you get my lean."

Daniel still meditated morning and evening, but dropped the dream meditation because he thought it might be the cause of his continued dreamlessness. He hunted and fished, occasionally with Mott but usually alone. He read omnivorously, stocking up on library books on the monthly trip to town. Some evenings he smoked dope with Mott and listened to Mott's plaster-cracking sound system, driven by banks of solar panels that would dwarf the average drive-in movie screen. Daniel learned to cook, out of necessity. He chopped wood. He went swimming. And when Mott wasn't around, he snuck into the greenhouse and whispered endearments to the chiles.

The weekly descent of Mommy's Commies added saturnalia to the routine. Mommy's Commies was a commune of thirty-two young women and one old woman who lived on the Godfrey Ranch seventy miles east. The old woman was a Sorceress of the White Fury and the most brilliant teacher of its arts. When the women were at the ranch, Mommy, as she was called, expected them to pay undivided attention to the lessons at hand. When they were away she encouraged them to play, and especially to explore—with proper precaution—their particular sexual energies. Though not formally af-filiated with AMO, Mommy's Commies had helped distribute their contra-band for fifteen years. Mommy felt a little danger and a chance to be bad were essential for fledgling sorceresses, and the money was good, too.

Eight women arrived every Thursday evening to make the pickup, and left the next morning to four different cities. Daniel never had a chance. Mott didn't want one.

After Mott had greeted them, taking all eight in his arms at once and bellowing some endearment like, "If God didn't want me to eat pussy, why'd he make it look like a taco?" they gathered in what Mott referred to as the pleasure dome, the outside of which looked like a melting cube, for a brief business meeting and a long party. The inside of the dome featured padded walls, a thick carpet, Mott's membrane-shredding sound system, and a bar that served Mott's homemade whiskey and absinthe, and any drug you could name. Occasionally, the synergistic effects of multiple drug ingestion would cause what was then known in hip circles as a bummer and among young sorceresses as a learning experience. But despite the occasional psychic cave-in, the party mood usually prevailed.

After the ritual exchange of dope and money, the stash was divided into four, and then each woman cut a small portion for the party, most of which went to Mott as sort of a king's tariff to protect their shares through the evening. Mott's notion of a party was to take all available drugs and liquor, listen to some loud sounds, get naked, form a pile, and screw till you passed out. It never happened that way, but as the night burned on Mott usually convinced one or a few to repair to his place. Daniel, shyly, would ask one of those remaining if she would like to go to his cabin and talk awhile. After an hour of nervous chatter he would try to seduce her. His high success rate was more a tribute to their understanding than his style.

The women called them Boy Poet and the Grizzly Bear. A tawny blond half in love with Daniel caught the essential difference—"Mott loves us equally, all at once. Daniel loves us specifically, one by one."

But, unfortunately, once only, for as Daniel soon discovered, after a single orgasm with a woman, he was impotent with her thereafter. Try as he (and they) would, which was considerably, he couldn't get it up for any of them twice. The women were confused and understanding. Daniel was just confused. By the end of summer he was depressed, and at harvest, when all the Commies had arrived to help pick, dry, clip, and bag the powerful sin-semilla, the drying sheds were so erotically charged with the fragrance of ripe females—plant and animal—that Daniel could hardly bear it. Though he feared Mott might react with laughter or disgust, Daniel turned to him for help.

Mott listened to Daniel's hesitant description of the problem and simply nodded. "Thought you'd been looking puny lately. Wondered what was going on."

"That's what I'd like to know," Daniel said glumly.

Mott said, "This is going to take some massive thinking, and that means hitting the special reserves."

They were in the main room of Mott's house, the trapezoidal interior hung with animal skulls suspended from the ceiling on delicate silver wires. Mott jerked hard on a wolverine skull and Daniel heard a latch open behind him. Intrigued, he watched as Mott lifted a four-by-eight panel from the wall, revealing a storage space containing shelves of guns, ammo, grenades, and four gallon-jars of a greenish-tinged liquid. Mott took down one of the jars, rummaged in a box till he came up with a large, clear-plastic meat baster with a bright red bulb, and set them on the table in front of Daniel.

"What's that?"

Mott unscrewed the cap and bent over to savor the bouquet. "Something special I had Charmaine brew up in her spare time. Call it Ol' Wolverine."

"Is it like your chili?"

"Better." Mott dipped the baster in the jar and drew up a few inches of liquid. "It's whole extract of coca leaf, peyote buttons, and poppy heads, then she centrifuges 'em or some damn thing to get the essence, and after that she makes a ten percent solution." Mott tilted his head, stuck the narrow tip of the baster in his nostril, and squeezed the bulb. "Razoooolllii!" he cried, swaying slightly. He wiped the tears and handed Daniel the baster. Daniel, cautious, half-filled the tip. The effect of Ol' Wolverine on the sinuses was much like that of Mott's chili on the palate.

Thus fortified, Mott addressed Daniel's problem. "What ya got," he explained, "is a weird case of Shrivel Dick. Nobody's sure what causes it. Some docs think it's physical, some mental. In your case, having taken some shrapnel to the brain, I gotta think that's the reason. Don't matter if it was a *sliver* of metal, cause even if you blow a speck of fly shit through a bowl of jello, it's gonna have *some* effect, right? And I'm assuming you actually *do* want to diddle these girls, and don't suffer from some sorta unnatural pussy aversion."

"No, I'm sure," Daniel said.

"So the message is gettin' from your heart to your brain, but it ain't making it from your brain to your dick—that's the problem right there."

"It does *once.*"

"Maybe the switch is weak, and one blast of desire fries it shut?"

"Maybe so."

"What you've gotta do, Dan, is take the *scientific* approach. Do a fucking experiment. Get three or four of the Commies, blindfold yourself so you don't know who's who, then have 'em take turns on ya."

Dolefully, Daniel shook his head. "I tried it two weeks ago with Helen, Jade, and Annie. Once each."

"Yeah? Is Jade that one with the tits that'd make your heart stand still?"

"I guess."

"Maybe you shouldn'ta used the blindfold."

"Maybe not."

Responding to Daniel's glum tone, Mott said with sudden brightness, "But hey—what the hell? Women are *awful hard* critters to please. 'Long with always wanting everything to fit their mood at the moment, they want you to pay attention to 'em and be nice and give 'em credit cards. Once could be plenty. Blessin' in disguise."

"Right now it feels like a curse."

"Well, short of *brain surgery*, you're gonna have to live with it, and since you'd be stark motherfucking *crazy* to let someone cut on your brain, that leaves living with it—and you might as well start now. So what say, pardner, we take a moonlight ride up on Bleeker Ridge? Nothing in the world Pissgums hates worse than a night ride."

"No thanks, Mott, but I appreciate your asking."

"Think about it, Dan. Sitting up there on Bleeker Ridge watching the snow fall in the moonlight."

Perplexed, Daniel said, "It's not snowing."

Mott seemed startled by the information, then smiled. "Well, maybe it'll start."

"Thanks anyway, Mott," Daniel said, rising from the table, "but I think I'll go watch it from the river. You and Pissgums have a good time."

Daniel sat by the river, dejected by the one thing he hadn't mentioned, the fear that his condition made love impossible. He hadn't felt like discussing that with Mott. Mott was friendly enough, but never let friendliness cross the line into intimacy. Wild Bill was like that. Aunt Charmaine, too. All these AMO people with their guarded, friendly openness. Volta wasn't even that friendly.

He caught a flash of light downstream, then heard the distinctive growl of Charmaine's Chevy panel truck gearing down for the bridge. His mother had always claimed that old women knew everything important. He wondered if he would have been able to talk to his mother about his problem; it cheered him to feel certain he could have. He decided to consult Charmaine. As an older woman, she might have some insight. As a chemist, maybe she could make him a potion. When he stood up he felt a faint twist of nausea. Daniel took a moment to connect it with mescaline, and about the time he recalled that Mott's Ol' Wolverine contained peyote, he realized he was ripped.

Charmaine was in the kitchen, reading the paper and eating toast. Daniel, aided by the coca-mesc-opium combo, liked the way she held her toast.

"Daniel," she said pleasantly putting down the paper. "How are you?"

"I have a problem."

"Yes?" There was neither apprehension nor cajolery in her voice, just the usual open neutrality.

"It's a sexual problem. I talked to Mott, but I wanted to ask your advice, too."

"You're loaded," Charmaine said, looking at him intently, toast still poised in her hand.

"Being loaded and talking to Mott are the same thing. He was riding Pissgums in the snow." Daniel paused, his train of thought derailed, then added awkwardly, "But I want to talk to you independent of being loaded."

She gestured with her toast. "Sit down and talk."

Daniel sat at the table and began to explain, absently turning a jar of marmalade between his hands. Charmaine reached over and lifted it from his grasp. Daniel stumbled, embarrassed. She listened with a calm focus that unsettled him.

When he'd concluded, Charmaine said, "So it's not a problem of having one orgasm a night, but of being limited to one orgasm per partner, whether that night or next month?"

"Yes ma'am, that's it."

"Can you masturbate twice?"

Daniel nodded, stunned. He hadn't even thought about that.

"If you can make love with yourself twice but not anyone else, I doubt the problem is physiological." She stood, delicately brushed toast crumbs from her fingers, and started for the back door.

Daniel watched her go as if she were falling, either away from him or toward him, he couldn't tell. He blurted, "I'd like to sleep with you. I think I could do it with you twice."

Charmaine stopped and turned around, a hint of warmth in her smile. "I'm absolutely flattered, Daniel, but I'm just as absolutely not interested. I'm in the middle of some very demanding work, first of all. More importantly, I'm not the solution to your problem."

"Well, since I've already made a fool of myself, I might as well ask you something I've been wondering about. Whose aunt are you, anyway?"

Charmaine replied easily, "Nobody's really. It's a name Mommy's Commies gave me years ago. It's not widely known—and I'll trust you to keep it that way—but I'm Polly McCloud's daughter."

"Mommy of Mommy's Commies is your *mother?*"

"Yes. Though it doesn't make me an aunt to the girls, clearly."

"Why don't you ever visit your mother?"

"I do."

"Oh," Daniel said. She acted as if he should have known, but how could he if nobody ever told him anything and were evasive if you asked?

Before Daniel could think of anything to say, Charmaine concluded, "I have work to do, and you have company waiting. Good night."

Since he half expected Volta would be waiting for him in his cabin, he was mildly discombobulated to see a stocky woman with snow-white hair standing at his door. For an instant he thought it might be Polly McCloud, but then he recognized her—and was as shocked to see her as he had been the first time.

"Goddammit, you *better* remember," she threatened.

"Dolly Varden."

"I can show you my buckshot cherry if you don't believe it. And don't just stand there, come over and give this ol' frame a squeeze—I need all the young action I can get."

As he hugged her, he realized she was the first person he'd seen since his mother's death who'd known her while alive. "My mother's dead, you know," he said as evenly as he could.

"Yes, I know. It made me sad in a real simple way. It's also the reason I'm here. I'm acting as a go-between."

"Between who?"

"AMO and Shamus Malloy."

Daniel shook his head. "I'm a little dumb tonight. You'll have to explain."

"Volta put the word out that you claimed your mother's death was not an accident, that she had yelled for you to run before the bomb exploded, and that you wanted the names of Shamus's accomplices since they might be responsible. When Shamus finally heard, he called Volta and said he wouldn't give him the names until he was satisfied that you really had heard your mother scream for you to run. Obviously, Shamus thought it might be a ploy on Volta's part to either extract privileged information or to keep Shamus feeling miserable. Volta suggested a go-between. They agreed on me."

Daniel said, "You can tell Shamus it's true, and that we'd appreciate the names of the others involved."

"So you don't think it was an accident?"

"It may have been. I don't know. She yelled and then the bomb exploded—the same second. My gut feeling is that somebody killed her."

114

"Any ideas?"

"No. That's why Volta and I want the names of the others."

"I'll tell Shamus personally."

"Where is he?"

"Daniel," Dolly chided, "that's confidential."

"Well, *how* is he?"

"Torn up—he loved Annalee."

Trembling, Daniel said, "So did I. Tell him if I didn't do it and he didn't do it, we should talk to the other three people involved, the bomb-maker for sure."

"Shamus asked me to warn you that Volta is a very strong and cunning man who didn't want the theft to occur."

"Do *you* think Volta had anything to do with it?"

"Personally? No. But he is a powerful and perceptive man."

Daniel rubbed his eyes. "Dolly, do you mind if I ask your opinion on an entirely unrelated matter?"

"Hell, I'd be honored."

Dolly listened as he explained his problem. When he finished, she said, "So you can only make love with the *same* woman once—if I got it right?"

"You do."

"Well, you best make it good."

Dolly left the next morning with Charmaine after assuring Daniel that if and when Shamus provided the names, Volta would contact him.

At about the same time, seventy miles upriver, Jade Lavelle and Annie Sawyer waited for Mommy to return from her morning dip in the Rouge. They met her on the trail. Her short silver hair was still wet from her swim. She listened as they explained Daniel's problem, her clear hazel eyes shifting from one speaker to the other.

Mommy's response was swift and definite. "Don't get involved with him. He's going in a different direction."

Annie and Jade were startled. Mommy seldom spoke so directly or emphatically.

As they thanked her and turned to leave, Mommy added, her voice much softer, "I know—oh, how I know—they *are* attractive."

Over the next month, as the harvest was cured, clipped, and distributed, Daniel tried to follow Dolly's advice. But he was still limited, for whatever reason, to one orgasm with each woman. All the Commies soon knew of Mommy's comment, and those who hadn't slept with him hurried to do so. By Thanksgiving, he'd just about run out of Commie lovers.

Fishing for steelhead, Daniel nearly leapt in the river when Volta appeared behind him and said, "Any luck?"

"None," Daniel said.

"Well, here's some. We're fairly certain we know who killed your mother. The man who made the bomb, Gideon Nobel."

"Why?" was all Daniel could say.

"He was in love with her, had been for years."

"It doesn't sound right," Daniel said. "For one thing, I'm sure she never mentioned him." He began to reel in.

"That's part of the reason—the feeling wasn't mutual."

Daniel started to say something, but Volta held up his hands. "Let me apologize for the cheap drama—it's an old show-business habit. Let's go on up to the house and I'll start from the beginning. That is, if you're done fishing."

They walked back to the ranch house and sat in the living room. Volta began, "Dolly contacted Shamus, gave him your assurance that your mother had shouted a warning just before the bomb exploded, and Shamus, after considering it for a few weeks, sent the names of the other people involved." He handed Daniel a piece of paper. Daniel recognized Shamus's scrawl.

Carl Fuller—driver
Olaf Ekblad—inside
Gideon Nobel—bomb

"What does *inside* mean?" Daniel asked.

"Going inside with Shamus, for the actual theft. As soon as I received the names—I've been in Mexico—I put some of our best people on them, and they've found out quite a bit in the short time they've had.

"Carl 'The Throttle' Fuller is an old wheelman, a real pro. We found him in Minneapolis without any trouble. He claims all he knew of the setup was his end—procuring the cars, arranging the switches, times and places for picking up the others. He didn't know about the diversionary bomb, and never met anyone else involved except Shamus.

"Basically the same story for Olaf Ekblad—absolutely trustworthy, no nerves, and he could have written the manuals for most alarm systems. In fact, AMO has used his services in the past and we've found him utterly reliable. He knew a diversion was planned, but not what or who was involved."

Daniel interrupted. "But this Gideon Nobel did?"

"Listen for a moment. Gideon Nobel met your mother when she was sixteen or seventeen—it was in San Francisco, during one of her visits."

"I was too young then," Daniel said, disappointed. "I won't be able to remember."

"They met in North Beach and he fell in love. For over a year they were occasional lovers—much too occasional for Gideon. Your mother, it seems, was something of a street legend at the time, showing up for a few days a month and then disappearing. At any rate, their affair is still remembered. Gideon was evidently captivated; your mother, less so. She went out with other men, and there were a few public scenes that leave little doubt of his jealousy and anger.

"Gideon was a highly regarded sculptor then, at least among the avant-garde. His most memorable work is a set of twenty-four pieces sharing the central image of Mickey Mouse. In fact, it's called *Mickey Mouse Time in America,* and pieces of the set still exist.

"While there may be aesthetic arguments about the value of his sculptures, there's none about the artistry of his bombs. Expert workmanship. Untraceable connections for the explosives. The highest-quality components. Excellent safety features. And *no* mistakes that anybody ever heard about. Gideon also had a certain panache in his demolitions, always using a Mickey Mouse clock—sort of his signature, even though he replaced the clock mechanisms with more sophisticated timers.

"Now this is important: Gideon, unbeknownst to Shamus, lived less than four blocks away from Shamus in Richmond. It is easily conceivable that he saw your mother and Shamus together, or even that Shamus told him about her—though Shamus denies that anyone but you and he knew of your mother's involvement. It is possible that Gideon deduced your mother would be delivering the bomb. He knew that it was merely for diversion, which meant that it would present a very low risk for whoever delivered it, yet would require someone completely trustworthy—in short, a perfect job for Shamus's lover.

"At this point it gets a bit trickier. Shamus swears that Gideon didn't know that the bomb was diversionary to a plutonium theft. However, Gideon knew something of Shamus's history, and no doubt sensed his current obsession with fissionable materials—Gideon was not without wit, and obsessions *are* difficult to conceal. So it's likely Gideon figured out what Shamus was after. There is evidence Gideon had reservations about his association with the heist, as he indirectly confided to certain friends days before the planned attempt—mentioning that he was involved in something that he regretted, fearing it would bring a great deal of scrutiny to his activities. It also seems Gideon had a particular antipathy to nuclear devices, considering them beyond the scale of intelligent control. Not unlike Shamus's position, really, but with the crucial difference that Gideon believed they are so poisonous to

117

the soul that you can't mess with them without contamination, whatever your motives.

"So. Between jealous revenge and a growing fear about his probable involvement in the theft of nuclear materials, Gideon decided to alter the bomb in some way—perhaps so that it would detonate moments after it was armed, or perhaps by a remote device." Daniel started to say something but Volta anticipated him. "So why did your mother know something was amiss in time to yell a warning to you? I'm not sure, but maybe it was something she felt when she armed the bomb or—and I wouldn't discount this as a possibility—she remembered Gideon's obsession with the Mickey Mouse image, probably knew he made bombs, did know a Mickey Mouse clock had been used in the one she was carrying, and came up with enough doubts and dangers to warn you."

Daniel was shaking his head.

"I know," Volta said, "the latter is fairly thin conjecture."

"Yes, it is—but more than that, it was the *way* she yelled for me to run. It wasn't like there *might* be danger; it was immediate, urgent."

Volta sighed. "I know. But by your own description she was extremely nervous, enough so that a vague connection might have become an urgent truth."

"What does Gideon say to all this speculation?"

"Nothing. Nor will he. He was killed in a car wreck less than a year later—hit head-on by a drunk driver, who is now serving an eight-year term for second degree murder."

Daniel said, "Circumstance, conjecture, a convenient death—it sounds awfully loose."

"I can't disagree. But how would you like to check it out yourself? Investigative work is excellent training. Besides, you must be ready to come out of the hills for some bright lights and big city. It's up to you, of course."

"I would like that," Daniel said. "I want some direct information."

"Done. I'll set up a money drop for you in the city to support your investigation. You take care of the rest—lodging, food, and so forth. You'll be on your own, but I'll give you a number to contact me if you're so inclined. I might be able to coordinate information and leads, and perhaps offer some instructions—suggestions, really."

"Why not give them to me now?"

Volta smiled faintly. "Because I'm not sure what they are. Things have been moving very fast lately."

"I noticed," Daniel said. He was just about to ask Volta's opinion on his sexual problem when he heard Mott railing at Pissgums down in the barn.

"I must leave within the hour," Volta said, getting to his feet, "and first I must talk to Mott and Charmaine."

"What do you have to talk to her about?"

Volta arched an eyebrow. "Business. She needs some supplies and new equipment for her lab."

"What does she make in that lab of hers anyway?"

"She doesn't always tell me, and I never ask."

"You just supply the materials and equipment on faith, right?"

"Exactly. The same basis on which we provide your training. Please call and check in when you get to the city."

Daniel left the Rocking On a week later, three jars of chili and a quarter pound of trainwreck weed in his pack, farewell gifts from Mott. Charmaine was gone for the month, so he left her a good-bye note thanking her for her help. He promised Mott he'd call if he ran across any new drugs or happened to hear about a vintage bazooka for sale.

Transcription: Telephone Call Between
Volta and Daniel

DANIEL: Hey, this is Daniel. I just went by the drop and there's only a hundred dollars.

VOLTA: We're not a *rich* organization, Daniel.

DANIEL: A hundred dollars won't even pay *rent*. This is *San Francisco*.

VOLTA: I understand. It's a dismal situation. But frankly, the finances are in shambles. Our accountant fell in love with her secretary. There's a hundred-dollar limit on all nonessential outlays.

DANIEL: And checking out my mother's death is nonessential?

VOLTA: Since it's already been done to some degree by others—who were paid *eight* hundred dollars—it's difficult to justify financially. And people besides myself are involved in these determinations.

DANIEL: Am I supposed to sleep in the park?

VOLTA: It's been done to good effect.

DANIEL: I get it—part of the training.

VOLTA: Not specifically, no. We do, of course, assume that any of our students has the wit to survive in an affluent society.

DANIEL: What if I need to bribe someone for information?

VOLTA: Bribery is the failure of persuasion. And you're certainly not being trained to acquire information that could simply be bought.

DANIEL: All right. A hundred a week is good enough.

VOLTA: A *month*.

DANIEL: You're kidding. I'd rather devote my attention to investigating my mother's death than finding out what garbage cans in which alleys are the best to eat from.

VOLTA: Perhaps you'll find attention sharpened by necessity.

DANIEL: I thought I was supposed to get twenty percent of the truck farm profits?

VOLTA: You are. A hundred dollars a month for fourteen months is fourteen hundred dollars.

DANIEL: *Fourteen hundred!* It should be more like fourteen *thousand!*

VOLTA: Daniel, you've confused *gross* with *profit*. Gross is total income. Profit is the gross minus operating expenses, which include everything from land payments and taxes—it is three thousand acres, remember—down to kerosene for the lamps. It also includes ceremonial expenses, like burning hundred-dollar bills, and instructional salaries—Wild Bill's, for instance. Plus, of course, the five percent dues you're supposed to pay as an AMO member. We assume your honor, so take it out at this end to save the tedious and entropic transactions of sending it to you only to have you return it. It makes life easier for our accountants.

DANIEL: Maybe if they had more work, they wouldn't have time to fall in love with their secretaries.

VOLTA: If, out of some notion of formality, you insist on receiving the 5 percent we've withheld, I'll send it tomorrow. I believe it's around ninety-three dollars.

DANIEL: (after a pause) No, keep it. Buy your accountant and her boyfriend a wedding present.

VOLTA: That's very thoughtful. You're a credit to Wild Bill. And Daniel, do let me know if you turn up anything interesting.

The first interesting thing Daniel turned up was a spirited blond named Epiphany Chantrelle. He met her in City Lights Books his second day in town. She took him home to a communal house on Treat Street, a Victorian three-story. The number of residents on any given day varied between two and twenty, depending on who was in town, or jail, or had just been released, or had left for Nepal, or returned from Chile. Nobody asked too many questions, and an almost self-conscious spirit of cooperation prevailed. There was always something cooking in the kitchen and the dishes got done. A neatly lettered sign over the sink read: "We're all guests here." Beneath it someone had added Wild Bill's familiar phrase, "One hand washes the other."

He slept with Epiphany that first night, after explaining as straightforwardly as possible that he probably couldn't have sex with her again. And he couldn't, though he tried several times before she eventually left for Detroit with a drummer from Rabid Lassie. He made love—once—with six other women, but when he found he couldn't repeat, decided to try celibacy awhile. Perhaps the problem would solve itself.

To anyone who asked, Daniel said he'd been working as a ranch hand since he was twelve, saved a little money, and had come to San Francisco to find out how people could live so close together.

Gathering information on Gideon Nobel proved frustrating and tedious. He couldn't find anyone who'd even admit they knew Gideon made bombs. He did manage to see the highway patrol report on Gideon's fatal accident. Gideon's Volkswagen had been hit head on by a Chevy driven by a drunk pipefitter named Harlan Maldowny, whose wife had left him a month earlier. Harlan was still in Vacaville on the second-degree homicide rap. Daniel thought about visiting Harlan but decided it would probably be a depressing waste of time. It clearly hadn't been a hit.

He checked out the list of Gideon's North Beach friends that Volta had given him, or at least those that still remained. They recalled his passionate infatuation with Annalee, and some of the scenes he'd caused when rejected, but nobody thought he was the sort of man who would carry a torch or a grudge for very long.

Daniel's investigation took a diligent five months, two pairs of shoes, and too many bus rides. And it all checked out pretty much as Volta had presented it until he met Charlie Miller.

He turned up Charlie Miller through Quentin Lime, an art critic who refused to believe Daniel's line that he was an intern reporter considering writing a piece on Gideon Nobel.

"First of all, Gideon Nobel was, if not an outright charlatan, the worst sculptor west of New York. Secondly, you're much too young to be a reporter, even for an abomination like *Teen Arts*."

"I skipped a few grades," Daniel explained.

"Whatever. It doesn't matter. I refuse to discuss Gideon's alleged work."

"Actually, I'm not so much interested in his work as I am in his life and his particular Bohemian lifestyle—you see, the focus of the article is on different artistic lifestyles."

"Well, that shouldn't be difficult to uncover: He suffered quite publicly and volubly. I'm sure hundreds of people in North Beach alone could still provide you with the squalid details."

"What about his series of sculptures with the Mickey Mouse theme?"

"Drivel," Quentin Lime sniffed, "pure, witless, kitschy drivel."

"It received some good reviews."

"Most reviews are written by morons about morons. Sensibility is at a premium in American culture these days."

"Did you know him personally?"

"Never," Quentin Lime said icily. "We tended to frequent different social circles. Gideon considered himself a beatnik. He and Charles Miller wrote a miserable piece of self-promotion called the *Three M Manifesto*—essentially the *crucial* culture concept of "Mickey Mouse Moment," which they, with childish illogic and grand infelicities of expression, advanced as a beatific state."

"I thought the *Three M Manifesto* had been published anonymously?"

"I assure you that my sources, while I'm not at liberty to disclose them, are impeccable."

"This Charles Miller—who's he? I haven't heard him mentioned before."

"You've probably heard him referred to as High Life. Do you get it? Miller High Life. Bohemians are *so* witty."

"High Life, right, I've heard about him—but he's in Spain isn't he?"

"Unfortunately, he returned two days ago, which means that in about a half hour he will be slouching at a back table in Cafe Trieste, holding court to an empty house. I hear he's now billing himself as the Last Beatnik. Let us fervently hope so."

"Sit down, man," High Life motioned before Daniel could even introduce himself. "You know what the *real* work of art is, man? Life. Not just human life, but *all life.*" He leaned forward confidentially as Daniel took a chair. "I used to be a painter. Now I'm the paint. You digging that?"

Daniel said carefully, "I think I know what you mean."

"But do you dig the *tragedy* of it?"

"I thought it sounded fine."

"No, man. And you know why? There's no canvas. They're all turning into fucking robots out there. Power-suckers. Women are buying electrical vibrators to fuck themselves with, man. Personal appliances—it's a whole new market. You see, man, Marx got it right for his time, but hey, who could have imagined *advertising*? A *whole industry* devoted to the creation of desire! Like we didn't have enough, right?"

"I really don't know," Daniel said. "I've spent most of my time in the mountains."

"Go back, man. It's your best shot at sanity."

"I probably will, but right now I'm trying to gather some information on a sculptor named Gideon Nobel."

High Life looked blankly at a spot just over Daniel's head.

"I'm not a cop," Daniel assured him.

"Man, everybody's a cop or a reporter. Anybody that *calls* the cops is a cop. Anybody trying to write their way into the fame game is a reporter. You know what I'm saying? I mean, a person that calls the cops is a person that doesn't have any friends. I don't need that action, dig, 'cause I have friends. Maybe even this Gideon cat was a friend. Why would you want to know?"

Given High Life's clear antipathy to reporters, Daniel tried a different cover. "I'm writing a graduate paper on his life and work."

High Life cocked his head. "Oh yeah? Where you studying?"

"Cal."

"Who's department chair in art over there now?"

"Polansky."

"You read the right catalogue, man, but Polansky had a stroke about three months ago." High Life started to rise from his chair. "See ya later."

"Actually," Daniel said, "I want to know about Gideon because I think he killed my mother."

High Life sat down. "Hey, that's *too* much. What was her name?"

"Annalee Pearse."

High Life looked at Daniel sharply, then shook his head. "Let's fall by my pad, man. Do a little of the good shit and see if we can't get this back on track."

Charles "High Life" Miller hadn't been properly stirred in the melting pot. He had General Custer's flowing blond hair and the dirt-brown eyes of Sitting Bull. His upstairs apartment on Columbus was furnished with a mattress, three orange-crate bookcases, wine bottles shoved in a corner, and a refrigerator that ran constantly and noisily. High Life sat on the mattress and rolled a joint. He lit it, sucked down a little hit, passed it to Daniel. As he exhaled he said, "Brought this shit back with me from Spain. Basques grow it in the highlands. Best kept secret on the planet, this weed. It'll knock your dick in your watchpocket."

Daniel took a few hits and passed it back, imagining Mott snorting in derision at the size of the joint. Mott's, usually rolled in newspaper in the Rastafarian mode, required both hands just to hold on.

High Life asked abruptly, "Your mother now, she the Annalee who Gideon had the bad hots for back in the late sixties?"

"So it seems."

"How'd she die?"

"A bomb exploded."

High Life nodded, staring at the joint in his hand. "Well, man, you know how it is—accidents happen."

"Not this time."

"I knew them both. Your mother couldn't have been sixteen, seventeen. Stunning chick. Mysterioso. Make the scene for a few days and—*poof*—gone till you saw her again. Gideon was what? Early thirties? Very hip, definitely knew the scoobies from the doos. He went for her hard. He thought she might be an actual Moon Goddess. I mean, Gideon truly believed there are gods and goddesses who assume human form in order to increase their understanding of us. Anyway, I was in Vesuvio's the night Gideon pulled a gun on Johnny Gilbert and threatened to blow him away if he didn't quit porking your mom—that wasn't very sensitive on my part, was it? But that's what he said to Johnny Gilbert, who was a poet. She dug poets. But I'll tell you, Gideon loved her as real as you can. He might have killed *for* her, but he'd never have killed her."

"She was in love with someone else."

"When are we talking about?"

"Early 1980."

"No way. Me and Gideon were tight into the late seventies." High Life held up his thumb and index finger pressed together to illustrate how tight they'd been. "He'd gotten over your mother by then. He was an artist, and artists are passionate people. He wasn't *happy* unless he was obsessed, taken with some glory vision, some monstro-truth, and when he was in it, he was *in it*, over his head. And when he came up, it ended. Like when he knew your mother, he was obsessed with moonlight. He used to go up on the roof at night and fucking *moonbathe*. He wrote letters to NASA threatening to kill any asshole astronaut that dared to set foot on the moon. He called your mom Diana—believed to his bones, man, that she was a genuine Moon Goddess. All he talked about was her and the moon. It lasted about two years. Then he got into Marx."

"Karl Marx?"

"Don't ask *me* how he made that leap, but he read every word of and on Marx for about two years. Then it was clouds."

Daniel asked: "What about Mickey Mouse—was that another of his obsessions? He did a series of sculptures, didn't he?"

"Oh yeah, he got into Mickey deep. He gave me the second sculpture he did. They all represented an hour of the day, dig, and mine was midnight. A little painted bronze of Mickey Mouse with his head up his ass, and his ears kinda reshaping his lips. Best one in the series, I thought. But I had to sell it when I hit some hard times. You know, in some ways Mickey was his last shot. After that he became extremely interested in, uh . . . *sonic* sculptures, if you follow me—*loud* noises. I mean, after Mickey Mouse, what's left?"

"When did he do these Mickey Mouse sculptures?"

"Umm, let's see? Must have been around seventy-seven, seventy-six. Yeah, seventy-six, the Bicentennial, because that Christmas he gave everybody a Mickey Mouse watch with the hands pulled off."

High Life began a long rant against cultural idiocy, but Daniel tuned him out. In late 1976 they'd still been at the Four Deuces, but Annalee hadn't been making her monthly city trips for a long time. It was highly improbable she could have connected Gideon to the bomb. And then Daniel surprised himself by immediately deciding not to tell Volta the new information, or not until he had thought it through.

It wasn't pleasant thinking it through. He lay on his mattress in the basement of the Treat Street house resifting evidence, considering motives, entertaining the improbable, trying to seize the obvious, taking each person carefully, starting with himself.

He knew he hadn't betrayed his mother, but it *was* possible that the girl who'd wandered into the house the night before the theft attempt and who'd so wonderfully sucked his cock might have been an agent investigating the phony paper they were producing. Maybe she'd found something in the house, a note or something his mother had left. The trouble with that was he didn't think his mother knew where the bomb would be planted until the next morning.

He eliminated Shamus mainly on instinct. What he had learned didn't contradict his gut feeling that Shamus had been the one with the most to lose. Volta's suggestion that perhaps Shamus had changed the bomb so that it would kill Annalee seemed utterly farfetched; Daniel might have entertained it if Shamus had gone ahead with the theft, b·· he hadn't, nor had he tried to eliminate the others involved.

Gideon was more problematic. A faulty bomb was possible, but Daniel had to doubt, in light of the information from High Life, that the blast had been intentional on Gideon's part. High Life had claimed Gideon had never said much about nuclear devices one way or another except to insist they were possessed of such horrible karma it was best to not even think about them. Daniel wasn't sure what that meant, since it could be taken as a mindlessly blithe dismissal or an aversion as deep as taboo.

He provisionally eliminated Carl Fuller, the wheelman, and Olaf Ekblad, the alarm specialist. Shamus had said whoever was involved would deal only with him and know only the part assigned, and evidently that was the case.

That left his mother. She, he thought ruefully, would have done just about anything to stay with Shamus, and whether the theft was successful or not, she was going to lose. Only by preventing it could she have stayed with Shamus. And though she certainly had her sacrificial side, it was insulting to think she would kill herself to save the relationship. She wasn't crazy. And even if she would have endangered herself, she wouldn't have put him in peril. But what finally convinced him it couldn't have been his mother was the memory of her scream telling him to run: It had been terrified. Whatever had happened, she hadn't expected it.

Daniel, heeding Shamus's message to be careful of Volta, decided Volta should be considered as well. There were just too many unknowns. First of all, Volta would have had to know what was happening—where and when— which meant somebody would have had to tell him. Only Shamus and, for a few hours, he and his mother had known where the bomb would be placed. Of course, Volta had been strongly against the plutonium theft, and knowing how Annalee and Shamus felt about each other, he might have put tails on them. But it's the nature of tails to follow, not anticipate, though perhaps there had been a way to get to the bomb *before* it got to Shamus. The other thing was, none of it felt like Volta's style. But he knew exactly what Shamus meant about Volta. Even when discussing the weather, Volta always seemed to say just a little bit less than he actually knew.

After ten hours of hard solid thought on every possibility he could imagine, Daniel gave up. There were too many unknowns, too many improbable sequences, and all the evidence pointed to the obvious: a faulty bomb, probably a malfunction in the timer.

Transcription: Telephone Conversation Between
Volta and Daniel

DANIEL: Hello, Volta? This is Daniel.

VOLTA: And how are you, Daniel?

DANIEL: Broke and nowhere.

VOLTA: (chuckling) At least you're making progress.

DANIEL: You'd have to convince me.

VOLTA: The last time we talked you were merely broke.

DANIEL: (sullenly) I suppose.

VOLTA: Have you made inquiries?

DANIEL: Yes, but without any startling discoveries.

VOLTA: Are you satisfied Gideon killed your mother?

DANIEL: Not completely.

VOLTA: I'm not satisfied at all. The more I've thought about it, the more it seems too improbable that your mother connected the bomb with Gideon just moments before it exploded. As I mentioned before, it seems far more likely she heard something inside the case—some sound, the timer connecting—that convinced her the bomb was about to explode.

DANIEL: That's my tentative conclusion, also.

VOLTA: Have you explored it at all? The possibility of a faulty bomb?

DANIEL: No.

VOLTA: I have. I've talked to four demolition experts who all said it was virtually impossible there would be a warning sound, though it would depend on the type of bomb. One of the experts, "Blooey" Martien said that if your mother was a particularly receptive soul she may have "sensed" imminent death—he entered it as a possibility, but noted it was highly doubtful. However, when I attempted to obtain the police report on the bomb, it was missing. No record. Gone. So while you may indeed be nowhere, you're not alone.

DANIEL: What do you mean the police record is gone?

VOLTA: I'm not sure I can be more explicit. The bomb report is not on file. With every bombing, there's a lab analysis of the traces to determine the composition of the bomb, the type of explosive, so forth. Either the report was never filed—highly unusual—or it was removed. Or, mostly likely, it was misfiled in the bureaucratic paper shuffle. You're welcome to look if you choose. I must say, though, we have an exceptional contact inside the department, and she's gotten nowhere. Also, your inquiries will no doubt excite their curiosity about you, thus their scrutiny, and perhaps their wrath.

DANIEL: How do I know that you're not making this up?

VOLTA: You don't. But you're free to verify the information. In fact, we'll increase your pay to $120 a month to do it. It's a rather strange arrangement, paying you to verify our honor, but AMO has traditionally delighted in strangeness.

DANIEL: I'll take your word for it. But thanks for the raise. I can afford lunch twice a week now.

VOLTA: Really, Daniel. Like most human beings, sniveling does not become you.

DANIEL: (quickly, trying to catch Volta off guard) Did you know my mother was seeing Shamus in Berkeley?

VOLTA: No. But I clearly surmised the possibility, since I did request your mother to call me should he appear.

DANIEL: What made you think he'd show up?

VOLTA: His eyes when he talked about Annalee.

DANIEL: Were you having Shamus watched? Or us?

VOLTA: (patiently, but with some snap) No, Daniel. You must understand that while I didn't want Shamus stealing nuclear materials, and would have tried to dissuade him, I would not have physically intervened, and certainly not by killing your mother. If you think differently, we're wasting each other's time and spirit.

DANIEL: I'm sorry if I offended you. I've been asking questions for the past few months and I'm a little hungry for some answers.

VOLTA: All I can give you is my word that I knew nothing of the plutonium theft until the day your mother died in the explosion.

DANIEL: One of the reasons I ask is that Shamus says not to trust you. I wonder if *you* trust *him?*

VOLTA: Less so lately than before. He's not doing well. He's evidently drinking heavily and taking drugs—one of the painkillers, Percodan or Dilaudid.

DANIEL: That's not like him. Does he still wear a black glove?

VOLTA: Yes, but with the fingertips cut off. All this comes from Dolly, by the way.

DANIEL: It's depressing about Shamus.

VOLTA: Alchemy is full of cautions about becoming fascinated with the powers of decay. It is also traditionally held that a man burned by silver is marked by the moon.

DANIEL: (abruptly, but not demanding) I'm tired of thinking about all this. I don't see anywhere left to go with it. What's next, if anything?

VOLTA: Take a three-week vacation. The man I want to connect you with won't be back till the twenty-eighth. Call around then and I'll put you in touch. His name is William Clinton.

DANIEL: What will I be studying?

VOLTA: Concentration.

DANIEL: I thought that's what I studied with Wild Bill.

VOLTA: Indeed. I trust you're well prepared.

William Rebis Clinton was the ace safecracker west of the Rockies. Willie the Click, as he was known to his cohorts, could drill or blast any lock devised. However, as he repeatedly and vehemently pointed out, the highest expression of the safecrackers' art was opening combination locks by touch alone, by becoming the spinning wheel, the tumblers and pins, by disappearing through your fingertips into pure sensation. On his fortieth birthday, Willie had resolved never again to use anything but his hands to open a safe. He hadn't, and he was pleased. Drills and explosives did what Willie believed all technologies did: They killed feeling. By assassinating time and space under the guise of saving them, they keep people out of touch when the better state of being, according to Willie and others, is in touch. In his more delirious screeds, Willie claimed that industrialization was a Christian plot to destroy the pagan reflex between sensation and emotion.

Willie was a short, wiry man with intense brown eyes. His most notable trait was his tendency to speak in whirling bursts of proverbs, obscure quotations, metaphors, speculative observation, and oblique conceits. When Daniel had arrived at Willie's apartment in the Mission District, Willie had taken Daniel's offered hand and scrutinized it a few minutes before ordering Daniel to sit down and spread both his hands palm up on the worktable. Curious, Daniel complied, and then became suddenly anxious when Willie sat down opposite him and opened a case containing five silver needles, needles so slender they flirted with invisibility.

"What are those for?"

"The obscure by the more obscure, Daniel, the unknown by the unfathomable. To gauge sensitivity. Synaptic discrimination. Your particular neural awareness. It's painless. Though I believe it was Carlyle who noted, 'The tragedy of life is not so much what men suffer, but rather what they miss.'" Willie lifted a needle to the light. "Now shut your eyes and tell me when you feel something—the slightest pressure or other sensation."

Daniel shut his eyes and concentrated on his upturned hands on the table. He felt a tingling in his left index finger and told Willie.

"Yes," Willie muttered, "continue."

Daniel felt a burning sensation on his right ring finger. Then his left thumb itched, then his left middle finger tingled. Willie said, "Bah. Poor summation. A plus B, but no C. Clogged thresholds. You can open your eyes." Willie was glaring at him. "Virtual tactile insentience. A turtle has more feeling in its shell. So be it. As they say in Yugoslavia, 'Tell the truth and run fast.' I'm afraid we'll have to start with the absolute fundamentals. You do understand that opening locks is an art, and that a necessity of art is to intensify the organs it employs?"

"No," Daniel said hesitantly, not without a touch of perversity, "I'm not sure if I do understand that."

"Muddy mind, troubled water. All right. Consider what Sickert had to say: 'The whole of art is one long roll of revelation.' And it is revealed only to those whose minds are what Horace called 'vacant'—though he was actually speaking of a woman whose heart is free. Get rid of yourself, Daniel. To open locks you must open yourself. Disappear through your fingertips."

"Suppose I don't come back?"

"A door always opens."

Daniel started to say something but Willie cut him off. "No. No more abstractions for you. You are the kind who can swim in them, but you should be bathing in water squeezed from stone. If you'd please close your eyes, and place your hands palms upward on the table again."

Daniel immediately felt something light and papery settle on each palm. Willie commanded, "All right, open them."

In his right hand Daniel saw a hundred-dollar bill. In the left, a slip of paper with a series of numbers.

Willie explained, "The phone number belongs to Oriana Coeur. The money is to pay her."

130

"For what?" Daniel demanded.

"For her profound sensual dimensions. You will see her every Thursday until you develop tactility. From seven o'clock in the evening till three o'clock in the morning on the other six nights of the week, you will meet with me here for study. We will start with alarm systems. Locks must await your work with Oriana. As an Estonian proverb has it, 'You can't expect the mute to sing.'"

"What did you mean about Oriana's 'sensual dimensions'?"

"Ah ha! You see? Attention begins when the imagination is seized. Oriana is a woman of the evening who has a remarkable sensitivity to touch. The fee for her company is usually five hundred dollars a night, but since she and I developed the exercise together, the charge is considerably less."

"So what will she and I be doing exactly?"

"Oriana will give you the *exact* instructions, but essentially you will touch her where she directs you, using a variety of pressures and movements. You will practice until Oriana is satisfied. *She,* please note, not you. You keep your clothes on. Your purpose is not only to please her, but to literally have her life put in your hands. *Literally.* If her pleasure is the answer, your task, as Krause put it, is 'to provide the riddle.'"

That evening, Oriana, her reddish-gold hair spilling over the pillows, arms flung wide, gave much more explicit instructions on where and how she wished to be touched—everywhere and any way she could imagine. At the height of her pleasure, Daniel imagined she was touching him, and for a long spinning instant lost all distinctions between their skins. Afterward, his hands felt like globes of light. But when Oriana, still flushed, began kissing his fingertips, asking what *his* pleasure was, he said he'd like to wait.

Oriana bit his middle finger gently. "So Willie told you to keep your pants on, huh? He's such a purist."

Daniel said, "It's not really that. In the past, I've only been able to be with a woman once."

"What do you mean *be with*? That you could only come once a night?"

"Once, period."

Oriana was interested. "Then you can't get it up again for her, ever?"
Daniel nodded.

"Not even a little tremor of a twinge?"

"Nothing."

"These ladies knew what they were doing?"

"They were extremely desirable, and remarkably patient."

"So what do you think is going on?"

"I don't know. It could be from an injury. A tiny sliver of metal was once blown through the right front quadrant of my brain."

"Good Lord! What happened?"

"It's complicated, Oriana. My mother was killed in an accident and I almost was, too."

"Oh honey," Oriana said. She took Daniel's hands in hers and pressed them to her face.

Daniel felt a tear against his palm. "Don't cry," he asked her. "Please?"

Oriana flung his hands off her face and sat up on the bed, facing him. "Fuck you," she spit. "I'll cry when I feel like crying."

Daniel fell in love. He told her, "I want to wait to have sex with you because I'd rather have a future than a past."

In reply, she embraced him in her bare arms. "Any time and all the time you want."

Every Thursday evening Daniel was a brilliant student, but the rest of the week he was dunced by distraction. His mind wandered over Oriana's lush and astonishingly responsive body. Willie's mind was as interesting as Oriana's body, but not nearly as provocative.

Nonetheless, over the next three months Daniel learned to disable fifty different alarm systems and pick almost any lock that could be opened with a key. As they entered the fourth month of instruction, Willie introduced him to combination locks. At the first week's session, Willie made him sit for two hours blindfolded, ears plugged, wearing thick gloves before allowing him to attempt the simplest $3.95 combination lock. As Daniel twirled the dial, Willie coached him. "Feel *inside* the lock through your fingers. As if they were root tips seeking water. Feel for the slightest drag, the friction between molecules. Trust your fingertips. They are closer than your brain, far less busy, and immensely less complicated. You need to open this lock to see yourself, and as Edgar Davis Dodds said, 'Freedom resides in being equal to your needs.' But first you must comprehend the difference between necessity and desire."

Daniel wondered if he merely desired Oriana or actually needed her.

"Daniel," Willie scolded, "is that a pretty sunset you're watching up there on Jupiter?"

Daniel went back to work on the lock.

That night Daniel got some homework—a cheap combination bicycle lock. It was locked. When he returned it the next evening open, he received two locks to take home. Willie promised they'd begin the field-work portion of their study when he could open twenty at home overnight.

Willie scouted the first few jobs, and put Daniel through his paces, from disabling the alarm system to locating and opening the safe. Soon Daniel's responsibility expanded to include scouting and planning. They made about one field-trip a week, or about as often as his visits to Oriana. Daniel had suggested to Willie early on that he thought working with Oriana twice a week would be doubly helpful. Willie said he was sure it would, but that he couldn't afford it. Oriana, when Daniel asked if he might see her more often, had claimed that the pleasure center in her brain would fry shut if she saw him more than once a week.

Daniel, with Willie's guidance, opened twenty-three safes during his apprenticeship. To Daniel's utter dismay they never stole anything. The rule against theft had been firmly established on his first job, a dentist's wall-safe in Tiburon.

"Put it back," Willie hissed.

Daniel thought Willie was kidding and didn't even pause as he stuffed the sheaf of bills and an ounce baggie of cocaine into his jacket pocket.

"Daniel," Willie roared, "did you fail to hear me or fail to understand? *Put it back. We're practicing.*"

"Be serious," Daniel pleaded. "If we get busted, is that what we tell the cops—it's okay, officer, we're just practicing."

"We don't tell the cops shit, ever. And we don't steal unless it's necessary. And we harken to Salinius's observation that 'the great enemies of honor are greed and convenience.'"

Daniel returned the drugs and money to the safe. "So what is this?" he sneered. "Art for art's sake?"

"You flatter yourself. It's merely practice. After much such practice, it might become art."

Daniel fired at him, "Hey! I've been living on a hundred dollars a month for almost a year!"

"That's plenty," Willie said. "Besides, you've been living on *five hundred* a month—a hundred for room and board, four hundred for Oriana."

"I get it," Daniel said wearily, "I suppose it's charged to my account. You guys are merciless."

"Not really. We're just playfully fair."

"*Playful?*" Daniel repeated. "That's twisted thinking." Daniel started to swing the safe door shut.

"No," Willie stopped him. "Wait. Not only do we not take anything, we *always* leave them something for their trouble." He handed Daniel a small, elegantly printed card. On it was a quotation from Rilke:

> *. . . there is no place*
> *that does not see you.*
> *You must change your life.*

Smiling to himself, Daniel dropped the card on the baggie of cocaine, closed the safe, and gave the knob a carefree twirl.

For Daniel, the most illuminating aspect of cracking safes was the things people chose to keep secret. Money and drugs were the most common items,

133

with jewels, documents, and guns close behind, but after those the list got strange:

> A quart jar of glass eyes
> A flattened typewriter
> A pair of black panties tied around a pair of roller skates (Oriana had howled when Daniel told her)
> A tree-sloth fetus floating in a jar of formaldehyde
> A small twenty-four-carat gold yo-yo with a string of finely braided silver that Daniel had wanted so bad he could taste it
> An old coffeepot
> A piece of chalk
> A petrified loaf of French bread
> And Daniel's favorite, a neatly printed note in an otherwise empty safe: "Eat shit, George. I've taken it all and I'm on my way to Paris with the pool boy." (This was Oriana's favorite, too)

Transcription (Partial): Telephone Call Between Volta and Willie Clinton

VOLTA: A certain large library in our nation's capital has come into possession of some old documents that rightfully belong to us.

WILLIE: I'm on my way.

VOLTA: What about Daniel?

WILLIE: You know I always work alone on jobs like this. To cite a popular Southern California proverb, "Just because everything's different doesn't mean anything has changed."

VOLTA: Fine. I just thought it might make an interesting final exam.

WILLIE: He doesn't need a final exam. He's proficient, but that's all he'll ever be as a safecracker. Granted, he has some feel for it, but not wholeheartedly. My sense—and I may be wrong—is that Daniel doesn't want *in,* he wants *out.* And it was Schiller, I believe, who said, "Blesséd are those whose necessities find their art." In my opinion, safecracking isn't Daniel's art. It hasn't helped that his attention has been confounded by a lovely young woman.

VOLTA: I've never been a foe of sweet confoundings. After all, who's to say what the lesson is unless you learn it.

WILLIE: You're shameless! You stole that from Sophocles!

VOLTA: William, as T. S. Eliot said, "A good poet borrows; a great poet steals."

WILLIE: I don't have time to listen to you mangle quotes all day. When do I leave?

VOLTA: Twenty hours. Bruce on Castro is making the arrangements. What about Daniel? Any suggestions?

WILLIE: Give him some money and some time off. A hundred a month really *is* a bit grim. Otherwise, I fear San Francisco will be hit with a spate of B&E's.

VOLTA: Well, as they say: "You can lead a horse to water, but you can't make him do the backstroke or suck blood from a turnip."

When Daniel arrived at Willie's Friday evening he found the door locked and a note pinned to the sill: "Daniel—Come on in." His brain still floating from the previous night's session with Oriana, Daniel took a moment to comprehend the note.

He picked the lock and went in.

There was a safe on the worktable, a small Sentry combination. It was a snap. Inside was a stack of cards with the Rilke quotation, a handmade set of vanadium picks, and another note from Willie:

> I'm sorry I can't give you my personal farewell and good wishes, but some urgent business has usurped my attention. Please accept the picks as a graduation present. It's been a privilege to work with you. I could go on, but, as Auden has chided, "Sentimentality is the failure of emotion."
>
> Volta asked that you call him asap through the Six Rivers exchange.
>
> May the doors open on what you need,
>
> Willie

As Daniel finished the note his first thought was *now I can fuck Oriana.* But the first thing he did was call Volta as requested. Volta, who seemed preoccupied, told Daniel a five-thousand-dollar cashier's check was waiting for him at the Hibernia Bank, and that in two weeks he should meet Robert Sloane in Room 377 of the Bathsheba Hotel in Tucson.

Daniel cashed the check in the morning and took a cab back to Treat Street, instructing the cabbie to wait. He took only a few minutes to pack his gear. As he passed through the kitchen on his way out, he stopped to count out a thousand dollars in twenties, leaving them on the table. He directed the cab to the Clift Hotel, tipped the driver a hundred-dollar bill, tipped the doorman twenty for dealing with his luggage, and rented a suite for ten days, paying the full $1500 in advance. The suite was elegantly comfortable. He sat at the cherry-wood desk and dialed Oriana's number. A computer-generated voice informed him the number had been disconnected.

He spent the next three torturous days wondering if she'd gone with Willie and why she hadn't said good-bye. He tried her number over and over and the same hideous voice gave him the same bad news. He wondered if maybe she'd been hassled by the cops or a john. He thought about asking Volta to find out what was going on. He thought about Oriana's long body, the curve of her flanks, the warmth of her inner thighs. He hurt.

When he stirred from a fitful sleep early the fourth day, he saw the red message light glowing on the phone. The desk informed him a letter had been left for him. In a few minutes, the concierge himself delivered it.

The note from Oriana was brief:

Now you'll always have a future.

Daniel started laughing, and right in the middle of laughing he burst into tears. He couldn't stop until he burned the note.

Six days later, on the night before his flight left for Tucson, Daniel relieved the Marina Safeway's vault of ten thousand dollars and left it on the kitchen table at the Treat Street house before returning for his last night at the Clift. He believed it had been Willie the Click, quoting Schiller perhaps, who'd noted, "If luxury doesn't inspire generosity, the luxury is undeserved."

Bad Bobby Sloane—tall, lean, greying at the temples, always neatly and conservatively dressed—looked more like a savings-and-loan vice-president than a gambling fool. If you'd been around him in his early twenties when he'd succumbed to the only burst of flamboyance in his life, he might have handed you one of his business cards—and there it was, right under his engraved name:

ROBERT SLOANE
Poker Player & General Gambling Fool

I will play
Any man from any land
Any amount he can count

EARTH

> At any game he can name
> Any place, face-to-face.

Bad Bobby had started playing poker for keepsies when he was nine years old, just after the Second World War. He'd played his first game around a migrant campfire in a Georgia peach orchard. He'd bought into the game with his father's new boots, for which one of the men gave him fifty cents. His father had died a week earlier, beaten to death in a barroom brawl. Before sunrise, Bobby had turned five dimes into sixty-seven dollars.

Almost four decades later, Bad Bobby Sloane was generally regarded as probably the best all-around cardplayer in the United States, especially in Texas Hold-'Em and, since Johnny "He-Horse" Coombs had recently cashed out, perhaps the best at Five-Card Stud.

Daniel's knock at Room 377 was answered by a hotel steward. Behind him, through the drifting smoke, Daniel saw a card game in progress. He told the steward he was looking for Mr. Sloane, and after a few minutes' wait, Bad Bobby stepped into the hall. He had flat blue eyes and large, bony hands. He was wearing a well-cut houndstooth jacket, brown slacks, a lighter brown shirt, and a black tie with a gold stickpin fashioned in the face of the Joker.

"Glad to meet ya, Daniel," Bobby said in his sleepy Georgia baritone. He took a room key from his jacket and tossed it to Daniel. "Go on down to the room and get the clouds outa your head. I'll be along when I get there. Whatever you need, call room service and put it on the tab."

Daniel nodded toward the door. "You playing in that game in there?"

"Yup," Bobby sighed, "and I'm stuck and bleeding. That's why it's likely to be a spell."

Bad Bobby wasn't there when Daniel went to bed, but he was there in the morning, talking on the phone, when Daniel woke up.

"Denver by *four!* What happened? The Raider cornerbacks get caught stealing cars? The defensive line busted at customs? Sweet Jesus, I may be an old coondog but I still know what a bone is. Shit, give me twenty grand on the Raiders. What's the overs? Well mark me down another five on the unders."

Daniel heard him hang up and then begin dialing again. "This is Robert Sloane in 377. Could you please send up some Eggs Benedict, two crisp-fried pork chops, and a quart of fresh-squeezed orange juice." He saw Daniel was awake and said into the phone, "Just a moment, please," and then to Daniel, "You eating breakfast?"

"Your order sounded good to me."

Bobby doubled the order and hung up.

Daniel said, "Is the card game over?"

"Broke up about a half hour ago."

"Did you win?"

"I lost twenty thousand."

Staggered as much by the amount as Bobby's nonchalance, Daniel said, "That's an awful lot of money, twenty thousand."

"Not if you say it fast," Bobby grinned. "Besides, you gotta remember you're not playing for *money,* you're playing for *chips,* and chips is just the way you keep track. The reason they make chips round is because they're *supposed* to roll. And speaking of rolling, we best get our gear together. We're leaving right after we watch the Raiders kick some Bronco ass."

"Where are we off to?"

"El Paso. Promising Seven-Stud game."

"Am I going to play?"

"Not for a bit. First you've got to learn the rules and manners, the different games and strategies, basic principles and moves. And since you'll be playing my money till you're good enough to win some on your own, I'll be calling the shots. That's the deal whenever I take someone on to teach. I call the shots until you can beat me heads-up in a gambling game, and then you're free to do as you please. Any time you challenge me and lose, it costs you ten grand for my effort. That's the game, Daniel, and it's your choice. It's also your first lesson, a bedrock gambling truth: If you don't like the game, don't sit down."

"Suppose I can't beat you?"

"Well, you'll probably be so poor and frustrated and fucked up that I'll cut you loose outa mercy, if you beg nice. That makes me out mean, but actually I'm about the easiest man in the world to get along with, 'cept for two things I can't abide—sniveling and gloating. Don't snivel when you lose or gloat when you win."

"Do you mind if I ask about your connection with AMO?"

"No—though it's not good card manners to press a man for information on his private life."

"I didn't mean to offend you."

"You didn't." Bobby ambled over to the TV and switched it on. "When I first moved up into the high-stakes games, I went bust occasionally—well, more often than not, to tell the truth—and Volta offered to back my action. Most backers naturally want a chunk of the cake, fifty-fifty being about standard, but Volta only wanted five percent a year—of the *net*—with me to do the accounting. Can't hardly beat that with a stick. Plus, I agreed to take on students now and then if Volta thought they had promise. You're only the third one. First two mighta made it, but they went crazy 'fore they got there."

Daniel started to ask where "there" was, but Bad Bobby raised a finger and pointed toward the football game. "We're gonna have months to talk on the road. Right now we got twenty-five grand that says there's no way the Broncos can whup the Raiders by more than four points and that together they don't score over forty-two. Let's eat breakfast and watch our money."

The Raiders won outright in a defensive struggle, and later that afternoon Bad Bobby left town as he usually did—ahead of where he came in.

El Paso. Houston. Dallas. New Orleans. Nashville. Omaha. Cheyenne. Denver. Reno. San Francisco. Always the best hotels, the finest restaurants, and the fastest action in town. Daniel watched as Bad Bobby played. He loved Bobby's style, a balance of discipline and impulse, imbued with an aesthetic that fell neatly between plantation manners and swamp-rat savvy. He heard hundreds of Bad Bobby stories from players and spectators alike.

The most frequent story concerned Bobby's youth. He was already making a good living playing cards from town to town by the time he was sixteen, but he was illiterate. So Bobby took a cut of his winnings and hired tutors to travel with him, paying them wages and expenses in exchange for teaching him reading and writing, and, later on, arithmetic, geography, and history. It took Bobby nine years to read and write at a college level. He attracted tutors who liked the thrill of an occasional wager, whether it might be on the turn of a card or how many road-killed armadillos they'd see between Lubbock and Galveston, and thus was able to complete his college education at a modest profit.

Daniel learned that Bad Bobby's nickname had been given him by Barbwire Bill Eaton when he'd beaten Barbwire's set of aces with a low straight in a Texas Hold-'Em game, causing the usually unflappable Barbwire to bang his head on the table and babble, "Goddamn, lots of players beat me, but you beat me like an ugly stepchild. Gettin' so when I see you come through the door, I say to myself, 'Fasten yr asshole, Bill, cause here comes Bad-Beats Bobby.'" The name was soon shortened to Bad Bobby.

When the game was over and they were back on the road, alternating at the wheel of Bad Bobby's perfectly restored '49 Cadillac, Bobby shared his poker wisdom and general card sense with Daniel, explaining rules, odds, strategies, how to properly shuffle and deal cards, and the small niceties of etiquette, like playing quickly and in turn. Daniel learned, if only theoretically, how to play position and manage money, when to raise, call, or fold, how to quickly assess the strengths and weaknesses of other players, the best times to bluff, how to calculate pot odds, how to spot tells, and cheaters, and marks. They reviewed recent hands as Bobby explained why he'd played them that way and what he might have done in different circumstances. He constructed practice hands for Daniel, questioning him on his decisions. He illustrated the lessons with copious stories and lore picked up in forty years on the road and at the tables.

"I tell ya, Daniel, there's *no sure thing*. Why, I was in a big-stakes Five-Card Draw game in Waco—we were playing with the joker—and I saw a hand with five aces get beat for everything the guy had."

"Wait a minute," Daniel said, "nothing can beat five aces. What'd the other guy have in *his* hand?"

"A Smith and Wesson. A thirty-eight, I believe."

When they swung through Las Vegas two months later, Daniel was burning to play. He told Bad Bobby he was ready.

"Told ya, Daniel, you play your own money any time you think you're ready. You can play *my* money when *I* think you're ready."

Daniel said, more challenge than question, "You don't think I'm ready."

"Nope. I think you'd get sucked down like a little muskrat swimming in a pool of 'gators. Fact is, you're still making too many mistakes on the problems I've been giving ya."

With passion, Daniel said, "That's because I'm *sick* of theory. From watching you play it's pretty clear that every hand is a unique situation, because you're involved with people, *real* individual players, and one of them is on a hot streak, and one just had a fight with his wife, and one has just finished his sixth whiskey in two hours. I *would* play my own money if I had any left, and I can always get what I need if I have to—"

"No you can't," Bobby cut him off cold. "*No* thieving, not even an ashtray—that's an iron rule with me. Offends the poker gods."

"I think I'm ready," Daniel said firmly.

Bad Bobby scratched his nose. "All right," he said without conviction, "I'll front you five grand. But the deal is, if you lose so much as a nickel, you don't play again for a month and you don't badger me about being ready."

"You're on," Daniel grinned.

"We'll get us some dinner and head downtown to the Antlers. They've got a hundred-dollar-limit Five-Stud game that's about your speed." Bad Bobby gave him a laconic smile. "It's a real character builder."

Daniel bought in for a thousand dollars and built some character immediately, his three sevens crunched by three jacks—set over set, one of the toughest beats in the game. He called for another thousand.

It took him an hour to lose the second grand. In a pot with six players, Daniel raised himself all-in on the fourth card, which had given him a second pair to go with his aces, only to get beat on the last card by both a low flush and a straight.

Bad Bobby chuckled behind him. "Now Daniel, remember what Ol' Jake Santee used to say: 'Don't hurt to get it all in. What hurts is getting it broke off.'"

Daniel took out the rest of his bankroll and called for three thousand dollars in black chips. Five hours later, having discovered a tell on a player named Frog Jorgenson and having caught some good cards, Daniel had twelve thousand dollars in front of him. When the player to his right busted out, Daniel was surprised to see Bad Bobby slide into the vacant seat and call for twenty thousand dollars in chips.

Daniel played cautiously whenever Bad Bobby was in the pot. Bobby played his usual game, steady with erratic eruptions, though he juiced the action by betting the limit from first round to last. An hour before dawn, Daniel had about seventeen thousand dollars and Bad Bobby had doubled his stack. As word spread that Bobby was in town, players dropped by the Antlers to check out the action. When the sun came up, there were four times as many railbirds as there were players.

Bad Bobby stretched lazily as the deck was shuffled. "Gentlemen, I'm only good for a few more hours. Any objection to putting some guts in this game and raising the limit to a thousand?"

Everyone except Daniel immediately agreed.

"Thousand it is, then," a player named Mad Moses announced.

"Just a minute," Bad Bobby said mildly. He turned to Daniel. "How about you, Daniel?"

"Hell," Mad Moses said, "he's winners. If he don't want to jack it up he can cash 'em out—there's a whole herd of high rollers drooling to git in the game."

"No," Bobby said flatly, "that ain't how it's done. He's been in the game over twelve hours, and if he says no, that's all it takes as far as I'm concerned."

"A thousand limit is fine with me," Daniel murmured. Twenty minutes later he wished Mott Stocker had been there to cut out his tongue.

Daniel started with the seven of hearts in the hole and the eight of hearts up. Bad Bobby was high with the king of hearts showing and when the low man brought it in for the minimum hundred, Bobby raised a thousand. Daniel and three other players called. Daniel caught the eight of diamonds for a pair on the board, Mad Moses caught an ace to go with his offsuit jack, the two others didn't visibly improve, and Bad Bobby caught the ten of hearts. When the bet reached him, Daniel raised a grand. Moses and Bobby were the only callers. Daniel caught the seven of clubs to pair his hole card, Moses was dealt the six of hearts, and Bad Bobby the trey of hearts, giving him, at best, a pair of kings or a flush draw. Bad Bobby, now low, surprised Daniel by betting the limit. Daniel raised the same. Mad Moses, after long deliberation, folded.

Bad Bobby reraised a thousand dollars. Daniel hit it again. So did Bad Bobby. "I'm not stopping," Daniel said, pushing his call and another grand raise into the pot. "You've got to catch me and I love the odds on that."

"Well," Bobby said, "count your stack down and we'll get it all in right now, 'cause I intend to keep raising you back." When he'd counted down what remained of his seventeen thousand and shoved it in the pot, Bad Bobby matched it. Counting Mad Moses money and the initial bets, there was over forty thousand dollars in the pot.

"It's up to the cards now," Bobby said. "Let's take a look and see if I can snap your two pair."

The dealer turned up the jack of hearts for Daniel. Bad Bobby caught the queen of hearts. He had the ace of hearts in the hole. Heart flush.

"Take the pot," Daniel said, trying to control the shocked disappointment in his voice. He smiled ruefully at Bad Bobby, who was stacking the chips. "You deserve it, Bobby, catching that queen with so many hearts out, raising all the way—that's luck."

"No, Daniel, that's knowing *when.*"

"You want more chips, Daniel?" the floor man said at his shoulder.

Daniel started to rise from his chair. "I guess not."

"If no one objects," Bad Bobby said, "you can play ten grand off my roll." There were no objections.

Bad Bobby cashed out at noon, thirty-thousand dollars winners. Four hours later, his eyes stinging from smoke and exhaustion, Daniel cashed out twenty-one thousand five hundred, fifteen thousand of which he returned to Bad Bobby, who was still awake when Daniel got back to the hotel.

"You come out, huh?"

"I won sixty-five hundred."

"Good, but don't forget you can lose."

"I would have if you hadn't staked me that extra ten grand. Thanks for the confidence."

"Well shit, I wouldn't have much of an opinion of myself as a teacher if I didn't think you could hold your own in a little pissant game like that. Besides, you caught Froggy's tell about ten minutes after I did. You might be relying a shade heavy on odds, but I suppose that's my fault. Just remember that if you're playing Russian Roulette, one chamber loaded out of six, about seventeen percent of the time you're going to be dead. Technically, you know, you lost our side bet when I broke you, because if I hadn't extended more credit, you'd be washing windows with your tongue. Now you have enough money of your own to do as you please. If you run short, you can play my money any time."

But Daniel, with his sixty-five hundred dollars profit, played his own, and he played it well. At the end of a year he had almost two hundred twenty thousand dollars, eighty thousand from a single pot in a Seven-Stud game in Albuquerque, beating Dumpling Smith's four nines with a low straight flush in diamonds. Between games, as they traveled the circuit (what Bad Bobby called hard-assing the highway), Bad Bobby critiqued Daniel's play. Aside from the lack of polish and occasional lapse in judgement, he saw only one major flaw. It wasn't so much a repeated mistake as it was a general disposition—Daniel liked to gamble. He was seduced by the needle-thrill of action, the excitement and hope and abandon.

Bad Bobby told Daniel that a friend, a famous stock-car driver, had told him what he considered the greatest danger of racing: " 'When you're driving hard out on the edge, and the love of speed comes over you so true and deep and real, you don't *want* to slow down. You know you ought to. But you're locked into something so awesome and consuming you can't back off. It's always the same—the faster you go the less you care about being able to stop. Ever.'

"And that's bad shit, Daniel. Don't step in it."

But to sustain the high, thin edge of concentration gambling required was costly in itself. Along with the constant travel, there were days without sleep, an almost constant isolation from the natural world, adrenalin solos dancing on the blade. Against the discontinuities of the gambling life, Daniel developed portable routines. He read the paper with breakfast to remind himself daily there was a world beyond the cardtable. He took a long bath before every game. He wore, interchangeably, ten identical white shirts. The routines gave him a sense of stability, of a quotidian infrastructure that could survive the winds of chance. Occasionally he wanted a woman, and most often she was a five-hundred-dollar call girl. Daniel liked call girls. They were adventurous, usually independent, often beautiful, took pride in their erotic charms and understanding, and there were no complications.

Daniel agreed with Bobby's claim that the simple life was essential if you hoped to sustain the ferocious concentration cardplaying demanded. Bad Bobby practiced extreme simplicity. Besides the restored '49 Caddy, his worldly possessions were his father's straight razor and an old Ruger .38 that "Jack-'Em-Up" Jackson had given him to discourage cheaters and highwaymen. Bad Bobby slept and bathed in hotels, ate in restaurants, and bought new clothes when he was tired of the ones he was wearing. He also bought books—he was studying history—but when he finished one he either passed it along to Daniel, if he was interested, or left it for the room's next occupant and the vagaries of chance.

After fifteen months of steady playing, Daniel became restless and vaguely depressed. They were halfway into their Lo-Ball swing through northern

California, and the familiar land forms reminded him of the clear balance of ranch life. Gambling also had its balance, but it was forever shifting, erratically brilliant. He was bored with the game. He'd learned what he could, and it left him strangely dissatisfied. He told Bobby he wanted to move on.

Bad Bobby wouldn't let him. "I've spent over eighteen months working with you, and I'm not done because you're not ready."

"I appreciate that," Daniel said. "I've learned a lot. But I'm beginning to burn out."

"Daniel, that's just when you learn things you'd never know otherwise. It's that long, precise discipline that holds it together when it wants to fly apart. That's when you develop some bottom to yourself, but you've got to be tough. You've got to patiently practice what you don't enjoy if you want to make yourself a whole player. Like a wide receiver who's the best there is going long, but who stays after practice every day and works on those three-yard outs that he has trouble with. That's why they invented dues, Daniel—to pay 'em."

Daniel sighed. "I appreciate what you're saying, but I can quit any time I want. Don't make me do it."

"Actually," Bad Bobby grinned, "you can't quit whenever you want, 'cause I got it on your honor that you have to beat me in a gambling game to call your own shots."

"Fine," Daniel shrugged. "Tomorrow. Five-Card Stud."

"You chose your strongest game, even if your timing is off. I just got a call from Stan Wurlitzer down in Gardena. Seems both Guido Caramba and Rupert the Limey are in town, and there's heavy sentiment developing for a hundred-thousand-dollar freeze-out game if Stan can put it together. I'm supposed to let him know by tonight."

"How's it set up?"

"Everybody buys a hundred thousand, and you play till somebody has it all. You lose your buy-in, you're eliminated; no second buys."

"The game?"

"Lo-Ball Draw, exactly like we've been playing the last coupla weeks. I personally think Lo-Ball will eventually be your best game, because a big edge in that game is hitting it on the come and playing power position. 'Course, this will be no limit, and you don't want to be raising too much to draw cards."

"Are you suggesting I could play in a game like that?"

"That's up to you. I'm sure going to, so I don't really want to waste my energy whipping on you tomorrow. But here's a proposition: If you win the freeze-out, you're free to go. If you don't, you'll still have enough money left to take a shot at me later."

"Knowing your propositions, I assume the other players will be good."

"You got that right."

"So, if I'm the winner, I not only get to leave, but I take eight hundred thousand dollars with me."

"It'd be nice to tip Stan ten grand or so for holding the stakes and letting us use his facilities—unless, of course, you *don't mind* being known as a no-class tight-ass." Daniel started to defend his tipping—generous by most standards, though hardly equal to Bobby's extravagance—but Bobby rolled right over him. " 'Course, you're long odds to win. You've got to beat seven other players, and they include Guido, Rupert, and me. My advice is to start early and bring extra grub."

Daniel had known Bad Bobby long enough to sense a proposition. "What are you laying now?"

"Even money you don't make the final four. Your eight to my one that you're exactly the third player eliminated. And twenty to one you don't win it."

"You're hurting my confidence."

"Can't help it. Real is real, and I call 'em like I see 'em. And what I see is that you're a damn good player, but not good enough yet."

They were sitting in Daniel's room at the Eureka Inn. Daniel pointed at the phone on the desk. "Call this Stan guy and reserve two seats. And I'll take a grand on the first two propositions, and five on the twenty to one that I win it all. So then you'd be out two hundred thousand plus change, and I'd be on my own."

Bad Bobby gave a number to the operator. He grinned at Daniel. "You'll love Guido. He's a character-builder all by himself."

The next morning, they left for San Francisco. As Daniel drove, Bad Bobby analyzed the players and discussed the strategy of no-limit Lo-Ball freeze-out. It would be a full game, eight players. There were only two Bobby hadn't gambled with before.

"Clay Hormel is a movie producer, lots of bucks, and Hollywood all the way. You've seen the type in Vegas—silk shirt unbuttoned to his navel, six pounds of gold chain, sunlamp tan. He may know how to cut a movie deal, but he don't cut shit as a card player. His ego's as big as his bank account, and I figure they'll both get flattened some in this game.

"Charley Li is an old Chinese guy, over seventy now I'd guess. Knows Lo-Ball as well as anyone and can be double-tough if he catches a heater. I think he may be a little too conservative for this action, a tad too predictable. But he's solid, and he's a real gentleman.

"There's two guys I don't know, but Stan gave me a line on their play.

First guy's named Paul Schubert, known as 'Rainbow.' Gather he's something of a hippie, one of these new-age types with the ponytail and turquoise. Stan says he's about thirty years old, and he's either pretty high up in some drug dealing or there's bread in the family, 'cause he doesn't play well enough for the roll he packs. He's probably an action freak, a good example of what I warned you about. Can't pass up a big pot and makes terrible calls. Which means he's hard to bluff.

"The other guy is Johnny 'The Rake' Russo. I've never met him, but I've heard a lot about him. East Coast guy. Got his first stake together lagging quarters in the Bronx when he was twelve—that's the line anyway. He's not much older than you—twenty-one, around there—and seemingly deserves his rep for being double tough. He's not afraid to put chips in the pot. Stan says he plays a lot like me when I was his age. That means he'll be too aggressive on marginal hands, bluff in the wrong situations, and not pay enough attention to position.

"Rupert Mildow is a middle-aged English gent down to his tweeds and walking stick. Everybody calls him 'Limey,' which he thinks is vulgar, which is why everybody calls him that. If he has a weakness, it might be he doesn't trust his instincts, especially the killer one. But if you beat him, you've beat somebody. He's good.

"Guido, though, is probably the best. He's tougher than a junkyard dog, and since he came up from the bottom, he loves the top. He's part Mexican and part Italian. He comes on like he's got stones the size of boulders—and he does—but he's also got fire and finesse. He likes to give you this exaggerated Mexican bandito accent to annoy you and twang any latent racism. Likes to make you *want* to beat him. An uncanny ability to find your weakness and show it to you for lots of money. Probably the best psychological player I've ever seen. Pay attention to his play and don't listen to his mouth."

"So, how does he play?" Daniel said.

"*Real* good."

"You're overwhelming me with helpfulness."

"It'd be foolish to say more. Guido plays the players, the chemistry, the mood, the rush, and the moment as well as he plays his cards. I've beat him a few times, but if this ol' Caddy was full of the money I've lost to him playing Lo-Ball, the axles would snap with the load."

"Does he play Stud or Hold-'Em? I mean, you're supposedly the best around at those."

"Well," Bad Bobby said, "I got enough of it back that I still have the car." He gave the horn a long echoing blast as they passed through a grove of redwoods, then smiled contentedly as he watched the road unwind.

* * *

The players met Friday night in the lounge of Stan Wurlitzer's cardroom to discuss rules and format. Except for Guido, everyone was there promptly at nine. He arrived twenty minutes late, accompanied by an entourage of four lovely young Chicanas, each in a white silk dress of alarming décolletage, and a thin choker of opals and pearls. The jewels were a proper complement to their skin, which had the sheen of melting caramel.

Daniel stared, remembered he was going to play Guido, not them, and shifted his attention with difficulty.

Guido was greeting the other players with gusto. He was a large man, well-bellied to the point of corpulence. His face was broad and swarthy, the cheeks slipping into jowls. It would have appeared frankly corrupt if not for Guido's eyes, eyes the color and same hard gleam of obsidian. He was wearing a tuxedo and silk top hat. His cuff links were twenty-dollar gold pieces. Large diamonds sparkled from his wristwatch and rings.

When Stan Wurlitzer introduced him to Daniel, Guido frowned. "Mr. Wurlitzer," he said playfully, "there ess a leetle boy in the lounge who has loss hees momma. You find her queek to lead thees young one to safety."

Daniel, assuming that somehow Guido had heard about his mother's death, said calmly, "Fuck you."

"So *bold!*" Guido shouted, stumbling backward as if overwhelmed.

"*Really* Guido," Rupert said dryly, "save it for the game."

"Ahhhh, but I can't help it," Guido apologized. "I feel so *wonderful* thees evening. I jus feenish loving all my girlfriends and it makes me so happy to be there with them I am late being here weeth you. And you, young Daniel, I was only keeding, for I hear all over you are an *hombre* at the table, that even so young you already have the hairs on your ass and gallons of *cojones*. But"— Guido's booming voice dropped to a sad murmur—"I weel run over you like water runs over the lowlands."

"That's why we're playing," Daniel nodded, "to find out."

"Stanley," Rupert rolled his eyes, "may we proceed?"

The rules were standard: open or out in turn; checks could call on the second round but not raise; you had to bet a 7-6-5-4-3 or any hand lower. The format Stan suggested was likewise agreeable to all: rotating deal; a five-hundred-dollar ante to begin with, increasing as players went bust; a half-hour break every three hours and an hour every six, with twelve hours a day limit on playing time. Stan collected the stakes, each player except Guido counting a hundred grand off their rolls or presenting, in Rupert's case, a cashier's check.

Guido said disdainfully, "I do not soil my hands weeth cash or waste my time at the banks." He snapped his fingers: each of his beautiful young friends hiked her dress and removed a wad of bills from her garter. Guido, gnashing his teeth at the sight of their supple thighs, announced, "I tell you people, Guido Caramba weel not gamble money that has not known the warmth of a woman's skeen. Now, eef our meeting ess done, I must take my friends here and return to my training. I weel see you *mañana.*"

"You weeel indeed," Daniel murmured.

The players gathered in Stan's cardroom just before noon. They cut cards for seats, going around the table in order of low cards. Daniel cut the Joker, a propitious sign, he felt. He couldn't have been happier with the final positions if he'd deployed them himself. From Daniel's left, taking their seats around the clean felt table behind one hundred thousand dollars stacked in black and gold chips, were Charley Li, Rupert, Johnny Russo, Clay Hormel, Paul Schubert, Guido, and Bad Bobby—which meant that Guido and Bobby, the two strongest players, would usually be acting before him.

There were already close to a hundred spectators seated well away from the table. Clay Hormel, perhaps to rattle Guido, had arrived with his own bevy of young starlets. Guido's caramel-skinned beauties, still in bridal-white silk, sat behind him. Guido had added a black cape to his tuxedo.

Daniel whispered to Bad Bobby on his right, "Guido looks like a fat Dracula."

Bad Bobby barely nodded, drawling, "Yeah, and he plays like a werewolf."

They cut for the deal, Guido winning the honor with the ace of diamonds. Each player anted a black five-hundred-dollar chip, Guido shuffled, and "Rainbow" Schubert cut the deck. Guido shut his eyes and lifted his face heavenward, solemnly intoning, "God, I ask You for mercy on their doomed asses," and dealt the first hand.

Daniel held a 9-8-6-5-3. When Bad Bobby passed, Daniel opened for four thousand. Charley Li, Rupert, and Johnny Russo passed.

"Hell, I always play the first pot," Clay Hormel said, calling. "If you don't win the first one you can't win them all."

"I like your philosophy, man," Rainbow Schubert said, also calling.

Guido looked at his cards belligerently. "What ees thees? A full house? I play the wrong game. But I call anyway because maybe the poker gods weel get eet straightened out." He set four thousand-dollar gold chips into the pot. "Teekets?" he inquired sweetly, burning the top card face down in the pot.

Daniel rapped the table softly, indicating he was pat.

"Nooo!" Guido wailed. "Please reconsider."

Daniel said sharply, "No cards."

Guido shrugged with hopeless fatality. "Are you also pat, Meester Hormel?"

"Not now. Send three." He discarded and Guido dealt him three cards. Rainbow Schubert drew one.

Guido set the deck down, capped it with a chip, and looked at his cards for nearly thirty seconds. Finally he said, "I can't play thees mess. I have two aces, two deuces, and that funny leetle man riding the bumblebee with hees finger up hees ass." He smiled at Daniel, appealing, "Help me play my hand." Guido turned it over: two aces, two deuces, and the joker.

Obviously he would draw two cards to ace, deuce, joker. Daniel suggested mildly, "Throw away your two pair and draw to the joker."

Guido looked at Daniel with implacable fury. "I tell you sometheeng right now, my young one. You can fuck weeth Guido's money because Guido, being a happy man, does not care about money. You can play weeth Guido's wimmens because Guido, being a generous man, would never deny you their immense pleasures. *But!*" he thundered, dramatically isolating the contradiction, "you *cannot* fuck weeth Guido's *mind!*" His voice softened to a reflective murmur. "You cannot fuck weeth Guido's mind because Guido has no mind. He feed it to hees guts thirty years ago starving in Tijuana."

"I was just trying to be helpful," Daniel said, acting vaguely hurt that his intentions could possibly be misunderstood.

"I will take *two* cards," Guido decided, discarding and drawing.

Daniel was slightly worried, not by Guido's mouth, but his hand. Though a pat nine was the favorite against any two-card draw, ace deuce joker was the best two-card draw in the game. Daniel bet another four thousand, not a strong bet, but better than checking, since they would know he didn't have a seven or lower.

Clay Hormel and Rainbow folded. Guido was squeezing out a peek at his draw. "Ah," he beamed, "a *stranger*. Look, I don't lie." He laid down ace-deuce-joker-four, keeping the last card hidden.

Six cards will beat me, Daniel calculated, *seven won't. Damn near down to even money.* He watched Guido's eyes as he tipped the fifth card for a look. They glittered with excitement.

"Yaaaaasss," Guido shrilled, *"hello* leetle seex!" He glared at Daniel. "I call your puny bet and raise whole handfuls." Guido pushed in the ninety-six thousand dollars he had remaining.

Daniel looked at his hand again. It hadn't changed. The odds slightly favored him, but it was far too early to risk it all on what he held. "Take the pot," he told Guido, folding his cards face down.

Guido glowed. "I don't bullsheet you. I make a hand." He turned over his last card, the ace of hearts. He'd paired aces. "See? Two ace, three counting the joker." Suddenly he looked worried. *"Three ace?* No, I forget again!" He slapped himself lightly on the side of the head. "Guido, you dumb one, wake up! Eet ees *Lo-Ball!* But," he quickly forgave himself, "take the cheeps anyhow."

Next to Daniel, Bobby asked softly, "Rough eight or nine?"

"Yup."

"You played it right. No need to risk it all early on a slim edge."

"That's why I laid it down," Daniel said curtly.

"Don't let him get in you, now," Bobby warned, gathering the cards to deal.

Clay Hormel was the first to go broke, calling a raise from Rupert before the draw and then, when Rupert rapped pat, drawing two cards. When Rupert checked to him, he'd foolishly tried to bluff a pair of fives with his remaining twenty thousand. Rupert called immediately with his 8-4-3-2-1, and Clay sheepishly joined his flock of starlets on the sidelines.

The next few hours moved slowly. Daniel played conservatively, paying careful attention to position. He was down to sixty thousand when he realized the thousand-dollar antes were beginning to dent his stack. He began to open pots for ten thousand, trying to win the antes. At the end of five hours he was nearly back to even, as were most of the remaining players except Guido and Rupert, who each had about a hundred seventy-five thousand, and Charley Li, down to fifty thousand, his cautious play eating up his antes. Charley realized it too late, began playing catch-up hands, and steadily went broke. Daniel took Charley's last eight thousand, making an eight against Charley's pat nine.

Rainbow Schubert went broke ten minutes later. He'd reraised Bobby with a pat 10-9-8-2-1 before the draw. Bobby had only called, then rapped pat. That put the pressure on Rainbow, who after toying with his turquoise bracelet and tugging on his ponytail, finally threw away the 10-9-8 and drew three, catching a 9-4-3. When Bad Bobby uncharacteristically checked, showing weakness by not betting into a three-card draw, Rainbow bet the twenty-five thousand he had left. Bad Bobby called with his 8-5, springing the trap.

As the next hand was dealt, Bobby told Daniel, "I owe you a grand."

Daniel gave him a quizzical look.

Bobby explained, "You weren't the third player eliminated."

"That's right," Daniel said. He'd forgotten the side bets.

The action picked up as each of the five remaining players looked for an edge. Though there were a few good pots, the hands broke close to even. As they approached midnight and the end of the first day, Daniel, Bobby, Guido, and Johnny Russo all had about a hundred eighty thousand with Rupert down to eighty grand.

Just before midnight, Daniel took fifty thousand of Rupert's. Daniel was dealing. Rupert opened for ten thousand and everybody passed to Daniel. Daniel raised forty thousand. Rupert called and drew one card. Daniel played pat. When Rupert checked, Daniel bet thirty thousand, all that Rupert had left. Rupert considered for a moment then shook his head. "Take the pot, sir," he said with his usual crisp formality. "I was drawing to a six-four with the joker, and I caught a notch outside." He turned over his hand—10-6-4-2-joker—then threw it in the discards.

Daniel said, "When you checked, I knew you didn't have a seven or better, and I had all the eights." He turned over his hand, four eights and an ace.

Rupert nodded glumly. "Good hand."

Guido squealed, "Someone call the weather station and please see for me if thees ess true. I don' believe my eyes but I think I jus' see some snowing."

The last hand before midnight, Rupert tapped out.

Daniel and Bobby ate a late-night dinner in the lounge. Bobby reviewed the pro football games coming up the next day, idly asking Daniel what he thought of the spreads. Daniel wanted to talk about the card game. "Forget football. How am I doing?"

"Who's got the most chips on the table?"

"I do," Daniel said. "I've got about two hundred fifty thousand, Guido two hundred forty, you're around two ten, and Russo's about even."

"Well, whoever's got the most chips is doing good."

Daniel ignored Bobby's sarcastic grasp of the obvious. "I think I'm going to win it all. That snow hand broke me loose."

"It was a good play," Bobby said, "but it sure would have been interesting to see what you woulda done if Rupert had rapped pat in front of you. Beside crap your pants, I mean. But like I told you a thousand times, a good play is the one that wins the pot. That's the measure of it."

Daniel was about to reply when Clay Hormel approached their table. "Bobby, Daniel—good to see you both still in there." He squeezed Daniel's shoulder. "Kid, that was a helluva snow you put on ol' Limey. He's *still* talking to himself. Tell you what, though—I sure as hell would have called you."

Practicing his social graces, Daniel said, "I wouldn't have tried it on you. You're too tough."

"If I could have caught a few cards, I'd still be in it."

Bobby agreed, "Yeah, you gotta catch the tickets."

Clay said, "Like the ol' saying goes: 'When you're hot, you're hot; and when you're not, you're colder than a motherfucker.' And speaking of hot,"

Clay winked, "you guys are invited down to my place in Malibu for some serious party-time when the game's over. Lots of gorgeous women and other fun things. Can't tell, maybe even play a few hands of cards."

"We'll be there with bells on," Bad Bobby grinned.

Daniel said more loudly than necessary, "It depends on how I feel."

"No matter how you feel," Clay patted him on the back, "my parties make you feel better. See you there, and good luck to you both."

When Clay was out of hearing, Daniel leaned forward and said so evenly that the control in his voice was obvious, "Don't fuck with my head when we're not playing."

"You ain't beat me yet," Bad Bobby replied without a trace of defensiveness. "Till you do, I call the shots. Clay's Hollywood games are world renowned for a shitpot of lawyers and producers with big money, bigger egos, and just a tiny little talent for poker. And personally speaking, if I don't win this freeze-out game, my bankroll will need some pumping up. So that's the shot I'm calling for us. And till you beat me, you come along."

"Till then," Daniel said.

"And besides all that, Daniel, I'm your *teacher*. I'm *supposed* to fuck with your head."

Guido came on strong when play resumed the next afternoon. He'd changed from his tuxedo into a chambray work shirt and jeans, explaining, though nobody asked, "Now eet ess time to go to work."

He went to work on Johnny Russo's chips the fifth hand, taking half of them when he beat Johnny's one-card 8-5 with his pat 8-4. He took a raised pot from Bad Bobby, making an 8-6 to Bobby's pat 9-8. Daniel recognized Guido was hot and stayed away from him, the four-thousand-dollar antes slowly eroding his stack. But he couldn't avoid Guido forever.

Bad Bobby dealt it. Daniel opened for twenty thousand with a one-card draw to ace-deuce-trey-four. Johnny Russo passed. Guido raised fifty thousand. Bad Bobby passed. Daniel had an impulse to raise all he had left, around a hundred fifty thousand, and either force Guido to fold or, if he called, let it all ride on the single card. He decided just to call, sliding two stacks of gold chips into the pot. He drew one card. Guido, after some thought, rapped pat. Daniel noticed the hesitation; Guido usually declared himself immediately. Daniel looked at his new card: he'd caught an eight, making an 8-4-3-2-1. But he didn't know what to do. If he bet a lot and Guido raised, he'd have too much in the pot not to call. If he checked and Guido bet a bunch, he'd have to call. He decided to bet a little, hoping Guido might think he was trying to sucker him into raising. "I bet ten thousand," Daniel announced.

Guido looked at him curiously. "You don't bet very much. You don' like your hand?"

"You can raise if that's not enough," Daniel told him.

Guido thought a second. "No, I jus' call."

"I have an eight-four," Daniel said, spreading his cards face up on the table.

Guido shook his head dolefully as he turned turned over his, a 7-5-4-3-2. "Put eet een a Glad Bag, keed, and set eet out on da curb."

"A seven-five?" Daniel said with disbelief. "And you don't *raise*? Guido, what's the matter? You don't *like* money? Or did you think it was a suction bet?"

"No, no, no," Guido passionately denied it. "Eet ess jus' that you play so bad I feel peety on you. But peety ess not a good thing for you or me, so soon it must be like God and the dwarf."

"God and the dwarf?" Daniel repeated, immediately knowing better.

Guido slapped himself on the forehead, bellowing, "What! You have not been told of God and the dwarf?"

"No," Daniel said, "but I have a feeling I will be."

"Yes, I weel gladly tell you how eet ess weeth God and the dwarf. Thees dwarf ess sitting one day in the cantina with many, many other people when God walks een the door, looks 'roun', and says, 'I'm going to shit on all the peoples een thees cantina—except for you, leetle dwarf.' The dwarf he ees very happy and he jumps down from hees chair and cries, 'O thank you merciful Lord for sparing me, for already I have suffered very much being a dwarf.' And God tells heem, 'Hey, I don' spare nobody. I'm gonna use you to wipe my ass.'"

Guido laughed wildly while Daniel, without a word, tossed his hand in the discard. Guido's laugh bothered him more than the story. Guido was crazy; he might do anything. Daniel decided to play cautiously until he regained his sense of balance.

Perhaps too cautiously. With Bad Bobby again dealing, Daniel opened for ten thousand dollars with a pat 8-7-6-5-3. Johnny Russo, who'd dropped to about seventy thousand, called, as did Guido and Bobby. When Daniel rapped pat, they each drew a card. Daniel wasn't in love with his chances: A rough eight was good odds against one player drawing a card, but not against three. Daniel checked, prepared to call any bet. Johnny Russo pushed all his chips in, close to sixty thousand. Guido cursed the king he'd caught and pitched his hand in the discards with disgust. Bad Bobby announced, "I raise," adding another sixty thousand to the call.

"I got nothing left," Johnny said, tipping up his empty rack.

Bobby reminded him, "There's still another player in the pot."

"No there's not," Daniel said. "I might have called sixty thousand, but not a hundred and twenty." He threw away his hand.

"You got me," Johnny told Bad Bobby. "I paired fours."

"I caught a queen," Bad Bobby said, spreading his hand.

Johnny said, "Good call. I didn't think anyone would expect a bluff." He pushed himself back from the table and stood up.

"Don't feel bad," Daniel told him, "I threw away the winner." He counted his chips. He had a hundred sixty thousand dollars, Bad Bobby three hundred thousand, and Guido around three-forty. He would have to play careful to catch up, look for a good clean shot and gamble on it.

Down to a hundred twenty thousand after Bobby snowed him with three nines, Daniel took his shot. He was dealing. Guido opened for a modest ten grand, Bad Bobby passed, and Daniel, with 9-5-joker-2-1, raised fifty thousand.

"Well dwarf," Guido smiled, "I wipe my ass early. Please put in *all* your cheeps eef you weesh to play." He called Daniel's raise and added another sixty thousand.

Daniel looked at his hand again. It wasn't likely he'd get a better one to play. "I call," he said, and put his remaining chips in the pot. "Cards?" he asked Guido, picking up the deck.

"Cards?" Guido repeated, as if he'd never heard the word. "Guido Caramba does not put a hundred and twenty thousand dollars een the pot and then draw a card. Only a fool would do such a thing." He rapped the table violently. *"No cards!"*

"Shit," Daniel muttered. He'd been hoping Guido would draw; if so, he'd play pat. Guido's big production over drawing cards made Daniel think Guido wanted him pat, which meant he likely had a rough eight or seven. Bad Bobby had taught him it wasn't a sound practice to break a pat hand if you couldn't win any more money if you improved it, and since he was all in, there was no more to win. But any eight would beat him. It was a gut judgment. He threw the nine face up on the the table and said to Guido, "I'm going to get off this smooth nine." He dealt himself one card.

Guido feigned astonishment. "You are *craaazzy*. Now you must ween the pot twice." He spread his hand on the table: 10-9-8-7-4.

Daniel slowly turned over the card he'd drawn. It was the jack of hearts. "You win," he told Guido, "take the money." He rose numbly from his seat.

"You are good player, dwarf," Guido smiled hugely as he stacked the chips. "You will grow."

Still numb, Daniel watched the game continue from one of the front-row seats reserved for the eliminated players. An hour later, Bad Bobby, who'd started making hands, had pulled even with Guido, each close to four hundred thousand dollars. Next to him, Johnny Russo said, "Looks like it might go awhile now."

"I was just thinking the same thing," Daniel agreed.

It ended on the next hand. Guido opened for forty thousand. Bad Bobby, dealing, raised a hundred sixty thousand.

"That ees mucho dinero," Guido murmured. "Before I call, there ees one card left I must look at een my hand." Squinting, Guido peeked. "Oh my God you weel not believe, but eet ees the yoker. I don' even believe thees myself. I must call your raise and then raise all my cheeps I have left. Let us do eet now and go home."

"Sounds good to me," Bad Bobby said cheerfully, stacking off the rest of his chips. He picked up the deck and burned the top card. "You drawing any cards, Guido?"

"*Of course* I draw cards," Guido said with umbrage, as if he would never think of putting four hundred thousand dollars in a pot with a pat hand. "Thees nine ess not good." He flicked it into the pot. "Geeve me uno."

Bobby slid him a card and picked up his own hand. Since they were all in and he was last to act, he turned it over to look at it: 9-6-5-3-2. "I'll draw with you," he said, and threw away the nine.

Daniel, suddenly wired to the action, couldn't believe they'd both broken pat hands.

Bobby dealt his card face down, set down the deck, then flipped his new card over—the ace of hearts. "I caught inside on the bottom," he told Guido. "I have a six-five."

Guido spread his own hand on the table. "I too have a seex, but I like my seex very very much because eet ees seex-four-trey-yoker-ace."

"Take it down, then, Guido—you win it all. Congratulations."

Guido grinned benevolently as the crowd burst into applause. "Thank you, Bad Bobby. You are an *hombre* of spirit and grace, and I admire very much your gamble. You got down weeth me on that last hand. We catch alike, but I draw a leetle smoother. We will play again, amigo."

Getting to Malibu the next day was easy. They flew in Clay Hormel's Lear jet to the airport, where a limo was waiting to whisk them to Xanadu, the producer's "little beach house," which had a Jacuzzi and round, revolving bed in each of the thirty guest suites, and a kitchen staffed and provisioned to serve the crew of an aircraft carrier. Johnny Russo and Rainbow Schubert accompanied them on the flight. Guido had regretfully declined, citing a prior engagement with his bevy of lovelies for a religious holiday, the observance of which seemed to involve rolling naked on large-denomination bills. Daniel, in a funk, hadn't been interested in the lurid details.

Noticing Daniel's mood on the flight, Bad Bobby told him, "Just 'cause they beat on you don't mean you have to get bent. Yesterday is history. Today's brand new."

Daniel muttered, "I don't know why I broke that pat nine against Guido."

Bad Bobby said softly, "I ain't gonna sit here and listen to you snivel." He moved to the rear of the plane and sat down with Johnny Russo.

Getting to the party was easy. Getting away proved difficult. First there was his "personal hostess," Linda O'Rahl, whom Clay had introduced as "maybe the next Meryl Streep." Linda showed him to his room and informed him that there was a full bar right behind the movie screen if you lifted it (she demonstrated), that weed, coke, and 'ludes were available upon request, and that "Sexually, I'm into whatever you're into."

Daniel felt a powerful, implacable despair gathering in the center of his brain. It was difficult to keep his tone civil. "Thanks, Linda, but what I'm really into at the moment is a long walk along the beach, all alone except for a bottle of whiskey. I need to sulk and sort and think and scheme. You go play with someone who can do you some good. If Clay says anything, tell him I'm gay."

Linda said helpfully, "I have a gay girlfriend. We could put you in a pussy sandwich?"

"In another mood, I'm sure it would be delightful. Right now I need walking, water, and whiskey."

"You want water with your whiskey?"

"No. I meant the ocean."

"Sounds romantic."

"It's not," he assured her.

Even though Daniel left by his private exit and went around the back, he still couldn't get away. He had to cross a long, terraced patio thronged with people. Just below them, on the beach itself, a nude coed volleyball game was in progress. That stopped him. In the intense, late-October light, every naked body seemed young, tanned, perfect, and doomed to perish.

"Sweet Jesus," Bad Bobby suddenly groaned beside him, "stark-naked volleyball. Seems California just gets stranger and weirder every time I pass through."

"I'm going for a walk," Daniel said. "If it's all right with you, of course."

Bad Bobby looked out toward the horizon. "I made me a deal with the ocean when I was a scrawny little twelve-year-old cracker-ass kid—no folks, no kin, nowhere. I'd scraped my way down to the Gulf because I'd heard about the ocean, but I'd never seen it; and I wanted to see it real bad. And I stood there gawking at it, water as far as I could see, and I said real fast, 'Ocean, let's work out a deal. If you don't fuck with me, I won't fuck with you.'"

"Sounds fair," Daniel said. He took a step to leave.

"Goddamn, Daniel!" Bobby boomed, stopping him. "Don't matter how big a snit you're in, it's piss-poor manners to be holding a bottle of whiskey in your hand and not offer a thirsty man a drink."

Momentarily disconcerted, Daniel remembered he had a bottle of Jack Daniel's in his hand. "Sorry," he mumbled, offering the bottle.

Bad Bobby unscrewed the cap and lifted the bottle: "May you get 'em when you need 'em, and sometimes when you don't." He took a long swig.

Daniel nodded to acknowledge the toast. He realized he was tired of looking at Bad Bobby, tired of his voice, his strong and constant presence.

Bad Bobby handed the bottle back. "There's a hell of a card game shaping up inside. If you need to find me, start looking there." He turned and walked away.

Daniel fumed as he walked down the beach. "He's *always* the one who walks away. *Always* gets the last word. *Always* has the hammer and the high ground."

Heading up the beach, he was forced to admit that Bad Bobby was simply sharper—more experienced, more aware, more determined—and Daniel arrived at the understanding that if he played cards heads-up with him, Bad Bobby would hand him his ass. The understanding didn't cheer him up.

When he was out of sight and sound of the party, Daniel sat against a wave-smoothed drift log and drank slowly and steadily. He watched the ocean, each wave driving him deeper into depression. Even the fiery sunset seemed bleak. He felt like he was trapped inside himself, a ragged rat in a maze.

He stood up shakily and took off his clothes, the night air balmy against his skin. He waded out in the creaming surf and dove into an oncoming wave. As he felt himself tumbled in its force, his depression vanished. He swam out till nearly exhausted and then floated on his back, watching the stars, giving himself to their vast indifference. It was exactly what he'd been missing—stars, rock, water, wind. For over a year he'd been living sealed in smoky rooms, perfumed suites, and moving cars; rootless, wired to the action, tightened down to the turn of a card. Too small, too narrow. It wasn't what he wanted. He wanted to expand, to roar. He wanted to be a furnace of light.

Every clear night at Nameless Lake Wild Bill had spent at least half an hour staring at the night sky. When Daniel had asked him if it was some sort of meditation he was doing, Wild Bill had claimed that the stars were actually alchemists' forges and he just found it reassuring to see so many souls at work.

Floating, Daniel tried to see the stars through Wild Bill's eyes, but couldn't. He tried to imagine he was the first primitive man who'd ever looked up and beheld them. With an oblique leap, he thought of a warm autumn afternoon when Johnny Seven Moons had showed him how to play Indian stick gambling. Stick gambling was clean and simple. Which hand held the stick. Left or right; right or wrong. Pure intuition, the grace of guessing. Daniel smiled at the starry heavens. He had his game. It eliminated Bad Bobby's major edge in cards, his years of experience. Daniel doubted if Bad Bobby, despite that experience, had even *heard* of stick gambling.

Daniel swam back in slowly, riding the waves, then sat on his log drying off. He felt fresh, happy, confident—an actual sea change. He could see the lights from the party far down the beach. He decided not to go back. Scooping a hollow against the log and rolling his clothes into a pillow, he curled up and in moments fell asleep.

He dreamed for the first time since the explosion.

A card was dealt to him face down across the green felt table. He flipped it over. The jack of hearts, the knave, the hook, the sweet bastard himself. He focused on the image. It was Guido's face. He turned the card upside down. Now it was Bobby's face. He ripped the card in half.

Another was dealt immediately, skimming face down across the felt. Slowly, he turned it over. The jack of hearts. He ripped it in half.

Another was dealt. Jack of hearts. He tore it in two.

And another, and another, and another, the invisible dealer sending them as fast as Daniel ripped them up.

The next card he turned over was blank. Stunned, he stared at the glossy white surface. A bird cried. He touched the card. It turned into a window. He strained to see through it but he was looking into an empty sky.

He touched the glass, and when he lifted his finger he saw a black stone hurtling toward him. But as he watched, entranced, he saw it wasn't a stone at all, it was a bird, a raven, and it had a small, brilliant object clasped in its beak, a spherical bauble of some kind, a glass bead, but no, it was too brilliant, too clear. A diamond, a slender spiral flame burning in its center, and then the bird hit the window and it froze into a mirror and he heard his mother scream, "Run, Daniel, run," but there was nothing he could do, he was falling toward the mirror. He curled into a ball to protect himself, then changed his mind, opened himself, arms spread wide; the instant before he hit the mirror he saw it was empty.

The mirror shattered into a million diamond splinters and Daniel floated on his back in the moonlit water, watching the darkness and the stars.

He woke in the late morning. Except for a raging thirst, he felt wonderful. He was dreaming again. His luck had changed. He picked up the whiskey bottle to celebrate. Under it, side by side in the depression, were two stones, virtually identical, each a flat, smooth, elongated oval, one black, one white. He hefted them, one in each palm, then closed his hands into fists. He stood with his eyes closed, the stones warm against his palms. Bad Bobby was in trouble.

Transcription:
Denis Joyner, AMO Mobile Radio

Hang on, honey, we're going up high! Yasss, sweetness, wrap your ears around me and I'll get you there. Yup, and you didn't even have to guess it, you got the DJ, the Devil Jubilee, coming at you hot and heavy on mow-beel, multiple-frequency, pirate, jack-your-ass-up, ray-dee-oooo—and oh my goodness, talk about diversity, you got me if you want me on KPER, KINK, KUZZ, KLUE, and KYJL (the only gay station in Malibu). And now that you got me, just try turning me loose.

You figure on that while I cue up tonight's musical treat. Hold still now, cuz for the next three hours you're gonna hear something so old, so moldy gold, you're gonna remember back through seven lifetimes at least. Three solid hours—count 'em, Jack—of uninterrupted Voodoo Trance Jam that I recorded live, scared to death, on my recent trip to Haiti. And while you're digging the movies on your skull walls, the DJ here is gonna be getting comfortable with a little sweet thing who just dropped by the van to discuss the price of opium in Shanghai. So I'll catch you 'round 'bout midnight with DJ's bedtime story and quasiphilosophy lesson, yet another installment in this metaphysical potboiler he's beginning to suspect is his life. So spoon June's moon and stay attuned. Be here now or there later. This has been the DJ babblin' in your ear. Till then, all over and far out.

After he'd showered off the sand and changed clothes, Daniel found Bad Bobby where he'd said he'd be, playing Hold-'Em in Clay's game room. Bobby had towers of neatly stacked chips in front of him, so he was either doing well or had bought a bunch. Before Daniel could say a word, Bad Bobby stood up, said to the table of players, "Deal me out a few hands," and motioned Daniel outside on the patio.

"Daniel, we've blundered into Poker Heaven. There's lawyers, producers, actors, directors, drug dealers—and they are all *loaded* with cash money and hot to prove they have the *huevos* to play no-limit Hold-'Em." Bad Bobby glanced around and leaned closer, lowering his voice. "And about half of them, it's maybe the *third* time they've played Hold-'Em in their entire life, and they didn't learn shit from the first two. They think a pair of treys in the pocket is a mortal lock and that a kicker is some Hungarian who boots field goals for the Rams. The only reason *not* to be in that game is if you absolutely *hate* money. How much you have left in your roll?"

"I'm down to about twenty grand."

"Get it in there."

"I'm saving it to play you."

Bad Bobby blinked slowly, about the only sign of agitation he ever displayed. "Jesus, Daniel, not now."

Daniel reminded him, trying to keep any hint of mockery from his tone, " 'Any man, from any land; any game he can name; any amount he can count; any place, face to face; any time he can find.' "

"You got it close to right," Bad Bobby acknowledged, his drawl considerably tightened. "Now you go find the time and come back and tell me when it is, and I'll see if I'm available. In the *mean* time, I'm gonna keep on repairing the dent Guido put in my bankroll. And since I can flat fucking *guarantee* I won't be available till this game breaks up, you might as well sit down and get rich. You lose your twenty grand, your credit's good with me."

"Give me fifty thousand." Daniel was half bluffing. His credit line had always stopped at twenty-five, which Bad Bobby claimed was a safeguard against Daniel going so tilt he couldn't recover.

But without a word Bad Bobby dug out his roll and started counting. When he ran out of bills he shook his head. He handed the wad to Daniel. "Only forty-seven. Little short myself."

"Thanks," Daniel said, moved that Bobby had given him his last penny. "I'd use mine first, but if I lost it, I'd have to borrow from you to play you heads-up, and I'd feel bad about making you gamble against your own money."

Bad Bobby cocked his head. "That don't make a drop of sense to me. It's all money, and when it isn't, it's all chips. Like I told you, it's just a way of keeping track."

Daniel looked at him and said, "How do you always manage to get in the last word?"

"Same way I usually manage to get in the last raise. Why? You want to say something?"

"No, not really."

"All right, then—let's go shear sheep."

Good Shepherd Bobby destroyed the personal finances of a famous young actor, nearly drove a prominent Hollywood law firm into Chapter Eleven proceedings, and cost Clay Hormel a point off his next teenage horror flick. Definitely one of Bad Bobby's better days at the office.

Daniel won eight hundred fifty dollars, or, according to a chuckling Bobby, a little less than he'd tipped his personal hostess. Daniel had been ahead almost ninety thousand. With a pair of tens in the hole, the flop had brought another ten and a pair of sevens. He slow-played it, not raising till the end, but when Bad Bobby had reraised a whopping hundred thousand, Daniel had put him on four sevens and threw his hand away. He'd been right—Bad Bobby showed the hand down when Clay Hormel, with ten-jack, called what he thought was a bluff, thus losing one percent of his profit in *Torn Teenage Flesh VIII*. When Bad Bobby saw that Daniel had laid down tens full, he'd nodded with respect. "Besides being smart, that took some real balls. The more I see of you, Daniel, the more I see a player."

Daniel said, "Wait till we play the game I'm going to name. And I promise you it won't be cards, because you're the best."

"I'm looking forward to it, Daniel. I really am."

So when the game broke up Daniel was right behind Bad Bobby as they cashed out. Daniel handed him the fifty grand he'd borrowed and said, "You ready?"

Bad Bobby shrugged. "Sure. But you don't want me now—sweet Jesus, son, can't you see I'm on a *supreme* heater? There should be flames shooting out my ass, I'm that hot."

"Every heater burns out," Daniel said, repeating one of Bobby's axioms.

"All right. What's the game?"

Daniel thought fast. "Nomlaki Stone Gambling."

"And I suppose you wrote the official rule book." Bad Bobby was clearly dubious.

"As a matter of fact, it's the oldest gambling game on the North American continent."

"I thought Indian Stick Gambling was."

"Well, yes," Daniel gulped, "that's right, too. See, stone gambling is just like stick gambling, except you use stones instead of sticks."

"Makes sense," Bobby noted.

Daniel continued, "You use a white stone and a black stone. You mix them hand to hand behind your back and then hold your fists out to the other person, who can choose the hand that has either the black or white stone."

"Little more complex than stick gambling, but the same idea. I gotta think you chose it because you think it'll neutralize my vast card-playing experience. Which was smart of you." He draped his arm fraternally around

Daniel's shoulders. "But you're gonna be in a world of hurt, Daniel. I beat Tony Big Elk *so bad* stick gambling that he retired, and he was supposed to be the best."

Daniel hadn't heard that story before, so wasn't sure if it was fact or intimidation. "Maybe we shouldn't waste our time playing. I'll just *give* you the ten grand and listen to you call the shots for another year."

"Probably be efficient," Bobby chuckled, "but it wouldn't be as much fun. I haven't played sticks in about fifteen years now and I'm kinda looking forward to it. You want to do it here, or in one of our rooms?"

Daniel feigned dismay. "*Inside?* Bobby, this is *Indian* gambling. We do it *outside. Naked.* Right on the beach. First one to a hundred wins."

Bad Bobby plainly didn't like this. He blinked slowly, took his arm from Daniel's shoulder, and crossed his arms on his chest. "I assume you have the stones?"

"In my pocket."

Bad Bobby glanced at his watch, then at his personal hostess hovering nearby. "It's nine-thirty. I'll meet you here at midnight. I've got to stash my roll, wash off the smoke, get something to eat."

"Midnight's perfect," Daniel told him. "I was going to suggest it myself."

Naked, Daniel and Bad Bobby faced each other at the surf's edge, the waxing half-moon spilling phosphorescence on the wet sand.

"Okay," Daniel said, "let's get our wager straight. If I win, I'm free to go, to do as I please; if I lose, I stay, and it costs me ten grand for the fun of getting beat."

"That nails it."

"I have a little proposition," Daniel said, "a side bet."

Bobby said, "I won't know what it is if you don't tell me."

"First, I want you to know why I'm offering it. You see, all I can win is leaving you, and as a matter of fact you're good company, a fine teacher, and the best cardplayer I've seen in my brief career—including Guido. So I want to bet you another ten grand on the side, straight up, no odds. That way I at least stand to win something besides leaving, and if I lose I want you to take my whole roll."

"You want to give it away, I'll take it." A wave crashed a hundred yards out. Bobby glanced at it.

"Good thing you've got a deal with the ocean," Daniel said.

"You gonna talk this game or play it?"

"Play it." Daniel put his hands behind his back and began rapidly shifting the stones back and forth. "You're the champion," he told Bobby, "so you get

162

to go first." He kept trading the stones till he didn't know himself which hand held what. He thrust his fists out to Bad Bobby.

Instead of choosing, Bobby lifted his grizzled face heavenward and began a high, rhythmic chant: *"Hiya-Ya-Yee-Ah-Yah—"*

"Hey," Daniel said sharply, "what the fuck are you doing."

Bobby stopped chanting and looked at Daniel with plain surprise. "Why, I'm singing my gambling song. That's the most important part of the stick game, your song. You need it to open your circuits and mess up the other guy's. See, you probably think you don't know which hand holds which stone, but you do." He touched Daniel's left hand. "Black."

Daniel opened his hand. It held the black stone.

"One for the old guy," Bobby said, beaming as he accepted the stones from Daniel.

It was a slaughter. Daniel beat him one hundred to forty-seven, and that after trailing twenty-eight to twelve. When it had reached eighty to forty-four Bad Bobby had groaned, which was about as close as he ever came to sniveling. "You're hotter than a cheap pistol and I've turned colder than penguin shit."

It didn't help Bobby's concentration that—as Daniel had foreseen—the literal tide turned at five minutes past midnight, or that at about the time the surf began surging around their ankles, Daniel got an erection he was unaware of until Bad Bobby said, "Why don't you put that thing away?"

"Boy," Daniel said, "Nature sure makes you jumpy. Why don't you see if you can make it a deal?"

But what really hastened the rout was Daniel's discovery that if he emptied his mind, concentrated *through* instead of *on*, he could feel the black stone in one of Bobby's hands. Always the black, though often he'd point to the other hand and guess white so Bobby wouldn't suspect he'd somehow keyed in.

Daniel didn't know how he knew, but it didn't surprise him that he did. Wild Bill had hammered into his head that life was full of critical information that refused to pass through the rational circuits of knowledge. Or as Bad Bobby put it later, as he peeled off a hundred hundred-dollar bills and handed them to Daniel, "Simple arithmetic will tell you how much you lost, but only your ass knows how bad it's been kicked."

Transcription: Telephone Conversation Between
Volta and Bad Bobby

BOBBY: It's Robert. Called to tell you Daniel's ready to move on. Beat me the first try in some version of stick gambling. Whipped me bad.

VOLTA: That didn't take long. You must be getting old, losing your edge.

BOBBY: You were right—he's good. He'll stand in and take his best shot. No seasoning, of course, and he's got a weakness for the long odds and big moves, but there's somebody home, know what I mean, even if he's not sure who it is.

VOLTA: Any suggestions where to send him next?

BOBBY: I don't know. I'm not good at figuring what's next. Have enough trouble figuring out what's now. And Daniel's hard to read. He's got gamble in his blood but no heart for the road—he was burning out on the life, not the game, but you really can't separate them. Thing I can't figure is how he can be such a restless soul and not have a taste for the road.

VOLTA: Maybe he doesn't have a taste for the game and can't admit that to himself.

BOBBY: (after a pause) I don't know. He's either a helluva quick learner or he's got some card sense on the natch, because in eighteen months he was holding up against some of the best, and that was starting from scratch. He don't have to admit *that* to himself; that's just a stone fact. And the bigger the money, the better he plays.

VOLTA: Any indication where his interests lie?

BOBBY: He mentioned the focus was too tight in gambling. He said he wanted to expand. Maybe send him back to the mountains for a while—he says he misses them. Maybe turn him over to Slocum Wright for a couple of years to learn boats.

VOLTA: Not enough challenge.

BOBBY: Well, you got me. By the way, before my senile ol' mind forgets it, he said to be sure and tell you he had a dream and wants to talk to you about it.

VOLTA: Tell him I'll talk to him later, unless it's something urgent regarding his mother.

BOBBY: Sure, but where does he go? He seems real anxious to know.

VOLTA: Probably because he's thinking of quitting.

BOBBY: (chuckling) Haven't we all.

VOLTA: True enough. But okay, give him these instructions. He should fly to New York two weeks from tomorrow, on the twenty-seventh. Wait in the Silver Wings bar for a man named Jean Bluer. If Bluer isn't there by six P.M., he should take a taxi to the Wild-wood Hotel and register as David Hull. If he hasn't heard from Jean Bluer in three days, he should call me at the Six Rivers number.

BOBBY: Who's this Jean Bluer? Sounds like a Frenchy.

VOLTA: A recent addition. I just decided a few seconds ago he might be the one to open a different dimension. Could take me a few days to find him, though—that's why the convoluted and contingent instructions.

BOBBY: You have anyone lined up for me?

VOLTA: No.

BOBBY: There's a kid named Johnny Russo that looks good. Care if I take him on for a few months?

VOLTA: Not at all. But I'm a little surprised. I thought you preferred traveling that mean ol' hard-ass gambling highway by your lonesome.

BOBBY: Guess it turns too lonely when a man starts losing his edge. Hell, I only won about half a million this week.

VOLTA: That's nothing. I heard some guy named Guido Caramba won seven hundred thousand in two days.

BOBBY: Probably a good thing you have me to rag, otherwise you'd go around putting the boots to puppies. You know, Volta, any time you think you know something about playing cards, I'm sure you can find me and show me how it's done.

VOLTA: You know I don't gamble, Robert.

BOBBY: Right. And Pancho Villa couldn't hide a pony.

Daniel sat in the Silver Wings Bar at Kennedy International drinking whiskey and waiting for Jean Bluer. He'd parted company with Bad Bobby in San Francisco twelve days earlier and hiked and fished in the Sierras till his departure for New York. He'd made his flight in Oakland with barely enough time to cadge a shower in the employees' lounge and change his smoke-tanged clothes. Now, seven hours later, he was on the other side of the continent, his head still in the Sierra high country, New York at his feet, his heart dislocated and confused.

In the mountains he'd considered giving up his training. He didn't feel it was going anywhere. Every teacher had demanded strict attention and ferocious concentration, but to no real point, or none he wanted. That, he decided as he ordered another whiskey, was the problem: He didn't know what he wanted. He had no family, no lovers, no close friends. His vocational skills, essentially solitary occupations, were illegal in most states. Growing dope, cracking safes, and playing poker were potentially lucrative, though if nothing else, he was comfortable with risk. The ten days in the Sierras hadn't refreshed him as he'd hoped they would. As he waited, he decided if he didn't like Jean Bluer, or if it was more of the same work in a different form, he would ask Volta for a two-year vacation. If Volta refused or resisted, he'd quit AMO. No. He would *tell* Volta he was taking a few years off for independent study, not ask. He was still hurt Volta had shown no interest in his dream.

At six, Jean Bluer hadn't arrived. Irked, Daniel downed his drink and made his way through the crammed terminal as the PA boomed static-fractured announcements of arrivals and departures.

"I'm departing," Daniel, at least one sheet to the wind, muttered as he followed the arrows for ground transportation. But when he stepped outside into a raw dusk, he didn't see any buses or taxis around. A porter whisked by with a rack of luggage.

"Taxi?" Daniel called.

"Do I *look* like a fucking taxi?" the porter snarled without breaking stride.

Daniel, scrambling to make the leap between high country solitude and the teeming arrogance of New York, fell short. An infinitely sweeter voice behind him purred, "Are you going into the city?"

Daniel turned. The speaker was a striking young woman with long, glossy black hair. She was barely an inch shorter than Daniel's six feet, wearing a skirt the color of terra cotta and a loose red-silk blouse. The colors went well with her dark complexion and the lines complemented her body, more sleek than thin.

"I'm looking for a taxi or a bus or something," Daniel told her. The whiskey and a rush of lust thickened his tongue.

"So I gathered. These porters are becoming absolutely loutish, their insolence matched only by their capacity for obscenity."

"Yeah," Daniel said. He looked at her closely, trying to fix her nationality. She was wearing lots of makeup.

"You didn't say if you were going into the city, but if you are, you're welcome to ride with me."

"That's very kind of you," Daniel said, trying to muster a formality equal to her own. "I accept with gratitude."

"Where are you staying?"

"The Wildwood."

Her large brown eyes looked pained. "There *are* better hotels in New York."

"I wouldn't know," Daniel said. "I've never been here. I'm meeting an old friend."

"Business?"

"Indirectly. We've done a lot of gambling together." Inspired, he added, "That's why we're meeting at the Wildwood—there's supposed to be a rather promising poker game there. Poker, you see, is my business."

"A gambler! How fascinating. You must tell me more."

Daniel started to oblige when a black limousine hushed to a stop beside them. A chauffeur ushered her inside, inquiring, "And how was your trip, Miss Haruh?"

"Work, as usual." Then, indicating Daniel, "This gentleman will be riding into the city with us, Phillips. Please drop him at the Wildwood Hotel."

"Of course, Miss Haruh."

The limo was opulently appointed. "You travel very well," Daniel said as they pulled away.

"When you travel as much as I do, luxury becomes a necessity."

"I can appreciate that, though in my business forsaking luxury is more often the necessity, especially if you play badly. My name, by the way, is Daniel Pearse."

"Mine is Imera Haruh," she said, bowing her head slightly.

There was something about her that Daniel suddenly didn't trust. Her speech and gestures seemed too self-consciously graceful or formal—as if rehearsed. "Haruh?" he said. "Is that Pakistani?"

"Close. Indian."

"Your English is exceptional."

She smiled. "It should be. I was born and raised in Madison, Wisconsin. My parents were Brahmins who did not like Gandhi any better than the British."

"So, what takes you on these travels where luxury is a necessity?"

"I'm a model with the Sebring Agency. I just shot a spread for *Elle* with Raoul Villela—it seems only an hour ago I was in Madrid—and next month I'll be on the cover of *Vogue*. Look for it. I'll be wearing Oriental make-up, a bamboo hat, and halter-top pajamas. It's their Vietnam Remembrance Look or something equally tacky." She arched her lip in distaste. "The editors, the advertisers, even the photographers—none of them have souls."

Daniel said, "You don't have to do it."

"Mr. Pearse," Imera said tartly, "the world gives women very little of financial value other than their beauty, which it then wastes. I intend to—how do you gamblers say it?—*cash in* while I can."

Daniel thought, *That explains the brittle, practiced grace. A model, a Brahmin, and a pound of righteous feminine bitterness.* "Miss Haruh," he said gently, "please don't mistake my intentions, but after I've finished making arrangements with my friend at the Wildwood, would you be my guest for dinner? And not merely to reciprocate the generosity of this ride, but to sustain the pleasure of your company." *That was good,* Daniel thought, impressed.

Imera's smile seemed more relaxed. "As long as it's no place where I'd usually be recognized by the fawning flesh-dealers of this city."

"Anywhere you choose."

She cocked her head slightly, a gesture that would have seemed coy if not for the strength in her voice, "And please, Mr. Pearse, don't mistake *me.*"

"I won't," Daniel assured her, thinking, *I dreamed; now maybe I can make love to the same woman twice.*

They ate at a small Greek restaurant, then, having dismissed Phillips earlier, took a taxi to her Upper East Side apartment. He didn't wait for her to turn on the lights. Taken with the sudden dizziness of desire, he put his arms around her.

"Daniel," she warned, breaking away. "Don't. You'll be disappointed, I'm afraid."

"More likely, that would be *your* complaint, not mine."

"I doubt that sincerely," she said, flipping on the lights.

Daniel, whose attention had been riveted on her, was startled to see her apartment was more like a small warehouse, most of it devoted to makeup tables and racks of clothes. He looked at her, the intimation of betrayal like a weight in his lungs. But before he could even imagine what it was he hoped she could explain, Imera swept off her wig and hung it on a nearby rack. She was bald.

And when she spoke, it seemed her voice had dropped thirty-nine octaves. "Daniel, allow me to introduce myself properly. I'm Jean Bluer, Master of Disguise." Jean Bluer smiled hugely at his little joke.

"I'm going to kick your ass," Daniel promised, taking off his coat.

"I seriously doubt that will occur. Besides being a master of disguise, I am also a master of Tao Do Chaung, the almost extinct art of Ninja foot fighting, and I *will* defend myself."

"I think you're the master of bad jokes and bullshit." Daniel lunged.

Jean Bluer spun sideways, whipping his right foot around into Daniel's thigh with an excruciatingly precise force. Daniel went down screaming.

Jean Bluer looked at him as he writhed in pain. "Daniel," he said, vaguely disappointed, "you must develop a larger appreciation for the essential humor of identity."

Since Jean Bluer was never entirely himself, any description was provisional. His eyes most often were blue, but through the adroit use of contact lenses and the application of special drops he prepared himself, they might be twenty shades of hazel, brown, or grey. His hair color, length, and style were a function of whatever wig he chose for the day, just as his nose and ears depended on putty and makeup for their shape. He altered his body with girdles, lifts, padding, postural changes, and the warehouse of costumes, many of which he'd sewn or otherwise assembled himself. When Smiling Jack had called Volta's attention to Jean Bluer, Jack had claimed that given enough preparation time, Jean could pass for *any* adult from twenty-nine different cultures—and Jack was notoriously frugal with exaggeration.

Daniel received his daily lessons in the warehouse where Jean dwelt among his manifold identities. Jean was a passionate and exacting teacher. Study began at seven in the morning and lasted till nine in the evening. At Daniel's insistence, instruction in Tao Do Chaung was added, beginning at five A.M. After the smoky rancidity of the gambling life, Daniel embraced the physical exertion of Tao Do Chaung's dervishlike exercises.

Daniel had revered—even loved—Wild Bill. Mott Stoker he'd admired for the exuberance of his excesses. He'd hated and adored Aunt Charmaine's glacial grace and piercing mind. He'd respected Bad Bobby's skill, style, and raptor's eye. He was enthralled by Jean Bluer. The warehouse, like Jean's psyche, was a hall of mirrors, and while Jean, like his student, examined each image for its elemental accuracy, teacher and student were both compelled to look into themselves for who they might possibly become.

Jean Bluer distinguished four stages of disguise: the photograph; the dance; the poem; and the person. The photograph, as the label implied, centered on visual accuracy. Under Jean's severe tutelage, Daniel learned how to use skin tints, crepe beards, putty, sponges, false eyelashes, contact lenses, paint-on tooth enamels; a variety of wens, warts, and beauty marks; and molded latex masks which, worn overnight, pulled his features to their designs.

Initially they worked from a file of photographs. When Daniel finished his makeup, Jean Bluer inspected the face, offering a barrage of criticisms and suggestions.

"The seal between the nose putty and lip line is faulty—use a bit more glue, and mix a touch of Max Factor Number Nine in with it.

"The beard is inept, much too sparse below the jaw. The powder on the cheekbones is excessively dark, thus exaggerating the hollow; in sunlight you'd look like a zombie. And *smear* the lip gloss; it's blinding. Small amounts, smoothly applied—that's the proper application. Small and smooth. Suggestion, not statement. The harmonious integration of details."

After a month working from photos, they moved to the street for an hour every morning. Jean Bluer would pick out a model for Daniel to reconstruct back at the warehouse. Jean commented as Daniel, squinting into the semicircular mirror on the makeup table, reproduced the face from memory. As Daniel soon discovered, each face Jean chose as a model presented different problems.

"*No!* Never! The eyes are too far apart. You couldn't fool a blind man," Jean Bluer would admonish, picking up the eyeliner. "Like *this,* you see—a bolder line, and a little more arch to the brows. The eyelashes, now, curl them *away* from each other. Notice how it widens the placement of the eyes, thus broadening the forehead, harmonizing the illusion."

Or another day: "Acchhh! The scar is terrible. *Atrocious.* Like scars little kids paint on their faces playing pirate. Utterly one-dimensional." (One-dimensionality was, for Jean Bluer, the only unforgivable fault.) "Wipe it off before its stupidity paralyzes us both. Now try this: a whitish-grey liner, a hint of silver, a faint streak of blue for the highlights. Then, the little bottle next to the Max Factor Flexible Collodion that you've used to hold wigs and seal putty—no, next to it, yes, the little bottle that says *Non*flexible Collodion. Now, paint over the scar. See? It shrinks the skin and draws it inward. Notice how the lower lid of your eye is just *slightly* pulled down? Yes, yes—excellent. You did especially well on the coloration. That *is* a scar. Merely looking at it one can feel the pain of the original wound, the pain of healing."

When Daniel was proficient with makeup, Jean introduced him to costume. From Amish hats to zebra-striped panties, Daniel learned materials, cuts, padding, and the conventions governing them. Women's clothing in particular confounded him.

"Heavens," Jean Bluer howled at his first attempt, "you'd be arrested in a moment as a transvestite, and any self-respecting drag queen would *assist* the police. The nylons are baggy. If your upper lip were any thinner you could slice salami. The purse was out of style seven years ago, and you are holding it like a dead baby. Your breasts have ridden up around your collarbones because you have not imagined their weight, thus are holding your shoulders too far back. Also, your feet are too far apart and your center of balance seems to be around your knees rather than between your hips. This is bad, Daniel. This makes me ill."

After school, Daniel, who lived in a rooming house down the block, was free to do as he pleased, as long as he observed how people looked, walked, talked, and thought. Daniel kept notes, and while he practiced the morning's lesson in Tao Do Chaung, Jean critiqued them aloud.

" 'Waved.' Which hand? Was this coat buttoned, open, or partially buttoned. You note a blue-striped dress shirt. What sort of collar and cuffs? *'European* laugh?' *'Southern* accent?' Meaningless descriptions. The laughter of the French and Italians is completely different. There are well over a hundred southern accents. Precision, Daniel. Detail. Nuance. One perfect gesture or inflection will carry even a hasty physical disguise."

When Jean Bluer was satisfied with Daniel's progress, he introduced the second stage, the dance. He started Daniel at the center: muscle, bone, integument—what was connected to what and how it worked. From that center, Jean explained, posture, movement, and gesture naturally expanded.

"Physique is the deposited history of our forebearers, and thus a component of character. Any voluntary movement is, naturally, a gesture of consciousness—certainly our main interest—but always pay initial attention to the arrangement of muscle, bone, and skin, for they determine the actual form of the movement."

Daniel learned ten basic walks, each emphasizing a different center of gravity, and therefore a different balance. He worked barefoot to sense the precise distribution of weight and strain. They spent the lunch hour on the street, observing the way people moved their bodies, endless variations on a few skeletal themes. Jean emphasized hands—the position of the fingers, angle of the palms, the speed and force of movement, continually reminding Daniel to look for each person's *pattern* of motion, not just isolated moves. And at the end of eighty strenuous days, Jean, pleased with Daniel's abilities, announced they would move to the third stage of disguise, the poem.

Daniel started with breathing exercises, first establishing a "regular" breath as a median from which to explore different rhythms. "Accent, pitch, inflection"—Jean dismissed them with a wave—"they can only be added *after* you have the basic cadence. Listen to how people breathe when they talk, and the rest falls into place." As usual, his advice was amazingly helpful.

From breath cadence, Daniel moved into sound, the vibrating air of vowels and consonants, the bare phonetic minimums and the corresponding placement of teeth and tongue, the subtle variations in pitch and duration. Daniel practiced from Jean's vast catalogue of tapes as Jean listened for flaws in Daniel's imitations.

"Not 'you-all'; it's 'yawl.' *Roll* the jaw—it's a broad elision. . . . More drag on the gutturals and more hum in the nasals—you're in New Mexico territory, pahdnah. Pay attention to that tongue! Northern, more forward; southern, let it loll back a little. And diction, Daniel, *diction!* You're supposed to be an Irish hod-carrier, not a British barrister."

Daniel's favorite of these admonitions was "More mumble, please, more mumble."

When they entered the last stage of disguise, Jean gave a short speech about what he was after. "So far we have been involved in the duplication of appearance, movement, and speech. Duplication requires craft. Now we enter art, for the fourth stage requires not merely a physical extension of identity, but its assumption. *Real* imagination, where you become what you create. And this needs to be stressed: Those identities are *already* within you. We think of identity as being singular, unique. But it is only the expression of one possibility. Think of identity as a braid of many identities through which the force of life flows—like an electrical wire composed of many smaller, intertwined wires coated with a rubber insulation that keeps them intact, coherent. You are both the Ancient Mariner and the wedding guest, the bride and the groom, minister and derelict. Every person dead, alive, or to be born is within you. Tap that storehouse of selves, draw upon your own body of metaphor."

The exercises for the fourth stage of disguise, the person, were challenging to the point of absorption. At seven each morning Jean gave him a problem to solve. Daniel had till noon to find a solution, which he performed for Jean. If Jean approved, he sent Daniel out on the streets to present it under real circumstances. The problems were people.

The first was easy. "Daniel, become a thirty-seven-year-old union electrician, born in Chicago, with a wife and two children. You fell from some scaffolding two years ago and shattered your left shoulder, living on disability insurance ever since. You're on your way back from seeing the doctor and have stopped for a drink in an unfamiliar bar. I'll be taking the part of the bartender."

The problems soon became more difficult. "You are a twenty-year-old female journalism student at Columbia University. You were born in Lubbock, Texas, lived there till you were fourteen, then moved to Newark. Your father is a mid-level executive with Standard Oil, and your mother is a closet alcoholic. You have been increasingly depressed the past few months and have sought help from the university counseling center. I will be a psychologist.

"You are a thirty-year-old male Puerto Rican cocaine dealer. You've been in prison once for three years for assault on a peace officer. You have a scar on your right cheek. I will be a new buyer, whom you suspect may be a narc. You want to be careful, but you could also use a new customer."

172

Although Jean always sent Daniel to the street with each solution, it was nearly four months before the sharp, continual criticism gradually gave way to praise. The day Daniel passed through a welfare interview as a fifty-year-old female Colombian immigrant with four children and little English, Jean told him, "As you know, you are my first student under my agreement with Volta, and I'm either a much better teacher than I ever hoped, or you are a natural talent. I can find very few flaws lately, and they are flaws only experience, not instruction, can correct. You are good enough to leave any time you choose. I will notify Volta."

"Thank you," Daniel acknowledged the praise, "but I won't leave until I can fool you as you initially fooled me."

"Ah, but Daniel, that was much easier on my part, since you'd never seen me before or suspected I would be in disguise. Do remember that I can spot a disguise very quickly, especially when I'm looking for one. Your chances of getting past me are extremely poor."

"With all respect, I believe I can do it."

"Very well, if you insist. At the end of Tao Do Chaung each morning, I will tell you where I plan to eat lunch and the route I'll take to get there. Assume the disguise of your choice and engage me along the way. If you can fool me for thirty seconds, consider yourself successful."

The first day Daniel disguised himself as a window washer, renting a van and equipment. As he began washing the windows of the restaurant, Jean emerged, laughing, and told him that most professionals used some sort of detergent in the water since it seemed to get the windows cleaner.

The second day he joined a group of winos huddled in a doorway. As he passed by, Jean put a quarter in his hand and whispered, "It would have been a twenty if you'd fooled me."

That night, Daniel had a brainstorm. He would disguise himself as the one person Jean might not expect, might not even recognize: He would disguise himself as Jean Bluer.

Daniel left early for the studio next morning, still excited by his plan. There were very few people on the street. An old black man, so drunk he'd entered another dimension, lurched past with his eyes rolled back in his head. A sturdy Ukrainian woman stood at the bus-stop. A sawed-off, pot-bellied army sergeant carrying a duffel bag fumed by, muttering to himself, "Fuckin' reveille motherfucker and no fuckin' sleep—*fuck* the fuckin' army!" Daniel hurried on.

Daniel crossed the kitchen toward the large dressing room where he usually changed into a jock and sweatpants for Tao Do Chaung. Volta was standing at one of the mirrored makeup tables, idly examining a color chart.

The moment Daniel saw him he realized he'd just passed Jean Bluer on the street, and that he would most likely never see him again. It was an appropriate farewell.

Volta glanced up. "Daniel, how have you been?"

Daniel said, "Was that fat sergeant I just passed on the street Jean Bluer?"

"It was indeed. Jean's talents are required elsewhere. Not an emergency exactly, but a *pressing concern,* you understand. Your work here is through."

"Not quite," Daniel said, shifting his center of gravity into the Tao Do Chaung stance known as the Wounded Crane and simultaneously unleashing a flawless Do Rah Ran, a powerful side kick that swept Volta's feet out from under him.

Volta, however, controlled his fall, tucking himself midair and rolling on his shoulder as he hit. He was on his feet instantly and assumed the .38 Colt Python stance, the front bead locked on Daniel's navel. "Don't make me defend myself," he said calmly. "I'm no match for your youth. I'd have to shoot you."

Daniel said with certainty, "You wouldn't kill me."

"I didn't say I'd *kill* you; I said I'd *shoot* you. In fact, since the gun is full of snake-loads—birdshot instead of a bullet—I doubt if I *could* kill you, but I could probably perforate about a half mile of small intestine, which would slow you down enough to make it a fair fight."

"No," Daniel said in the same implacably certain tone, "you wouldn't do that either."

Volta shrugged. "You're right." He released the hammer and tossed the pistol to Daniel.

Startled, Daniel grabbed awkwardly.

While he was still fumbling, Volta started talking. "What are you so ferociously peeved about anyway? That I've been neglecting you? Daniel, I'm not your father. I have responsibilities to many others as well as you. And I have my own life, too. Or is this because I didn't have either the time or inclination to hear your dream? I told Robert to convey my congratulations, which I trust he did." Daniel began to say something but Volta rolled on. "Or was that spiteful kick the result of my high-handed presumption in ending your work with Jean and sending him to attend other business? Daniel, your work with Jean, by *his* report, was finished a week ago. Since then, again by his report, you've been trying to convince yourself that you're adept enough to fool him—that is to say, his equal. You're not. Though having said so, I hasten to add that I think you have the talent and passion to surpass him eventually. The opportunity is there. And have you noticed how opportunity seems to expand as it narrows?"

"I sure have," Daniel said. "That's why I'm quitting AMO."

"You're welcome," Volta snapped. "Bye."

Daniel flipped open the .38's cylinder and ejected the shells into his palm. They were snake-loads. He looked at Volta. "Maybe you would have shot me." He tossed Volta the gun.

Volta caught it by the butt and in virtually the same motion flipped open the cylinder, magically producing a speed-loader in his other hand, and had the pistol ready to cock again before Daniel could blink twice. "I'm a man who draws lines, Daniel. That way I know where my edges are. One of those lines is a refusal to be brutalized for petty reasons, especially youthful petulance. If you were a Zen master, I would be bowing to you. But you're not. As you've no doubt noticed."

Daniel took a deep breath, and for a moment seemed to be gathering himself for a heated reply. "Okay," Daniel said. "I'm sorry. I apologize."

"Accepted and forgotten," Volta said. The gun disappeared into his jacket.

Daniel said, "It was a bit of all the reasons you mentioned, but the work with Jean especially. You think my work here is done, Jean thinks it's done, but *I* don't. Today I was going to try something that may well have worked—I was going to disguise myself as Jean."

Volta sat down at the makeup table, turning the chair away from the bank of mirrors to face Daniel. "That might have proven difficult, since there is no Jean Bluer."

"I thought I sensed one."

"Possibly you did."

They were silent a moment and then Daniel said, "I need a vacation, a serious rest. A year at least; maybe two."

"You quit, remember? I assumed you quit in order to do exactly as you please. Do so."

" 'Accepted and forgotten?' " Daniel reminded him. "Don't beat me with my apology."

"Your apology was for the kick, not your resignation—for that, no apology is necessary. We couldn't very well call AMO a voluntary alliance if one wasn't free to withdraw."

"I want to stay. It was an addled act. Jean gone, you here telling me what to do . . . it was too much at once."

"I'm truly glad to hear that, Daniel, because right now we need your help."

"*My* help?"

"I don't understand why you seem startled," Volta said with more than his usual dryness. "We haven't been providing your training without some expectation of return. We consider you what we call a free agent. We assume you will listen to various requests for assistance, though of course you retain the right to refuse, or to suggest alternatives. No more teachers, unless you wish to arrange further study on your own. And remember one of Wild Bill's better lines: 'When the teaching ends, learning begins.' "

"So what am I *needed* for? To grow dope? Gamble? Crack safes? To disguise myself as an Italian waiter and find out what the Secretary of State discusses with his mistress over the scallopini?" Daniel's sarcasm belied his excitement.

"Nothing so mundane. This is much more in tune with your romantic nature: a jewel theft. An extraordinarily difficult theft, I warn you, but it is an extraordinary jewel. To steal it, you will have to surpass Jean Bluer."

"You just finished saying—" Daniel began, but Volta cut him short.

"What's the ultimate disguise, Daniel?"

Daniel considered a moment. "Invisibility, I guess."

"Exactly."

"I'm not quite able to do that yet."

"I am," Volta said. "Or I was at one time."

"Actually become invisible, right? Dematerialize? Poof?"

"*Vanish* is the term I use. And no poof. It's more like slipping underwater."

"You're telling me you could *vanish* into thin air?"

"Or thick."

"No offense," Daniel said, "but I'd have to see it. And then I'd still probably have to believe it."

"You'll have to take it on faith. I gave up the practice years ago. It was too dangerous for me. And it might be even more perilous for you."

"Why?"

"Because I think you'd like it."

"First I'd have to do it."

"Let me assure you, Daniel, if I didn't think you were capable, I wouldn't mention it. Do you think I'm unaware what an outlandish claim it is, especially when I'm not prepared to demonstrate? And I'd be remiss if I didn't mention that I've never met another human being who had the power to vanish. I've tried to instruct six people before you, without success."

"Not even an arm? A finger?"

Volta ignored him. "I discovered it by accident. I was near death, adrift on the ocean. A woman on the boat that rescued me claimed her mother, a Jamaican shamaness, had vanished once in her practice and found it such a dangerous and treacherous state of mind that she never tried it again. When a woman accomplished in the spirit arts says a practice is dangerous and treacherous, that should command your attention. This is for real, Daniel, this is for keeps. School's out."

Daniel held up a hand. "Wait a minute, now. I thought you said you were going to teach me."

"I couldn't call it teaching. That would be an insult to people like Wild Bill. All I'm going to do is share my experience, which might be wholly inapplicable. The best I can do is point at the mountain and hope you find a trail."

"How long would it take me to learn?"

Volta shook his head. "No idea. None. The other people I've tried to teach all gave up within a week."

"I suppose it's arduous and requires great concentration."

"Naturally. Immense concentration; pinpoint focus; enormous clarity. It takes everything you have."

"Is this jewel worth it?"

Volta said, "Properly, that's for you to decide."

"Have you seen it?"

Volta hesitated. "Well, I've *dreamed* it."

Daniel shook his head. "I'm getting lost. You want me to vanish into your dreams?"

"Good Lord, *no,* " Volta blanched. "That's exactly what I *don't* want you to do."

"So, what is it *exactly* you *do* want me to do?"

"Steal the diamond."

"So, it's a diamond?"

"Yes, though it's a bit like saying the ocean is water. The diamond is perfectly spherical, perfectly clear—though it seems to glow—and it's about two-thirds the size of a bowling ball. I think of it as the Diamond. Capital D."

"Who owns it?"

"No one. The United States government has it at the moment. We want it. And to be honest with you, Daniel, *I* particularly want it, want it dearly. I want to look *at* it, *into* it, hold it in my hands. I had a vision involving a spherical diamond, a vision that changed my life, and I want to confirm that it was a vision of something *real,* the spirit embodied, the circuit complete."

Daniel was smiling. "You're going to love this. That dream I wanted to talk to you about, my first since the explosion? It just happened to feature a raven with a spherical diamond in its beak. Obviously, it wasn't as big as a bowling ball, and there was a thin spiral flame running edge to edge through its center, which made it seem more coldly brilliant than warmly glowing, but it sounds like the same basic diamond to me."

"And what do you think it is?"

"I think it's beautiful."

Volta gave him a thin smile. "If I were more perverse than I already lamentably am, I would say it is the Eye of the Beholder. In fact, I don't know what it is."

"It might be a dream," Daniel said.

"Very possibly," Volta agreed, "but I don't think so. I think—*feel*, to be exact—that the Diamond is an interior force given exterior density, the transfigured metaphor of the *prima materia*, the primordial mass, the *Spiritus Mundi*. I'm assuming you're familiar with the widely held supposition that the entire universe was created from a tiny ball of dense matter which exploded, sending pieces hurtling into space, expanding from the center. The spherical diamond is the memory, the echo, the ghost of that generative cataclysm; the emblematic point of origin. Or if, as some astrophysicists believe, the universe will reach some entropic point in its expansion and begin to collapse back into itself, in that case the Diamond may be a homing point, the seed crystal, to which it will all come hurtling back together—and perhaps through itself, into another dimension entirely. Or it might be the literal Philosopher's Stone we alchemists speak of so fondly. Or I might be completely wrong. That's why I want to see it. If I could actually stand in its presence, I'm convinced I'd know what it is. I would even venture to say, at the risk of rabid projection, that it *wants* to be seen and known."

"But you're not even sure it exists," Daniel said. "Right? And hey, it's tough to steal something that *doesn't* exist, even if you can be invisible. The more I think about this the less sense it makes."

"Then think about this: Two days ago, Navy divers searching for the wreck of the *Moray*—you might recall it was a nuclear submarine that vanished without a trace in 1972—found a mysterious object on the ocean floor exactly on the Greenwich Meridian. According to our information, the object appears to be a spherical diamond that 'glows'—whatever that means. It has been taken to a government lab for tests and observation. We're not sure where it is at the moment; there are rumors it's being moved. That's what Jean was called away to work on, as well as Smiling Jack and some of our other best people. Including you, I hope."

"And you really think I might be able to do it? Actually vanish?"

"I think you're the most likely candidate I've ever known."

"Why's that?"

"A number of reasons, but essentially because you *want* to vanish."

"I do?"

"I think so, yes. But what concerns me is that I'm not certain you will want to come back."

"Suppose I don't. Or can't. What happens to me then?"

"I don't know, but I suspect you might truly discover what lost means. Not confused, or disoriented, or displaced. Lost."

"Is that a challenge?"

"It challenged me."

"Is that why you quit?"

"Yes, one could say that."

"What did you steal when you were invisible?"

"Nothing. I used the ability to perform escapes in my magic act."

"Sounds like magic to me, all right."

Volta said emphatically, "It's *not*. Vanishing is a tool, a technique, another manipulation of appearance. Magic is the expropriation of the real."

"Well, hell, let's get started. I can't wait to see if I can vanish into nonexistence and magically expropriate a reality you dreamed."

"You've forgotten *your* dream; you might have to battle that raven for the Diamond."

"I suppose I'll find out. Are we going to start soon?"

"Early tomorrow morning. Meet me at the Oakland airport at midnight, Pacific time. You can pick up your tickets and itinerary at the Gilded Lily Pawn Shop at the top of President Street. You'll be leaving this afternoon. I have some business, so I'll be taking a later flight. We'll meet at Gate Seven and then catch a private flight north to the Eel River, and from there to my place. We'll get started after breakfast."

"That's not much sleep," Daniel noted.

"Daniel, I can only tell you what I know. And one thing I know is that exhaustion encourages vanishing."

Daniel and Volta took the interfacility shuttle to the private hangars. On the way, Volta told him, "Our pilot will be a young man named Frederic Malatest. Red Freddie, we call him. Don't bait him on politics. He takes them seriously."

"Red Freddie and Low-Riding Eddie—that's quite a crew."

"That," Volta sighed, "is our entire western air force. No wonder we're forced into imagination."

Red Freddie was in his mid-twenties. His lanky frame and laconic movements were in contrast to his piercing brown eyes and the message emblazoned in black letters across his motorcycle helmet: *Smash the State*. While Volta sat with his eyes closed, Daniel started Red Freddie on politics before they'd even taken off.

Over Ukiah Daniel expressed serious reservations about Red Freddie's

179

claim that the highest revolutionary act available to a middle-class people in the 1980s would be piling their television sets in the middle of the street and setting them ablaze with their front doors. They argued for a few minutes, until Red Freddie warned, "Reconsider your position," and put the twin-engine Beechcraft into a steep power dive.

Pressed back in his seat, Daniel watched the town lights below rush toward him. He was too stunned to speak until Volta, with a trace of reproach, said in his ear, "I told you he takes his politics seriously."

Daniel immediately leaned over and screamed in Red Freddie's helmet, "You're *right!* Build a bonfire with those front doors. And while you're at it, throw on all the word processors, too!"

"Right on!" Red Freddie bellowed, lifting the nose back up and leveling it before beginning a series of exuberant snap-rolls, each punctuated with a scream of "Yes! Yes! Yes!"

"Another thing," Daniel yelled. "After the televisions and typewriters, every speck of paper in the country."

"You got it, bro! You think something is important enough to write down to be remembered, important enough for others to know, well you can write it on a goddamn wall. Imagine it, man: motel room walls would be like poetry magazines."

Volta sleepily opened his eyes and said, "Did you two realize that Ukiah is haiku spelled backwards?"

Before Daniel could admit he'd missed that one, Red Freddie threw out his arms and dramatically declaimed,

> *When the last capitalist is strangled*
> *With the guts of the last bureaucrat,*
> *Cherry trees will blossom in our minds.*

Daniel said, "And when all the paper's burning, people should throw their clothes on the blaze and snake-dance around the neighborhood naked, then sit in a big circle and toast marshmallows and drink whiskey and smoke dope and trade stories, lies, and rumors."

Red Freddie nodded rapidly. "And the next morning form labor syndicates and call a general strike."

As Daniel and Freddie raved back and forth, Volta eased back in his seat. He admired youth and ambition, the seizures of endless possibilities and unqualified enthusiasm, but lately they were making him tired. He tried to relax and let everything go, but he couldn't shake an image of Daniel looking at himself in a mirror. The boy was bright, maybe even brilliant, but he was not wise.

For the thousandth time Volta wondered whether he would have offered Daniel the chance to vanish if there was no Diamond to steal. He remembered how Madge Hornbrook had touched his sleeve just before the ceremony when he'd replaced her as a member of the Star, whispering "Just remember that the crucial decisions are always too close to call." He was encouraged by Daniel's claim that he, too, had dreamed of the Diamond—a good sign. Yet he found little solace in it. He was getting old, he realized. Old.

Twenty minutes later, Red Freddie set them down on a fog-shrouded strip along the Eel River. He kept the motor running as Daniel and Volta quickly unloaded. In minutes he had the plane turned around, gunning it down the strip.

When Red Freddie lifted off, Daniel picked up his duffel. "All right, what do we do from here? Walk?"

"Right," Volta said absently.

"Which way and how far?"

Volta looked at him, then bent to pick up his own suitcase. "Northeast. About a hundred yards. To my truck." Volta started walking, Daniel falling in beside him.

Daniel said lightly, "Your *truck*? Given your position as a senior member of the Star, I thought a limo would be waiting."

"The truck was indulgence enough."

"What is it? Something along the lines of Smiling Jack's Kenworth?"

"You'll see," Volta said.

To Daniel it looked like any other old battered pickup, though it had new rubber all the way around. He told Volta, "Bad Bobby would book it eight to five that the tires outlast the truck."

Volta took Daniel's duffel bag and swung it into the bed on top of his suitcase. "No he wouldn't. Robert has a discerning eye for the deceptions of appearance."

"Well," Daniel allowed, "maybe even money."

"I intended to let you drive, but since you persist in insulting a work of art, you merely ride."

Not until Volta turned the engine over and Daniel felt the whole truck shimmying with an almost erotic anticipation did he understand the work of art under the hood.

Volta smiled, a boyish gleam in his eye. "The music you hear is a 427 Chrysler. This is an authentic moonshiner truck—not much to look at, granted, but since it's a rocket on the road, all you see's a blur." Volta tapped the gas.

"You like power, don't you?" Daniel said.

"Properly applied." Volta slipped the truck into first and applied some.

It was just as well Daniel couldn't think of a reply, for it would have been lost in the engine's chattering howl.

The narrow road soon left the river plain and began twisting up a long ridge. An hour later they dropped down and crossed the north fork of the Eel, its water shivering with starlight. A few miles farther on they turned onto a dirt road blocked by a sturdy metal gate. Volta pushed a button under the dash and the gate swung open. Daniel assumed they'd arrived, but it was another chucked and rutted seven miles and three gates before the road sloped down off the broad point of the ridge, curving slowly north as the land leveled, ending abruptly at a small frame house with an adjacent barn and scattered outbuildings. Volta touched another button under the dash and the house and yard lit up.

Daniel drawled—a fraction too slowly, Jean Bluer would have noted—"I got it figured 'twernt any ol' moonshiner done did your 'lectronics."

"No, it was a young electromagnetic genius, a German anarchist in love with waves."

"I heard Wild Bill claim more than once that 'German anarchist' was a contradiction in terms. That the best you could hope for was a Hegelian Baptist."

Volta laughed. "Bill's prejudices are notorious. But let me welcome you to my retreat, which is known locally as Laurel Creek Hollow. I wouldn't forbid you to reveal its location, but I ask you, as I do all visitors, to exercise the utmost discretion."

"You may depend upon it," Daniel promised, vaguely mimicking Volta's formality.

"Tell me," Volta said, "do you find me a bit grandiose and dramatic?"

"A little," Daniel answered.

Volta leaned toward him, his gaze so intense that Daniel was surprised when he whispered, with a mixture of apology and exasperation, "That's show biz, Daniel. Pure show biz." Before Daniel could respond, Volta pointed out the window, adding, "And that's the house. It's four fifteen. I suggest you unload our bags while I start a fire and cook us some breakfast. It'll be your last meal for a while, and I'd like to make it special."

It was. Air-light buckwheat pancakes with fresh butter and Vermont maple syrup. Ham from the Blue Ridge Mountains, cooked with a peach glaze and sliced thin. A fruit dish of apples, grapes, and slivered pecans, barely sauced with curried sour-cream. For beverages: Gravenstein apple juice and a choice of Vienna Roast espresso or Volta's own blend of tea, the latter with a squeeze of lemon and a dollop of fireweed honey.

As Volta cooked, he told Daniel about the origins of the ingredients. The buckwheat was grown and milled by a Montana woman named Jane Durham.

She sent him a fifty-pound sack every year because Volta had personally tracked down her grandfather's grave—he'd been a Wobbly organizer—and purchased a headstone for it. Tick Hathaway cured the ham, the last of twenty Volta had received in exchange for the 1925 Honus Wagner baseball card Tick needed to complete a collection. The apples were from a feminist commune in coastal Sonoma County, juiced on an old screw press. Smiling Jack had brought him ten gallons of maple syrup from the Hewlitt Jefferies' farm near Burlington. The honey was from the five-percent dues of another commune, whose members rejected the use of money—Dead President Trading Cards, as they called it.

Although Daniel felt both the urge and obligation to savor each morsel, it was all he could do not to wolf the food. It had been almost twelve hours since the airline dinner of gooey Yankee pot roast and boiled vegetables. Daniel was eyeing the last slice of ham, half listening to Volta recount the geological history of the Eel River watershed, when suddenly Volta stopped and delicately pushed the ham platter toward him.

"I'm sorry," Daniel said. "I'm so hungry I'm afraid I can't really appreciate how good it is. But I do appreciate you cooking it for me; I really do."

"I'm sure the food appreciates your hunger as much as my preparation. Hunger, you know, has always fascinated me. I have seen people on the verge of starvation standing in line to give food away. This was in Tibet, in a small mountain village. There was a holy man who lived in a cave higher up the mountain. Every full moon, for as long as it was visible in the sky, he would receive petitioners at the mouth of his cave. Each petitioner brought him a gift of food. In exchange, he would answer one question. When the holy man had enough food to last the month, he would start giving each gift to the next person in line. It was a rough climb to the cave, remember, and food was scarce, but the line of petitioners would begin forming well before sunset. There were often over a thousand people in line, and all of them knew that the holy man would withdraw when the moon set.

"The first time I visited I asked him, 'What is reality?' Without hesitation he replied, 'A handful of rice.' Sort of your standard holy-man answer. The second time, I asked, 'What is the greatest obstacle to wisdom?' He shut his eyes a moment, and when he opened them they had this wonderful delighted twinkle. 'Wisdom is easy,' he said. 'The mind is difficult.' "

Daniel wiped his lips. "I don't know about how easy wisdom is, but the mind being difficult, he got that right."

"Indeed. But I mention it because I'm experiencing some of that difficulty. I have reservations about your attempting to vanish. Gut reservations, nothing I can explain—except to assure you that they reflect uncertainties regarding my judgment, not yours."

Daniel, surprised by the turn of the discussion, said, "I *want* to try it. That's *my* judgment, *my* call. You're relieved of the responsibility of the decision."

Volta said, "I don't accept responsibilities that can be absolved. Clearly, since your approval is necessary to the attempt, and my instruction may be critical to your success and safety, it is a mutual decision. I'll be responsible for my part; you take care of yours."

"That's all I was trying to indicate—that I intend to."

Volta leaned back in his chair and looked at Daniel closely. "All right. From this moment onward, Daniel, don't speak to me. Don't speak at all. If you do, or if you violate any subsequent instructions, our work will end there, and along with it, my responsibility. Now please, finish your tea."

When they'd cleared the dishes, Volta took a six-volt flashlight from a shelf and told Daniel to follow. He led him out the back door and along a wide trail toward the cedar-shingled barn. Stars still glittered overhead, but the sky had begun to pale in the east. Volta followed the trail around the barn, then down a gradual slope to a small shack. Volta opened the door and entered, shining the light back for Daniel. When Daniel was standing beside him, Volta shined the light around the room. Along the far wall was a narrow bed. Three thick quilts were folded and stacked on the foot of the bed, a small white pillow on top. The only other furnishing was a straight-backed wooden chair.

Volta held the light on the chair and told Daniel, "Sit down."

When Daniel was seated, Volta held the light on a door in the wall Daniel was facing. "The door opens on a small compost toilet. If you'll remember to sprinkle a small can of wood ashes when you use it and replace the seat cover, there shouldn't be any odor."

The light flicked back to the bed. "Against the wall at the foot of the bed are three one-gallon jugs of local spring water. I advise you to use it sparingly."

Volta snapped off the light. "I want you to shut your eyes, Daniel, and I want you to listen well, listen as if your life depended on it. This is where I make my speech."

Volta began pacing around Daniel in the chair. Daniel shut his eyes and sat up straighter, concentrating. He felt fatigue evaporate as his attention sharpened. But as Volta continued his silent circling, an image of a jackal formed in Daniel's mind, then a vulture. Circling, waiting for his flesh. His heart started pounding so hard he couldn't breathe, so hard he thought it would explode, and he felt himself lifted to another plane, a plane of glassy power, smooth, translucent, solid. It wasn't a mystical experience. From his days with Mott Stocker, he recognized the feeling as the first rush of excellent amphetamine. He shook his head—not to clear it, but in mild disbelief. Volta had dosed him with crank! It made sense—Volta wanted him exhausted but alert. But Volta could have asked, or suggested.

Daniel was approaching righteous anger when Volta stopped in front of him and said, with an irony not lost on Daniel, "I know you trust me, but I can feel you don't trust me deeply. That's fair enough. You don't know me well, and you may think I've withheld information on your mother's death, or that I may have brainwashed you while you were in your coma, or that I have otherwise controlled your behavior and limited your expression. You're wrong, but I understand your caution. However, *do trust me* in this: What you're about to attempt is extremely dangerous—more so if you succeed than if you fail. Banish frivolity, boredom, self-pity. They can only compound the peril. The states of mind you may enter are almost impossible to imagine. They make drugs look silly."

Volta paused, started pacing around the chair again, but this time speaking as he moved. "Daniel, I want you to know I'm not speaking symbolically when I claim you can dematerialize your body and *literally* vanish, move unimpeded through concrete walls and steel doors. I don't have any idea how or why it is possible to spontaneously convert—perhaps invert—mass to electromagnetic waves, not so much jumping a frequency as leaping a dimension. I liken it to a phase change, the same essential configuration in a different form. Solid to liquid to gas; ice to water to air. Perhaps invisibility is one of our possible states. I don't truly know. I've ridden every metaphysical twist, and to me it remains an incomprehensible fact.

"As I mentioned before, I vanished many times in the past, usually in connection with magical performances. I'm the only person I know who's done it, though I have heard of another—the Jamaican shamaness—so please, Daniel, *please* understand that all I know is limited to my experiences. In short, what I tell you might be inapplicable to your own circumstances. You must absolutely trust your own instincts and intuitions as you approach the threshold. However, *my* intuition tells me that the experience is archetypal, and so I'll tell you how it felt, hoping it will be close.

"First, though, let's set some ground rules. You must, as noted, remain silent. You can talk to yourself—or scream or sing—when you're alone, but not when anyone else is present. You must fast—nothing but water. You are not allowed to leave this room. If you do, for any reason, that ends it. Finally, you must follow my instructions to the best of your ability, though actually that may be a measure of mine. Each day I will slip a set of instructions under the door.

"As to my pedagogical method, Wild Bill claims I'm a practitioner of the Kamikaze Socratic school, with a strong influence from the Marquis de Sade, but you know how fiercely judgmental William can be. I assume what he means is that I fly at the heart of the lesson and am not afraid to make you suffer. I build the raft. You run the river. I draw the map. You make the journey. If you don't trust me, clearly you should say so now and not waste our time and spirit."

Volta fell silent, still slowly pacing around Daniel on the chair. After three circuits, he continued. "Here's how I experienced the transformation from matter to electromagnetic energy. It begins with an empty moment. Blank. Null. To me it was exactly as if time had stopped. And I think that's just what happens, because you escape its force, not by transcending it or obliterating it, but by finding a still point within it, like a trout finding the point of hydraulic equilibrium behind a boulder in the flow.

"The next sensations come quickly. First, there's a very brief feeling of wetness, then a sense of light and warmth on your skin, and then a sudden and horrible confusion of all sensory information—a synesthetic snarl, an electrical storm in the brain. It's at that point, I think, you actually begin to vanish, or begin the neural transition. It coheres as suddenly as it started, and you're immediately sorry, for you find yourself falling, and you experience—or at least I did—terror that is unimaginably intense. It's a paradoxical fall—you know it is endless and you know you're going to hit. I'm sure you're familiar with the folklore about falling in dreams, that you always wake up before you hit because if you *do* hit, you'll die. As usual, folklore is correct.

"To vanish, you must consciously resist the terror and stop the fall. You resist the terror by recognizing it without reacting, accepting without judgment, becoming light moving through space. Again paradoxically, you cleanse the terror of falling by falling. You *stop* the fall by conscious imagination. What I did was form an image of myself falling, and then I concentrated on that image with every scrap of power I could summon, concentrated so deeply the image dissolved.

"When the fall stops, you are invisible, and everything returns to 'normal,' or at least one's familiar sense of space/time coherence and one's usual perceptual and emotional sets. Except the body is not visible. You can lift that electrical field you call a hand and scratch that whirling constellation of energy you call your head, but you are not flesh and bone, ashes or dust. You are released from the constraints of matter, and as that recognition deepens, a powerful serenity wells up and surges through you, and at the quick of that serenity is a magnificent clarity—you understand everything and know exactly what to do.

"That is when it becomes dangerous. And not because the clarity is delusional. On the contrary, it couldn't be more real, more true. And one thing you see most lucidly is that everything is necessarily subject to flux, and you're about to undergo a wrenching reversal. That the powerful serenity you felt surging through you was actually you surging through it; that the clarity isn't yours, but belongs to a center you are passing through. You can't keep it. And because you try to sustain it, try to hang on, it's worse. It's ecstatic, and it's all you want to feel forever. You are free of purpose, pain, obligation, consequence; dialectic and dynamic; life; death.

"The ecstasy is consuming. There's nothing you desire more than the annihilation of that last speck of concentration holding consciousness together. And though I obviously can't know for sure, it's my strongest intuition that if you succumb to ecstasy and fail to reclaim your concentration, your center, you'll vanish forever. Just as the terror is experienced as falling, the ecstasy is experienced as rising, soaring—but unchecked, it's the same as falling. So watch for that moment when clarity swerves toward the ecstatic. Catch yourself and return as soon as possible. I mean immediately. The further you soar, the further you fall."

Volta quit speaking but continued to pace. Daniel, who had been wired to every word, opened his eyes when Volta passed behind him. The room seemed much brighter. He wondered if there was a skylight. He glanced up. There was a skylight, but it wasn't much—a small panel of corrugated plastic, clotted with detritus from the surrounding trees. The amphetamine made his jaws ache and his mind race; he wanted to babble hundreds of questions. It took an effort to maintain his silence.

Volta stopped directly in front of him, put his hands behind his back, and continued. "It is impossible to overestimate the power and glory of that ecstatic leap, but if you surrender to it, I believe you'll be consumed. I repeat: *Return immediately.*"

Volta smiled thinly. "The reason I'm repeating myself is not simply to stress its importance, but to forestall having to explain how you escape ecstasy and return to the visible. I'll tell you how I did it, but I also must tell you that while I feel *crossing* into energy is roughly the same for everyone, each person's return is unique. I don't know why I feel that's the case, and I trust that you don't expect me to offer reasons for intuitions.

"Now before I tell you how I returned, let me refresh the principle, which I'm sure you're familiar with. The principle is contained in an ancient alchemical forge-chant, which Wild Bill refers to as 'that ol' cornball Babylonian mantra.'

To be yourself,
see yourself.

187

> *To see yourself,*
> *free yourself.*
> *To free yourself,*
> *Simply be."*

Daniel agreed with Wild Bill's aesthetic assessment. He almost shook his head in dismay.

"I feared you'd share William's antipathy for civilized wisdom, but surely you understand that clichés endure because they're repeated, and they're repeated because they've proven accurate. But I won't pursue it.

"Here's what I did to escape the ecstasy and return. I imagined a mirror. I held the image of the mirror ferociously in mind until I could see my face within it. And then I smashed the mirror. The return was immediate and wrenching, and the further I'd sailed, the worse it was—almost in direct proportion.

"When you return, you feel distant from your body, weak, witless, disoriented. It passes quickly, but you're exceptionally vulnerable to poor judgment, physical miscues, and general fuckups while you're reintegrating. Be careful.

"Basically, then, vanishing first of all involves a feeling of terror as you fall, then a brief and serene lucidity, which in turn opens into a soaring ecstasy. All three states of the transformation have their dangers, and your only defense is consciousness and concentration. Nothing really changes except form into formlessness, flesh into air. If you're thirsty when you're visible, you'll be thirsty when you vanish. Again: consciousness and concentration. You must work from the center of yourself. Use it to stop the fall. Sustain the clarity. Salvage yourself from ecstasy. Dilute the melancholy that invariably accompanies returning.

"The longest I was able to sustain invisibility was sixteen minutes, and I almost didn't make it back. Ecstasy doesn't encourage concentration. I have no idea if it's possible to sustain it longer, but I wouldn't try it for over ten minutes if I were you.

"I've told you what I can, but there are things I haven't told you. Some I haven't told you because you must discover them for yourself. There are things I haven't told you whose omission may seem cruel as the work unfolds, but it would be wise to withhold judgment until we're done; appearances and disappearances are equally deceptive. There are also things I haven't told you because I don't know them.

"That's not all I haven't told you, but I will tell you this, with my honor behind it: Nothing you'll be instructed to do is dangerous, up to the point of vanishing. Difficult, exacting, perhaps painful—yes. But not dangerous. Vanishing *is* dangerous."

Volta looked in Daniel's eyes to be sure the point was clear. "So, we begin. Your instructions today are simple, derived from an ancient exercise that I'm sure you're familiar with. I want you to acknowledge, *without response,* every piece of sensory data, every thought, every image, every feeling. Accept and let pass; see and release. Don't get caught up; don't follow; don't cling.

"I met a Chinese magician in Tangiers years ago. His name was Fang Chu, and he was the best fire eater I've ever seen. He claimed the 'acknowledge without response' meditation is the only one you really needed to understand magic. Fang Chu had this wonderful smile and not much English, though more than my Chinese. Whenever we talked about the meditation he would grin hugely and say, 'O yes! And so easy!' Then he would turn the grin up a notch and open his hands like this"—Volta grinned and opened his hands and then, imitating Fang Chu's sharp nasality, said, " 'Not'ing to it, as your cowboy say.' "

Volta held the pose a moment, still grinning. In his own voice he said, "So cowboy, nothing to it. Ride straight on through. There will be further instructions in the morning. Oh yes, and I almost forgot: No one knows what we're attempting here, and I believe it should remain that way. Until I say differently, this is *solely* between you and me. If you succeed in vanishing and wish to teach others, you must get my permission. When I die, the judgment of transmission shifts to you. I must have your honor on this, Daniel. Agree by remaining silent; if you don't agree, say so. We can still stop—no blame, no shame."

Volta waited. When Daniel had remained silent for almost a minute, Volta squeezed his shoulder. "I wish you the three things you will definitely need: strength, grace, and luck." He crossed to the door, closing it softly behind him.

Daniel leapt to his feet. The room was cold enough that he could see wisps of his breath. There was no sign of a heater or fireplace, nor could he find any lamps. The murky skylight was the only source of illumination. Its bright rectangle of light was beginning to lengthen on the bare western wall. The light did little to take off the chill. Daniel paced, flapping his arms for warmth as well as to burn off the manic energy of amphetamine meeting exhaustion. He tried not to think, to let all sensation simply loop through, fly away home. He tried to imagine his mind as a hole in a net, but thousands of speed-amped fishermen repaired it faster than he could rip.

"That motherfucker *dosed* me!" It felt so good to hear his own voice aloud, to move his speed-jammed jaws, that he began babbling to drain off the flitty, jangled, ganglia-scorching rush of amphetamine.

"I'll hire Mott, goddammit. Mott said a guy dosed him once, STP, B-1 brain-bomber of psychedelics, twenty-seven hours of spiders crawling out his nose and his great-granddaddy—shrunk down to miniature, inch tall at most—standing out on Mott's dick, digging his caulks in as he revved up his chainsaw. So Mott would take care of Volta for dosing me, I know he'd do it, I'm sure he would, Volta, that arrogant prick deserves it, fucking power freak, dumps crank in my tea and then tells me to empty my poor fucked mind, sure, right, so wired I can feel my pores open and shut, right, you bet, make it more amusing, mix in some mumbo-jumbo soul-and-spirit shit for the mystery/romance crowd, then tie their brains to the track."

Daniel listened to himself with the faceless intimacy between confessor and priest, feeling both the mechanical emptiness of sin and the weary forgiveness. He listened, heard, let it go, a lake barely ruffled by the breeze until suddenly he doubled over with a pain so complete and consuming he couldn't tell at first where it was coming from. It left him trembling in a cold sweat. He'd just started to straighten up when a grenade went off in his small intestine. He jackknifed to the floor, flopping like a clubbed fish.

When the GIFLUV X-27 1-20 PSB virus took full effect an hour later, flopping became a luxury. Gastro-Intestinal Flu Virus (GIFLUV), Experimental Lot Number 27 (X-27), had, as its code explained, an hour lapse between ingestion and full release, a twenty-hour duration (1-20), and with the general effect of making the victim puke and shit *bad* (PSB). Daniel's stomach and bowels emptied their various loads in the compost toilet as he whirled helplessly. When he pulled himself up on the bed at last, shook off his pants from around his ankles and piled the quilts over his quivering body, Daniel looked up at the grimy plastic skylight and moaned to the heavens, "Only a monster would double-dose another human being with food poisoning and amphetamine. Making sure you're awake for the misery. Only a monster. A fucking *fiend.*"

Sometime after sunset the savage bouts of vomiting and diarrhea gave way to a deep, steady, skeletal ache accompanied by flashes of fever and chills. Daniel was forced into a state of nonresponse. He felt himself shivering under the quilts, saw and released the image of himself shivering in an instant, let it pass into the parade of sensation. He began to feel calmer, almost floating. He desperately wanted to sleep, but the pain and the falling edge of speed prevented him.

Daniel tried harder to focus. He saw himself sitting in the straight-backed chair in the center of the shed, fishing through a hole cut in the floor. He didn't remember a river under the shed, but he could hear the water and feel the current carry his line. The drift paused and his rod-tip twitched. He set the hook instinctively and moments later lifted a golden fish from the water.

He had to show Volta. Holding the fish in his left hand, he headed for the door. But when he opened it, expecting to step outside, he found himself in another room, a duplicate of the one he'd just left. He crossed the room and opened the door into another empty room. And another, room after room. He held the fish tightly. When he opened the next door, a faceless man holding a small automatic pistol shot him in the head. Even though he knew he couldn't possibly survive the wound, Daniel put his hand to his temple to see how bad it was. Pieces of his skull moved under his hand like continental plates. His shock-bloated tongue couldn't form words. His ears roared as his sinuses filled with blood. He sagged to his knees and, in almost the same motion, toppled forward. Still clutching the golden fish, he tried once to push himself up but his body was too heavy. The last thing he felt before he died was the fish thrashing in his hand.

The fever finally broke an hour before dawn the next day. Daniel slept into the early afternoon. He woke with a raging thirst. He gathered himself and threw back the sweat-damp quilts, but when swinging his legs to the floor proved too complicated, he crabbed himself around and reached over the foot of the bed, uttering a small moan of pleasure as his hand circled the neck of one of the gallon water jugs. He had to use both hands to lift it. He leaned back against the abutting wall, legs splayed for balance, and drank greedily.

A dull headache was getting sharper, and his eyes felt like they were on stalks. *Better than yesterday but worse than shit,* he decided. A few moments later he burst into laughter, spraying a mouthful of water through the rectangular shaft of light from the skylight. The droplets of water hung suspended for an instant, round and molten in the swath of light, then disappeared.

Daniel tried to imagine himself as a droplet of water hurled into light, but he couldn't come close.

He wiped a dribble from his chin and lifted the jug for more. He was light-headed, he realized, almost giddy—but not disoriented. He knew exactly where he was, why, what had happened yesterday, who was responsible, and how he might take his revenge. He considered whether he should give Volta a Mott Stocker chili enema before he skinned him alive with a dull linoleum knife, or apply the enema as the *coup de grace* once Volta was flayed. He'd about settled on the former when he realized that if Volta had put the double-whammy dose on his breakfast, drinking the water was probably on the dumb side of chancy. However, he was still thirsty. He drained the jug. As he set it down, he noticed the envelope shoved under the door.

It was a journey across the Sahara to get out of bed and go pick it up.

He brought it back to the bed before opening it. The message was in a neat hand.

> I hope you're feeling better today, Daniel. I also trust you appreciate the force of necessity. Extraordinary undertakings require extraordinary means. Be assured, on my honor, that the water is untainted.
>
> Your instructions today are again simple. By sevens, count to 63,000 as smoothly as possible, and then, without pause, count backwards by sevens to zero. When you finish or fail the exercise, relax or sleep as you will. Let your mind glide.

As he wondered how long it would take to count to sixty-three thousand by sevens, Daniel opened the second jug of water and enjoyed a dread-free pint. He set it back on the floor, sat up on the bed, closed his eyes, and began aloud, "Seven, fourteen, twenty-one . . ." He started swiftly to establish momentum, and in a few furious minutes had passed a thousand, but the addition of one thousand before each number soon slowed the pace. Without missing a beat he began saying the numbers silently. That sped him up briefly, but it was still slow. At 2,401, he quit saying the numbers silently and tried to see them in his mind, a digital display progressing smoothly and quickly in increments of seven. It was like gliding on ice as the numbers flew by, and he almost skated past sixty-three thousand in no time at all.

He paused a moment, looping a circle around the figure, then headed back. But the shift to subtraction lurched him from the groove. He had to retard the rhythm to the point of slow motion before he could pick it up again, quickening it to a pulse, then speeding till it nearly blurred. He felt like he was sailing through a tunnel without walls. As he passed 490, he slowed down to savor his return, and then celebrated with a long drink of water.

Daniel was pleased. As far as he was concerned, he had completed the exercise efficiently and close to flawlessly. He acknowledged there'd been some shaky moments the day before when the poison hit—*very* shaky, actually—and his recent attempt to imagine himself as water in light had been a bit feeble. But such a reaction to systemic poisoning was certainly understandable, and the attempt to vanish like a water droplet was at least an attentive seizure of possibility, an error in the right direction. Alert and boldly decisive, disciplined enough to move on a flicker of instinct—that was the spirit Volta had indicated was necessary. Daniel was just about there. Very close. He could feel it.

He laid back down on the bed and watched the skylight darken. When he saw the first star's murky glimmer in the night sky, he folded his hands across his chest and shut his eyes.

He looked down into a circular pond. A golden fish swam languidly in the shallows, the water so clear, so still, he could see the fish's scales. Daniel plunged his arm into the pond and grabbed the fish behind the gills. He lifted it thrashing from the water and started running. He wanted Volta to see it before it died. He threw open the shed door expecting to find Volta meditating in the straight-backed chair. Instead his mother was laying in bed exactly as he was, and he sensed her nakedness under the quilt as his own. She ignored the fish in his hand and asked him, smiling, "How many sides does a circle have?" It was a riddle she'd asked him one April Fools' Day at the Four Deuces. He knew the answer but said, "You got me."

"Two," Annalee said, her eyes glittering. "An *in*side and an *out*side."

Daniel fought an impulse to weep. He said, "That's a great riddle from a great mom."

But he couldn't wait for her smile. He had to get the fish to Volta. He didn't have to explain his haste; she understood. He waved and bolted out the door into a duplicate room, only his mother was in bed with a man he didn't recognize, straddling him, her hands touching her own breasts, her back arched with pleasure. Daniel turned and ran into another room, this one empty, and then into empty room after empty room until he opened the door and a faceless man raised a pistol and shot him in the head. The last sensation Daniel felt was the fish slipping from his hand.

He read the day's instructions back in bed, the quilts mounded over him. The instructions were brief: "Count your bones till they glow."

He assumed it was the same practice he'd learned from Wild Bill. But this had a different focus: *"till they glow."* He had no idea what that meant. It was still early. He could sleep on it.

When the rectangle of light touched his outflung hand, Daniel woke. Except for a nagging thirst and a growing hunger, he felt exceptionally clear-headed. In his work with Wild Bill, Daniel had developed a variety of ways to do the bone-counting exercise. He started with the simplest, moving upward from his feet. He didn't really count the bones—just touched and moved. When he ended at his skull he felt sweetly refreshed, but far short of glowing. Taking a clue from the counting exercise, he reversed direction, skull to feet, but the rhythm was sprung. He decided it was his arms; he had to move down them and then back up. He concentrated on his arms, thinking he could perhaps blur the awkwardness with speed. It was better, but needed more power behind it. He tried to bring his mind to a single point of concentration, a dense mass, holding it till he trembled with the effort, then unleashed its pent force down through his neck and shoulders into each arm, converting it to energy. And rather than turning around at his fingertips to course back up his arms, something happened Daniel didn't expect—the energy shot through the ends of his fingers, arced through space, and returned through the soles of his feet, rushing up through his legs and pelvis more powerfully than it had started. He was afraid his brain would be obliterated, so he slowed it slightly, gathered the force, shot it back around the circuit, and then again. With each passage through his bones the power increased. When his skull could no longer contain the force, he let the surge shoot through the top of his head; it looped back through his fingers. He split it into two circuits, then four, and each new circuit clarified the power. He effortlessly added more until he felt as if he was enmeshed in a silken light. He felt his bones begin to glow. The light squeezed him out of his body. He floated above it, watching in amazement as it coalesced into a spherical diamond, the light now a spiral flame in its center. But it coalesced until it collapsed back into itself, through itself, roaring into emptiness. He felt a terrible suction pulling him down. He turned and ran. He had to warn Volta. But what had been light was now black water, a whirlpool spiraling him irresistibly downward to its vacant center.

In the dark suction, a golden fish flashed before him. He lunged. The instant his hand closed around the fish, Daniel was running uphill toward Volta's house. Volta had to see it. When Daniel opened the door he saw himself standing across the threshold. He didn't realize he was looking into a mirror until a faceless man stepped from behind it, raised a pistol, and shot him in the head. Daniel collapsed to his knees. He felt the fish flop out of his hand. Even though he knew he was dead, he could still see. The pool of blood spreading from his wound was almost like the surface of a lake at water-level. The golden fish flopped into view. When it reached the edge of his blood, it righted itself and started swimming toward him. Suddenly, it disappeared into the depths. Daniel kept watching, waiting for it to come back up. The cooling blood began to congeal.

Daniel dressed quickly in the cold room. The water was running low. What he really wanted was some food. He hadn't eaten in four days. He thought of buckwheat cakes with maple syrup and Virginia ham, and almost swooned.

Daniel walked softly across the room and knelt in front of the door. In a minute he heard Volta moving down the trail, humming cheerfully under his breath. He quit humming as he approached the shed. Daniel waited, poised. When the edge of the envelope appeared under the door, Daniel snatched it. He growled softly at first, letting it build in his gut, rise, hold, suddenly erupt into a roar, and as suddenly cut off. He listened. He could hear Volta humming as he walked back up the trail. *Well,* Daniel thought, *at least he has something to think about.* And added aloud, dolefully, "Yeah, like what a fool I am."

> Under the bed, bolted to the frame between two sheets of plywood, is a mirror. Prop it up securely and position yourself comfortably in front of it. Count your bones until they glow, then relax for about ten minutes, until you're breathing calmly and evenly. Shut your eyes and try to empty your mind. When you open your eyes again, look at yourself in the mirror. Look deeply into your own eyes. See yourself through yourself. The point of integration is the surface of the mirror. When you join yourself there, you will vanish.
>
> These are your final instructions. Try as often and as long as you want. I maintain my faith in your success.

As Daniel slid under the bed, he would have given twenty to one that the mirror would be round. He would have lost. As he discovered when he spun off the wingnuts and pulled the plywood sheets, the mirror was rectangular, roughly two feet by four, in a slender maple frame. He propped it against the western wall and, after folding one of the quilts under him, sat down about three feet away.

He closed his eyes and imagined his skeleton. He started counting his bones, quickening the rhythm until the circuit blurred and energy looped through his hands, feet, loins, spine, and skull. His bones began to glow as if the marrow was aflame.

The glow faded into an empty tranquillity. Daniel opened his eyes and looked into his own eyes looking back. He saw his skeleton stretched out on the bottom of a lake, his bones the glossy black of ebony. He wanted to lie there forever, but a resonant drumming from the surface seemed to summon him. He felt his skeleton float upward. But it didn't break into light. The lake surface was frozen; Daniel's bones rattled against the ice. The drumming was almost deafening now. People were banging the ice with shovels in the hopes that the vibrations would raise his body. He could hear them calling to each other but the ice muffled their words. He tried to call out, to tell them it was all right, he liked the bottom, but the thick ice made it hopeless.

He'd started sinking when Volta, calmly and distinctly, said "Life." Daniel stopped his descent and floated, gathering what strength remained. He kicked back toward the surface, feeling the cold water rushing through his eye sockets, ribs, pelvis. As he neared the frozen surface, he balled his right hand into a bony fist and slammed it upward through the ice, shattering it into a geyser of diamonds. His bones were fleshed when they touched the air. He pulled himself out of the lake through the hole he'd opened. Severely disoriented, he turned in circles, looking for the shortest way to shore, but fog obscured his view. His flesh felt wet, but he wasn't cold. In fact, it seemed balmy. He turned and faced what he hoped was west and started walking. He hadn't taken three strides when he stepped over the edge of a cliff.

Volta had just finished decoding a long message from Jean Bluer when he heard Daniel scream. He stood on the backporch in the early morning light listening intently. When there were no further sounds from Daniel, Volta glanced at his watch. It was seven-thirty. At seven-fifty, another scream shredded the silence. Volta turned and went back inside, leaving Daniel's bewildered cry echoing away across Laurel Creek Hollow.

Daniel's terror was reflexive, powerful, total—"cellular," as Volta had called it. Daniel was irked at himself for being surprised. Volta had noted that the feelings of wetness and warmth were precursors to the drop.

On his second attempt, Daniel had no previews of coming attractions, no sense of wetness or warmth. He met himself on the surface of the mirror and immediately fell. Though startled, Daniel managed to form an image of himself falling. He could control the fall with the image, but his grip was shaky. The sound of the wind planing over the shed roof cracked his concentration.

He was focusing too slowly, caught in movement rather than anticipating it. He needed to leap to the moment of transformation, catch the fall as it started. But first he needed rest. He felt so confident he drank the rest of the water, then took an hour nap.

The third time was the charm. The instant he merged with his image on the mirror's surface, Daniel imagined himself falling with a concentration so powerful and precise that the terror never really began. He opened his eyes.

The mirror was empty. The quilt cushion was bare. Amazed, Daniel stood up and walked through the mirror, the wall, the laurel tree outside. He walked up the trail thinking, *How can I walk without a body? Without feet? Why don't I just sink into the ground or float off?* He wasn't troubled by the questions, just curious.

Volta was sitting on the porch, trying to read a bundle of letters fluttering in the strong easterly breeze. He seemed less interested in the messages than the shed.

Watch this, Daniel thought, even though he wasn't sure what he would do. Not that it mattered. He felt serene, powerful, invincibly wise. He began to dissolve in pure pleasure. He understood this was the danger Volta had warned him about, but he wanted to feel it forever, wanted to stay there, pouring into joy. He almost flirted too long. With immense concentration he imagined a mirror, then his image in the mirror, and, when their eyes met, himself.

Daniel's return was wrenching. As he staggered sideways on the lawn, right in front of Volta, he felt a searing pain, followed immediately by a rush of melancholic exhaustion. Confused, he looked up at Volta.

Volta's eyes glittered with delight. "Daniel," he called, rising from his chair, "you *did* it. Excellent. *Excellent!* Finally, someone to compare notes with. Come in, come in—you must be hungry."

Three: WATER

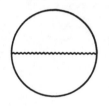

Sensitive Chaos.
—Novalis

*In its unbounded state, it's water's nature to seek
a spherical form. That's why rivers meander.*
—Schwenk

GURRY DEBRITTO STARTED WITH THE CIA WHEN HE was twelve years old. His father, a marine colonel, served as a CIA liaison officer. When they needed a young boy to pose as the son of a female agent, the colonel suggested Gurry.

Gurry trained all winter at Norfolk with Claudia Lord, the woman agent who would be posing as a bitter war widow and Department of Defense secretary with a child to raise and some information to sell. They were hoping to flush a Russian agent.

It went down in a Baltimore hotel. Claudia fumbled pulling her gun. She'd just flipped off the safety when the Russian shot her. He stepped up quickly as she slumped to the floor and shot her again to make sure. Then he turned the gun on Gurry and pulled the trigger, but Gurry was diving over Claudia's body and the bullet grazed his calf. Gurry picked up Claudia's gun and kept rolling as three more slugs tore chunks from the carpet. As the Russian bolted for the door, Gurry came up kneeling, the gun held steady with both hands. He shot the Russian in the neck. Hearing his father's war stories, he'd wondered what it would feel like to kill someone. Now he knew. It felt good.

With his father's blessings, the CIA put him on salary. His training was thorough, his teachers the best. At sixteen, he performed his first solo hit, a Dayton reporter about to reveal some bad news about cash movements in the Cayman Islands—not that Gurry cared why. But when he was twenty he did ask himself why he was killing people for a loutish bureaucracy he had come to despise for the monthly pittance of sixteen thousand dollars.

Gurry declared himself independent. The agency graciously gave him his leave, sending two men to kill him. When their bodies were found mummy-wrapped in scarlet ribbon at the bottom of a dumpster two blocks from the director's house, a truce was negotiated: Gurry would continue to take on special assignments for them at a reasonable wage, but could accept or reject assignments as he chose.

Gurry Debritto's career wasn't limited to assassination—he did security work and general demolition as well—but assassination, he often said, was "the biggest buck for the bang." His fees grew in direct proportion to the narrow legend he became. The most he'd received was twenty million dollars for poisoning Jack Ruby. The least was the twenty thousand for killing Annalee Pearse. That one still pissed him off. It wasn't his fault it was botched.

"We're drunk in a Motel 6 in Stockton, California. You didn't find Miss Rainbow Moonbeam Brigit Fifth Bardo or whatever the fuck her name is, but we know enough already, don't we? Other people at the party said she wandered back around dawn and announced—it was the sort of thing people remember—'I just went around the block to the Horsehead Nebula and sucked a boy's dick till his skull caved in.' That boy had to be Daniel, and we know he must have told her—bragging, probably—about Livermore. Or maybe she gave him drugs. Or found something in the house. Or convinced him it was wrong and he should call the cops. But maybe he called Volta. Annalee said they'd been given a number to call if they saw us. But we don't need all the pieces to solve the puzzle. We can *feel* the truth. We can *feel* Daniel's fear and hatred, and Volta's cold, neutral touch. You were right to advise our independent investigation, right to sense their dissembling. Volta is brilliant. To suggest—after coaching Daniel—that it wasn't an accident. The best lie is always the truth. He's worthy of us."

Shamus Malloy was talking to his horribly burned hand. He always took the white glove off now as soon as they were alone. He had the thumb tucked under his index and middle finger, making an opening like a mouth. Above it, on the knuckle joining the index finger to the hand, stray splatters of molten silver had left pocked scar-tissue that resembled two blank eyes. Shamus looked into them. "You have to help me. What should we do now? What should we do about Daniel and Volta?"

His hand said, "Destroy them."

Transcription:
Denis Joyner, AMO Mobile Radio

Time to ID down to a bottom line: you got the DJ, the Direct Jolt, wired to fire some juice in your ear, and if you got the DJ, you know you have KUSH fuckin' rollin' ray-dee-ooo, natural as a six and five, and where you are is where it's at, and who I am's a mystery to me too.

Let's run that bunny down to an illogical conclusion. I mean, *come on* people! Why are you covering me up with this deluge of cards and letters asking, 'Hey, who are you, and what's going down, and is this for real, and wow, who pays for your folly and where can I get me some?' Asking, 'What does DJ *really* stand for?' Asking, 'What does it all mean?'

My marketing consultants must be taking drugs. They must think demographics are some kind of visual aid. *Who* am I? Hey, *who* are you? And who are we if we're turning the table together? Why is it wise to question all answers and stupid to answer all questions? Face it: Sometimes you have to beg for an answer. I mean get right down on your bony little knees and beg your heart dry.

But friends and countrymen of the roaring night, you don't have to beg me. Answers I don't know are my specialty. So, let me take your questions from the top:

My real name is Doe John. I was born of gypsy spawn and motion is my home. I am the Voice of the Blur and the Breath of Song. Hang on, honey—I got the pedal to the metal and I won't be long.

Everything is going down, unless it's rising or signed a short-term contract with equilibrium.

It's for real and for sure. A true fucking story, friend. You can bet it with both hands.

When you lose the bet, AMO shoots some vig my way, keeping me on the air like some alternative PBS for the sorely bored and seriously demented. In the long run, I come out of your pocket when you're asleep at night and tell you all the good ways to be bad.

DJ stands for disc jockey, as in I'm riding the wheel just like you and I guess we'll just have to see for ourselves where it stops. If it does. If it's moving to start with. Because if wishes were wings we'd all be risen, and if cream was butter we wouldn't have to churn.

Don't mean shit.

Churn on that.

And next time send me some tough ones.

This has been the Devout Jester whispering sweet nothings in your ear.

Three days after Daniel's first disappearance, he came in for breakfast, sat down, squared his shoulders, shut his eyes, and instantly vanished.

Volta, who'd been chopping tomatoes for salsa to accompany his re-nowned *huevos rancheros,* laid the knife on the cutting board and applauded, murmuring, "Bravo." Then he went back to chopping.

He was aware of Daniel's presence but tried mightily to ignore him. He was glad to get rid of him, if only for a few minutes. From the moment Daniel had reappeared and stumbled toward the porch, he'd showered Volta with questions. The only one Volta could answer with certainty had been the first.

"What did you put the poison in, the wheatcakes or the ham?"

"Daniel! I take pride in my wheatcakes, and I would never insult Tick Hathaway's ham."

"Where?"

Volta couldn't tell if Daniel was demanding or pleading. "I injected it in the apple in your portion of the fruit salad. I was in a Christian mood."

"*What?* Christian?"

"The Tree of Knowledge. Forbidden fruit. Temptation and the Fall and all of that. Some tastes of the forbidden are rapturous; some make you sick."

"What's sick," Daniel gasped, "is dosing somebody. And what's really sick is mixing speed with it."

"I've offered the apology of necessity. I can only repeat it. And please—it wasn't *poison.* It was a virus that took Charmaine weeks of intense work."

"She hates me," Daniel said.

Volta noted with surprise the disconsolate edge in his tone. "No, she doesn't. She highly recommends you, as a matter of fact; and as you undoubt-edly noticed, she is extremely aware and uncommonly insightful."

Daniel doggedly shook his head.

After that first question, Volta had no certain answers. This uncertainty seemed to provoke Daniel into fusillades of more questions, as if answers simply awaited the right inquiry.

"Why do your clothes vanish with you? And your fillings? Why don't they just fall on the floor?"

"I don't know," Volta patiently replied, a reply he would often repeat. "I can only tell you, based on my own limited experience, that anything in intimate connection with your force-field for longer than thirty to forty hours will disappear with you and reappear when you do—depending on its own strength of field and its harmony with your own."

"What do you mean exactly by this *force field?* Your body?"

"Daniel, I can only speculate. I think of it as the sum of vitality—flesh, soul, psyche, or anything else you consider a constituent of being."

"Wait a minute now. Let's take a practical example. Say my pocketknife disappears with me and I walk outside and set it on a rock and then go back inside and reappear, the knife would still be in my pocket?"

"No, not in my experience. It would reappear on the rock, right where you left it."

"Why? It wouldn't be in my force field anymore."

"I don't know. Perhaps there's some principle of dimensional or field exclusivity. Or as Smiling Jack is fond of saying, 'You can't be in two places at once if you're not anywhere at all.'"

"Wait a minute. How can you see? You don't have eyes. How can you hear when your ears have vanished? It just doesn't make sense."

"That's because it's impossible, Daniel. If the impossible made sense, it wouldn't be impossible. I assure you I made long and serious inquiries— discreetly, of course—from physicists to shamans. The only conclusion among those few who would even *entertain* the notion was that sensory integrity is not limited to somatic existence. Think of it this way: You briefly turn into your ghost."

"I don't believe in ghosts."

"Don't tell me. Tell your ghost."

"All right, all right. So what you're saying is that the physical self turns into spirit."

"I don't know. What I'm suggesting, if anything, is that we're born to be amazed."

"But I wonder . . ." and Daniel would ricochet off on another line of questions.

To spare himself, Volta added another four hours of solitary meditation to Daniel's daily post-graduate regimen. It didn't matter. There were still as many questions; Daniel just asked them faster.

"Why did you experience the ecstasy as contraction while I felt it as expansion?"

"I don't know. Perhaps we were experiencing different things, or the same things differently."

"And that's why I didn't go through that still, empty, stop-time sensation you did when you vanished?"

"So I assume, yes."

"But some things we experienced were the same. Why some in common, some unique?"

"I don't know. To make it more interesting?"

But the interrogative reversal didn't work. Daniel ignored the question and bored on with his own until Volta said pointedly, "Daniel, ask yourself. You know as much about it as I do, and I have no doubts that soon you will surpass my meager understanding."

Volta wiped the cutting board. Daniel had been vanished far longer than his program prescribed. Volta resisted an impulse to check the clock. Daniel was beyond him. He must have simply imagined a mirror, making a leap that Volta had never considered. That didn't surprise him, for he'd felt from the beginning that Daniel wanted to dance on the threshold. Thus far Daniel had displayed discipline and respect, but his passion to understand what was essentially a mystery could easily fuse into obsession, and that worried Volta. As he cracked eggs, he decided to relinquish his position on the Star. He was weary of constant decisions, weary of questions he couldn't answer or had already answered too many times. If they stole the Diamond, he would have found what he'd sought. Then he could spend his remaining years watching the wind blow, visiting friends, tending the garden, savoring a cup of afternoon tea, standing in the Diamond's center.

Volta glanced at the clock. Serenity would have to wait. Daniel had vanished fifteen minutes ago, clearly ignoring Volta's suggestion that he limit disappearances to under ten minutes. He tried to sense Daniel's presence in the room. He felt, but only faintly, that Daniel was still at the table. Just as Volta was about to abandon nonchalance and yell at Daniel to return, Daniel reappeared, still seated at the table. He showed no evidence of disorientation. His smile was almost indecent with triumph.

"Forgive the theatrics," Daniel said. "I've been around you too long."

"Indeed," Volta said, his throat tight. He could feel his anxiety collapse through relief into anger. Anger was pointless.

"Not bad for a beginner, wouldn't you say?" When Volta said nothing, Daniel added, "It's all in the imagination, and a million mirrors."

Volta walked over to Daniel. "No it's not," he said evenly. Before Daniel could react, Volta slapped him hard across the face. "It's a dance, and you better watch your step or you'll fall through one of those mirrors and keep on going."

Daniel touched his numb cheek and lifted his eyes to Volta's. "Fuck you," he said.

Volta swung but his open hand never touched flesh. Daniel had vanished.

Swiftly but without apparent urgency, Volta moved to the center of the kitchen. He rolled up the sleeves on his faded denim shirt and waited, trying to sense Daniel's whereabouts. Before he could bring his concentration to the necessary point, Daniel appeared behind him, locking his hands behind Volta's neck and pushing his head forward and down, virtually immobilizing him with a full nelson. Applying just a bit of pressure for emphasis, Daniel grunted, "Well my, my—*imagine* that. I mean, who would have even *imagined* the *possibility,* or ever *imagined* it would come to this? Do you *imagine* I'll accept your apology?"

Volta started laughing. Daniel increased the pressure but then he began laughing too and eased off slightly. The instant the pressure relaxed, Volta shot his arms straight up as he pushed backward, neatly slipping the hold and knocking Daniel off balance. Before Daniel could react, Volta produced a deck of cards and tossed them fluttering at Daniel's face, who instinctively raised his arms to protect his eyes.

"Dharma combat!" Volta shouted joyously. "Real magic!" He tickled Daniel along his exposed ribs.

Daniel brought his elbows down to pin Volta's hands, simultaneously shifting into position for a Tao Do Chaung shin-kick. Volta escaped him and tossed a fine gray gritty powder in Daniel's face that instantly blinded him and set his sinuses ablaze. Pawing at his face, Daniel staggered helplessly while Volta followed close behind, almost yelling, "It's really all in the imagination? Come on, is that for *real?*" He timed his words between Daniel's vicious sneezes, but found little pleasure in Daniel's discomfort. He put his hand on Daniel's shoulder and guided him to the sink.

"You win, Daniel." He pushed Daniel's head down tenderly and turned on the cold water so Daniel could rinse his eyes.

Daniel burbled, "Jealous."

"Wrong," Volta said softly, but with such conviction that Daniel shut up and gave himself to the soothing water.

Volta patted him on the back. "I don't want you pouting about this. I applaud your abilities, but I won't be taunted or demeaned. We have important work to do together. Obviously, and to your credit, you've surpassed my abilities at vanishing, have done in a week what took me years. I readily admit you may well have a genius for it. However, I am responsible for sharing the secret, and I wouldn't have assumed that responsibility if I hadn't thought you would grant me some rights in the matter, some control, some respect."

He quit patting Daniel's back, and leaned down to whisper in his wet ear, "I can feel your hunger, Daniel. I can feel how you want to lose yourself. I felt it too. Expanding, contracting—it makes no difference. Vanishing is not the way out. There is *no way out,* Daniel, no final, astonishing escape. That's the cold, magical fact."

Daniel nodded almost imperceptibly.

"Good," Volta said. He paused a moment, his hand still on Daniel's shoulder. "And don't ask me any more questions today. Practice your right to remain silent. If the theft fails, you may need it."

Over the *huevos rancheros,* Volta briefed Daniel as usual on the previous night's radio transmissions regarding the Diamond.

"Last night's only news was that we can expect some real news this morning. We know the Diamond is in New Mexico, probably the White Sands Proving Grounds—or that's my guess."

"No progress," Daniel translated.

"If I'm reading correctly between the lines, it means someone's gotten in close. Probably Jean or Ellison Deeds. I don't think you've met Ellison, but he's as accomplished as Jean in his own right. Patience is crucial, Daniel. You've been with us long enough to know how highly we value quality information. Lacking guns and numbers, intelligence is our most important weapon. And as I'm sure you appreciate, the closer one gets to the source, the more reliable the information. If you don't appreciate it, you should—your life may depend on it."

"I didn't say no progress was unsatisfactory," Daniel said primly, a tone at odds with his damp hair and red eyes, which gave him the look of a half-drowned gargoyle at the end of a bad drug binge.

Volta nodded, pleased that Daniel, if a little testy, seemed willing to regard their recent clash as a mode of clarification. "We're just at one of those plateaus," Volta said. "After all, we've learned about where it is, though not exactly—White Sands is a large installation. But the exact location and the security arrangements will likely come as a single breakthrough, so it could all coalesce very quickly."

"You said White Sands was a military testing ground for bombs and other weapons, right?"

"Correct."

"You think they're going to nuke it?"

"Who knows? A national government is bad enough, but this administration is the largest collection of scoundrels and morons in recent memory, perhaps ever. I wouldn't even guess what they might do. However, I'm not convinced they could destroy it, even with a nuclear device."

"You still think it's the diamond you saw in your vision."

"I hope so," Volta said, noting Daniel had replaced bald questions with tentative assertions.

"Well, *you* want to see it for your own purposes. It would seem you're being greedy too."

Volta smiled. "Of course I'm being greedy, but my greed is pure: I want to see it, not possess it. I think it's not real greed if you don't think anyone should have it, including yourself."

"You should run for president," Daniel said.

"I'm already a president of sorts, and serving the Star seems to have exhausted my ambition as well as my strength."

"That still leaves you your wisdom and charm," Daniel smiled thinly, lifting a salsa-drenched forkful of the *huevos rancheros* in salute.

"Plus, I can cook," Volta said.

And precisely at that moment a solo harmonica began the opening strains of "Amazing Grace."

Daniel slowly lowered the fork to his plate. "How did you do that?"

"I didn't. Coincidence did. It's a signal that an EU transmission—Essential and Urgent—will follow in fifteen minutes. Why don't you let the dishes wait and come down to the barn with me. You haven't seen the communications center yet, and this is probably the information we've been waiting on."

As a monotone voice recited numbers and letters in clusters of three—"A-O-seven—Niner-Double L—Z-one-four"—Volta wrote them down. Daniel noticed Volta was taping the message, or at least had the *record* button pushed down on a tape deck jacked into the radio. "B-eight-N—G-O-Niner—I-two-Zero . . ." The code fascinated Daniel. It sounded like Bingo on mescaline.

As the voice settled into a drone, Daniel glanced around the barn, nearly half of which was a communication center—phones, CBs, shortwave radios, tape decks, two computer stations, a row of locked filing cabinets, and a long worktable. A huge bank of solar-charged nickel-cadmium batteries lined the far wall.

The transmission abruptly ended and Volta sent a brief response, also in code. When he clicked off the shortwave, the tape deck stopped.

"That must be a secret channel," Daniel said, avoiding a direct question.

"No," Volta said, "we use legal frequencies: 21.000 to 26.450 Megahertz in the daytime, 7.000 to 7.300 at night. The CIA has computerized scanners that monitor unauthorized frequencies. If it picks up an illegal signal, it can easily triangulate the point of origin."

"But if it's on a legal frequency, anyone can listen."

Volta shrugged. "Let them. All they'll hear is the code, and code is fairly common on the air—smugglers, amateur cryptographers, paramilitary groups. We use what's known as a shift-cipher code, which means it shifts from one code set to another—we use nine—at intervals that can also be changed. It's extremely difficult to crack it by frequency-of-occurrence methods. We use one set of nine for a year, and to our knowledge we've never been cracked or compromised. And besides, the band we use has over a thousand frequencies available. So first someone would have to find it, monitor it continuously, and then break the code. And they still might not understand the message. Here, let me show you."

Daniel watched as Volta transcribed: OBJAY THIRTY K CARROT C CRUSH ZROW GLO DFORM U HIRNOW XTR CBR 1BLT T GO CECIL.

"I don't get it all, but I think I caught the important part."

Volta read it aloud, explaining the shorthand: "The object is a thirty-thousand-carat diamond—'C Crush' being crushed carbon—a zero being round or, in our case, a sphere. This one glows. However, DFORM is our standard phrase for 'the defense is formidable,' so I should go there and confer—'you here and now.' XTR is again standard, meaning further information—usually nothing more than where to meet—is available through the CBR station, which it might please you to know is the *City of Baton Rouge.* And that's basically it."

"What about the 'One BLT to go Cecil.'"

"That's Smiling Jack's signature. In the unlikely case the code gets broken, a signature phrase makes it far more difficult for the codebreaker to transmit disinformation back to us. Everybody has a signature phrase; the names are nulls, dummies. So a transmission with a name but no signature phrase indicates the code has been compromised in some way. Even so, it probably would have been judicious to switch to a new set for this project. We've been using this set almost eleven months. I just hate to make the change at a critical juncture, since it takes a while to get fluent in the new set."

"I don't understand you," Daniel said. "You just got it confirmed that it *is* a large spherical diamond that glows—exactly like your vision. Right on the money. You should be pleased, or grateful, or at least vaguely happy."

"I am," Volta said. "I'm also worried."

"Why?"

"Because when I'm not having visions confirmed, I have to make decisions, the right ones I hope. And when you have to be hopeful, you should be worried."

"What do you have to decide right now that couldn't wait on a few minutes of satisfaction?"

"Whether to leave you here to practice by yourself or take you to New Mexico for the meeting."

"Take me. I can practice anywhere."

"At this point, only one other person knows you'll be involved—that's Smiling Jack. If you attend the meeting, six more will know."

"But they're trustworthy, right?"

"Daniel, it's not a question of the knowledge being safe with them, but of them being safe with the knowledge." Volta paused, then added more forcefully, "You *do* understand the Feds are going to want it back?"

"I haven't been dwelling on it."

"You stay," Volta decided. "I'll be taking the truck, so you'll be without a vehicle. Unless, of course, you can imagine one. Now, if you'd do me the favor of cleaning up the kitchen, I'll send some routing messages and gather my gear."

Daniel was rinsing out the sink when Volta called him into the living room. He was standing near the door, looking at himself in the oak-framed mirror under the cuckoo clock. A Bulgarian anarchist had given Volta the clock for helping him during an illegal stay in the U.S. It kept excellent time, but the cuckoo appeared randomly.

Daniel thought Volta was referring to the cuckoo clock when he said, "I should have warned you about this earlier." But he took the mirror down, tapped the exposed nailhead as if it were a telegraph key, then pulled outward and up, lifting a veneered panel out of the wall. The panel was about half the size of the mirror that had concealed it. There was a narrow vault behind the panel.

Daniel had never seen a safe so skinny, six inches wide and two feet high. Nor did it appear to have a lock. "What's the point of a safe without a lock," he said.

"The lock's inside."

"Well, that's certainly a provocative approach to security."

Volta opened the safe door and removed a small black cubical box with a short aerial mounted on one side.

Volta held it up for Daniel's inspection. "The lock. A radio-controlled nerve-gas canister. You noticed my tapping the nail. I was sending a coded radio sequence to deactivate it; otherwise it fires automatically when the door is opened. Solar trigger. Fires at the faintest hint of light. The gas isn't lethal, but it's instantly incapacitating and makes your recent bout with the flu seem like a Tahitian cruise in comparison."

"*Another* of Aunt Charmaine's concoctions from the concrete bunker?" Daniel said with distaste.

Ah ha, Volta thought, *Charmaine's really got a hook in Daniel.* He wasn't surprised. Charmaine could make you feel like she knew you better than you would ever know yourself, a feeling that simultaneously attracted and repelled. Nodding as much to himself as to Daniel's question, Volta said, "Yes, Charmaine. But I trust you appreciate that Charmaine's genius for synergistic associations extends beyond mere potions."

"But probably also includes that powder you threw in my face this morning."

"No, I'll take credit for that. It's the inner bark of a species of Peruvian pepperbush that is dried to parchment, then finely ground."

"Where did that and the cards come from anyway? I saw you roll up your sleeves."

"I'm a magician, Daniel, remember? When a magician rolls up his sleeves, it should arouse your suspicions, not lull them."

"I'll watch that," Daniel said.

"Do." Volta removed three flat black plastic boxes from a stack inside the safe.

Daniel said lightheartedly, "You don't trust me alone with the family jewels?"

"Actually, two boxes are the family crystals—we use them to modify our CBs. The other is a taped transmission to Ellison from a group in Canada."

"What sort of transmission?"

"Confidential."

"To me, but not Ellison."

"You weren't included in the confidence."

"I see."

Volta closed the safe door and turned to Daniel. "I honor confidences. Sometimes it seems silly, given the information. Sometimes it's literally torture—not physically, or not yet anyway, but heart and soul. But we can't live without secrets and the trust that bears them. You've asked that your ability to vanish be held in confidence. It will be. Our Canadian friends requested their information be kept confidential. It will be. How could you possibly expect me to keep your confidence if I betray theirs?"

"I didn't, not really. Ever since I've been vanishing, I seem to want to know everything that's going on, and act against what's expected. In a weird way it's made me sort of playfully impulsive."

"I thought that might be what was going on," Volta said. "But you're fortunate. Your reactions—curiosity, perversity, and goofiness—are much sweeter than mine, which were fits of morbidity and crushing doubt."

"Another difference."

"Yes. You're innocent, and I'm experienced."

"This morning we were equals."

"And so we are. And so are innocence and experience. As are space and time. But as much as I enjoy our little metaphysical chats, I must go explore possibilities for practical application in circumstances we do not control."

"And I stay here, working to improve our control and the possibilities for imaginative application. Any instructions?"

Volta said, "Walk down to the river and back every morning."

Daniel waited for a moment before asking, "That's it?"

"Yes. Beyond that, proceed as you deem wise or as you damn well please or any combination thereof. You take responsibility now. It's yours to do or fail. Just don't mistake your abilities for the truth. Don't worry about the transmissions coming in; they'll be shuttled. I'll be back within a week. Don't run amok. Don't delude yourself. We need you."

Volta drove slowly down the mountain. Red Freddie, flying in from Big Sur, wouldn't arrive at the airstrip till dark. Volta had left early to get away from

Daniel and radios and his own weariness. He planned to wait down by the river at the airstrip. Just sit in the sunlight and watch it flow. The summons to New Mexico meant everything was going to start moving fast. He didn't think Daniel was ready and he wasn't sure he was either. He hoped the daily trek to the North Fork and back would slow Daniel down. Daniel was too enthralled with the power of vanishing. Certainly Daniel seemed to have the gift for it, if not always the necessary understanding. That was the trouble with youth: power without point. And Daniel still didn't trust him. Volta smiled behind the wheel. Daniel would trust him even less if he knew that nerve-gas canister was actually one of Mott's polyresin sculptures from his True Cubism period, a birthday present from ten years ago. But that was the good thing about youth: it was gullible.

It was a steep two-hour scramble down to the North Fork and a tough four-hour pull back up. Daniel had expected to see the river gliding smooth and bright along a wide plain; instead, high with the late winter runoff, it was brawling through a narrow, boulder-strewn gorge. The roar of the coffee-colored water was so loud he didn't hear the bear crashing through the thin screen of stunted willows toward him. Fortunately, he saw it. He threw a piece of handy driftwood at the bear, and in the same moment vanished. He moved behind the willows, reappeared, and watched. The bear was standing motionless, peering at the stick Daniel had thrown, occasionally wriggling his nose along its length. He touched it with a paw. When it didn't leap at him, he picked it up in his jaws. Daniel was astonished when the bear shambled down to the river's edge and almost delicately released the stick into the swift current.

Going to the river each morning was Daniel's favorite part of the program he developed for himself. Food was a close second. The fresh air and exercise, coupled with a full recovery from Charmaine's flu, unleashed a tremendous hunger. He ate a huge pre-dawn breakfast before he left for the river. When he returned at noon, it took at least two hours to prepare and demolish lunch. From two to five he read from Volta's small but excellent library, followed by three hours of dinner. That left eight to nine for vanishing practice. He wasn't sure if it was perversity or respect, but he followed Volta's program, vanishing once a day for an additional minute each time. He did this with an ease that quickly became boring. Though Volta hadn't seemed overly impressed, Daniel felt he'd found the secret—imagining himself invisible by recreating his state of mind, bypassing the mirror, the fall, the fear, leaping the wall instead of drilling through it. If he didn't have to fight his way through, the energy saved could be used to sustain his stay in invisibility. Daniel was confident he could vanish for an hour easily. The twenty minutes he'd done to impress Volta hadn't even strained him.

Jump out.

Jump back.

Simple.

Returning from his seventh trip to the river, wondering how much longer Volta would be gone, Daniel spotted a huge deer browsing in a clearing across the draw. It was the biggest deer he'd ever seen. His intuition told him it was a buck, but he couldn't see any horns. It moved like a buck. Chagrined, he remembered it was late March and the antlers shed in mid-winter would have barely started growing back. He decided to take a closer look. The draw between them was choked with brush, but was no obstacle to those with powers. Daniel vanished, and instead of walking through it, walked it through him.

Daniel's odor evidently vanished with him since the deer continued feeding, apparently oblivious, as he approached. Daniel noted the swollen, velvety knobs where the new antlers were forming and congratulated his intuition. He thought, *If nothing else, this invisibility gets you in close, lets you see the world without the influence of your presence.* Yet the closeness was wrong somehow—a voyeur's intimacy, hollow because it wasn't reciprocated, sterile because it lacked permission.

Daniel spread his arms out wide and reappeared, announcing cheerfully, *"Good* morning, fellow creature!"

The deer replied by leaping twenty feet straight up, executing a ninety-degree turn in the air. It was already running before it landed. A rear hoof nailed Daniel squarely in the center of his forehead, dropping him to his knees. Hands covering his face, fingertips pressed to the wound as if to hold back the pain, he listened to the buck crash loudly downhill through the brush.

Daniel was examining his forehead in the living room mirror when Volta walked in. Daniel jumped as high as the deer.

"Pardon me," Volta said, "I didn't know you were back."

"Me either," Daniel yammered. "That you were."

Volta narrowed his gaze. "What happened?"

"I hit my head."

Volta stepped closer, took Daniel's head firmly in his hands, and tilted it toward the light. "It looks like you were hit with a cloven hoof."

Daniel twisted his head free and stepped back out of reach.

Volta shot his right arm out, pointing a trembling finger inches from the wound. He bellowed, "You bear the mark of Satan! I leave you for *one week* and you're claimed among his hellish clan, flesh for his flames, fuel for his sick desires!"

"All right, goddammit," Daniel snapped, "a deer kicked me in the head."
He waited, expecting Volta's laughter.

Instead, Volta said wearily, "Well, are you all right?"

"Yeah, fine," Daniel grunted. He looked at Volta more closely. His eyes
were raw and glazed with exhaustion, his face haggard. "I'm fine," Daniel
repeated, "but you don't look so good."

"I shouldn't. It's been seven long days of nervous waiting for bad
news. I'll give you the grim details after dinner, and we'll consider possible
approaches."

"Is it really that grim?"

"Look at it this way, Daniel: *you* are the only break we're getting."

Daniel wasn't sure what that was supposed to reveal. He was still considering when Volta said, "How's the deer's hoof?"

"It bounded away nicely, thank you."

"That deer must have been truly startled—as if you appeared right in front
of him, out of nowhere."

Daniel wanted to discuss more successful applications of invisibility.
"Vanishing saved me from a bear."

"I wasn't being critical, Daniel. I'm glad to see it wasn't all work and no
play in my absence."

"Other than the bear—which was necessity—and the deer—which was
convenience and curiosity—I stuck exactly to your program."

"Thank you. Was that out of perversity or respect?"

"I'm not sure. Probably some of each."

"I appreciate your candor. I would also appreciate it if you would cook
dinner this evening and not disturb me till it's ready. I've been up thirty hours
and have spent the last three on the radio making thousands of tiny, inter-
linked decisions, some of which may prove crucial to our success. It has lately
been forced on my reluctant attention that I'm getting old. No complaints—I
am ready to be old—but I can no longer go two days without sleep. I'm tired,
Daniel. I'm going to bed."

"Dinner around six?" Daniel said.

Volta nodded in gratitude. "Bless you."

While he was mashing potatoes, Daniel thought of a foolproof way to
steal the Diamond. He could hardly wait to cheer up Volta. But when Daniel
announced at dinner that he'd thought of a way to steal the Diamond, Volta
brusquely said, "It can wait. Let's devote our dinner conversation to a subject
appropriate to the season, the erotic unfurling of Spring. Let's talk about blow
jobs."

Daniel nearly dropped his fork. "What?"

"Blow jobs. Cock-sucking. Fellatio. Let's talk in particular about two blow jobs: the one you received the night before your mother died and one I was forced to witness while in jail."

Daniel said, stunned, "You sent that girl, didn't you?"

"Daniel, think. I absolutely lack the imagination or style to garner information through sexual duplicity, sweet though it might have been. I'm convinced you didn't tell this Miss Bardo anything that might have compromised the plutonium theft or jeopardized your mother, otherwise you wouldn't have told me that you thought your mother's death wasn't accidental. But that doesn't mean Miss Bardo couldn't have found something—a note, a diary— or, acting as an agent for others, placed a bug in the house, or planted an electronic locator in a pocket of your lowered pants."

Daniel was shaking his head. "How do you know she was there if you didn't send her?"

"I didn't until you just confirmed it. Shamus talked to a McKinley Street neighbor of yours who had hosted the party from which your young lady-friend wandered. The same young lady who announced, upon returning, that she'd just 'come back from the Horsehead Nebula down the street' where she'd 'sucked a young boy's dick till his brain tore loose,' or words to that effect."

"How did you find out?"

"Dolly Varden. Shamus called to use her as a go-between again."

"Between who?"

"I'm not sure. I think he just wants you to know he knows, see how you respond."

"So he thinks I told Brigit, or that she was an agent. An agent for who?"

"I have no idea how he's thinking, Daniel. Dolly says he's gone insane— not obviously, but she has an unerring sense for madness. He's evidently been drinking hard for the past year, and the whiskey, grief, and guilt have dragged him over the edge. It wouldn't surprise me if he thinks *I'm* somehow implicated, having brought you into AMO and favored you as a student, or for any number of demented reasons."

"I have no response," Daniel said, "except to say I didn't tell her anything. We hardly talked. She was stoned. Really stoned. And if she was an agent, she wouldn't have gone back to the party and announced it."

"I think that's a fair and measured reply for the circumstances. You can talk to Dolly directly if you want, or I can just radio your answer."

"Go ahead. I have other things to concentrate on."

"Indeed. The second blow job, for instance." And Volta proceeded to recount the sergeant's savage humiliation of the young boy, and how he'd been tempted to vanish and intervene, and why he hadn't, and then seeing the Diamond in the mirror.

Daniel listened, sickened, slowly coming to understand the Diamond's importance to Volta. "I think I get it," he said when Volta concluded. "If the Diamond is like the one you saw in the mirror, then it in some way confirms your decision not to vanish and try to stop it?"

"Or rewards it. But something like that, yes."

"I think I would have tried to stop it. I'm not judging *you,* though, or no more than I'm judging myself."

"Of course you are. Not that you can. I was at a point with vanishing—a point you haven't reached, and perhaps won't—where I felt certain that if I disappeared even once more, I would not come back. Which meant I could have only borne invisible witness to that boy's degradation, just as helpless as I was locked in my cell. If and when you come to that point yourself, see how you judge me then."

"I don't believe it," Daniel said. "You sound defensive."

"Perhaps you've mistaken it for my annoyance at your glib judgments."

"Nope, I know *that* tone well. And really, I wasn't criticizing your decision so much as . . ." Daniel let the thought trail off, having realized Volta's defensive tone had nothing to do with the decision he'd made in the cell.

Volta cocked his head. "Yes?"

"The sergeant. Whatever happened to him?"

Volta nodded slightly and gave Daniel a weary smile. "I'm not sure if I should commend your insight or lament my transparency."

Daniel waited for an answer.

Volta pushed his plate back. "The sergeant crawled under his bed, put his service revolver in his mouth, and pulled the trigger. This was four years later."

"Why?" Daniel said.

"Because I poured terror on his guilt."

Daniel remembered Wild Bill's mention of Ravens. "How did you do it?"

"Slowly," Volta said. "It was almost a hundred days before he snapped, a hundred days believing that the kid's ghost had sent me to exact revenge, a hundred days of raw fear to convince him justice would not be denied."

"I wouldn't argue about the justice," Daniel said, "but it's still murder."

"I won't dispute your judgment—except to say AMO has been debating the fine moral points of the issue for centuries, and to no conclusion."

Daniel was shaking his head. "No, not the fine points, just the fact: You drove him to do it. I can understand that. But why torment him? That's different. That's cruel. Why not just walk up and shoot him? A hundred days . . . that's what I don't understand. I just can't believe you could do that."

"Could *you,* Daniel? Suppose your mother was set up, with cold premeditation, to be killed in that alley. What would *you* do?"

"Try to find out who did it."

"Assumed. And when you were certain who'd done it?"

"I don't know," Daniel sighed. "I really don't know."

"I didn't either," Volta said, "till I found out. Let me tell you what I learned. I didn't enjoy it. I'm not proud of it. I'm not ashamed. I never did it again. And I want you to know you're the only person I've ever told. It wasn't sanctioned by the Alliance; it was personal business. I obviously trust you'll honor it as a strict confidence."

Daniel said with a flash of anger, "Yes, sure, you know I will. But *why* are you telling me all this stuff about Shamus and the girl and that poor kid and killing the sergeant? *Now,* of all times? When I need to keep focused on the work?"

"Because you're the only other person who has vanished, and thus might be capable of understanding the particular nature of my decision and the state of mind in which it was made. And I'm telling you now because you're going to see the Diamond, and perhaps be forced to make some impossible decisions, and I want you to know you're not alone. Our ability to vanish changes nothing but our form. While it gives us a rare perspective, it offers no exemptions. It doesn't make us wise or powerful or compassionate. And what understanding and compassion we do earn from our efforts only makes some decisions more painful—though perhaps we suffer them more gladly."

"Then what's the point? A finer appreciation of inescapable suffering?"

"No. The point is life. Its facts and meanings and mysteries."

"Okay," Daniel said breezily, "tell me the facts of life."

"I can offer a condensed version of the first statement of principles in the *Emerald Tablet,* ascribed to Hermes Trismegistos, the protoalchemist. 'As below, so above. As above, so below. It is thus to accomplish the miracles of one thing.'"

"'Miracles of one thing?' Shouldn't that be 'miracle'?"

Volta looked at Daniel and shook his head. "I wish that deer had kicked you harder; I really do. Maybe seeing the Diamond will help. Perhaps we should abandon our metaphysical inquiries and turn our attention to the more mundane task of stealing it."

When the dishes were done, Volta spread a large map on the table. He used his pencil for a pointer. "As we now know, the Diamond is being kept at the White Sands Proving Ground. More exactly, right here, in the Tularosa Valley, roughly between the San Andres and Capitan Mountains in the old lands of the Mescalero Apache. The closest towns are Tularosa, Mescalero, High Rolls, and Bent. However, we have allies on the Mescalero reservation, so we'll use that area for staging the raid, with our field headquarters in El Paso. So far, no problem."

Volta replaced the map with an aerial photo of what appeared to be a volcano rising from a plain. Daniel interrupted: "It might save us time and explanation if you want to hear how I think I can steal the Diamond, whatever the defenses."

"I think it would be more efficient if I describe the security and you listen, judging its effects on your approach. You'll have to know it anyway. Tell me when your plan is compromised, if it is." He pointed at the volcanic cone. "This is Sunrise Mountain, a cinder cone as you no doubt see, and though it appears taller, its elevation is five hundred forty-five feet—which would hardly qualify as a knoll around here, but then we aren't surrounded by alkali flats." His pencil moved to a dark rectangular speck at the base of the mountain. "This is where the bad news begins. That speck you see is the entrance to a horizontal shaft that runs to the center of the mountain. It's approximately seven hundred yards long, with a five-degree declination from entrance to center. At the end of the shaft is a large vault. The Diamond is in the vault."

"What sort of lock?"

"We'll get to that. First, let's go down the shaft, which has four separate checkpoints, each manned by a marine machine-gun crew. The guns are in concrete bunkers built into the tunnel. The watch changes every six hours, but the old shift stays in place until the new one occupies its positions, so the changing of the guards, traditionally a vulnerable moment in all security arrangements, is well covered."

"I'm beginning to see what was meant by 'formidable defenses,' but none of that affects my plan."

"Keep looking." Volta slid a diagram of the shaft over the aerial photo. "There are four alarm systems in the tunnel, one at each checkpoint, each on an independent circuit, each monitored at Holloman Air Force Base twenty miles to the south, where, at any alarm, a squadron of F-15s and an entire company of marines in helicopter transports can be airborne within fifteen minutes—the jets perhaps sooner."

Daniel said, "I don't like that at all—not that it hurts my plan."

"Just on general principles then?"

"Right. Especially the principle that a mistake could really be punished."

Volta nodded. "Also, the airspace above Tularosa Valley is under routine radar surveillance from the air base, but only above five hundred feet, so a small plane or helicopter could come in under it, though again the margin for error is substantially narrowed.

"Back to the shaft for a moment. It has tracks for electric carts to carry people and supplies. There's been a lot of activity lately, technicians shuttling back and forth with equipment, and we're concerned our information may already be outdated. I'm sure you understand the difficulty of *close* scrutiny, since there's no concealed vantage point on the flats. So let me tell you for the *first* time now what you will hear from me a hundred times more: If you encounter *anything* that is different than expected, don't try to improvise. Retreat; report; and we'll revise the plan."

"Assuming mine wouldn't work. I still haven't heard anything that would prevent it."

"Well, we haven't got to the bad part yet: the vault. It was custom built for the CIA by Seabrook Security. It's a perfect cube, thirteen feet on a side, each wall composed of a two-foot slab of stainless steel."

"Great," Daniel said. "It'll give me more room to work in."

"There's more," Volta cautioned. "Each wall, except the door and the floor, is wired on the outside with an electrical sensor grid that can detect a pressure change of five hundred pounds per square inch and a temperature change of thirty degrees Centigrade. The door and floor are sensitive to changes inside the vault of *five* pounds p.s.i. and *ten* degrees Centigrade. Makes it difficult to blast or drill your way in. The grids are independently wired to each checkpoint, air base security, and a nearby CIA installation— and of course it's a doubled system, sounding when it is broached as well as when it's shut down by any other means than a coded sequence, which changes every day." Volta smiled at Daniel. "And how does your plan look now?"

"Fucked," Daniel said disgustedly.

"I'd have to infer you were planning to stay in the vault with the Diamond long enough that it would vanish with you."

"You got it. I figured I'd just walk into the vault and hang around for the thirty to forty hours you said it takes to capture an object in my force field, or whatever you call it. I guess you'd already considered that possibility."

"It crossed my mind, yes, but I rejected it even before I learned of the pressure-sensitive floor."

"Why?"

"You risk yourself too much. Suppose you were in the vault when they came—as they often do—to take the Diamond to the CIA lab nearby?"

"I'd vanish."

"And how long can you vanish for?"

"Well, you saw me do twenty minutes, and I think I could do more."

"What if they stayed an hour? You'd be forced to reappear."

"But," Daniel countered, "not necessarily in the vault. I could go right out through the mountain, reappear, wait till they were gone, and vanish back into the vault."

"You might be spotted outside, since there's virtually no cover. Besides, you'd have to break field congruence with the Diamond, forcing you to start over. It could be months before you had forty uninterrupted hours with the Diamond, and I assure you you'd be exhausted long before then. All assuming, of course, that forty hours would be sufficient to enmesh the Diamond in your force field. That forty-hour figure, as well as my purely speculative notions of intimate force fields and their powers, are based on my limited experience with ordinary objects. The Diamond, clearly, is *not* an ordinary object. You might well be taken into *its* field—a glowing six-pound spherical diamond likely exerts a considerable force.

"*Six pounds!*"

Volta raised his eyebrows. "Well, you can check my calculations, but thirty thousand carats at two hundred milligrams per carat is roughly six pounds, or about the size of a bowling ball."

Daniel said carefully, "This glowing—do you know the source?"

"None of our people has seen it, and the information they've been able to gather is extremely sketchy. All we know is that light emanates from the Diamond. Very few people have actually seen it so far, and I gather they're still having a difficult time believing it. Even the spooks are spooked. They seem to be divided into two equal factions. One faction thinks it's some weird KGB espionage ploy. The second faction of U.S. Intelligence, if you'll excuse the oxymoron, thinks the Diamond is from outer space, likely placed here as some monitoring device, though there's some sentiment that it's an artifact from a lost civilization, Atlantis being the leading candidate. In short, they know what the Diamond is made of, but they don't know what it is, what it means, or how it can be real.

"There've been some hard swallows and weak smiles in the intelligence hierarchy the last few weeks. Nobody is eager to assume responsibility. You know how bureaucracies function—their most compelling concerns are always 'Who else knows?' and 'How can we cover our asses?' Which right now works to our advantage, though we should act soon."

"How soon?"

Volta smiled. "I think the Hour of the Wolf on April Fools' Day would be both propitious and appropriate."

"Not to mention whimsical."

"Appropriate," Volta repeated firmly. "But you're entitled to your opinion, however misguided."

"I have to admit I don't know what the Hour of the Wolf is, though it sounds good."

"It comes from the late Paleolithic, the Great Spirit tradition. It's the hour before dawn, a time of particular magic for the hunter, a heightening of psychic powers. It's also the time when other creatures, whether asleep or tired from a night's feeding, are most vulnerable."

"I've sort of lost track of time here, but April first couldn't be much more than a week away."

"A week from tomorrow."

"But," Daniel said innocently, "we don't have a plan."

Volta feigned dismay. "Daniel, you couldn't possibly believe that *I*, the Great Volta, wouldn't have a plan? Plans are my specialty. My delight. I'll outline it. You listen for flaws.

"From the drop-off point—as yet unselected among four possibilities— you hike seven to nine miles, packing all necessary equipment, across the alkali flats to the base of Sunrise Mountain.

"You vanish and enter the shaft, moving directly down to the vault, reconnoitering as you go.

"Inside the vault, you reappear. As you do, you leap in the air and attach yourself to the ceiling. Remember, all the pressure/temperature alarm grids are on the *outside* of the vault, with the exception of the floor and door."

"I remember that," Daniel broke in, "but what I don't remember is how I attach myself to ceilings."

"A suction cup the size of a dinner plate will hold eight hundred twenty pounds."

Daniel wrinkled his nose. "You mean like a toilet plunger?"

"In form, but of superior design and materials. We have allies who can engineer the unusual on short notice. I brought it with me, in fact, so you would have ample opportunity to practice."

"Okay," Daniel said, "so I'm stuck to the ceiling with a suction cup."

"Actually, it's attached to a harness; you'll be in the harness."

"Like a spider dangling on a silken thread. I like that. So, what next?"

"You *gently* attach a charge of plastique to the *inside* of the locking mechanism—it's both combination and double-key—and set the timer, depending on this variable: the position and protection of the Diamond. If it doesn't seem adequately protected—I'll give you some guidelines later—you pick it up with another suction cup, this one double, molded back to back, and you attach it to a predetermined position on the ceiling, where, based on the calculations of our physicists, the blast will have the least chance of damaging it.

"When the Diamond is secured, you vanish again, go back into the tunnel outside the vault, reappear, don a protective mask, and shoot two small canisters of nerve gas *up* the tunnel. It should *deeply* reassure you that Charmaine considers the gas among her finest work. A single whiff almost instantly paralyzes the voluntary nervous system, immobilizing the victim. It is also odorless and disperses quickly and evenly. Moreover, it penetrates every known gas mask. Yours, of course, is fitted with neutralizing filters. One thing

I admire about Charmaine is her policy of never releasing a toxin until she develops a neutralizing agent. By the way, she calls this nerve gas Medusa Seven."

"That's nice," Daniel said. His tone was decidedly neutral.

"It will take about thirty seconds for the gas to incapacitate all guards. Immediately after you fire the gas, you disappear. The charge should detonate within four minutes, blowing the door. You step inside the vault, reappear, grab the Diamond, and run up the shaft and around to the west side of the mountain. There, Eddie LaRue will pick you up in his helicopter, fly you to a waiting car on a nearby county road, and you'll drive away to meet me in El Paso, where you and I alone will decide what to do with the Diamond. After examining it, of course."

Daniel said, "I have questions."

"You should."

"Why not knock out the guards *before* I go down the tunnel? That way if I come unsuctioned or drop the Diamond or something and set off an alarm, the guards are already incapacitated?"

"A number of reasons," Volta said. "First, if you find something awry and have to abandon the mission, we don't want it known that an attempt was made. Secondly, because of the tunnel's pitch and the fact that heat rises, there's a noticeable upward draft, which would substantially slow or possibly prevent the nerve gas from reaching the third or fourth checkpoints. This way, if you do set off any alarm, you can simply vanish and walk through the mountain to your pickup site."

Chastened that he'd missed those points, Daniel said less aggressively, "But the charge will set off the alarm regardless, right?"

"There is no way to remove the Diamond from the vault without opening the vault, and no way to open it without setting off the alarms—short of defeating the alarm system itself, which is virtually impossible. Though we may attempt it if all else fails."

"And when the alarm sounds, there'll be jet fighters and a horde of marines on our ass in fifteen minutes. You have to expect roadblocks."

"If the timing goes right, you have an excellent chance of getting away undetected. All they have is an alarm. They have to cover every direction, while you know exactly where you're going. Further, the truck will have a place to hide the Diamond, and you'll be provided an identity and an alibi. So will Eddie in the helicopter, who will be attached to an actual film crew, a second unit shooting sunrises for Axel Koch's newest epic, *Roper Man.*"

"Is this Eddie LaRue the Low-Riding Eddie I've met?"

"Yes. My apologies—I assumed you knew."

"Don't you have doubts about my abilities to deal with explosives after what happened to my mother? Maybe I'll break down, choke."

"The way to conquer fear is by facing it. I obviously have confidence in your courage or I wouldn't have introduced you to vanishing."

"But you did consider it?"

"Naturally."

"What about the fact that they'll know the vault was blown from inside?"

Volta smiled. "That's my favorite part, Daniel. All loss should be instructive. In this case, perhaps we'll help expand their rather narrow conception of reality."

Transcription:
Denis Joyner, AMO Mobile Radio

Hello, baby. I bet you were just twirling along, looking for a solution for these springtime, no-bang blues, and you got this paradoxical precipitate instead, the DJ himself, the ol' Dharma Jewel, and now you can't decide if I'm the Real Dazzling Item or just another Rhinestone Cowboy jacking his jaws to soothe the circling coyotes and keep the moon afloat on the dark waters of the human soul. All day you faced, the barren waste, without the taste, of water: cool—clear—water. Parched. Shrunk to the nut. Well, you've made it to the Last Mirage; welcome to the waterhole. Drink deep and sail on refreshed, real as the diamonds on your grandmother's wedding ring, real as the ineluctable weirdness that whips us all around the circle, real as a sun-ripened grape about to get pressed. I'll stay with you till I'm gone, 'cause you got mow-beel radio babbling in your ear, shaking it down to separate the gold from the dross, and you're finding it all right here on KRMA, just another station on the cross.

Shamus's scar-twisted hand was angry. The tucked-thumb jaw was almost a blur as it yelled in his ear, "Annalee told him, you idiot—he was her son, she loved and trusted him. She did everything but admit it that night in Richmond when she mentioned Daniel was beginning to suspect something. She'd already told him. If you hadn't been so love-blind you'd have known right then. But you can't blame her. She couldn't distinguish between love and trust. Daniel is the maggot in your heart. Daniel and Volta. Quit looking for this stoned girl who sucked him off. He's probably telling the truth when he says he didn't tell her anything, because he'd already told Volta the minute he'd found out what you were planning, and Volta, that jealous, jealous man,

224

arranged for it to go wrong; maybe even talked Daniel into going along to make it look good. Then Daniel almost got killed, so Volta, with his perverted sense of honor, took the lad under his wing. Daniel is the Judas, but Volta is the devil. It doesn't need *proof.* I can taste it, I can smell it, I can feel their darkness burning in my bones, hear their treachery in every word, see them through my scars. If you get Daniel, you'll get Volta. Do you hear me? Quit crying, goddammit! Do you hear me? Get them soon. Soon."

THE THERAPEUTIC JOURNALS OF JENNIFER RAINE:
MARCH 24

My name is Jennifer Raine, Judy Snow, Emily Dickinson, Amelia Empty, Wanda Zero, Clara Belle. I live in room 28, Apan Hospital, Valley of the Moon, California. Apan is a mental care facility. I am here under the care of Dr. Putney, who suggested I keep a journal since it's good to express your feelings. But actually, except for being bored shitless, I feel fine.

The court committed me because I have an imaginary daughter named Mia. Dr. Putney keeps referring to her as my invisible *daughter. Of course she's invisible: She's imaginary. But Doc Putney isn't too hot on the obvious. Except for the logically obvious, that is, like how can I be 23 and have a daughter who's 11, and why can Mia laugh and cry but not speak. Because, Doc, I imagined her the way I need her. Someone I can talk to without words. An ally. A witness.*

I try to make Dr. Putney understand that since I imagine her, since I am her mother, I have a responsibility to her. So when that Safeway clerk caught me stealing food for her, I was absolutely justified in destroying three aisles of bottles and cans allegedly containing food. I'm not crazy, Dr. Putney, I'm hurt and one reason I'm hurt is exactly because there is no food in the food stores. Too much telly, not enough vision. It's not crazy to know that. I am not crazy. I have scars to prove it. I'm hurt, that's all, and Mia is helping me heal.

The moonlight glittered on the alkali flats as the Hour of the Wolf approached. Daniel checked his watch and trudged on toward Sunrise Mountain. He felt anxious, giddy, ridiculous, and absurdly serene, as if such wildly mixed emotions were exactly what he should be feeling while on his way to steal a six-pound spherical diamond from his government, equipped with nerve gas, plastique, and a large suction cup, armed only with his wits and the ability to disappear.

Practice had been a snap. Volta had set up a stainless-steel plate nine feet off the ground with a pad to break his fall. But he'd stuck the suction cup to the target on his first attempt and hadn't missed in fifty subsequent tries. A rope between the brass ring on the back of his special harness-vest and the suction cup kept him from falling to the floor. At first he had trouble "controlling the dangle," as Volta said, but with a little practice, as Volta noted, he got the hang of it. Daniel found that by imagining himself as a spider swaying on its own silken thread, he didn't feel quite as stupid.

At Coach Volta's instructions, he'd practiced vanishing and reappearing at one-minute intervals. "Think of them as metaphysical windsprints," had been Volta's advice. They hadn't winded Daniel at all. He was sure he could vanish at fifteen-second intervals if he wanted and perhaps fast enough to strobe between the two states. He intended to explore the possibility after the attempt on the Diamond.

He'd also practiced his new identity, which he would inherit from Jean Bluer, who was now driving across Texas as Isaiah Kharome, freelance preacher and editor-publisher of *God Shots,* a religious magazine. Jean had sent a set of photos and a tape of the voice; the proper makeup and documents would be waiting in the getaway truck, which also served as the Reverend Kharome's Mobile Temple. When Daniel mentioned that such an outlandish guise didn't do much for his sense of seriousness, Volta said it wasn't supposed to.

Various objects had taken different amounts of time to mesh with Daniel's force field and vanish with him. The suction cup disappeared with him in less than twelve hours; the plastique had taken almost forty. Volta attributed the differences to field congruity, pointing out that Daniel's field welcomed suction and resisted—understandably—explosives. Daniel wasn't convinced, but had no explanation of his own—though again he intended to explore this after he'd stolen the Diamond.

But first he had to steal it. He looked at Sunrise Mountain looming in the moonlight, shifted the weight of his equipment-laden vest, lowered his head with a giggle that surprised him, and plunged onward.

Volta had just poured a modest shot of cognac to accompany his coffee when a call came in at 2:30 A.M. He answered immediately, "Allied Furnace Repair, night service."

"Mr. Deeds did not go to Washington. He's fresh from a Bent bar where he's had about fifteen drinks with an engineer from Closed Circle Security Systems, a Pennsylvania company doing some local consulting work."

It was Ellison Deeds. Volta sighed; it had to be bad news. "Changes?"

"Additions, evidently. That's all I could learn. The man could hold his liquor. He did talk a bit in general about his particular specialty, camera surveillance."

"I understand," Volta said softly. He paused a moment to consider, then added, "Well, our night man is out on call now. I'll let you know as soon as he gets back."

"I'll be at home," Ellison said.

Volta hung up the phone, leaned back in his swivel chair, thought a minute, then leaned forward and flipped on the radio. He sent the message in code. THINGS FALL APART. HAVE RIDE READY FOR EARLY DEPARTURE OR VERY LATE IN SCHEDULE. SEND IMMEDIATE WORD ON CONCLUSION. CHANGES POSSI-BLE. STAND BY.

When the transmission was acknowledged, Volta sipped his cognac and watched steam wisp from the coffee cup. He hoped Daniel had the sense to call it off if they'd added cameras.

Daniel vanished. He waited a moment for the clank of any equipment that hadn't gone with him, then started down the tunnel. The bunkered checkpoint was twenty feet from the opening. He was passing it when someone whispered, "Check."

Daniel stopped. Then, realizing it couldn't have been meant for him, he looked in the bunker. One of the guards was watching TV. The other two were bent over a board. Daniel stepped through the wall for a better look. Two guards, one thin and rangy, the other built like a stump, were playing chess. Stumpy, playing white, didn't have a prayer.

"Fuck it," Stumpy hissed, "my ass is grass. I tell ya, it's that damn pill they're making us take—fucks the shit out of my concentration."

"I took one, too," Rangy said. "All it is is atropine, and if you think *it* fucks up your concentration, someone lobs gas down here you'll find out fast what fucked concentration is all about."

"Hey man, no way any dude's gonna rain gas on us. I've been in the fucking Corps since 'Nam, and I'm telling you this is jacked-up, jerk-off duty. We don't even know what the fuck we're guarding. Whole duty, all we've seen is a little box go by once. Fucker's probably empty."

"Right," the thin one said disparagingly, "that's why the place is crawling with federal spooks. That's why Keyes, the Region Supe, has been here himself for three weeks. It's probably plutonium."

"That's wonderful fucking news," Stumpy muttered. "Lay a little radiation on the Agent Orange I got in 'Nam and throw in this anti–nerve gas atropo-fucking-feen or whatever the hell it is and my balls will probably drop off."

"Don't sweat it. From what I hear, Keyes knows his shit."

"Keyes is an asshole; asshole's 'sposed to know shit."

"Hey," the guard watching TV hissed at the other two, "this is a silent watch, remember."

"Eat my dick, Orvis," Stumpy said, but he quit talking.

Daniel felt something missing in the silence. It took him a moment to realize there was no sound from the TV, and less than that to see it was a monitoring screen displaying a static view of the vault. Neither cameras nor the atropine were expected. The mission was canceled.

Daniel doubted that the atropine was any defense against Aunt Charmaine's Medusa brew, but if he was wrong he was dead or in prison. And the camera cut at least five minutes on the getaway. He turned and started walking toward the tunnel mouth when he suddenly started laughing so hard he nearly lost his concentration and lurched back into visibility. Prison? How could they keep him in prison? How could they shoot him if he was invisible? If it fell apart he could always shoot a flare to warn Eddie off and use his invisibility to give him a big edge on pursuit. Volta was right, though—better to leave and try again. But he should look around for other security surprises. And see the Diamond. He turned and continued down the tunnel.

He reached the vault without incident. He spotted the camera quickly, but was so anxious to step into the vault that he almost missed the photoelectronic eyes. That's what he assumed they were until he examined them more closely. Perhaps they were lasers. No difference—either way it was some sort of grid. He quickly noted their positions. He'd been vanished twelve minutes already. He could feel the edges of his concentration beginning to erode.

He examined the vault door impatiently and then stepped through into a room of unimaginable light. Bars of gold stacked along each wall bathed in the steady, dense, incorruptibly clear light from the spiral flame, slender as a thread, burning through the Diamond's center. Daniel felt his concentration begin to dissolve, its force subsumed by the greater coherence of light. He grabbed the suction cup at his waist, desperately thrusting it upward as he leapt back into flesh. The suction held. Visible, he swayed above the Diamond, arms and legs reflexively outstretched to stabilize himself, like a man about to plummet down a well transfixed in midair. Dazed, he looked down into the the Diamond's center. The spiral flame had vanished but the light's unflickering clarity remained, neither terrifying nor serene, particle nor wave.

Daniel wanted to hold the Diamond. It was perched on a columnar pedestal in the center of the vault, just out of reach. He would have to vanish again and reposition himself. He didn't know if he could muster the concentration to vanish in its field or, if he could, whether he could sustain the focus necessary to reappear as he leapt and slap the suction cup back on the ceiling. But he didn't care. He had to touch it.

He closed his eyes but it was hopeless. He could not gather himself out of the light. Couldn't separate his center from the Diamond's. He kept his eyes shut and tried to imagine the Diamond in his hands. He could see the Diamond clearly in his mind, but not in his hands, not touching. He opened his eyes and looked into the center of the Diamond, surrendering his concentration, his will and desire. When he vanished, the Diamond vanished also, though its light remained constant. Daniel picked it up gently, slipped it into the velvet pouch he'd brought, and walked quickly through the gold bars and the western vault wall and through the mountain. Even inside the velvet pouch, which had a thin lead sheet between the doubled material, the light was undiminished. He lifted it to his face and looked deeply into the light. At its center was the spiral flame again, the Diamond in the raven's beak, the open window, the mirror shattering, Annalee screaming, "Run, Daniel!" And then he was staggering on the moonlit plain, the pouch heavy in his hand, the light gone. He opened the pouch and looked inside. The Diamond was still glowing, but he couldn't see the spiral flame. He lifted his hand and touched a face, a face he couldn't imagine as his own.

Daniel started running toward the setting moon. Before he'd taken three strides there was a roar above him and what seemed to be a huge locust descended, blocking his way. Daniel's first thought was to vanish again but then he realized it was Low-Riding Eddie and that the locust was Lucille. Daniel ducked his head against the prop wash and stumbled toward the chopper, the pouch clutched to his chest.

Low-Riding Eddie reached across the cockpit and helped yank him aboard, gunned the chopper into the air, backed off the throttle for a second as it stabilized, then whipped into a 180-degree turn. He kept it wide open as they flew fifty feet above the alkali flats below.

They'd covered five miles before Eddie glanced over at him and yelled, "Hey, you all right?"

"Yeah," Daniel said weakly. Realizing Eddie probably couldn't hear him over the engine's howl, he nodded.

"Fuckin' near landed on ya, man—you come outa nowhere."

Daniel shouted, "Lots of room. No problem."

"Get the goods?"

Daniel pointed at the pouch on his lap, then raised his thumb.

The Low Rider grinned his merry approval, his eyes sparkling like the silver studs on his leather jacket. "What kinda jump we got on the heat?"

Daniel was dreamily watching the flats slip by. He looked over at Eddie and shook his head.

Eddie assumed he hadn't heard the question and yelled it again.

Daniel leaned closer and shouted, "No problems. I got by the alarms."

"Fuckin' A-Okay!" Eddie bellowed, pounding him on the shoulder.

Daniel leaned back smiling, his hands on the pouch. He could feel the Diamond's warmth through the velvet. He remembered then that he hadn't checked the inside of the vault for a camera. But he figured he would have noticed one, and recalled that the checkpoint monitoring screens had shown only the outside of the vault. "Clean," he murmured to himself, then turned his attention to the fading stars. A few minutes later Low-Riding Eddie set him down along a county road and was gone again, it seemed to Daniel, before his feet touched the ground.

The Chevy pickup with camper was where it was supposed to be, keys taped under the dash, a small toolbox on the front seat. The sight cleared Daniel's head. There was work to do in the logical world. He opened the toolbox and found, on top, already snapped together, a ratchet, extension, and a half-inch socket.

The bolts on the front differential were loose. Lying on his side, he spun them off, then lifted the cover. The empty differential had been lined with mink. Daniel stared, then started to laugh. He couldn't stop. Finally, choking, he had to crawl out from under the truck and get up on his hands and knees. It took a minute to catch his breath, and when he shimmied back under the truck with the pouch he tried to ignore the mink lining and concentrate on the task at hand. He took the Diamond from the pouch, marveling again at its light, noticing that the spiral flame wasn't visible. Now he felt certain he could only see the spiral flame in his vanished state, and was tempted to check his theory. Instead he lifted the Diamond gently into the differential casing. It fit perfectly. He replaced the cover and cinched the bolts down tight. He returned the ratchet to the toolbox and picked up his harness-vest from where he'd left it on the floorboard.

The white flag was exactly where Volta had diagrammed it, forty yards down a shallow drainage gully to the right of the road. The buried disposal drum was directly below it. He lifted the sand-covered lid without difficulty. The drum was half full of a clear, odorless liquid. He set the harness-vest on the ground, then stripped down to his gloves, dropping each piece of apparel into the vat. Shivering in the chill dawn air, he picked up the harness-vest, gave the attached suction cup an impulsive kiss, held it over the dark maw of the drum. He was about to let go when he remembered that the unused plastique and nerve gas were still in the vest's special pockets. The disposal plan assumed he would have used them. He was deeply unsure about how they'd react with the chemicals in the drum, another product of Aunt Charmaine's bunker industry. He removed the gas and plastique from their pockets and dropped the harness-vest into the solution. He buried the gas and plastique farther down the gully, threw his gloves and the white flag into the drum, and then repositioned the lid, smoothing sand over it till it was well concealed. Bent over, bare ass pointed at the rising sun, he shuffled backward toward the road, erasing his tracks as best he could.

Back at the truck, he climbed inside the camper. Most of the camper was piled with cardboard boxes of *God Shots* religious tracts. The small makeup table was just to the left of the door near the bed, the wardrobe on hangers suspended from a ceiling hook, the makeup case under the bench. Jean had been easy on him; the face was essentially Daniel's own, with the addition of five more years and a scar on his neck. In ten minutes Daniel was Isaiah Kharome.

The only thing he didn't like about Isaiah Kharome was his sense of sartorial style. He assumed it was Jean's idea of an April Fools' joke. The florid Hawaiian shirt, a tangle of scarlet and lime, fought the blue-and-white-checkered polyester slacks, and the wild-plum blazer clashed with them both, though he was forced to concede a subtle coordination between the white socks and white embossed lettering—MIGHTY SPIRIT TOUCHDOWN CLUB—that encircled his hand-tooled belt, the buckle of which was a large single star. He did approve of Isaiah's wallet, chocked with credit cards and crisp twenty-dollar bills. He checked the briefcase of emergency funds stashed in the camper's false top. He didn't have time to count it but if it wasn't the twenty-five thousand dollars Volta had promised, it was close enough.

The sun had cleared the horizon when Daniel reached the highway. He stopped and tried to make sense of the cluster of road signs: Denver, Phoenix, Kansas City, El Paso. An early morning thermal lifted a dust devil off to his right. "Dust to dust," Daniel said in Isaiah's voice, "ashes to ashes."

Phoenix sounded good. Daniel pulled out slowly and headed west.

Volta had difficulty adding the hours he'd gone without sleep. Forty? The last eighteen, waiting for Daniel's call, should count double, he decided. Or triple. He took another sip of coffee, then reached for the blue phone.

Smiling Jack answered immediately.

"Anything?" Volta said.

"Nothing you haven't heard four times already."

"No sign of pursuit?"

"Nada. The guard changed at six o'clock like another day at the office. Either that gas erases memory, or he didn't use it. No alarms. No nothing. You want my opinion?"

"Of course," Volta said.

"Daniel didn't get it. He caught the changes and canceled out."

"And he hasn't called in because he saw the changes and thought we might be setting him up. Is that it?"

"He *should* know better, but yeah, that's how it looks to me, too."

Volta said, "Don't include me in that claim; I believe he got it. He told Eddie he did, and he had something the size and shape of the Diamond in the pouch. It wasn't his lunch."

"It might have been sand. Eddie said he just pointed at it and gave him a thumbs-up sign. Eddie was flying balls-to-the-wall. He admits he just glanced at the pouch. I mean, maybe Daniel can't admit that he missed, that he—" Smiling Jack stopped. "Hang on, Volt, I got something on the red line."

Volta waited, certain what it would be.

Smiling Jack returned. "Well goddamn, good thing we didn't get to betting on it. There's a shit-storm of commotion around the tunnel, and some jets just got off at the air base."

"They discovered it's gone," Volta said.

After a long pause, Smiling Jack asked almost angrily, "So how the fuck did he do it? No gas, no charge—I mean, where was it, on a silver platter in front of the tunnel?"

"No telling," Volta said. "He might have seen a way to get by the alarms. That only leaves the lock and the guards. Maybe they all fell asleep, or were in one place shooting dice or doing drugs. Daniel's sharp and resourceful."

"So we're back to why he hasn't called."

"Full circle," Volta agreed.

"Listen," Jack said earnestly, "you're a lot closer to him than me. What do you think? Think we got burned?"

"I think I'm going to wait till he calls."

"He might not. I have a couple of other bad thoughts."

Volta said, "Let's hear them all."

"They may have already nailed him. Quietly, of course."

"It's possible. But they either don't know what they have, or the sudden excitement around the tunnel is a ruse."

"Or maybe Shamus found him. If our information is good, he's been looking."

"I know, but Shamus would've had to get extremely lucky, or one of us in close betrayed him."

Smiling Jack sighed. "So, you wait for a call. What about the rest of us?"

"Get some sleep. In the morning, pick up Jean in Alamogordo. Chisholm Smith and Davy will be with him. Try to find out what happened in the vault and what the CIA is going to do about it. I imagine whatever they do will be done quietly—no APBs or sweeps involving state and local law. Probably a few hundred of their own agents, all with no idea who they're looking for. If nothing else, we'll find out how they handle such a problem. You know where help is if you need it."

"And you'll wait for him to call?"
"He'll call. We might not like what he has to say, but he'll call."

THE THERAPEUTIC JOURNALS OF JENNIFER RAINE
APRIL 1

My name is Jennifer Raine, Emily Snow, Wanda Zero, Zephyr Marx, April Fulsome, Annabelle Lee. I have a private unpadded room here with dull green walls, a radio, and all the Thorazine I can eat. I don't like Thorazine. It makes me feel like a package of frozen broccoli in the supermarket. That's why they put me here. Or perhaps I should say that's way I took off my clothes in the Safeway and destroyed a few aisles of alleged food. I had to. I could have gone over into lightning. It's all packaging, you see.

I do have to say this is the best of all the hospitals I've been in, especially since it's for my own good.

Doc, you've got to learn to take a joke. It was an April Fools' joke when I said in answer to your question, nothing particularly painful happened when I was eleven except maybe getting raped by the North Bay High football team right after my older brother hung himself in the garage wearing my panties. I expected you to laugh when I said April Fool. I didn't realize you had all that repressed anger and hostility. Don't you think I know that you can't help me if I won't help myself? Why else would I joke with you? Though I appreciate your efforts, I don't need help. *I need* time. *Time and space and a few breaks, Doc, that's what I need.*

But now you've got me feeling guilty. So I'll tell you what happened when I was eleven, but I have to make this fast because I can only tell it on April Fools' Day and it's almost midnight now.

Twelve years and a month ago my father and I took our little aluminum boat and went rowing on Lake Pauline. A storm came up fast like they do in March, and Dad was rowing for shore when we got hit by lightning. He was rowing, rowing, rowing (not merrily, not gently) and suddenly everything was absolutely white and my spine was on fire. No sound at all. No rumble, crack, boom, or blast. Just that silent solid endless alabaster flash and then nothing at all.

When I came to, it was almost dark. My father was lying twisted facedown in the bow, his left hand trailing in the water. He was dead. I'd seen a film in Junior High Health and Hygiene on mouth-to-mouth resuscitation and I tried, I tried so hard, breathing into him until I was exhausted. I can taste the tobacco and licorice in his mouth, smell his burnt hair, see Mia sitting where I had been, watching, struck dumb. Watching when I gave up and held his shock-white face to my breast as we drifted through the rain.

Do you understand why she's like a daughter to me now? When I kiss her goodnight after another day of nursing the wind, setting the empty egg, I can taste the ashes on her lips. And I kiss her goodnight every night. It takes courage to do that, Doc. It takes love. I'm not crazy.

My name is Jennifer Raine. Waitress. Typist. Would-be poet. Clerk. I have an imaginary daughter named Mia. When we were eleven years old, God exploded in my heart.

April Fools, Doc. April Fucking Fools.

APRIL 2 (12:04 A.M.)

No more joking now. My mother was there when they brought the boat in with Dad and me and Mia. For almost a month she just screamed, so they put her in a padded cell and finally she quit screaming and started begging. Begged them to bring her laundry. They finally had enough sense to bring her a big hamper of clean clothes. And that's what Mom's been doing for every waking moment of twelve years—sorting laundry. She sorts it into colors and then puts it back in the hamper and sorts it again. And every few minutes she stops and looks up with this happy expectancy and says, "Is that you, Philip?" Every time I go to see her it's the same. She'll smile at me very sweetly and say, "No, I'm sorry, you couldn't be my daughter because you haven't been born yet."

And I beg her to imagine me, please, imagine me. *But she can't.*

At a roadside flea market near the New Mexico border, Daniel handed out a whole box of *God Shots* magazines and impulsively purchased a dark green bowling-ball bag, bowling shoes, and a bowling shirt. The shirt was the same verdant green as the bag. On the back, in yellow letters, it read "Thrice Construction." Small script above the front pocket spelled out "Herman."

He stopped to rest several hours later. He pulled off on a dirt side road and slipped the Diamond out of the false differential into the bowling bag. He climbed in the camper. He stared into the center of the jewel for nearly ten minutes, concentrating, but couldn't see the spiral thread of flame. He vanished. The diamond vanished with him. The spiral flame was immediately visible. He emptied his mind and focused on the Diamond-center flame. He felt himself filling with light, becoming light, and he used the light to fuel his concentration. When he reappeared, he felt amazingly refreshed. Not until he put the Diamond back in the bowling bag to ride up front with him and stepped from the camper did he realize the moon had risen. He'd vanished for at least three hours. "No limits," he shouted to the moon. "Hang on, honey, I'm coming to see you."

* * *

Volta hung between trance and sleep. He could sense Daniel but not strongly enough to locate him. The only way Daniel could have taken the Diamond was to make it vanish with him, and he would have had to do it quickly. Perhaps he'd imagined it vanished with him. Perhaps the Diamond had been amenable. Or hungry. He couldn't imagine Daniel looking into the Diamond. He wasn't sure if the whisper of sense he felt emanated from Daniel or from some ghost-echo of his own fears that Daniel had been, at best, deranged, or, at worst, claimed by the Diamond. Daniel had powers. Indisputably had powers. But he was not as powerful as the Diamond.

Melvin Keyes, CIA Southwest Supervisor and a sharp-tongued man himself, would have enjoyed the sledgehammer wit of the director's dressing-down if he hadn't been its recipient. The director's rage dwindled at last, and now, as they stood in the looted vault, the director was reduced to repeating the list of Keyes's offences, less in anger than disbelief. "And you had the *entire* security forces of *every* intelligence office in this *country* at your inept disposal, on an *unlimited* budget, and they, or he, or she, or goddamn *it*—excuse me if I sputter—stroll right in and steal the diamond and walk right out. Pardon me, Mr. Keyes, if I just can't fucking believe it!"

Keyes, eyes averted, waited till he was sure the director had finished. "Sir, I share your distress, but consider the evidence: four checkpoints, cameras, laser detection grid, five-pound trip pressure alarm on the floor, double-key *and* coded lock untouched—it simply was not *humanly* possible to steal that diamond undetected. Therefore, I'm forced to conclude we're dealing with an alien species, one whose technology far surpasses ours. Consider, too, that our scientists have never seen *anything* like this diamond. Geologists, physicists, they all agree the probability of its occurring naturally are incalculably small. I think it was an information-gathering device of some kind, and they simply took it back."

"*They?*" the director curled his lip.

Keyes wasn't anxious to say it again. He looked at the vault floor. "I think we're dealing with alien beings, sir. Nonhumans."

The director said icily, "I don't believe in little green men. Nor does the president."

Keyes gave up. "Well, if it was taken by humans," he said crisply, "they'll be caught. We have two hundred agents in the field as of this moment, another fifty on their way, and a number of specialists working on forensics and interviewing the guards."

"Wonderful!" the director said, his sarcasm so massive a D-8 Cat couldn't have budged it. "The agents will remain under your questionable command for the time being. However, after my humiliating conference with the president and the NSC this morning, Dredneau has been called in to take charge of the investigation."

Keyes was incredulous. "Paul-Paul Dredneau? Sir, the Diamond is classified as a Zero-Access Red-Line Secret! Dredneau is a Canadian—a *French* Canadian at that. Not to mention he's crazy, a schemer, a fraud, a notoriously—"

"As the *president* ordered," the director cut him cold, "Dredneau is in charge of the investigation. If you'd done *your* job, the president and NSC wouldn't have required his services."

"With all due respect, sir, in my estimation the man is a show-boating fool, untrustworthy, and utterly incompetent."

It was Dredneau himself, standing at the open vault door, who murmured, "*Your* estimations, Mr. Keyes, have already proven their considerable poverty."

Dredneau was dressed in early Alfred Noyes: a long claret duster, a spotless white shirt with a ruffle of lace at the chin, doeskin trousers, calf-length boots of Spanish leather, and silk gloves—also spotlessly white—that he ordered by the dozen from Paris. Barely an inch over five feet and slightly bow-legged, he looked less like a nineteenth-century highwayman than a jockey turned fop.

The director, momentarily taken aback, offered his hand in greeting. "Dredneau. I've looked forward to meeting you."

Dredneau, ignoring the director's extended hand, bowed. "Paul-Paul Dredneau at your service, sir. I understand"—he glanced pointedly at Keyes—"that your security has failed, resulting in the regrettable loss of a most valuable gem."

"It was stolen sometime between noon of the thirty-first and one A.M. on April second. As you may have already been briefed, it was seemingly stolen from a locked vault without tripping or bypassing five separate and quite sophisticated alarm systems."

"How *perplexing.*" Dredneau simpered. "Fortunately, I was in New York concluding a nasty case involving a planned terrorist attack on the city's Easter Parade—now foiled, thank goodness—and I was able to respond with alacrity to your president's urgent summons. But before I bring my faculties to bear on the case at hand, allow me to introduce Roshi Igor, my assistant, bodyguard, and valet."

Neither the director nor Keyes had noticed Igor standing outside the vault door, a surprising oversight. On hearing his name, Igor entered. Four hundred pounds of dense muscle, he had wrists like mahogany four-by-fours protruding from his frayed coatsleeves and a neck like a redwood stump. Igor's eyes, though, were more imposing than his bulk. Set close beneath the Neanderthal slope of his brow, they looked like the bore end of a sawed-off double-barreled twelve-gauge.

Dredneau said, "Igor only recognizes his name and a small number of commands, but he is extremely sensitive to any feelings of rejection, hostility, and—No!" he barked, as the director offered his hand to Igor. "I don't allow him to shake hands. He has no conception of his strength. I've seen him turn a baseball into a frisbee."

Keyes laughed nervously. "Did you make him yourself or rent him from Hollywood?"

The director said quickly, "Hell, he looks real sharp to me."

Dredneau smiled. "I'm sure you appreciate the relativity of intelligence"—again glancing at Keyes.

Keyes said, "Perhaps we could discuss your friend's infirmities sometime later and turn our attention to the investigation, which is *already* solidly underway."

Igor began slapping his buttocks with his massive hands.

"No!" Dredneau commanded.

Igor immediately quit.

"Jesus, what was that all about?" the director said.

"I've taught Igor to communicate his feelings to me through the use of gesture. He thinks Mr. Keyes here is a rectum." Dredneau smiled at the director. "I believe you were sharing a similar perception as we arrived."

Keyes took a step toward Dredneau and Igor took a step toward Keyes.

"Stop!" Dredneau ordered. They did. "Enough playful banter, even if it does mitigate a serious situation. To work, gentlemen, and my work is information and deduction. First, some information. Besides its obvious value as a gem, what is this diamond's importance?"

"The fact is," the director said, "we don't know. We brought it here for tests. The diamond is perfectly spherical but, as far as we could determine, uncut or unworked in any way. And our scientists say the probability of natural occurrence is infinitesimal."

Gazing upward as if into space, Dredneau said, "Have you entertained the possibility it might be from another part of the universe?"

"Of course," Keyes said derisively. "Only an inhuman intelligence could have circumvented the security."

Dredneau, still gazing upward, said softly, "You're wrong of course, Mr. Keyes." He pointed at a faint circle on the vault ceiling. "A member of an alien species with an advanced technology would not have found it necessary to hang from the ceiling on what appears to have been a common toilet plunger."

"Horseshit," Keyes said.

Dredneau ignored him. "Only two elements of this case truly interest me. The first, obviously, is the practical question of how our thief managed to open the vault door without sounding an alarm."

"We're waiting," Keyes interrupted.

Dredneau continued to ignore him. "The second question is philosophical." Dredneau swept his arm grandly around the vault walls stacked with gold bars. "What sort of man, upon entering a vault full of gold, would have the presence to see beyond it?"

"Yes indeed," Keyes said with mocking joviality, "that *sure is* some fascinating speculation, but we're more concerned with things like *who* is the thief."

Dredneau said wearily, "I've already deduced *that.*"

"Good God, man," the director said, "tell us!"

"He's jacking us off, sir," Keyes said.

"The thief's name"—Dredneau paused—"is Isaiah Kharome. He was, and perhaps still is, driving a camper truck of some sort, posing as an itinerant preacher and the publisher of obscure religious tracts, but apparently affiliated with some ancient magical cult."

Keyes said, "Just *prestoed* it right out of here, huh?"

"Send it," the director ordered Keyes.

"Sir," Keyes appealed, "you're kidding?"

"Now."

Keyes turned to Dredneau. "How can you look at some dim circle on the ceiling here and not only detect it was left by a toilet plunger, but *deduce* the identity and disguise of the thief?"

"Because I'm a genius," Dredneau said. "And now, I must refresh my faculties. If you find him, please notify me immediately at the Turquoise Hilton in Albuquerque, the only decent accommodations in miles. In the meantime, please send me a detailed outline of the security arrangements, as well as the vault blueprints. I'll be available for further consultation. Good day, gentlemen." He turned on his heel and headed out the door, pausing to collect Igor.

Keyes said to the director, "You don't really want me to put that Isaiah Kharome camper-truck bullshit on the wire, do you? Everybody looking for a phantom of Dredneau's vanity?"

The director exploded, "Goddammit, *yes! Send* it. I'm not going to tangle assholes with the president over this. If you don't like it, Mr. Keyes—well, *you* fucked it up, *you* fix it."

Melvin Keyes made three calls. The first was to issue the agency-only bulletin on Isaiah Kharome. Then he rang his staff assistant for complete record checks on Isaiah Kharome and Paul-Paul Dredneau, further instructing him to deliver the security system schematics to Dredneau, and to tell Dredneau a Seabrooke representative would be arriving within the day. The third call was to Gurry Debritto in California.

"Yes?" Debritto answered.

"Keyes. Are you available? It's for me only."

"If it's interesting."

"It's an interrogation. Somebody either knows more than he's telling or I'm getting jerked around."

"That's not interesting."

"A quarter of a million, with the possibility of more—say ten million—if you recover a certain object associated with the inquiry."

"What sort of object?"

"I can't discuss it until you agree."

"Two-five for an interrogation? He must be extremely reluctant, well protected, or dangerous."

"We can talk tonight at eight P.M. in Albuquerque. Mama's Cafe."

"Half in front, as usual. The Cayman account. You have the number."

Keyes chuckled. "I'm always glad to see a man save for his retirement."

"I don't save anything," Debritto said. He hung up.

The phone booth was freezing cold in the desert sunrise. By the time Daniel finished dialing, his breath had fogged the glass.

Volta answered after three rings.

"Allied Furnace Repair."

"Hello," Daniel said, teeth nearly chattering.

Volta didn't reply.

"I got it," Daniel said.

"Yes, so we heard," Volta said softly. "Good."

"There were complications."

"You knew there could be complications. There usually are."

"There still are," Daniel said. His voice sounded tight, jerky.

"So I'd surmised," Volta said. "Their existence, not the specifics. What are they?" Soft. Patient.

"How did I do it?" Daniel blurted. "You must know."

"No doubt you imagined it."

"No doubt? *None?* No, I have doubts. That should please you."

Volta didn't respond.

Daniel said, "I don't know whether I imagined it or it imagined me."

"Come visit. Perhaps I could be of help in understanding the distinction."

Daniel shuddered. "No. You don't even understand what I'm saying. *You* don't *need* to see it. I do. I need to see it. It's my responsibility now. I've seen inside it and I need to see more because it wants me to."

"I never considered the Diamond my responsibility," Volta said. "I considered it my *due*. We have both earned rights in this matter. I only ask that you honor mine."

"That's what I'm trying to do, don't you understand?"

"No, I don't," Volta said.

"You'd have to vanish with it to see inside, to see what you want to see, to even know *if* you want to see it."

"I respect your judgment, Daniel, and I truly thank you for your concern, but I have to reserve that decision for myself."

With his fingertip Daniel drew ragged circles on the fogged glass.

"Come see me," Volta said gently. "Take your time. They just discovered it's missing. As far as we know, you're clear. If it's too complicated, I can always come to you. Tell me where and when."

Daniel said quickly, "I can't think now. I'm freezing. I'll call again later." He hung up.

Volta eased the receiver back into the cradle. He shut his eyes and inhaled slowly. "You lost him," he said.

THE THERAPEUTIC JOURNALS OF JENNIFER RAINE
APRIL 2 (EVENING)

My name is Jennifer Raine, Malinche Cortez Rainbow, Sandra Dee, Emily X, Desiree Knott. Still crazy after all these years, huh girls?

This afternoon Doc Putney tried to be more aggressive with me. Wasn't surprised. Men have one of two responses to me—flight or fight. I was telling him about the lightning-strike scar I got when my father was killed. It's right at the base of my spine, shaped just like a lightning bolt. I was telling him I wasn't killed too because when the lightning hit my brain and shot down my spine, the small of my back was touching the boat, and pulled out just enough juice to save me. I mean, I don't blame the lightning. It just wants to get to the bottom of the lake. If it doesn't connect, it can't go home.

Anyway, Doc Putney challenged me about the scar, but he did it all wrong. He said, "You don't have a scar, Jennifer."

So I stood up and turned around and lifted the grey smock over my head. I wasn't wearing anything else. I like my body close. Nakedness is one of my highest powers. I don't mean the foxy chick-trick of turning slowly, arms crossed, lifting with a little wriggle and then dropping a dress on the floor. I'm not good at being sexy. But I know how to be naked, so naked you can't even see my body.

Doc Putney must have almost swallowed the pencil he's always chewing on because he kind of croaked, "Jennifer, put on your clothes."

I told him, "Look at my scar." I reached back with my right hand and touched it so he'd know where to look.

The Doc got agitated. "There is no scar," he said, hitting every word like he was talking to a child. I don't even talk to Mia like that.

I stood there so naked I could feel the scar begin to glow. Finally he came around his desk and picked up my smock and handed it to me. He looked in my eyes—with more courage than I thought he had—and said with real gentleness, "There is no scar. Put on your dress now. Please."

The "please" intimated what a glance at his crotch confirmed—he had a serious hard-on.

"I showed my scar," I told him. "Let me see your cock. Let's play, Doctor."

I couldn't resist. Scared him though—reminded him he was a doctor. Compromising Situation with a Female Patient.

"No," he said. "This session is over." And he walked out. It was more of a controlled bolt. At the door he turned and said, "You should write about your feelings toward men."

Depends on the man, Doc. And me.

Before he even opened his eyes, Volta could tell by the ring that the call was the inside line. Probably Smiling Jack or Ellison. He picked up the receiver without enthusiasm. "Allied Furnace Repair."

"Glad you gave it up and got some sleep." It was Jack.

"I didn't give it up. He called."

Smiling Jack waited. "And?"

"I don't know. More exactly, he doesn't know. I think the Diamond overwhelmed him. He said he'd call back."

"Where is he?"

"He didn't say. Sounded like a phone booth, so I'm assuming he's on the road and moving."

Smiling Jack said nothing for a moment. "Since you didn't call, I guess we're playing him loose. Or letting him loose."

"I think it's fair for now," Volta said. "Not that we have much choice."

Jack sighed. He hated to deliver bad news. "We have a choice now. They've got his cover, everything but the truck's make and license plate number."

Volta sat up in the chair. "How?"

"You're not going to believe it."

"I believe everything that happens."

"The president himself—though rumor has it the pressure came from his

241

wife, through her astrologer—insisted they call in that weirdo Dredneau. According to a reliable source, he fucking *deduced* it from the plunger mark on the ceiling."

"That's an astonishing deduction."

"Yeah," Jack agreed, "I thought so. Of course, I don't have much skinny on this Dredneau, except he dresses out of the nineteenth century, has a certain dramatic flair, and evidently knows his shit. Sounds like your kind of guy."

Volta was thinking. "That's an impossible deduction. Change the code right now. Damn—I should have done it a month ago. Keep the frequency rotation, though."

"If we're piped, might as well pour shit in their ear, huh?"

"And I think we should have a go-between ready with Daniel. He hasn't said so directly, but he doesn't trust me."

"Wild Bill."

"He'd be my choice, too, if we'd heard from him in the last five months."

"I'll do it," Jack said. "Or Dolly."

"Thanks, Jack, but we need you for Dredneau, and Dolly for Shamus, though he seems to have broken contact. Let's gamble. How about Charmaine? She has a hook in him somewhere."

"I thought you said a go-between, not a persuader."

"A go-between can take many roles. Not knowing which may prove appropriate, why not provide for diverse possibilities?"

"Hey," Jack said, noting Volta's testiness, "I'm convinced."

"I think I'm too old for this, Jack. And I think I'm glad."

"I second them emotions. Take me with you."

"Sure, if there's anything left of us when this one's done. Till then, I'll wait for another phone call, you and whoever you need can surround our cryptographic Canadian, keep Jean open for assignment, and let Ellison handle the rest. I'm assuming the code was blown, but it might have been a hole in the cover. Run it backwards just in case. Put Ashley Bennington on that. And Lyle."

"Anything else?"

"Not that I can think of. You?"

"Nothing to *do*," Jack said, "but there is something I'm curious about."

Volta knew what it was. "Jack, you don't have to be coy."

"Did Daniel happen to mention how he pulled it off?"

"I inquired. He said, and I quote entirely, 'I used my imagination.'"

"I'm really looking forward to retiring with you. Just drifting in a boat on a good trout lake while I listen to you tell me all about magic and the secrets of the art."

"I'll tell you everything I can."

"Uh-huh," Jack said. "And after that I'll have to use my imagination?"

"I'll ask Daniel when he calls," Volta said.

Roshi Igor, whose real name was Roger Kingman, was eating pizza—a Navajo Jumbo, the specialty of the hotel: salami, pepperoni, anchovies, and sausage, smothered with thinly sliced garlic under a half-pound of blue cheese. Roshi Igor was enjoying it immensely. Dredneau, on the other side of the table, was not. He looked up from the security diagrams. "Really, Roger; my eyes are beginning to water."

"Sorry, boss," Igor grunted. He moved over to the couch.

Dredneau sipped his claret. He'd figured out how Isaiah Kharome had gotten by the guards. The nerve gas had evidently caused total amnesia as well as paralysis. He didn't know how he'd negotiated the alarms, but Dredneau's electronic specialists had assured him any alarm could be bypassed. That left the vault, and for that he needed more information. Keyes had said the Seabrooke designer would arrive by midnight. It was already nine minutes past. And his radio monitors hadn't called, which meant dead air. If the code or frequencies had been rotated he'd need a compelling explanation for his sudden loss of deductive powers. He didn't like that prospect. Irritably, he opened his gold-and-ivory snuffbox and inhaled a delicate pinch. The phone rang just as he sneezed into his pale silk handkerchief. He let it ring again before he answered, "Paul-Paul Dredneau."

It was the desk clerk. The Seabrooke man was downstairs.

"Indeed," Dredneau said. "He may ascend."

"The vault guy?" Igor asked. He licked the last bit of sauce from his fingers.

"He'll be up in a moment. And Roger—do keep in mind there's no reason to overplay your part."

"It's boring being dumb."

"I'm sure. But persevere."

Igor jerked his head at the knock. "You want me to get it?"

"No. Intimidation serves no purpose here. Sit and listen."

"Paul-Paul Dredneau?" Gurry Debritto smiled uncertainly, blinking behind his horn-rimmed glasses.

"I am," Dredneau bowed. "And you must be the long-awaited Mr. Sahlin."

"Yes sir. From Seabrooke." He lifted the black attaché case in his hand a few inches, as if offering proof.

Dredneau introduced Igor, offered refreshments, and suggested they work at the table. As he sat down, Dredneau said, "I assume you've examined the vault?"

"Yes sir, a few hours ago." Debritto, still standing, set the attaché case on the table and worked the combination.

"Any preliminary conclusions?"

"I have my notes and some photographs, but it might be useful to match them with the blueprints you requested."

"Of course. Excuse my impatience, but the president expressed some urgency."

Debritto opened the case lid, removed a thin folder, and handed it to Dredneau, explaining, "These are the bare structural blueprints and these"—he reached into the case—"include the alarms."

Dredneau flipped open the folder. Before he could react to the blank page, Debritto knocked him unconscious with a sharp chop to the neck.

Igor was still uncoiling from the couch when the slug from the silenced .357 shattered his skull. He swayed uncertainly for a moment, as if trying to decide whether to sit back down, then toppled backward onto the couch as another bullet tore into his chest. He was still trying to rise when Debritto quickly crossed the room and finished him off.

When Dredneau opened his eyes ten minutes later the first thing he saw was the attaché case turned to face him. Neatly strapped on the upraised lid was a gleaming row of instruments—scalpels, pliers, scissors, and long stainless-steel acupuncture needles. In the bottom of the case, beside an assortment of vials and syringes, was a small, compact meter with a wire running from it. Still dazed, he traced the wire to the electrode taped to the inside of his thigh. He was naked, he realized, his hands tied behind him on the chair, his feet pulled back and bound to the chair's braces. He moaned, "Roger . . ."

"Roger is indisposed," Debritto whispered in his ear. "If you make another sound, you will suffer. We're professionals, Dredneau, you and I. I respect your intelligence enough to assume you know that you have lost. As you see, you are connected to a polygraph. You will answer my questions with the truth. If you refuse, or if you lie, I will remove a part of your body—a kneecap, say, or an eye, a testicle, a finger. Believe me when I say I know what I'm doing. I've kept men alive up to thirty hours as I've whittled them down to a head and torso. If you still refuse, it will make no difference, for in that case I'll use pentothal—vulgarly known as truth serum. I'd prefer not to resort to an injection; while the information would be forthcoming, it is occasionally garbled. If you force me to use the pentothal, when I have the information I seek I will treat you accordingly. Further, if you *once* raise your voice above a civilized conversational tone—which would be futile considering the Hilton's acoustical design—I will cut out your tongue and we will have to proceed with a primitive system of nods. *Please,* employ your legendary intelligence. You do understand that you're faced not only with a choice between truth and falsehood, but life and death."

Dredneau nodded.

"The first question, then: Who stole the diamond?"

Dredneau, trembling, bit his lip.

Debritto mused, "He must not have heard me. I better check his eardrums." He reached past Dredneau and removed a long silver pin from the case.

Dredneau quavered, "You're going to kill me anyway."

"You didn't listen, sir. *Professional?* A professional never kills unless it's absolutely necessary. In your case, it isn't necessary. All I want is information pertinent to this diamond I've been engaged to find."

Dredneau shook his head.

"Of course," Debritto whispered. "Given your situation, why should you take my word? Please note the polygraph." Debritto tipped the case so Dredneau could see it clearly. "The machine is state-of-the-art. Watch the needle—the red area indicates a lie. Is your name Paul-Paul Dredneau?"

Dredneau licked his lips. "Yes."

The needle didn't move.

"Have you ever killed a man?"

"Yes."

The needle jumped into the red zone.

Debritto chuckled softly. "I didn't think so. Next question: Are you a homosexual?"

"No."

The needle wavered near the red zone.

"Now see, this is interesting. You seem to possess some profound sexual ambiguity." He pointed the pin at Dredneau's groin as if to indicate the locus of confusion. "Let me rephrase the question: Have you ever had sex with another male?"

"No."

The needle shot into the red.

Debritto giggled. "Ah-ha! How many?"

"Two. When I was young."

The machine verified it.

"I could ask you about women, but truly I'm not interested in humiliating you, and I'm sure you understand by now the machine's capacity to discriminate. So, to my point." Debritto set the pin down on the table and deftly jerked the electrode from Dredneau's thigh and held it to his own wrist. "The inside of the wrist is actually more sensitive than the thigh, but since your hands must be bound, I'd no choice. Now watch the needle while I make my statement."

He paused, then with a calm formality said, "If you tell me the truth, I will not kill you, nor will I harm you in any way. If you don't, you will suffer unto death."

The needle didn't move.

"You see? The truth." He retaped the electrode to Dredneau's thigh and picked up the stainless-steel pin from the table, idly testing the point against his own index finger. "I repeat: Do you know who stole the diamond?"

"Yes."

"Very good. The truth is always good, isn't it? Now, who stole it?"

"His name is Isaiah Kharome."

The needle quivered at the red edge.

"That appears to be a partial truth. I asked for the complete truth."

Dredneau said thickly, "The name is an alias I think, a constructed identity."

"Go on."

"This is a guess."

"Okay."

"The man's real name is Daniel Pearse."

Debritto said, "The machine agrees, or at least that it's a truthful guess. On what basis do you make that guess?"

Sweat trickled down Dredneau's neck. "I broke a code, an extremely difficult code. From radio transmissions. It took me almost eight months. Cryptography is a useful talent for a detective. I pay listeners all over the world to monitor coded radio transmissions. Most of the codes are trifles, unraveled at a glance. This one was provocative—what's called a shift-cipher. I had to amass a huge sample before I could establish any sort of frequency count, much less discern the operative principles; with that, the code sets followed."

"You're doing well. My compliments on your work, one professional to another. So, what are these code sets?"

"Partial panagrams—a complete set is in my valise in the bedroom."

"*Excellent.* Who does this Isaiah Kharome–Daniel Pearse work for?"

"I don't know. It's a guess. Based on style and odd textual references. It's a group of alchemists or magicians, I think."

"A secret society?"

"Perhaps."

"No national, racial, political affiliations?"

"Maybe anarchists."

"There have always been rumors about such a group."

"If the code's difficulty is any indication, they're very careful."

"We'll see. Now Daniel Pearse—why is his name a guess?"

"Because early transmissions referred to 'Danny Boy' and then changed to 'Kharome.' Playing around one night, I reversed 'Kharome'—still in code sets—and came up with DPearse. Logically, given the earlier Danny Boy reference, the D was likely for Daniel. I ran Daniel Pearse and Isaiah Kharome through my information network, which stretches from Interpol to the local PD—and *voilà!* A Daniel Pearse, but no Isaiah Kharome. Or no Mr. Kharome right away. He began to show up on DMV and credit card screens. Clearly, someone was constructing an identity."

"Tell me about this Daniel Pearse."

"His dossier is in my valise with the code sets and frequency charts. What little there is is rather provocative. When he was fourteen, his mother, Annalee Pearse, was killed and Daniel was severely injured planting a bomb. He was suddenly represented by expensive lawyers and placed under the guardianship of questionable relations. From there—"

"Stop!" Debritto said. "I hope you're right about this, sir. I get to clean up a mess. I killed his mother."

Dredneau said nervously, "My reports say a faulty bomb. Check them, please."

Debritto ignored him. "It was a rush job. I wasn't supposed to kill her; just stop her. Foil it. Those fools don't want to punish. I mean, they didn't even want the police to know. They didn't say *why,* of course. But a bomb in a nowhere alley in Livermore? It had to be a diversion for a run on the lab. Going public would hurt nuclear interests. They didn't even trust their own field agents to handle it. By the time I was called in, getting there in time, much less setting anything up, was going to be tight. I barely made it. I'd just gotten on the warehouse roof above the alley when here she comes, bomb in hand. She caught the movement when I pulled my piece. She turned to run, yelling to somebody. I aimed for her legs, but just as I squeezed it off she slipped on the wet pavement and the bullet hit the bomb. I lost seven percent of my hearing in my right ear."

"Sure," Dredneau said wearily. "CIA. Did Keyes set me up or does it go higher?"

"Please, Mr. Dredneau. I don't take orders from *anyone.*" Dredneau nodded. "I like it," Debritto continued. "You see, when they paid me off, they told me the kid was in a coma and probably wouldn't make it. I tell you, this is something. Now I have a chance to finish the job. And so: Where is our Daniel Pearse, aka Kharome?"

"I don't know."

"Do you know anywhere he might be headed, any sense of a plan?"

"No."

"Do you know where the diamond is?"

"No."

"Your truths are boring me, sir. Surely if you had code access as the theft was being set up, you must at least have some idea of how he accomplished it."

"Some. They further disguise the code with their own idiom, but from what I gathered he was supposed to use a new nerve gas on the guards, blow the vault, and be picked up by helicopter flying under the radar. Those are the only elements of the plan—other than dates and names—I'm sure of."

"But he didn't use the gas or explosive, right? So how did he do it?"

"I don't know."

"But you knew it was going to happen. My, my, Mr. Dredneau, you might have warned us. But it's much more fun to waltz in and grab some glory with stunning deductions—and no doubt grab a little money, too, while you're at it."

Dredneau said nothing.

Debritto smiled. "It makes you uncomfortable to realize how much alike we are. You want the ten million just like me. Otherwise, you would have given the CIA his real name, rather than Kharome, which he's probably changed ten times by now. Meanwhile, you wait for another transmission to decode, then maybe you and your large buddy retrieve the diamond yourself. At least you get to make another brilliant deduction. And if they offer ten, we professionals know they'll pay twenty. Isn't that how you were thinking?"

"Yes. Yes it was."

"Anyone else have this information?"

"No."

"Are you withholding anything essential or pertinent?"

"No," Dredneau moaned. "Please, it's everything of value."

"I compliment you, sir. You're a wise man. Not a single lie. You spared yourself some unnecessary pain. Just let me gather up my equipment and your valise, then I'll be on my way."

"Yes," Dredneau begged, "it's all there."

"I will have to gag you—I'm sure you see the wisdom in a silent departure."

Debritto gagged him with a rubber handball, holding it in place with swatches of silver duct tape. Dredneau began to breathe rapidly through his nose. Debritto gently pulled the electrode loose and coiled it into the case. In the bedroom Debritto went through the contents of the valise carefully.

Satisfied, he returned to the living room, stopping behind Dredneau. "My goodness," he said, "I can actually hear your heart pounding. Relax." He put his left hand lightly on top of Dredneau's head, leaning down to whisper,

"I want you to know how I did it. Remember just before I held the electrode to my wrist, how I laid the pin down on the table? Did you notice it was touching the sensor? The pin is highly magnetized. It disrupted the electrical impulse on its way to the meter, and thus my lie went undetected. And you call yourself a detective." Dredneau shook his head wildly. Debritto dug his thumb and little finger into Dredneau's neck. Dredneau exhaled sharply, straining. With a flick of his free arm, Debritto shook a long wood-butted needle from his sleeve. He pushed Dredneau's head forward and drove the needle upward into the base of Dredneau's skull. Dredneau stiffened as if hit by a cattle prod, bucked once against his bonds, then slumped.

Debritto patted his head reassuringly. "It'll take a little while. The slower the brain, the slower the hemorrhage."

He picked up his case and Dredneau's valise and went to the door, pausing as he opened it to call back into the room, "Goodnight. I hope I've been helpful."

Debritto turned right and headed for the stairs. An old man was pushing a narrow carpet sweeper across the top stair, a transistor plug in his ear. He jumped back against the balustrade when he saw Debritto waiting to pass, jabbering, "Sorry sir. Didn't see you."

Debritto smiled and nodded toward the radio. "Who's winning the ballgame?"

The old man looked confused. "No one." He removed the transistor plug from his ear. "No games this time of night. Just listening to some music to ease the work. That's my whole job, the stairs. Sweep 'em top to bottom, then polish the rails bottom to top. There's an elevator, by the way, you know." He pointed.

Debritto smiled. "I need the exercise. Keeps the heart clean." He pointed at the old man. "Opera," he said. "I bet you were listening to opera. I've got an uncanny sense about people's music. Now tell me: I got you, didn't I?"

The old man turned the earphone toward Debritto. "No sir, no opera for me. Far as I'm concerned, only two kinds of music—country and western."

Debritto caught the strains of Waylon and Willie—"Mama, don't let your babies grow up to be cowboys . . ." He grinned at the old man. "You're just lucky." He shook his head and went on down the stairs.

Smiling Jack replaced the ear plug and returned to his sweeping. He gave it three minutes and then moved quickly to Dredneau's door. When he heard the high nasal wheeze inside he took out his passkey.

Debritto called Keyes from a phone booth across town.

Keyes answered on the first ring.

"Have you come yet, Melvin," Debritto asked.

"What?"

"He was jacking you off, Melvin. He 'deduced' this Kharome character from some shit-brained psychic named Madam Woo. He had a serious mental defect according to my machine. I corrected the defect. Raised his friend's IQ up to zero first."

"Nothing?"

"I bagged his papers. If anything looks promising, I'll call."

"*You* will? I believe *I* paid for them."

"Fine. I don't care. I just thought since I'd conducted the interview I'd be better able to evaluate them. I'll drop them off as we arranged."

"Tonight. He might have been loony, but he'd been getting some results."

"He used snitches, just like everybody else."

"Did he figure out I sent you?"

"Of course. But I would have done him anyway. Fucking queer."

"All smooth? No sightseers?"

"An old fart sweeping the stairs. Had a radio plugged in his ear. We chatted a moment. He'll never know that music saved his life."

"I thought you didn't save anything?"

"I had fun with Dredneau. I was in a good mood."

Volta had asked Smiling Jack to come to El Paso for a personal report and consultation, and had arranged a charter to deliver him. It wasn't like Volta to duplicate effort. Jack couldn't tell him more in person than he had on the phone. Smiling Jack thought perhaps Volta was doubting his own judgment. To Jack, who'd worked with him for twenty years, this only confirmed Volta's judgment, for it took wisdom to understand that your heart's entanglements might be affecting decisions. And courage to admit it.

Over cognac, Smiling Jack recounted what he'd heard through Dredneau's door during the detective's torture, and his encounter with the killer on the stairs. Volta listened intently until Jack concluded with the information that Dredneau was still alive when they loaded him in the ambulance.

"He died on the way to the hospital," Volta said.

Jack nodded. "Yeah," he said distantly, "no surprise."

Volta poured them each another shot. He lifted his glass. "We've worked together what seems like forever, Jack, and you still astonish me with your good sense and clear judgment."

"Shit," Jack said, "coming from you that's almost more praise than I can stand." He lifted his glass. "But I will drink to good sense wherever it shows up."

"As I told you, though you might have mistaken my seriousness, I intend to retire when this Diamond caper is resolved." Volta smiled wryly. "Assuming it can be resolved."

"You used to relish complications. You're the one who claimed you found them inspiring."

"That's when I was young and foolish."

"That was three years ago. In Montreal."

"When I was still young and foolish." Jack started to speak but Volta lifted a hand. "Let me finish before I dodder even further from my point. With your permission, I'm going to recommend you to replace me on the Star."

"Nope. I accept the honor and decline the nomination."

Volta sighed. "Daniel won't bring me the Diamond, Charmaine refuses to serve as a go-between, you won't accept what you've earned—no wonder I'm doubting my judgment."

"Charmaine wouldn't do it?"

"She flatly refused. She said it was pointless. I quote, 'Volta, it is not something between you and Daniel, but between Daniel and himself.' And she's right."

"Now there's my candidate to replace you on the Star when we retire."

"Her clarity is beyond question, but she needs to refine her compassion."

"You're just miffed because she told you what you already knew."

"Exactly. As I said, she lacks compassion."

Smiling Jack shook his head and smiled.

"Speaking of which," Volta continued, "I'd like to ask you a question. Were you tempted to kill that CIA agent when you met on the stairs?"

"No, but if he'd decided to look at the transistor, I might have had to try. I'm old and he was obviously good. If he kills me, we lose the information I just risked my ass to get—like confirmation that the code's cracked, that they have Daniel's real identity, that this guy killed Annalee. Another thing, too. This killer told Dredneau that he—the CIA, actually—was tipped about Annalee planting the bomb, and I figured he's our best way of finding out who did it. I liked that girl a lot. I brought her into the Alliance. I know the attempt had nothing to do with us, that it wasn't our action and was against our policy, but she was betrayed, and I'd like to know who snitched."

"I doubt he knows," Volta said. "He's little more than a freelance assassin, and to judge by what you've told me, he wouldn't even ask why. I think we can assume this is the elusive Debritto we've caught whispers about. The style's right, and he's supposed to work out of the Bay Area. Did you notice that he said his instructions were simply to foil the bomb being planted? And yet when Annalee saw him on the rooftop and began running—which indubitably foiled the diversionary bomb, and thus the attempt on the plutonium—he tried to shoot her, tried to shoot her *knowing* her son was in the car. He'll be punished."

"Ah," Jack nodded, *"now* I understand why you wanted to see me. You have a personal problem."

"I'd like to think it was because I value your advice. My appreciation of your company is sharpened by the realization you came very close to being killed tonight merely because I feel I've earned the privilege of seeing this Diamond, though for no reason beyond my own personal satisfaction. When the Star Council found out about the Diamond, I'm the one who argued we should commit our full resources to wrest it from government control and return it to the elements. I argued that its possession, especially by a government, might be a disaster of the spirit. And that well might be the case. However, Daniel somehow managed to steal it, so in fact the mission has been accomplished. I never once mentioned to the Star that I personally wanted to see it. But I did tell Daniel. Daniel knew and understood that in exchange for my help in his training and the Alliance's aid in resources and planning, he and I would return the Diamond together. You see—"

Smiling Jack held up his hands. "Stop. I see. You want to know if it's honorable for you to trade his mother's killer for the Diamond."

"Exactly," Volta sighed. "Except I wouldn't have said *honorable*—I would have used *fair*. Is it *fair?*"

"Yes," Smiling Jack said without hesitation. "More than that, if this Diamond has overwhelmed him somehow, it might bring him back to earth."

Volta said, disgust and sorrow in his tone, "There are better reasons than revenge."

Jack shrugged. "I would have used the word *justice."*

"Touché."

"Maybe just being forced to make the decision will bring him around."

"One hopes," Volta agreed.

"We'll hope together. But we should also be thinking about what we'll do if he chooses to keep running with the Diamond."

"What can we do but let him go?"

"I meant about Annalee's killer, this Debritto."

"We'll send a Raven to see him. Justice was your word, so you can set it up."

"Hey, be fair," Jack said. *"You* said *punish."*

"Precisely my point."

Jack was distracted by another idea. "Volt, I got it. If Daniel doesn't want to revenge his mother's death, let's offer it to Shamus. He's crazy with grief, thinks you and Daniel conspired somehow to kill her. Who knows? Maybe justice would be cathartic."

"No. Shamus isn't capable of the necessary judgment, either moral or strategic. Besides, like Daniel, Shamus really wants the traitor, the one who tipped the CIA."

"And you don't think this Debritto guy knows?"

"I'd bet on it. However, perhaps Mr. Keyes can find out for us."

"You want me to call him and ask, or do you want to do it?"

"You do it. Pay phones only, short conversations, and you always call him."

Smiling Jack frowned. "Well yeah, I understand basic security, but should I just ask him to please tell me, or should I try pretty please with mustard on it?"

"I wouldn't say please at all until you've exhausted your leverage."

"That's what I'm missing—leverage. If I tell him I was listening at the door they'll know that we know the code was compromised, and then we can't set them up for a dummy transmission. The way I see it, our strongest asset is their ignorance that we heard one word of what went on inside that room."

"True," Volta said. "But you might say you worked as a consultant to Dredneau, that he'd summoned you to the hotel for a briefing, and you just happened to see a man leaving with Dredneau's valise. You hurried to the room to find Dredneau dying. His last act was to point to the room key that had fallen from his smoking jacket and to hold up two fingers. From which you finally deduced Keyes. Tape residue on Dredneau's thigh led you to believe he'd been interrogated by polygraph. You ran a profile of the hit through your computer, and you're fairly certain the assassin was Gurry Debritto. Explain that you'd come to detest Dredneau, because you and your computer wizardry did the real brainwork, while Dredneau hogged all the glory. Then trade your silence for the name of the informant on the Livermore plutonium attempt. Keyes will want to know why. Tell him you need the information to collect a large fee elsewhere. This is your test of his good faith in establishing what might be a mutually useful working relationship. If he refuses, intimate that Mr. Debritto might make a more understanding partner. I assure you he doesn't want Debritto to even suspect they've been linked, because Debritto's only protection would be to remove Keyes from the chain of connection. On the informant, we want something concrete, verifiable—a taped call, a letter, or at least the name of the person who received the Livermore tip. They very well might not know who the informant was, but at least we'll find that out."

"They can just say they don't know," Jack said, "that it was an anonymous call just like mine."

"Perhaps. But it's sometimes surprising how pressure elicits candor. And even if it was anonymous, maybe we can find out if the voice was male or female, adult or child."

"Uh-huh. I'm slow this morning. You're afraid it was Daniel. Because when you tell him we've discovered his mother's killer, he might figure if we have that, we have the snitch: him. And then he'd really run. And you'd go and find him if it took the rest of your life."

Volta looked at Jack squarely. "No, I wouldn't. A year ago, maybe. Not now. And I don't believe he betrayed his mother, or only inadvertently if he did. Daniel's in jeopardy. I intend to help him to the extent of my powers."

"And the Diamond? You don't care about seeing it?"

"Jack," Volta said passionately, "I can't tell you how much I want to stand in its light. But it's the nature of such things that you must let them go. I haven't yet, but I'm trying."

Transcription:
Denis Joyner, AMO Mobile Radio

Like wow, I just dropped down out of the Sierras tonight and cruised into the lovely Apan Valley. I don't know what it is about coastal California—maybe that literally pacific ocean out there imposing its wavelength on mine—but every time I pass through on my spiraling circuit, I get this totally awesome feeling of cosmic mellowness. Blissed out, instead of my usual pissed off. Damn near tempts me to trade in this old funky-junk van and buy a Mercedes; maybe put a hot tub in the wine cellar. *Viva est magnum,* mama, especially if you're holding the magnum, but I guess if you're serious about racing the other rats, you want a comfortable ride.

You know who I'm talking to if I'm not talking to myself this sweet April night. Yea verily, you *do know* who I'm talking to, baby, vibing through silence into the whorls of your ear, but you *don't* know why. Let me tell you: One perfect mind isn't nearly as good as two imperfect minds.

Spin that around your cranium while I get down with some ID, though I haven't got a cold fucking clue who, Miss Owl, who-who I am. But I can tell you that this is KAMO Mobile Radio, somewhere between snake-eyes and boxcars on them tumbling dice, and I'm rolling right along with it all, flying at you high and alive, done in and turned out. Yes! It's the redoubtable DJ, and tonight he's doubled up: Dream Joker and Diarrhea Jaws, too. So, if you don't know what to believe, hey, stick with me. And if you don't like what you hear, call the sheriff. Call the whole fucking posse, for all I care. Give the FCC a jingle while you're at it. Ring up the National Guard, too, and the Air Force, and whoever else you think can save your poor doomed ass. But whatever you do, *don't* touch the dial, because I just clocked the time and Mickey has both arms straight up, surrendering to the moon, which means it's time to tuck you in with a bedtime story. Snuggle down while I light a pipe of killer to clear my golden throat.

Ahhhhh. Better. You all settled? Okay. The story is "The Snake." And before we begin, let me make it clear that the snake in this story is not symbolic. It's not a phallus. It's not the Tempting Serpent, the Wingless Dragon of Unspeakable Evil, the Devil's Lariat, or an emblematic metaphor of any form but its own. The snake in this story is a garter snake, a small, brightly striped, harmless, viviparous member of the genus *Thamnophis*. A critter of reptilian cast. A discrete expression of being. A life.

THE SNAKE

I was visiting friends on the northern California coast, two women I'd known since high school, Nell and Ivy. It was about this time of year.

Since I can't stand cultivating anything except bad habits, I'd been assigned to peeling potatoes while Nell and Ivy worked in the garden. I was rinsing the spuds at the kitchen sink when Nell and Ivy came banging through the screen door, clearly upset, each holding half of a snake writhing in her hand. One of them had accidentally chopped the snake with her hoe.

They laid the snake's thrashing parts on the table. Ivy looked at Nell. "What do you think?" Her voice had that tightness you hear at the edge of a bad car wreck.

Nell said, "I don't think we can stitch its insides together."

Silently fretting, they watched the parts twitch on the table, barely glancing at me as I came over for a look. It didn't look good.

"How about tape?" Ivy suggested.

"Sure," Nell said, "we can try. Maybe it'll regenerate."

I told them, "Snakes don't regenerate." I'm a realist. Nell and Ivy are usually realists too.

"Maybe this one will," Nell said, at once angry, defiant, hopeful, sad.

They used shiny black electricians' tape. I helped, holding the upper half still while Ivy carefully wrapped.

We stretched the snake out in a shaded redwood planter to recuperate. I promised to check on it occasionally so they wouldn't have to hike up from the garden.

When I went out a half hour later, the snake was dead.

True story, folks. I dedicate it to all of you realists as a reminder that some gestures transcend failure. I buried the snake in the planter box, fuel for the flowers. Because if you draw your breath down to its tattered center, dance with your ghost through the moonlit mountain pass, hurl your heart in the forge and your soul in the river, you can feel that the stone is a living fountain that dissolves and coagulates, sunders and joins; and then you can imagine that snake slithering through the high spring grass like a phantom glimpse of flame, and you can follow it if you're brave enough, crazy enough, foolish, desperate, daring, hungry, dumb. Enter your wounds. Heal. Escape.

And when you get loose, come join me. I'll meet you at Jim Bridger's grave as soon as you can get there. We'll make music we can't hear alone, celebrate beauty yet to be born, take the Devil by the fucking horns and wrestle him to the ground. We'll shoot for the stars, sweetheart. We'll waltz in the moonlit cemetery like fallen gods, stand revealed, naked as air, and kiss each other's scars.

Till then, my invisible friend, this is the Dream Joker bidding you his tenderest toodeloo. Dream on.

THE THERAPEUTIC JOURNALS OF JENNIFER RAINE
APRIL 3

Whhhhooooooooowweeeeeeeee! *And who, my goodness, is he? I'm in love! I can't help it and don't want to. The DJ done got to me.*

I couldn't sleep and was just lying there listening to Mia breathe, feeling our breath trapped in this room, how we just keep breathing ourselves, getting so down I had to get up. So I snapped on the radio and twirled the dial, looking for music or just another voice to get mine out of my head—and there he was, loud and clear. The boy can talk that talk, and it was like he was saying it straight to me. Magnificent gestures, the flame of snake flesh burning in petals, the stone river that sunders and joins . . . it was love at first flight.

Short flight, though—five minutes and he was gone. I listened to the spit-sizzle static on the blank channel for another hour before I let him go. I can't feel whether I should follow or wait. He's a bad-boy, which I like, and he does talk good. But sometimes wildness is only the fear of being held, and talking the talk isn't walking the walk. I don't feel he knows how lightning burns. I'm not sure he knows shit about birth, beauty, nakedness, or moonlight. But I love him anyway. I want to dream a real face for him. I want to feel him touch my scar.

THE THERAPEUTIC JOURNALS OF JENNIFER RAINE
TOO LATE THE SAME NIGHT

I never had a chance to dream. I woke as Clyde was crossing the room and before I could move he was on the bed, pinning me, trying to kiss me, he just wanted to kiss me, but I didn't know that, how could I—rape, murder—how could I know? Jesus, I'm still shaking.

Clyde Hibbard, the retarded man I met my second day here. They'd loaded me with Thorazine when I'd been admitted, and Mia had wandered off. I was looking for her in the lounge. Clyde was the only one there, sitting on a beige vinyl couch, picking at the armrest as he stared at the IBM clock on the wall. He looked scared when he saw me; caught. I apologized, said I hadn't meant to disturb him.

"No-no, no-no, no-no," he stammered, "you didn't, you're not."

I smiled to put him at ease because I hate to see people shrink up like that. Tried a little humor: "Guess I shouldn't have said disturb, huh? Gotta be disturbed already to be here, right?"

It confused him. He tensed, like he was about to bolt, his jaw working for traction on something to say.

I barged right ahead. "I'm looking for my daughter, Mia. She's eleven. Blond, blue eyes, wearing jeans, sneakers, navy sweatshirt with a hood. She's imaginary, my daughter—wouldn't think you could lose her, but they drenched me with so much fucking Thorazine I lost track."

Clyde wrapped his arms around himself and shook his head vehemently. "No-no, never, I didn't touch her, I didn't, no-no, I wasn't here."

The chopped skidding language, the childlike exaggeration of gesture, that opaqueness in his eyes—it was plain as his face he was retarded. And from the why he'd collapsed into himself at the mention of Mia, I figured he was here instead of a "home" because there'd been trouble with touching little girls. If I hadn't been gauzed out, I would have seen it immediately. But I didn't, and I felt like shit. I told him I was sure he hadn't touched Mia, not to worry about it.

I started to walk away but he uncoiled out of himself and grabbed my hand with both of his—not hard, not snared—and said, "I'm Clyde. My name is Clyde Hibbard. Hi. Hi, how are you?" He smiled uncertainly.

I let him hold my hand a moment, then gently slipped it free. I wasn't sure what to do, so I said, "My name is Jennifer Raine, Goldie Hart, Serena del Rio, Belle Tinker, Annie Oakley, Lola Montez. Mia and I are new here. Just checked in. Glad to meet you, Clyde."

He was nodding excitedly. "You-you-you are beautiful. You are. Just like the other men said. Beautiful."

I tried to tell him as clearly as I could: "I'm not what anyone says, Clyde. Either are you. It's complicated enough being who we are."

It only bewildered him. He fastened his gaze back on the clock.

"Nice talking to you, Clyde," I said. "I have to find my daughter now."

He swung his eyes to mine, pleading a case I didn't understand. "I'm thirty-three, thirty-three, thirty-three years old."

"Don't watch the clock, Clyde," I said. "Clocks lie. Watch the sun and moon." I squeezed his shoulder quickly, and left him there.

And I didn't see him again till he was on top of me tonight like some nightmare lover pecking my face with slobbery kisses. I think that's all he really wanted to do, kiss me, because he had his clothes on and wasn't choking me or anything, but just his weight had me pinned, my arms under the covers. But I didn't know what he wanted, and I was terrified, so I yelled for Mia to crawl under the bed so she wouldn't have to watch and then I tried to fight out from under him, twisting my face away from his mouth, finally squirming an arm loose, and when I turned to roll free my elbow caught him in the nose. The pain seemed to startle him, then scare him. He grabbed my bare shoulders hard, shaking his head as he looked at my face. "Please, please, please," he blubbered, each ragged breath spraying blood from his nose on my face, shoulders, breasts. He shut his eyes and lowered his head, moaning "Please, please, love, I love you, please."

When he started sobbing he let go of my shoulders and I slapped him as hard as I could. He flinched and ducked as I swung again, and I know if I had a gun it would have meant nothing to me, nothing, to blow his stupid fucking brains out.

"Love you," he cried, eyes closed, shaking his head.

"No. You have to ask, Clyde. You need permission. This is rape, Clyde; you're scaring me, hurting me."

He opened his eyes then, looking at me, and his eyes just kept getting wider, as if he was trying to open them far enough to hold what he was seeing in my face. He worked his mouth, a gummy white string of spittle at the corner, a wet, strangled whimper rising from his throat.

I realized he was looking at his blood on my face. "You hurt me, *Clyde," I hissed. "You did."*

He lifted his hands helplessly, beseechingly, his mouth trembling to speak what he found impossible to believe.

I helped him believe. "It hurts, *goddamn you, Clyde, you motherfucker,* it hurts!"

"No," he begged me. "Love you. I do. I do. I do."

It was too much pain and hopelessness and fear. I started crying.

"I hurt you," Clyde said, amazed, destroyed, lost. He slid off me onto the floor and curled up in a ball, sobbing. I jumped naked from the bed, looking for something to club him with, or to scream for help, or run, but instead I knelt down beside him, stroked his shoulder, whispered it was all right, it was over.

I promised him I wouldn't tell.

He promised he'd help me escape.

Daniel reappeared with the Diamond. He was sitting cross-legged, the Diamond before him, on a high desert somewhere in Arizona on a windless, starless night, with the moon close to the horizon. He was crying, but he couldn't remember why. Not because he couldn't see inside the Diamond-center flame. He would eventually. The Diamond needed to be seen as much as he needed to see it. He could feel the permission there, but not the way. He would just have to keep sitting at the gate, keep mapping the axis of light until it illuminated the way. He smiled at the memory of Wild Bill trying to hammer into him that the map was not the journey.

"Okay, Wild Bill," he said aloud, "until it illuminates the territory."

He looked at the Diamond in front of him and told Volta, "It's not a metaphor. It's not the seed of the next universe. It is not a beacon. I think the Diamond is an entrance, a door, a portal—into what, I don't know, but I will find out. When I do, and if I can, I will bring it to you."

Since the telephone call nearly a day ago, Daniel talked aloud to Volta to discover and rehearse what he wanted to say the next time he called. He'd been too rattled from the theft the first time, less certain. One part of Daniel's new certainty was the understanding that the Diamond wouldn't permit him full passage until he honored his agreement with Volta or could explain, to his satisfaction and Volta's, why he couldn't bring him the Diamond. Daniel's failure to fulfill his part of the agreement upset him deeply. He wondered if that was why he was crying when he reappeared, or if it was because he'd had to return. He checked his watch: They'd been gone five hours.

He'd discovered that when the Diamond vanished with him in daylight, he couldn't see the spiral flame inside. The flame either dissolved in the sunlight or fused with it. The spiral-flame center was only visible when he vanished at night, and Daniel was convinced the flame was the threshold he needed to cross to enter the sphere.

He wiped his tears. As he got to his feet, he was seized by a vision of two moons on the horizon, one setting, one rising to meet it in mirror image. For a spinning moment he thought the moon was setting over the ocean or a lake, but unless the desert had turned liquid this was physically impossible. But so, supposedly, was vanishing. He thought his tears might be refracting the light and wiped his eyes again, this time with his sleeve. When he looked up, the moons were almost touching, as if a ghost twin were rising to join the real moon. He watched them melt into one. The moon seemed to brighten as it set.

Daniel shook his head. "What do you say, Volta? Was that a vision, an optical illusion, a hallucination, or a nightly occurrence I just haven't noticed before?" He didn't wait for an answer. He put the Diamond in the bowling bag and headed for his truck. When he pulled onto the highway five minutes later, he was laughing.

When Smiling Jack called Volta the next morning he had something besides his essential good humor to make him cheerful. "We have made Melvin Keyes 'extremely uncomfortable.' That's his description of how he felt about providing the identity of the Livermore snitch, but I thought his discomfort came from the idea that we were about to start running downhill with his nuts in our hand. I gambled that the guy was this Debritto shit, and it was. I could almost feel the phone trembling in poor Melvin's hand. I told him I'd get back to him soon, and while I understood he could fabricate any name he pleased, dump it on anybody, I knew it was one of three people as sure as I knew Debritto did Dredneau—and I also mentioned that solid documentation brightened my disposition and excited my gratitude."

"Excellent," Volta said.

Jack's smile broadened. "Let's make it a roll—you give me some good news."

"He hasn't called," Volta said. "However, the sun rose this morning."

"Now, you got it, Volt—look on the bright side."

Daniel had driven an hour west, watching the mountains take form in the rising light, when he caught some words in the corner of his eye, a blink, subliminal, but enough to shatter his reverie. He hit the brakes and fishtailed to a stop, then slammed the truck in reverse and backed up the highway.

The sign was written in sun-bleached red paint on a piece of whitewashed plywood wired to a cactus:

TWO MOONS REST STOP
1 mi. right on dirt road
Cabins Food Pool T.V.

Daniel decided the two moons he'd seen earlier were a vision from the Diamond instructing him to rest. The last time he'd slept was before the theft. The last time he'd eaten, too. He'd been drawing energy from vanishing with the Diamond, and now maybe it wanted some back. He drove on slowly, turning right at a rutted dirt road marked with an arrow that lanced two circles.

A dusty mile farther on was a weather-beaten building with OFFICE VA-CANCY lettered in peeling white paint. Behind the office, arranged in a ramshackle circle, were twelve cabins, none of which had been close to a paintbrush in the last decade. Daniel stiffly dismounted from the cab and looked around. If not for some tire tracks near the office, he would have thought the Two Moons Rest Stop had been abandoned. He knocked on the office door.

A short, strong-shouldered man wearing black cotton slippers with plastic soles, jeans, and a short-sleeved red-and-yellow checked shirt opened it immediately. Daniel thought he might be either American Indian or Mongolian: of all the faces Daniel had studied with Jean Bluer, this would have been the most difficult to duplicate. He judged the man to be in his early fifties, but realized he might be off twenty years on either side.

The man looked past Daniel. "Nice truck," he said. "That three-fifty's a good engine." He turned his attention to Daniel. "You want a cabin?"

Daniel, about to slide into his Isaiah Kharome voice, looked into the man's shrewd black eyes and decided to play it straight. "Yes, I do. I know it's a little early to be checking in—wanted to make Phoenix, but I'm too tired to drive. Safer to stop."

The man nodded. "Figured you were a guest. The bill collectors never drive campers. They like those compact foreign rigs. I'll get you a key." He turned back into the office, saying over his shoulder, "Welcome to come in if you want."

"Thanks, but I could use some air." Daniel glanced around as he waited. The cabins didn't look like much, but as long as they had a hot bath and a bed he didn't care. He didn't see the pool or the coffee shop.

The man, moving silently in his slippers, returned holding a large leather cup and a feather.

Daniel indicated the feather. "That from an owl?"

"Great Horned. Found it on the door step the day after we bought the place." The man squatted on the porch and slowly swept the owl feather back and forth above the sun-bleached planks, shaking the cup and chanting softly to himself. Abruptly, he spilled the cup's contents onto the decking: twelve small brass keys, various small bones and claws, a flat silver disc, a small gold nugget, obsidian shards of various shapes and transparencies, a pig tusk, and four dried seeds, each different, and none that Daniel recognized.

The man studied the arrangement a moment, then decisively picked up a key and gave it to Daniel. "Number Five." He pointed to the cabin. "That one there. Park in back."

Daniel hefted the key in his palm. Hesitantly, he said, "I didn't notice the coffee shop."

The man looked up blankly. "Coffee shop?"

"I mean, I just assumed—the sign down the road said food."

The man tilted his head. "You hungry?"

"A little."

"Got some jerky and half a loaf of pumpernickel bread in the house. I'll bring it over as soon as I get the keys put away."

"Don't bother yourself, really—I have some stuff in the truck."

"No bother. I'll bring it over in a bit. You go ahead and get started on your rest."

"Thanks," Daniel said. He felt he should go, but stood there watching the man return the various items to the cup. "I've been told my curiosity often lapses into rudeness, but I can't help asking how you can tell which key to select."

The man dropped the last seed into the cup and rose to his feet, facing Daniel. "I don't know how I do it. Kept trying, and after a while got a feel for it, I guess."

"Uh-huh," Daniel said, "I see. So it's intuitive, right? I mean, there's no method."

"No, no particular method. But there are traditions."

Daniel plunged to the point: "Well, what exactly do you *feel?*"

The man cocked his head, sunlight catching his high, strong cheekbones. "What do I feel? I feel which key fits the guest."

"Ah ha," Daniel said, realizing no secrets were going to escape the tautology of the obvious, "sure—that makes sense. Thank you for indulging my curiosity."

The man shrugged. "I don't mind."

Daniel parked behind the cabin. As he came around to the front—there didn't seem to be a back door—he saw the swimming pool set in the center of the encircling cabins. It appeared to be about six feet wide, and sloped dramatically from three feet deep to nine. There was no water in the pool. Weeds flourished in the long cracks where the cement had buckled and slipped.

The cabin wasn't locked. The interior, though sparely furnished, seemed even smaller than the outside suggested. But it had four large windows and it was clean. A wood heater dominated the center of the room. The squat lines of the iron bedframe were softened by the sheen of its polyester cover. Half a cord of wood was stacked along one wall, and on the opposite side was a formica table with two straight-back chairs. A TV, a fat seventeen-inch Philco from the mid-sixties, occupied most of the tabletop, its rabbit-ears antenna giving it an odd sense of alertness. Daniel assumed the single door led to the bathroom, but found only a toilet and washbasin behind it. He pissed, then washed his hands and splashed cold water on his face. He soon discovered there were no towels.

Moderately annoyed, Daniel—face still dripping—was standing in front of the TV waiting for it to come on when the manager said from the open front door, "It's not plugged in."

"Oh," Daniel said.

The man set plastic-wrapped jerky and slices of pumpernickel on top of the TV. "Actually," he said, looking at the screen, "it wouldn't matter if it was plugged in, because we don't have electricity. And if we did, they would probably turn it off after a couple of months and send some righteous, brutal men around to collect money. I don't like to do business with such people. Their hearts are no bigger than mouse shit."

"Speaking of business practices, it seems to me that your sign out on the highway is sort of misleading."

"Maybe. We do have cabins, food, pool, and TV, but sometimes not all at once. Besides, did I ask you for money?"

"No, you didn't," Daniel acknowledged, surprised.

"We don't charge. It's shameful to accept money from guests."

Daniel didn't know what to do with that information, so he said, "Why don't you put *free* on your sign?"

"Because nobody would be surprised when they got here."

Daniel stared at him, then shook his head. "I'm sorry—I seem to be having comprehension difficulties. What's your name? If I'm your guest, I should know who to thank for this hospitality."

"Wally Moon."

"Mine's Daniel Pearse," Daniel told him, ignoring his cover. "If it's not too personal, Wally, could I ask your nationality?"

"My mother, Lao-Shi, was Chinese; my father was a full-blood Apache named Burning Moon."

"And may I ask why this place is called Two Moons? Did you have a vision?"

"No, I took up with a woman. She is part Apache and part Seminole and some Cajun. She is not a relative, but her name is also Moon. It's a common name."

"So: Two Moons."

"My wife likes it. Her name is Annie. She's not here right now because she's menstruating. She goes off to the mountains then. She doesn't like being around me when she's menstruating. Says I screw up the reception. Women are all a little strange, but Annie is really something. I love her."

Daniel felt his face distort as he fought back tears. When he tried to speak his voice cracked so badly there was no point in trying to hide. He quit fighting.

He felt Wally Moon's hand softly on his shoulder. "You just need rest, Daniel. There's a sweathouse outside and a cold shower. The lamps and kerosene are on the closet shelf. Come over if there's anything you want. You're welcome to stay as long as you need."

Daniel gathered himself and said, "Thank you." He tried to smile. "What is this, some halfway house for fools?"

"No. Simply a place to rest."

When Wally had left, Daniel brought in the bowling bag with the Diamond zipped inside. He laid down beside it on the bed. He tried to think about what he was doing or could do or should, but it whirled away like water down a drain and in moments he was asleep.

THE THERAPEUTIC JOURNAL OF JENNIFER RAINE
APRIL 5?

I numbed and dumbed it through the day, nibbled my mush, nodded through my half-hour with the Doc. He said I looked pensive and withdrawn. I told him Mia was sick. That's when he chose to make his stunning-insight move, so contrived and dramatic you could tell he'd been saving it till I was weak: "Jenny, do you know that in Italian 'mia' means 'me'?"

I sank my fangs in Doctor Putney's vanity and let it drip: "Doc, didn't it ever cross your feeble mind that Mia is the acronym for Missing in Action? I named her after her father. It was a great marriage, Doc. We were both Soldiers of Fortune—the only man-wife team in the world—but his 'chute didn't open on a jump over Borneo. No need to even look for his body in the jungle, but since there's no body, he's officially MIA. You get it, or you want pictures? How about some pictures of my pussy, Doc? Some mental spread shots? 'Cause this distressed little damsel do declare she don't know what scares you worse, her mind or her cunt."

I'll say this for the Doc, he had the class to say, "I don't know either."

Ain't that the truth. He suggested we take a week off to consider whether there was any point in trying to continue working together. He thought I might have better luck with a female Jungian.

Personally, I think I'm healing, and I'm doing it against a run of bad luck. What did that crazy gambler in Oakland always say? "Your luck's bound to change if your chips hold out." And I might be digging for the last handful, but I'm still digging. Or as my new loverboy, the Dharma Joker, says on his radio show, "Dig it all, *and when it's all dug up, little darling, put it on the line." He didn't actually say that yet, but he could the next time.*

I didn't tell the Doctor about Clyde. I promised Clyde I wouldn't, and I've learned how strong it makes me to honor promises. I don't feel Clyde will mess with other women, but he might, and her suffering will be marked on my soul. But I don't feel guilty about my silence. I've learned about guilt. It's an abscessed truth, rotting with denial. And I need every truth I can get if I want to get well. I need *the responsibility for my silence and for what I say. I want the consequences of my judgment.*

Maybe I shouldn't have hidden Mia. I don't know. She could feel my fear from under the bed, and since she has such a powerful imagination, that might have been worse. She cried most of the day, but is sleeping now. I'll talk to her about it in the morning.

As we'd arranged, I met Clyde after therapy, under the big oak on the side lawn. It was difficult to make him tell me how he'd gotten into the women's wing. He trembled the whole time, mumbled, wouldn't look at me. I looked at him with revulsion, and sorrow, and pity, and love, and helplessness, until the feelings whirled and blurred together and I had to freeze myself to concentrate on making him tell me how he'd got in. He gave me ten dollars, two crumpled, clammy fives—he said it was all he had but he could try to steal some from the other men when they were asleep. Touched, touched almost to tears again, I told him ten was enough, and enough was plenty.

Clyde started snuffling then, spreading his arms out in misery as if I might hold him. When I stepped back, he dropped to his knees like a broken pilgrim, a doom-struck suitor of my violated affections. I thanked him for his help, repeated my promise not to tell, and turned and walked away, hating him for taking what can only be given, loathing his damaged, presumptuous greed, and loving him because his shame was greater than my forgiveness.

The moment I turned from Clyde and started walking away, the lightning scar at the base of my spine started burning like dry ice. I can still feel it as I write this, but it's more like a numb warmth now. I feel an intense desire to open, to be known—I suppose it's some sort of balancing response to Clyde. No wonder I'm locked up.

But Mia and me won't be shut-ins much longer. I told her what we have to do before I sang her to sleep, and promised to wake her when it was time. Promises to keep and miles to go before we sleep, miles before we're gone. Everything's packed in a tight bundle, except this journal and the radio. I'm going to change the journal to a notebook. We'll need the radio to beam in on the DJ. I've been running the dial from one end to the other, but either the DJ's not sending or I'm not receiving. I need directions to the grave.

I'm leaving the Doc a note on my pillow: "Gone dancing with the DJ. Don't wait up."

Daniel struggled to open his eyes but he was being lowered into a fresh, clay-streaked grave, his naked body glowing in the alkaline light of the moon. Standing in a circle around the pit, twelve old women were singing a wordless incantation of wails and parched moans, their upraised faces shining like oiled leather, their bodies swaying to the feathered tambourines they played. But the music Daniel heard wasn't the thump and shimmer of tambourines, but the sound of shattering glass.

When his back touched the ground, the music stopped. Above him, framed by the grave, the moon slowly spiraled into itself till it disappeared, the stars following like flecks of foam. People whose faces he couldn't see began to file past, each silently dropping a white rose into his grave, flowers to cushion the fall of covering earth, flowers to sweeten his decay. Daniel's hands were crossed on his bare chest. He pressed his right palm against his ribcage, feeling for a heartbeat. Pressed harder when he felt nothing. Harder, beginning to panic, when a voice hollered, "Hey! Daniel!" and he bolted from the bed, heart racing, riding the adrenaline rush as it cleared his senses.

Another holler: "Hey, you alive in there?"

It sounded like Wally Moon. Daniel tried to make his voice gruff with sleep. "Yeah, hey, who is it?"

"Wally."

"Yeah, okay, just a minute." He picked up the bowling bag and slid it under the bed. He buttoned his shirt as he crossed the room, tucking it in before he opened the door.

He need not have been so formal. Wally Moon was standing on the porch naked, dripping wet. "The stones in the sweathouse are still hot if you want to get clean. Sorry if I woke you, but I don't like to waste heat. Besides, it's about your only chance for a hot bath till the next one."

"Thanks," Daniel said, "that was thoughtful. A sweat would be perfect. And no problem about waking me up; glad you did. I've got some work to do tonight anyway, and—"

Wally's squint cut him off. "You work at night?"

"I'm a writer," Daniel said quickly. "Religious stuff."

"Oh, a poet."

"Not quite, no, more like a scholar, sort of a religious anthropologist, I suppose—theological essays, research papers, that general vein."

"So you're going to stay here and work tonight?"

"If it doesn't stretch your hospitality."

"No, I meant it when I said you could stay as long as you like. But I just wanted to make sure you planned to work, because I need to borrow your truck till the morning."

"Ummm, gee," Daniel began, "I'd really like to let—"

Wally, more as if continuing than interrupting, said, "I told you my wife was off in the mountains menstruating? Well, she went in our truck and it broke down—she called me on the CB just before I headed to the sweathouse."

Daniel said, "The front differential on my truck is busted. No four-wheel drive."

Wally wiped a trickle of water from his cheek. "Don't need four-wheel. She broke down on the highway about thirty miles from here, not out in the hills. Just need to tow it in if I can't fix it, but Annie said it sounded like the engine was eating metal, so it might not be simple to fix." Wally shook his head. "Menstruating women should not be around machines. They confuse machines. But don't worry about your truck, because Annie says she is done menstruating. Annie is always very lustful when she returns from the mountains." Wally grinned, looking directly at Daniel.

It was a universal appeal: Let me borrow your wheels so I can get laid. The appeal demanded a generosity beyond the merely convenient. Daniel, feeling vaguely conned, reached in his pocket for the keys.

Daniel was in the sweathouse when he heard his truck rumble past and fade toward the highway, the music pounding from its radio the last sound to dissolve. Faint from hunger and the heat, he bent forward from his squat, lowering his head to his knees. He inhaled strongly, stretching his lungs, but his attempt to keep the exhalation smooth collapsed into a sigh. He tried to imagine Volta's face. The face flickered but wouldn't hold.

Daniel mumbled anyway, "I know, it was stupid to let Wally take the truck. He and his wife could get nailed, they might turn me, or take the truck and money. Hundreds of shitty possibilities. But even if stupid, it was the right thing to do, or at least that's how I felt it. I'm working on nerve alone now, out on the edges looking for the center, not a realm that rewards a rational approach. Thought isn't fast enough. Don't make me doubt myself, Volta, don't make me hesitate. Hesitation could be fatal. Let me do it myself. Don't stand between me and the Diamond. This one isn't yours. It has a spiral flame through its center, like the one I saw. It wants me to see inside, wants me to know. Let me go." He realized he was no longer addressing Volta but the Diamond.

Daniel started laughing and immediately felt faint again. He dipped his hand in the bucket of cold water at his side and flung a cupped handful on the hot stones. The water sizzled into steam. The steam curled through the slender shaft of moonlight from the small, heat-fogged window behind him, coiled, braided, swirled through itself, dispersed. Daniel looked for a pattern, a rhythm. He threw another handful of water on the stones. A dragon's tail lashed slowly through the light. The durable lines of a pig. A great blue heron ponderously lifted from its fishing roost and glided downriver. A lion's paw. The bash and plunge of a whale. A twisted question mark. A rose billowing into bloom. A thousand possibilities, but nothing that cohered.

Twenty minutes later Daniel half staggered from the sweathouse and made his way to the shower. When the cold water hit him, jolting him back into his skin, he saw a slender twist of flame flash behind his eyes.

His body steaming in the cool night air, he walked naked back to his cabin, slipped the Diamond from the bowling bag, and vanished.

Calm, steady, focus locked, Daniel gazed into the Diamond all night, waiting for it to open. He reappeared with the Diamond an hour before dawn, so exhausted he didn't think to put it away. He curled around its light and immediately fell asleep.

Smiling Jack Ebbetts punched the Play button and said to Volta, who was pouring them both a shot of cognac, "I don't know if it's something or nothing or a load of shit. You tell me." He sat down across the table from Volta in the basement of the Allied Furnace Repair building, swirled the cognac in his glass, tossed it back.

The tape began with a ringing telephone. Smiling Jack said quickly to Volta, "He gave me his direct line so it didn't go through the secretary."

The ringing stopped.

"Keyes."

"Hello, Melvin," Smiling Jack's voice boomed in a hearty Texas drawl, "this is Jacques-Jacques Lafayette, Dredneau's good buddy and brain trust. You got your half of this deal for me?"

"Yes. Or the best I could. I'm not really pleased with this *deal,* though. I'm—"

"Well, shit-fire, Mel, it's simple enough: You talk and I don't; you don't and I do."

"But suppose I talk and then you talk anyway? Or want me to keep talking so you don't? Let's talk about that."

"Mel, what you're talking like is a man with a paper asshole. Haven't you ever heard of *honor?* Human *trust?* Mutual benefit?"

"Yes. I've heard of blackmail, too. And coercion."

"Well, fuck ya then, son. I better do business with this Debritto boy. Besides the information, maybe I could get a few of them two hundred fifty Ks that my little ol' computer tells me were recently transferred from your very own Whole Corn Distributing Company to a numbered Cayman account. Shit-oh-dear, wouldn't the *Washington Post* have fun with that on the front page!"

"I'd like *some* guarantee," Keyes whined. "You can understand that."

"You got a guarantee, hoss! You got my *word.* Now quit dicking me around while you're trying to slap a trace on my call, 'cause the call's routed through an empty apartment in San Angelo. Shit or get off the pot, Mel. You're not playing with kids."

"Okay, I'm going to connect you with Shelby Bennett in our Denver office. The information came directly to him about four hours before the bomb was to be planted. His informant is named Alex Three. He'd called Shelby before. There's no tapes, and Shelby ran Alex Three and Al X Three, and like he expected, got a blank screen. It's a code name. Shelby says—"

" 'Scuse me, pardner, but why don't you let Shelby tell me hisself."

"Sure, I'm putting it through now. I'm going to stay on the line."

"You don't have a *real* bone in ya, do ya Melvin? Not *one* trusting bone. Reckon it must raise hell with your faith."

As Shelby Bennett's phone rang on tape, Volta said to Jack, "You're incorrigible."

Jack smiled, then he and Volta listened as Shelby Bennett confirmed the information Keyes had already given. On tape, Texas Jacques-Jacques said, "Shelby, I'd be obliged if you'd answer a couple of questions for me."

"I'll try, Mr. Lafayette," Shelby replied.

"How many times has this Alex Three hombre rang up you?"

"Nine, starting in seventy-five and ending a few years later with the plutonium tip."

"Why do you think that was his last call?"

"Because his conditions weren't met."

"What sorta *conditions* we talking about here?"

"Just one, really. That nobody get hurt."

"Who fucked it up?"

Bennett paused a moment. "Nobody, really. I couldn't handle it personally because I was here, in Denver. He said he understood, that he was trusting me to put it in the proper hands, but that I'd be responsible if his condition wasn't satisfied. I told him that anything involving theft of nuclear materials went straight to the director; I had no choice unless I wanted a career change. He said to do my best to retain control. But when I called the director he took it out of my hands."

"Why'd this good ol' Alex Three choose you for these friendly calls?"

"When I asked him that myself, he said, 'I hear you're honest and reliable.' That's the only reason he ever gave."

"He ever let on how he was getting his information, or why he was passing it on?"

"I asked his source the first time he called, and he said, 'Me.' I never bothered to ask again."

"He ever ask for anything in return?"

"No, but he said he might. I told him I couldn't make promises, but that I'd do whatever I honorably could."

"Ya get that, Mel?" Texas Jacques-Jacques yelled down the line. "This fella knows how to establish a professional working atmosphere. You lissen up and learn something, hear?" When Keyes didn't reply, he asked Bennett, "Now Shelby, I'm hoping you might be able to tell me what sorta other tips this Alex Three passed along."

"I'd rather not—and anyway, I doubt if they're germane. Nothing even close to the level of the plutonium theft. I *can* tell you that most of it involved small South American matters and internal government corruption. I'll give you an example: We had some of our own low-level people ripping off emergency medical supply shipments after a big earthquake down south. That sort of thing."

"His information always pretty accurate, was it?"

"Utterly."

"You never met him, that right?"

"Always by phone."

"Ever tempted to slap on a trace, see where he was calling from?"

"He told me not to bother. I didn't."

"Okay now, so all you ever heard was his voice. You can tell a lot about a man just listening to him talk. What did you hear?"

"Male, mid-thirties or a little older, faint Germanic accent—Swiss

270

maybe—good vocabulary, very precise. But these weren't long conversations, you understand."

"No tapes, huh?"

"No. He asked me not to. It was a request, not a condition."

"You think you'd recognize his voice if you heard it again?"

"I don't know. He hasn't called since Livermore."

"Well, thanks for your help, Shelby. 'Preciate it. Mel does, too, I'm sure."

Keyes said, "Yes, thanks Shel; I owe you one." He waited for Bennett to get off the line and said to Texas Jacques-Jacques, "That's all there is, cowboy. You satisfied with my end?"

"You know, my ol' Pappy, bless his wildcat soul, always told me that if a man's real anxious to sell, give it some hard, cold thinking 'fore you buy. I got to respect my Pappy's advice. I'll get back to you on it soon as I got it mulled over good. Keep your loop tight, Mel."

Keyes was sputtering, "Hold on now, you—" when the recording ended.

Smiling Jack hit Stop, then Rewind. He glanced at Volta, who was staring into his untouched glass of cognac. "You want to hear it again, Volt?"

"Later, perhaps."

"What do you think? Flowers or fertilizer?"

"Flowers. I think you got everything there was, the whole truth and nothing but, and you had fun doing it. Please reconsider giving me the honor of nominating you to replace me on the Star. The Alliance is losing that sense of fun; you could refresh it."

"Damn, Volt, I think you're getting maudlin in your old age—or else it's tougher than you thought to sit here waiting for Daniel to call. Maybe you should get some natural light and fresh air on you. Do a bunch of pushups. Jog over to McDonald's and get back in the world."

Volta barely smiled. "You're right, waiting has been tougher than I thought. The hardest part is that I've had four straight days with time to reflect, and what I see of myself doesn't please me. I'm losing my effectiveness, and I'm not having fun. I'm tired of excruciating decisions, balancing acts, judgments that must consider the welfare of the Alliance before the good of my heart—though truly they aren't often at odds."

"Jesus," Jack said, "you're turning sane."

"I'm beginning to cherish that infrequent state of mind, yes."

"Well, before your effectiveness peters out completely, how do you want to move on this Alex Three info?"

"I think we should follow your dear ol' Pappy's advice and mull it over *reeeal* good."

Jack looked skeptical. "Way you were just talking, didn't sound like your muller could take much more."

"Plenty of room," Volta assured him. "Throw it in there with the rest and sit back and wait for something to connect. I'm assuming, naturally, that you're having Alex Three run through our own sources."

"Yeah, got them on it pronto, but they haven't turned diddley yet."

"Alex Three," Volta mused. "Try it under Alexandra, also—and Xan. Maybe try working on Al Ex-Three, or maybe X as 'times,' a multiplier, or as addition. Al Triple? All three times? A.L.? American League? Three-time winner in the American League?"

"I told Jimmy and J.J. to run any combos they could come up with. And those boys are whizzes on them computers."

Volta lifted a hand. "I was just babbling out loud, not impugning their abilities. Actually, I was avoiding thinking about a tougher decision."

"Like whether to tell Daniel, right?"

"No. He gets the information when we receive the Diamond. The tough decision is whether to tell Shamus."

"Not much to decide, is there? He's gone loco, first of all, and besides he hasn't been in touch."

"Not recently, but he might. And Alex Three had to get his information from close to the source, so Shamus is the best one to ask. Maybe he even knows who this Alex Three is. Let's play it this way: Call Dolly and tell her that if Shamus checks in, she can tell him *only* that we've discovered the snitch, and how it went down in the alley with a trigger-happy agent. But don't tell even *Dolly* we know who the agent was, much less the name. Only you and I have that name at the moment, and that's enough."

"We can hope Daniel will make it three when he calls and decides to trade the Diamond for his mama's killer, and a lead on the snitch."

Volta said, without conviction, "Possibly." He smiled wryly at Jack and raised his glass of cognac: "To hope." He paused as he brought the glass to his lips and added, "And to faith."

When Volta set down the empty glass, Jack said, "Aw, don't worry. Things are just hanging fire right now. Pretty soon some pieces will come tumbling together, and you'll know what to do because you—more than anyone I ever met—*know* what to do. I mean, don't think you can shamelessly flatter me with this Star bullshit and get away unscathed."

"Scathe me," Volta said, "I need it." But he didn't smile.

"You don't think he's gonna trade that Diamond, do you? You really don't."

"Jack, I've been sitting here four days *feeling* that Diamond take him. It was the one imponderable, how he'd react to the Diamond. Maybe I just didn't ponder it deeply enough."

"Volt, would you quit whipping on yourself? I mean, how could you've considered that?"

"I could have used some imagination," Volta said.

In a rich baritone and a horrible Irish accent, someone was singing "Dannnny Boy, Dannnny Boy, the pipes are calling—"

Daniel bolted awake. He looked around wildly: naked, daylight, the Diamond beside him on the bed. He lunged for the bowling bag and stuffed the Diamond inside, yelling at the singer, "What? Wait a minute, goddamm- it!" He slid the bag under the bed, and pulled on his pants. It wasn't until his first step toward the door that a sharp painful yank made him realize he'd caught half his pubic hair in the zipper. "Arrrhhh!" he howled, clawing at his crotch for the zipper pull. At his howl, the singing stopped.

"Daniel?" Wally Moon called from the porch. "Hey! You all right in there?"

Daniel flung the door open, his face flushed. "Yes, Wally, I'm wonderful. Just got jerked from a sound sleep by some serenading Mongol-Apache and in my haste to get dressed I caught my pubic hair in my zipper, which caused the pained cry that elicited your concern. But other than that, top o' the morning to ya."

Wally winced. "Oooh, I've done that. Not only hurts like a son-of-a- bitch, but it scares you, too. Better than catching a fold of skin on your dick, though—you ever done that, zip up your dick?"

"No, not yet, Wally." Daniel's anger was dissipating rapidly, his confu- sion with it. He remembered Wally had borrowed his truck. He didn't notice any sign of the keys in Wally's hands.

As if to confirm the keys' absence, Wally spread his arms, his open palms upraised in a mild plea for forbearance. "I *had* to wake you to give you the news."

"What news?"

"Good news," Wally said merrily.

"Do you have my truck?"

"No," Wally smiled. "That's the good news."

"For who?"

"For you. See, we towed our truck in about sunup—it ate a valve—and after we had some breakfast, Annie went to Tucson for parts. We don't have much money, but we have lots of relatives between us, and Annie's cousin's brother-in-law has a wrecking yard in Tucson. Anyway, about an hour ago, two guys in a grey Chevy sedan, last year's model, came up the road. They were both large men with nice shines on their shoes. They said they were U.S. Treasury agents out looking for a man named Isaiah Kharome so they could give him a large tax settlement that he'd never collected. But to tell you the truth, they didn't look like men happy to be returning money. They looked like men who had terrible childhoods."

"I see," Daniel said. "What did you tell them?"

"I told them we hadn't had a guest in over a month and that I didn't recall seeing a seventy-two Chevy four-by with a camper, New Mexico license LXA 009. I wouldn't have been able to tell them that with much conviction if your truck had been parked here."

"Thanks," Daniel said. "They weren't Treasury agents, though, I can tell you that. The IRS is hunting me because I claim my writing is religious and therefore tax exempt, but they don't agree. They've been hounding me for months—Isaiah Kharome is my pen name."

"Ah," Wally said, as if he finally understood. "I didn't think they had money for you. Only trouble. But see how generosity encourages good fortune? You kindly lend me your truck, and it's gone when they're here. Not only that, I've always thought that when people are chasing you, the best place to be is behind them."

"So they've gone on, I take it. Toward Tucson?"

"That's what their car tracks show. I always take a morning run so I went down to the highway to check."

"I'm a little worried about your wife. They might see the truck on her way back from Tucson."

"Before my run, I used the CB to call my uncle in Dos Cabezas who has a phone and he called Annie's cousin's brother-in-law's wrecking yard to leave a message that she shouldn't drive on the interstate today. She will understand. Annie is strange even for a woman, but she possesses great intelligence. She also likes to drive fast, so I would expect her back by early afternoon with your truck, and also with some groceries. We will have a feast to good luck this evening if you would like to join us."

Daniel frowned and said ruefully, "No, gosh, I can't. I'm supposed to be in Phoenix tonight."

Wally said with a faint chastising edge, "I had a teacher, an Apache holy man named Two Snakes, who taught that the best place to hide was where they'd already looked."

"He sounds like a very wise man," Daniel said, "but I have obligations beyond my control, and I must honor them."

Wally nodded. "Religious obligations and family obligations are very important to keep things going right. But you should take the scenic route to Phoenix—Six sixty-six, to Seventy, to Sixty, and then Eighty. But of course these tax people are everywhere you go these days."

"Don't worry," Daniel assured him. "I'm difficult to catch and much harder to keep."

WATER

When Daniel heard his truck drive in two hours later, he was still sitting on the edge of the bed, his shirt in his hands. He was thinking about what to do next, given the news of pursuit. He felt tired, calm, and strangely content, as if something was coming inevitably to a conclusion, its trajectory locked. He admitted to himself that he wanted a conclusion, wanted one soon. He didn't feel he had the power to hold on much longer. He decided to call Volta at the first opportunity. His cover was evidently blown and he wanted to know why. That was a practical matter. But he also owed Volta an explanation, or as much of one as he could give. And maybe Volta could give him some advice on how to proceed with the Diamond, how to see inside it. Daniel didn't want to return it until he'd seen what it was the Diamond wanted him to see. Maybe Volta could offer him perspective. He felt like he was too close to see clearly, yet he couldn't back away.

Daniel pulled out of the Two Moons Rest Stop an hour before dark. He left five thousand dollars on top of the TV, more an endowment to the notion of rest than a tip for services. Wally Moon had his head under the hood of a battered pickup when Daniel drove by. Daniel tooted twice. Without looking up, Wally Moon lifted the box-wrench in his hand and made a gesture that was, at once, forward and farewell.

THE NOTEBOOKS OF JENNIFER RAINE
APRIL

My name is Jennifer Raine Escapedangone; also known as you can kiss my sweet little ass good-bye. Me and Mia went out easy the way Clyde came in. Quick on tiptoes down the hall to the end of the wing and the unlocked janitor's supply room and then feet first down the laundry chute into the basement, kids on a slide, landing on a pile of fear-rank, night-sweat sheets that Clyde had mounded there for us. The basement walls were ringed with huge washing machines and dryers, and right above them was a series of narrow, ground-level windows. The fifth window on the eastern wall had a broken lock. I slithered through onto the cool lawn, then reached back for Mia. I felt our hands touching in the darkness, the pain and trust between us giving me strength, and pulled her through the window. We scampered across the moon-shadowed grounds to the brick wall, six feet at most, more a screen than a barrier, and from there, as my dear DJ says, it was simply a matter of over and out, out, out, out, and free, good gods, at last!

The first place we stopped was your standard all-nite drug-dealing diner at the edge of town—chafed plastic glasses, tape-scabbed stools at the formica counter, the waitress in a frayed, ice-blue rayon dress, bra and slip straps showing through, country-and-western on the radio in the kitchen, the spattering grill-grease and the radio's static indistinguishable, and four junk-grayed

275

men nodding to the same slow rhythm as they dunked donuts in their cold coffee.

I ordered a chocolate milkshake to share with Mia. We'd just finished when two young strutters came in, sleaze-boys, the kind who live on what they roll from junkies. I didn't like the way they looked at me. I wanted out of there so bad I left the whole five for the waitress and headed for the door.

The greasiest one waited until I'd passed before he called, "Hey mama, where you going? The party's just about to get started."

"Sorry, I have a date with the DJ to dance on Jim Bridger's grave." I walked away.

I hitched a ride around dawn from an old rancher in a battered flatbed who said he could only take me a little ways; I told him that was far enough. I lied to all his questions, and said nothing when he scolded me for hitching alone. "Lotsa bad men out driving. Drunked-up, too."

He took me almost to Fairfield. I went to a Salvation Army store and bought some faded Levis and a men's flannel shirt with my last five dollars.

After that I hitched a ride—another farmer—to here, somewhere in the central valley. I'm writing this by the scatter of moonlight through the cracked shakes of an abandoned barn. It's ramshackle and smells like old piss, but it's shelter enough on this warm spring night.

Ever since we got here (Mia's already asleep—she had a tough day) I've been trying to remember that yeasty odor of bread rising in my grandmother's warming oven from when I was four or five, and I just smelled it now, sharp and musky, and I remember my blue pajamas and the moonlight sheen on the goosedown quilt as soft as a goodnight kiss. And if I hold really still and forget myself, I feel the mist of my father's seed in my mother's pulse, can feel myself passing bodiless between them, my face erupting out of nothingness, my tiny mouth already hungry for a voice, and I can see my first dream shiver through the veins in my almost transparent eyelids, but I can't remember what I was dreaming. The first dream—that's what I want to know. I want to remember the first dream I ever had. And then I'll use that knowledge to ransom my ghost from the lightning.

Daniel didn't call Volta at the first opportunity, nor the hundredth. He couldn't figure out if the second thoughts represented prudent doubts or were merely allowing him to put it off. His cover was clearly blown, and Daniel had to consider the possibility that Volta had decided that the Diamond was safer with the government than with him, and had turned him to CIA, rolled over on him, "dropped a dime" as Mott said.

He had to consider it, but he didn't believe it. More likely, there was a tap, or maybe an agent inside the Alliance. A tap would make it risky to even call Volta, since they probably would set it up for immediate trace. That would provide his general location, if nothing else. He wasn't worried about being caught—he could vanish with the Diamond and walk through a wall of tanks—but he didn't want the annoyance. Nor did he want to leave them the truck with Wally's and Annie's fingerprints and a paper trail they could perhaps follow back to the AMO people who had set it up. But when all that convenient logic was exhausted, Daniel, with the fiercest honesty he could muster, knew the reason for his reluctance was a decidedly unreasonable intuition that he would be sadder for the call. Sadness would weaken him in his attempt to see what the Diamond wanted to offer.

He was thinking about drawing a blind *yes* or *no* from a hat when it struck him that he had never tried looking into the Diamond's center with his eyes closed. He pulled over at the next rest area and vanished with the Diamond. He looked into its center steadily and then closed his eyes. He saw an after-image of the spiral flame that faded quickly. He could imagine the Diamond, see the flame center clearly, but could not see inside it. After an hour, he forced himself to reappear with the Diamond and get back on the road.

He received two signs almost immediately. The first was premonitory: a mileage sign that read GLOBE 37. The second sign was so direct Daniel stopped the moment he saw it. The sign was on the wall of a fire-gutted gas station, written large on the outside face of the cinderblocks; the heat-blistered paint had peeled and fallen away, and of what was once a list of parts and services, all that remained were:

AKES

ARK PLUG

VOLTA REGULAT

The phone booth at the far end of the lot was unscathed except for a lingering odor of damp smoke.

Volta answered on the first ring: "Allied Furnace Repair, Night Service."

Daniel said, "The place I'm calling from advertises 'akes, ark plugs, volta regulats.' It left me no choice."

"Well," Volta replied mildly, "I'm glad to see you're beginning to develop a sense of humor. You're going to need it. First of all—"

"I have doubts about the privacy of this line," Daniel interrupted, adding, to explain his apparent rudeness, "before we get started."

"No, the line is secure. But I surmise by your doubts that you already know your traveling identity has been compromised."

"So I've gathered."

"Listen while I explain what happened. Listen carefully. It's a revelatory explanation."

277

Daniel listened as instructed. As Volta described Dredneau's torture, Daniel closed his eyes and slumped back against the phone-booth wall. He could feel what was coming in Volta's voice from the slight tremor at the end of each precise statement, feel it in the precision itself, and when Volta revealed that the man who'd tortured Dredneau had also shot his mother for no reason, Daniel softly cried, "Ohhh no. No."

Volta paused a moment, then continued, "Subsequently, through some inspired work by Smiling Jack, we learned the code name of the person who betrayed the Livermore theft to the CIA." Volta stopped and waited.

Daniel, too stunned to think, took a deep breath. "The killer and the snitch—you didn't mention their names."

"Daniel," Volta said evenly, "I will give you the names when you bring me the Diamond. I promised you in the hospital, the first time we met, that I would do everything I could to help you find your mother's killer, and now he is known. I've honored my promise. Daniel, you vowed that in exchange for my help you would share with me the privilege of beholding the Diamond and the responsibility of returning it to hiding, safe from us all. You haven't honored your promise, and even granting extraordinary circumstances, that shows an utter lack of respect for me, and yourself. If you want to revenge your mother, you must honor your promise with the Diamond. That's fair."

Daniel howled, "What the fuck am I supposed to do? Terrorize him until he kills himself?" Daniel hurled the phone at the glass wall but the cord was too short and snapped back against his wrist. He grabbed it and slammed it down on the hook.

He stormed back to his truck, started it, then turned it off and slumped back in the seat. "It's fair, it's fair, goddammit, it's *fair*. But I *didn't* want to know, don't need decisions." He walked resolutely back to the phone booth and redialed Volta's number.

Volta again answered on the first ring. He didn't seem surprised to hear Daniel say, "You're right, it *is* fair. But I'm going to keep the Diamond until I see inside it, or through it, or whatever it allows me to do. I want to see inside this Diamond a thousand times more than I want to revenge my mother's death—and even though Wild Bill cleaned out most of that cold frenzy, I would still revenge it. Do you understand what I'm saying? That as much as I would like justice for my mother, it's nothing compared to my desire to open the Diamond. I need you to let me go. I need your blessing."

"I've already let the Diamond go, Daniel, and I think the only way it will ever open for you is to let it go. You're free to do as you can, free to go, free to return. I have no claims on your soul. I wish you luck, and I wish you success. But I *will not* give my blessings because I believe the Diamond will destroy you. It may destroy you beautifully, magnificently, but it will destroy you, Daniel, and I will *not* bless pointless waste."

"It *wants* me to see. I can *feel* it."

"It's a mirror, Daniel. Just another mirror."

"I think it's a window. A door."

"Know thyself," Volta said, "and to thine own self be true. I have too much admiration for you to deny your right to explore as you must. But I wouldn't be true to myself—or you—if I didn't tell you I think you'll be destroyed, and that if you are, Daniel, it will break my heart."

"But you don't understand—"

"Perhaps not," Volta cut in. "I grant that possibility. But then, maybe *you* don't understand. Maybe you're obsessed, powerless against the Diamond, or simply too young to know better."

"It's possible," Daniel said. "But that's what I'm committed to finding out."

"May you find what you seek."

Daniel smiled in the dark phone booth. "That sounded like a blessing to me."

"Then may you find what you deserve."

"I'll take that as a blessing, too. I've *earned* this right, Volta, and though you truly helped me earn it—for which you have my endless gratitude—it's mine. And this is what I'm feeling in my marrow: It is mine not because I earned it or physically possess it; the Diamond is mine by destiny."

Volta said, "Be thrice blessed then. I'll add an ancient Estonian blessing: 'May your journey have an end.' The Diamond is your responsibility now."

Daniel said quickly, "I wouldn't have it any other way. But as part of my sense of responsibility, I vow to bring the Diamond to you when my work is finished, or if for some reason I can't and am forced to return it to hiding, I'd like to return it to wherever you had intended."

"No, Daniel. I let it go. I can't tell you how clean it felt when I finally released it from my grasp. And for *that* lesson, *I* thank *you*. I'm going to fold up this operation now, and go home to Laurel Creek Hollow. You have the routing numbers; the direct line is seven multiplied by the day of the month. Call if you want, or come visit. I'll guarantee your welcome but not my assistance; that will depend on the wisdom of what you need and my capacity and inclination to provide it. Let us take our leave as friends."

"That's all I wanted," Daniel said, his eyes burning with tears. "Thank you."

"Good-bye, Daniel," Volta said.

"Thank you," Daniel repeated. "Yes, good night. I'll be in touch."

They hung up at the same time.

* * *

Volta spent the rest of the night on the phone and radio dismantling the operation and reassigning people and resources to other projects. Ellison Deeds, Jean Bluer, and Smiling Jack were all in the field somewhere, so he left messages to call him upon their respective returns. He packed equipment till well after sunrise, then slept fitfully for a few hours. He lay in bed and tried to imagine what Daniel saw when he looked into the Diamond. Daniel had said he could only see into the Diamond when he vanished with it. Volta was skittish about even imagining himself vanished. He remembered the temptation to cross the threshold and keep going, consumed in some undreamable whirlpool of felicity, an ecstatic suicide. Instead, he tried a technique he'd learned from Ravana Dremier, slowly condensing himself to an essence and then separating it from his psyche, lifting himself out of himself as an objective witness, yet retaining his will to know.

He still couldn't imagine Daniel vanished and looking into the Diamond, but paradoxically—having abandoned rationality for empathetic imagination—he suddenly understood what he might have deduced through laborious reasoning. Daniel saw a spiral flame in the Diamond, just as he'd seen it in the vision he'd reported to Volta. That explained why he'd called it "mine," and why he thought it was meant for him alone. His vision, of course, had disposed him toward seeing it. Volta was the only other person in the world capable of confirming whether the spiral flame was indeed only visible to the vanished. And both of them knew Volta wouldn't vanish again. Daniel had perhaps chosen to spare them both the sorrow of refusal—whether out of kindness or pity, Volta wasn't sure.

And he wasn't certain Daniel could survive the situation in which he was so terribly alone. There was nothing Volta could do about it and remain true to himself, and probably nothing he could do even if he betrayed himself. Volta had let the Diamond go—not as joyously or as easily as he'd tried to make it seem to Daniel—but he couldn't release Daniel from his heart. Volta understood that he, no less than Daniel, had confused the ideal and the real, but he understood, in a way Daniel did not, that such a confusion seldom goes unpunished. Because Volta had no children, Daniel, orphan of fire, was an ideal son. And now it was going to hurt.

Volta closed his eyes and tried again to imagine Daniel vanished with the Diamond, tried to see the spiral flame through Daniel's mind. He was failing so badly he was relieved to hear a key in the lock and Smiling Jack's voice booming down the stairs, "Dreamers awake!"

Volta swung his feet to the floor, muttering, "One dreamer's not sure anymore if he knows the difference."

As he stepped from behind the partition, Smiling Jack advanced, waving a half-gallon of Ten High. "What do you say, Volt? Let's get really fucked up and full of sentimental despair and then finally decide life, despite every heartbreak and anguished cry, is worth each pulse and breath."

Volta tried to smile. "I'd drink to that, but you have work to do and I won't drink and get stupid without you."

"What work? Message I got said we're shutting this one down."

"We are, but I'm putting you in charge of loose ends. You tie such strong knots."

"What is this, an alliance of magicians and outlaws or the fucking navy?"

"It changes with every breath," Volta said.

"Maybe so," Jack sighed, "but I'm not going to try to change your mood. Be grim, glum, and gloomy."

"Jack, while I can't admire your alliterative abilities, I thank you for your thoughtfulness."

Smiling Jack sat down on the worn beige sofa. "How's Daniel? What'd he have to say?"

"He's emotionally ragged and spiritually lost—dangerously so. He's trying to see something inside the Diamond that he thinks only he can behold. He believes the Diamond wants him to see inside it. He intends to keep the Diamond until it opens and he understands. He said it is a thousand times more important to him to pursue the Diamond than revenge his mother's death. Other than that, our conversation was devoted to relieving each other of responsibilities for our stupid decisions."

"What do you think?" Jack said.

"I'm trying not to. That's why I want you to take responsibility for the follow-through. Two things: stay on Alex Three's identity, and do justice to Mr. Debritto. Set him up with the code as we've already discussed. When, where, and which Raven is up to you. I don't want to know till it's over."

"Okay," Jack said solemnly, "but there may be be another loose end. Shamus called Dolly this morning, claiming he has some crucial information he can only share with you and Daniel, so he wants to set up a meeting. He said he'd never heard of an Alex Three."

"How'd he sound to Dolly?"

"Nuts."

"No meeting right now. Have Dolly convey that we're both unavailable."

"Where are you going to be?"

"Home," Volta said.

*   *   *

Daniel woke in the front seat when the sun was high enough to blaze through the windshield. He had planned it that way when he'd parked the truck facing east, well hidden behind the burned-out gas station.

After talking to Volta he'd vanished with the Diamond. He tried concentrating on the twist of flame at the Diamond's center, focusing to a pinpoint intensity and then suddenly letting go, hoping the force of the Diamond's resistance would collapse outward—like someone holding a swinging door closed spilling into the street at the abrupt removal of the counterbalancing force. It didn't work.

He tried staring into the thread-thin, spiraling flame and praying with all his heart that the Diamond would open to him, let him see what he needed, let him step across the threshold clean. It didn't work.

An hour before dawn he took out his pocketknife and nicked his left thumb. He held his thumb above the Diamond, let the blood drip on the radiant globe before he sought to see inside. It didn't work.

Beaten and exhausted, he'd fallen into a dreamless sleep at dawn, not stirring until he felt the sunlight on his face. He sat up blinking, checked the Diamond in the bowling bag on the floor, and slid back behind the wheel.

Daniel drove straight through to Phoenix. He stopped at a Shell station for a city map, then checked the Yellow Pages in the phone booth's directory. He found exactly what he sought in the first listing under Auto Dismantling— *"Aura Wreckers . . . cash to smash."* When he noticed his fuel gauge showed less than a quarter tank, he unthinkingly pulled over to the pumps. When the attendant asked him, "Fill'er up, sir?" Daniel started laughing so hard he could barely shake his head and gasp, "No, empty 'er."

"Beg your pardon?"

"Nothing," Daniel said, more in control, "I thought I needed gas but I don't."

"Help you with anything else?" the attendant said. He eyed Daniel with wary concern.

"No, I guess not," Daniel told him. "I don't even know if I want in or out anymore, or if there's a difference."

"You look like you've been on the road awhile. Tired. It gets to you."

Daniel said earnestly, "I hope so."

The attendant nodded vaguely and said, "Well, take it easy. Have a good one."

Daniel thanked him and headed through Phoenix.

He stopped down the street from Aura Wreckers. In the camper, he dressed in his bowling shirt, jeans, and shoes, packed a change of clothes and toilet kit in a day-pack, and stuffed a thousand-dollar roll from the attaché case in his front pocket. He took the pack and attaché case back to the cab and set them on the floor with the bowling-bagged Diamond. He crumpled the phony registration and pink slip in the ashtray and burned them, tear-blind from the smoke before he cranked the windows down.

Daniel wheeled into the oil-splotched yard of Aura Wreckers and pulled up near a crane with a powerful magnet on its cable. The crane was picking up hulks from a pile of wrecked cars and dropping them into a forty-ton hydraulic crusher that turned each one into a small metal cube. A large beer-bellied man operating the crusher yelled at Daniel, "Hey, no parking! Office is back there." He pointed toward the building.

Daniel gathered the bowling-bag, attaché case, and day-pack and walked toward the man, who looked pained at his approach. Before Daniel was halfway there the man called, "C'mon, man—move your ride and put you in it—we don't have no insurance that covers fools. This is a heavy-equipment area, and I'm the yard boss."

Daniel stopped in front of him and looked into his eyes. "My truck must be destroyed."

The yard boss looked at the truck and then back to Daniel. "What for?" he said suspiciously. "It was still moving when you got here."

Daniel roared, "It is *possessed* of *demons!* I *know* because I am a man of God and a professional bowler. As a Minister of Faith with the Gospel Strike Church of Imperishable Bliss, I am under vows of frugality, and therefore drive from match to match on the PBA tour, spreading some of the Sun Lord's literature on the way. And as I travel these faithless states, I pick up every hitchhiker I see, some of whom are striking young women, many not even seventeen, wandering lost in this world, bereft of love and comfort. I swear to heaven my intentions are noble when I pick them up—to share the wisdom and consolation of The Word—but there are *demons* in the truck, vinyl warlocks, devils of chrome, and they tear my heart from the River of Light and hurl it into the Sewer of Raw Desire. I *know* it's the truck, because lewd and carnal desires seize those comely young women, too, and soon the demons have dragged us panting into the camper where we rut for hours like lust-crazed warthogs, and I *feel* their hot, tight, naked bodies move under me like a wave of ball bearings and my heart wants nothing more than the endless replication of our joined moment of release forever and forever!"

The yard boss gave the truck a more thoughtful appraisal. "Don't look like much of a pussy wagon to me." He shook his head. "But what the hell—if you got the pink slip and the registration's in order, I'll give ya a coupla hundred for it. Maybe take it for a drive. Fuck, ya never know, maybe something sweet'll jump on my bone."

Daniel thundered, "I want it *destroyed!* It is possessed by Creatures of Filth!" Daniel raised his fist and slammed it down into his palm. "The Creatures of Filth *must* be *crushed!*"

The yard boss stepped back and folded his arms over his protruding gut.

Tilting his head, he inquired with a trace of derision, "What are you, some kinda fucking wacko? You can't be for real. The real gets weird, sure, but not *this* weird. Huh? How about it? You for real?"

With an extended index finger, Daniel began thumping the center of his forehead. He smiled at the yard boss. "It appears I am."

The yard boss considered a moment. "Ya got the pink slip and reg?"

"The demons covered them with a green slime that sucked off all the ink. Turned that pink slip blank and snowy white."

"Get outa here," the yard boss muttered, pointing with his chin. "We don't touch fucking nothing without clear title, and especially from loonies who seem to have blown their mental transmissions but are still coasting to a stop. No title, no deal."

Daniel reached into his front pocket and took out the roll of bills. "Would a thousand dollars change your mind?"

"Completely," the yard boss said, counting it quickly before shoving the roll in a back pocket. "Get out what you want and pull it over. I'll go tell Jake there, running the crane, that you're next. And Reverend? Any more demons get to haunting your vehicles, bring 'em on in and we'll give them a Monster Mash that'll pop their little black hearts like rotten cherries. Same deal, same price."

"Bless you, son," Daniel said fervently, spreading his arms. "May you flow with the River of Light."

Daniel watched smiling as the cable-lowered magnet locked on his truck with a solid clank, rocking it on its springs. Cable reversed, the truck jerked free of the ground, sunlight exploding on its twirling chrome as the crane swung it toward the crusher like a fish being lifted from water to land. The magnet released and the truck dropped into the press, windshield shattering on impact. Then, with a breathy hydraulic hiss and the dry shriek of buckling metal, the press reduced the truck and its contents to a gleaming four-foot cube.

Daniel was impressed by this model of concentration, and fought a merry urge to try the crusher on his brain. He lifted his arms heavenward and cried out in joy, "Free, free, oh Blessed Light; free *at last!*"

He slung the day-pack over one shoulder and stooped to pick up the case and bowling bag. He hefted the bowling bag, imagining the Diamond burning inside. "How about it, huh?" he mumbled to the Diamond. "Free at last sound good? You and me together, baby, both of us, nothing but dense, wild, diamond light, stone solid and loose as flame. Marry me." He started giggling uncontrollably at the thought of giving the Diamond a diamond ring. It would be like giving Venus a rat's asshole for a wedding band.

Still giggling, he walked through the gate, turned west, and stuck out his thumb. From the churn of connections, he realized he hadn't slept with a woman since he'd been on the road with Bad Bobby. Over a year. With Jean Bluer he'd been absorbed in other identities, and after that all his energies had gone into vanishing, consumed in being nothing at all. He remembered thinking after he'd first vanished that he might be able to make love with the same woman twice, but he hadn't thought to try. His body, however, hadn't forgotten. A heavy current swirled through him. Bursting into tears at Wally's mention of loving his wife. Exceeding the demands of effective characterization with his description of all those lust-struck nubile teen-angels. Marriage. Conjunction. He was horny, so horny he could feel the Diamond's warmth against his thigh, or so erotically ripe he imagined he did. He let his arm drop to his side. He squared his shoulders; took a slow, deep breath; closed his eyes. He tried to imagine the spiral as a woman, see her face, gather her body from the spiral's burning curve, feel her opening with him, feel her heartbeat real against his palm, both of them bathed in light.

A deep male voice called, "Ya dreaming there, kid, or looking for an actual ride?"

An old Ford flatbed, dusty and dinged, rattled at idle where it had pulled over next to him. He hadn't even noticed. The short leather-faced man at the wheel pushed up a cowboy hat older than the truck and said, "You riding or hiding, son? Ain't going further than the Juniper Mountains, but you're welcome along if that's how your stick floats."

"What's that mean?" Daniel said.

"Old mountain-man lingo, from beaver-trapping. Means which way you're going, how you're inclined, what you hanker."

For a moment, Daniel thought of waving him on and waiting for a woman to stop. He wanted to be with a woman. But the old cowboy in the flatbed looked like he might know something. Daniel picked up the attaché case and said, "I'm riding."

THE FIRST NOTEBOOK OF JENNIFER RAINE
APRIL SOMETHING (7TH? 9TH?)

A long way from last night. I just hit Reno and things are good and bad, and probably that's "normal" if you're "sane" and "mature," but maybe because I'm none of the above, I'm down with the blues. Not depressed, Doc—blue. A touch of postpartum blues, the adrenaline of our delivery from confinement to liberty fading, from thrilling act to a new set of mean facts. It's tough to live in hiding or on the run.

I've got the mama-blues working on me, too. Mia woke up screaming last night in the barn. She had a terrible dream about fire-snakes falling on her in the darkness, their sizzling venom turning her to stone. I couldn't console her. I rocked her for hours, humming lullabies, but she just kept on sobbing until my helplessness overwhelmed me and I wanted to smother her to silence her cries. Instead, I left her weeping on the straw pallet and went outside to look at the moon and stars until I was small enough to go back in and rock her in my arms again and let her weep. I can't feel where she's hurt the way I could before; her pains have become too complex. I can only love her and hope she heals. Women hurt and heal differently.

I don't know about men. They seem to confuse permission and plunder. In my cosmology, the sun created itself and imposed a single rule of existence: Everything created had to create something in return. The sun, to demonstrate, created Earth. Earth created a mighty river fed from a bottomless spring. The flowing river hit a mammoth golden stone and forked into freshwater and saltwater, into rivers and oceans. At the exact point where water met stone, men and women were created. Men created the clock. Women created the moon.

See, Doc, I'm not crazy. I just know what's going on.

I have to admit some of my blues are the rejected kind. The only good news today was a ride from the barn to Reno, courtesy of an Alaskan fisherman named Billy Krough. I halfway fell in love as we rambled along. Billy, alas, was tall and strong, and while he wasn't really handsome, his face, especially his deep-set, sky-blue eyes, had character. Smart, too. I require intelligent men. Bright Billy knew where Jim Bridger's grave is—eastern Wyoming. I'd instinctively run in the right direction. The brain isn't the only organ that thinks.

Billy was headed for Las Vegas to play big-time poker, his last blast before heading back to Petersburg for the salmon and halibut seasons. He makes enough money in the four tough months of fishing to take off and travel the other eight. His two long-time loves broke up over his off-season restlessness and his months gone at sea. Seemed to actually understand their point of view and had remained good friends. And there we were in the front seat, Mia sound asleep in the back, and I wanted someone to hold me close, so I slid across and snuggled in tight and said, "Hold me."

He did, and it was tender and truly sweet, but without a trace of that wild carnal edge you would have to cross if you want to get so close together you can't tell each other apart.

I pushed it. I said, "I want to get closer. I want you to love who I am." Love doesn't do much for the powers of explanation, but since Love has never asked for one itself, that seems fair enough.

Billy was kind. He squeezed me a little bit closer and explained that he'd promised a certain woman not to play around, a promise he intended to honor despite what he was thoughtful enough to call a "delectable temptation like you." Me! But not so delectable the temptation couldn't be declined.

Shit. Why are the ones who are too good to be true always being true to someone else?

Billy let us off in downtown Reno. He wasn't even stopping to play cards since the action he wanted was in Vegas. He gave me a fifty-dollar bill, saying he wanted to treat me to a long bath and a night of safe rest, though I was absolutely free to piss it away gambling. A real gentleman.

I haven't decided what to do with the fifty. I'm writing this in a Winchell's donut shop while I think it over. Mia is still asleep. Poor little girl, she shouldn't have to go through this. She's exhausted. I'll let her sleep until she's done dreaming and wakes herself. It's no problem to carry an imaginary daughter around. They're light.

What we Crazy Jane's with imaginary daughters call "inside jokes."
Hee-hee.

Gonna laugh them blues away.

Eli Boyd, a semiretired ranch hand who worked his own twenty acres up near Hope Mountain when he wasn't working on somebody else's spread—which was too goddamn often as far as Eli was concerned—drove the old Ford flatbed at a steady fifty miles per hour and just as steadily told Daniel jokes, tales, yarns, and no-shit true stories of the Old West, back when a man could ride two days to hump the schoolmarm and never cut another human track along the way. Daniel listened, from Aura Wreckers in Sun City to the I-40 junction. One story in particular seized his imagination.

Eli began, "Cowboys are known fools for drinking up their wages, and I was doing my part till something happened that stopped me cold. Ain't a pretty story, but by God it not only saved me money on liquor, but all the expensive craziness that goes with it: dancing girls, bar repairs, bail, court costs, and them goddamn hospital bills.

"Happened in Colorado high country up outa Durango, musta been 'round fifty-five, fifty-six, somewhere in there. I was working for the Randall boys then, and me and one of their cousins was moving some horses up to summer pasture. We got 'em up to the line shack 'bout nightfall and put 'em in this little ol' barn the Randalls' great-great-granddaddy had built. Then me and Jamie—that was this cousin's name, just a kid really, nineteen or twenty—we went over to the line shack and grubbed up and shot the shit for a while before we hit the rack, pretty tuckered from being in the saddle since dawn.

"Jamie was a strange kid, a bit on the jumpy side and not real overwhelming in the smarts department. Stark fact of it is, Jamie may have been an in-breed somewhere in the Randall line. Folks 'round Durango used to claim the only virgin Randall women were the ones who could run faster than their brothers.

"For all Jamie's dumbness, he was good with horses. It was like he'd drawn what little brains he had all together and brought it down real hard on one thing, and that thing was horses. That kid loved horses. And he was *good* with 'em.

"So we're sacked out and sawing logs when these high, shrill whinnies out in the barn snap us awake. We both jump pronto in our boots and grab our shooting guns.

" 'Wolf?' " I whisper to him as we head for the door.

" 'I don't know,' Jamie says, and his voice is real thin and tight.

"We're just gettin' to the barn when these two young buckskin mares come bolting into the corral and I could see right away in the moonlight that their legs was chewed all to hell. I knew then what had happened; feller I used to ride trail with in the Junipers had seen it hisself when he was a young poke. The barn rats had gotten into some fermented silage and gone full-berserk frenzied, rampaging through the stalls eating the horses' legs from right above the hoof clean up to the knee—left it that flat, stringy, bluish-white color like you get when you skin out a deer. The horses looked like they all had white stockings, not much blood at all. Sweet fucking Jesus, it was ghostly!

"But what really froze my blood was them rats squealing, so high-pitched it could shatter your skull like cheap glass or at least leave you deaf from all the needle holes in your eardrums. The squeals from the trampled rats sounded different than the shrieks of those that only wanted to eat on some warm flesh.

"I mean to say my jaw's down around my knees, 'cause even though I'd *heard* of it, *seeing* it is something entirely different. Actually, being stunned stupid is about the best thing to do in that situation unless you feel like discharging a firearm against a herd of crazed rats in a dark barn full of insane horses. None for me, thanks; no sir. Let nature take its twisty course. I wanted to make sure Jamie saw the wisdom in letting it be. I didn't like what I saw. Jamie's eyeballs had rolled damn near 'round *backwards* in the sockets, same sickly white as them horses' legs, and stone blank, just like those Cuban what-cha-call'ems—them zoombies. *Gone,* know what I mean?

"And all of sudden Jamie screams, 'The horsies! The horsies!' Like a little kid. He runs for the barn.

" 'Don't, Jamie!' I yell. 'Don't shoot, it'll spook 'em worse.' Damn if he doesn't toss his gun away. But just before he goes in he stops and yanks out an old rusty icepick some hunter left stuck in a corral post.

"Now you notice I ain't running to stop him nor help him. It's right there in Article Twenty-two of the *Code of the West:* 'If some fucking in-breed wants to run into a bedlam of barn rats on a drunken feeding spree, that's *his* business.'

288

"I stood there in my boots and long johns and waited for the horses to get out in the corral where they had room to move. The noise died down enough for me to hear Jamie panting inside the barn, 'You fuckers, you fuckers,' and the thud of the icepick in the plank floor. I struck some fire to a hurricane lamp and went inside.

"Jamie was down on his hands and knees. The back of his right hand, the one without the icepick, was about chewed down to bone. An ugly sight, but it wasn't much compared to what Jamie was doing. He'd got a rat trapped in the corner of a stall and just kept stabbing it and stabbing it, fifty, sixty times, that icepick a blur in the lamplight.

" 'Jamie!' I yell, and he wheels to look at me, muscles in his cheeks jerking, white spit frothing from his mouth, his eyes turned back 'round normal but looking a thousand glazed miles away. And he roars like a goddamn mountain lion, 'Noooo! Noooo!' and goes scuttling after the rats, which are writhing in little squealing clumps eating their dead.

"He gets one his first stab and keeps stabbing it until another leaps at his face and he wheels and chases it into a stall where I can hear his sobs and the thud of that icepick like someone beating on a heavy door. All of a sudden he lets out a scream so powerful everything freezes to silence, the whole barn absolutely still. And he whoops, 'I got him, Eli! I finally got him.' And he starts laughing.

"I go in with the lantern and there's Jamie, grinning, his eyes locked on something far away. He's sprawled out against the back of the stall, and his right hand is icepicked to the wall straight through the palm. He says, 'Look, Eli, I finally got him.' "

Eli left Daniel thinking about this at the Junction of 93 and I-40, Eli's right rear turn signal erratically blinking as he headed east for his home on the range.

Standing with his thumb out for another ride, Daniel decided it was a cautionary tale, wisely taken to heart. Maybe Volta was right. Maybe he should just let it go. The old men seemed to think so, anyway, and he would be foolish not to consider their counsel when he was at a loss about what to try next. Maybe if he physically let it go, he could open it through memory and imagination. He looked at his upraised thumb, then opened his hand as if setting an invisible bird free. He imagined how it would feel to drive an icepick through his palm, imagined it so clearly he almost cried out with the pain.

Shamus was sitting at the tiny desk in a cheap Sacramento motel. His silver-scarred hand was pressed to his ear, dictating possibilities his free hand jotted down on a yellow legal pad.

"A.T. Al times three. Three Al's? Try that. Alalal. Allah? Swiss accent. Male, mid-thirties. Three *owls,* maybe? That budge anything loose in that compacted bowel you call a brain? Think, shithead! Help me out. Three owls. Awls? Laws? Three Laws? No, no, wrong direction. Al Triple X? Al to the Third Power—what's that, Al Nine? Third power. Al Thrice? Al Thrice! *That's it!* You get it, bumble-fuck?"

"No," Shamus said dully. He was very drunk.

"*Al* for Alchemy. Thrice-Great. Trismegistos. 'For this reason I am called Hermes Trismegistos, for I possess the three parts of wisdom of the whole world.' C'mon, Shamus—you tell me."

"Volta. That rotten, snitching prick," Shamus said, rage stirring him from stupor. "And it's just like that arrogant bastard to use Hermes Trismegistos and alchemy all scrambled into a cute code. That's his style, and he's so fucking confident, he gave it to us. And we knew it all along." Shamus wrote Volta's name so savagely the lead snapped when he crossed the t. "Volta the All Wise. Perfect sense. A Swiss accent would be a snap for Volta. And then he rubs our faces in it. Guess he forgot we studied with Jacob Hind. We're damn near the alchemical scholar he was. How could he think he could sneak that kind of cuteness by us?"

Shamus's scarred hand said in his ear, "Maybe he *knew* he couldn't, you idiot; ever think of that?"

Shamus was baffled. "What are you talking about?"

"He *wants* you to think it was him, to deflect you from Daniel. Figure it out, dildo—somebody had to tell Volta what was going on."

"It was them together, just like we thought. But where are they?"

The scarred hand moved from his ear to face him. "Listen: one will lead you to the other. Find one, you find them both."

Daniel's next ride was an hour coming. When he saw the Chevy pickup with a camper begin to brake, his first impulse was to run. It was his truck, somehow reborn from a cube of metal. With a rush of relief he noticed the Michigan plates and the reflecto-decal lettering arched above the camper door:

ERNIE & IRMA
Geritol Gypsies

Irma scooted over to make room for him in the cab. She was a tiny, delicate, white-haired woman, mid-sixties, in brown slacks, fresh yellow blouse, and a brown knit cardigan. She held a small poodle on her lap. The dog eyed Daniel tremulously. The poodle seemed somehow incomplete to Daniel but he wasn't sure why.

Ernie reached around the poodle to shake hands. Daniel could never have disguised himself as Irma, but Ernie would have been easy. Like Daniel, he was six feet and blue-eyed, but with forty years and as many pounds added. Daniel would have had to exhaust hundreds of wardrobes to match Ernie's polyester shirt, which had a line of Conestoga wagons running up his right arm, a cattle drive up the trail of his left, and a blazing pastel sunset across the back. Daniel found the shirt so improbable he blinked to make sure he wasn't hallucinating.

After Ernie introduced himself and pulled back on the road, Irma patted the panting little poodle and said, "This is Chester."

Daniel smiled at the dog. "Howdy, Chester."

Chester shivered, then wagged his haunches.

Daniel noticed that Chester either had lost his tail or it had been docked extremely close.

Irma explained: "A great big Doberman Pinscher bit off Chester's tail." She bent down and cooed, "We don't like big dogs, do we Chester?" Chester buried his head between her knees. Irma looked at Daniel proudly. "Chester understands everything I say."

"Where ya headed, Herman?" Ernie said a little too quickly, as if embarrassed.

Daniel, forgetting for a moment that he'd introduced himself with the name on his bowling shirt, wasn't sure who Ernie was addressing. He blustered, "Oh, you know, just on down the line for now. 'Frisco eventually, but the pro tour still is a while off, so I'm sort of making do with what action I can find. Heard they'll gamble on anything in Nevada."

"That's why they call it Lost Wages," Ernie grinned.

"So I've heard," Daniel said politely, having wearied of this on the poker circuit. He had decided to avoid Las Vegas. Too many people knew him and he didn't feel like working up a more elaborate disguise.

"So you're on the loose," Ernie said.

"Yeah, basically. And I'm not sure if I've got no place to go, or too many."

Thoughtfully, Ernie said, "Know what ya mean. I was like that when I was young and roaming, right before W. W. Two started. It was like I couldn't even *imagine* my life, know what I mean?"

With a faint smile Daniel said, "With me, it's more like I can't stop imagining it."

"About the same thing, huh?" Ernie said. "Just another way of looking at it."

Irma said to no one in particular, "Oh, it wasn't that bad." She turned to Daniel with a distracted smile. "Do you enjoy your work?"

"I don't know," Daniel said. When they glanced at him nervously, Daniel smiled and explained as well as he could. "I guess it seems strange not to know if I enjoy my work, but I'm honestly uncertain. I don't think of bowling in terms of enjoyment. I'm too busy concentrating on trying to do it right, do it well—do it *at all,* for that matter."

Irma smiled blankly, idly stroking Chester's thin back.

Ernie volunteered, "I worked for GM, thirty-five years at the Chevy plant in Detroit—what we call 'Motown.' Irma and me been married thirty-four years. I retired three years ago, kids gone, house paid for, so me and Irma just take off whenever the notion moves us. Going out and seeing things keeps ya young. Last fall we went and looked over New England. Real pretty in the fall, all them red and golden leaves. Now this country here strikes me as a little grim, but the light's nice, the sunsets and all."

Irma, with the same distracted smile, said to herself, "It always is."

Daniel said, "What'd you do at GM, Ernie?"

"I was just on the line. Mounted the spare, put in the jack and lug wrench, then shut the trunk."

"Did you enjoy it?" Daniel said.

Ernie shrugged his heavy shoulders. "Like ya said, it's a job."

Irma said to the poodle, "He enjoyed it, didn't he, Chester?"

Chester yapped sharply once.

Irma nodded with satisfaction.

"You know," Ernie addressed Daniel, "I didn't mind the routine. Gives life shape. And even if you're doing one thing all the time, it's never really the same. Like closing those car trunks—each one sounded different. Millions, and *every one* different. You know what I mean?"

"I think so," Daniel said.

Irma asked Chester, "Does Daddy know what he means?"

Chester yapped twice. "Twice means 'no,' " Irma translated, a smug glint in her eyes.

Ernie muttered, "Damn dog hates me. I was the one who thought he needed some exercise. Let him off the leash to go sniff around the park and the Doberman bit off all his tail and half his ass in one chomp 'fore I could nail him with a rock and run him off. Tried to tell Chester he was up against a rule of life: Big dogs eat. Being on the leash wouldn't have made no difference."

Daniel bent and said to the quivering poodle, "We don't like big dogs, do we, Chester?"

Chester hid his head. "He's so amazing," Irma trilled. "He understands everything he hears."

Ernie, Irma, and Chester said good-bye on the west side of Las Vegas during the sunset's fiery crescendo of gold and crimsons, the colors so pure and clear that the blinding sundown on Ernie's shirt paled to the edge of vanishing, so stunning that Ernie turned off the engine and they sat and watched in silence, Chester stretching his front paws against the dashboard to get a better view. Daniel was taken with how easily the air let the colors go, how inexorably Earth turned on the axis of darkness and light. He suddenly felt a panic to get out of the truck's cab, vanish, vanish or else start weeping. But he couldn't vanish with them there. He said, fighting the tightness in his throat, "Well, on that lovely, fiery note, I'l take my leave. Thank you for the ride and your splendid company."

Amid their farewells, he slid out. Just before closing the door, Daniel said, "Drop it in a river." Even Chester seemed puzzled by the remark.

Daniel stepped back to let the truck pull away, but it didn't budge. Muffled inside the cab, Chester barked frantically. Irma rolled down the window, calling excitedly, "You forgot your balling ball! Chester saw it! Understands everything, just like I told you."

Daniel lifted the bowling bag through the open window. "Wish I had Chester's mind," he said. "Pretty dumb to forget your means of livelihood. Thanks again. Take care."

He watched the taillights disappear back toward Las Vegas. He knelt to unzip the bowling bag, shielding the Diamond's light from traffic, though the road was empty. He looked into the Diamond. "You don't want me to let you go, do you? I'm the one, aren't I? If so, help me. Help me. Please, please help me." He vanished with the Diamond.

Around midnight, without warning, Daniel's concentration buckled and collapsed. He tried to tighten his focus but there was no power left. Overwhelmed, it took him a terrifying moment to gather himself and imagine him and the Diamond returned. The entry back was ragged. Daniel had no idea where in the world he was. On his knees, he stared at the Diamond, wondering where the spiral flame had gone. He heard a faint roar to his right. He turned, blinded by a ball of light hurtling toward him. He dove to the side, wrapping his body protectively around the bowling bag just as the driver of the black Trans-Am stood on the brakes and skidded into a one-eighty, stopping a hundred and fifty yards down the road. As the car headed back, Daniel zipped the bowling bag shut. The driver pulled onto the opposite shoulder and swung across the divider and stopped beside Daniel. For a moment the long blond hair made Daniel think it was a woman. He was sharply disappointed when a stocky man in his mid-thirties wearing cowboy boots, Levis, and an army fatigue jacket stepped around the car and said, "What in the name of fuck was *that* all about?"

"What?" Daniel said with puzzled innocence, getting to his feet.

"Didn't you *see* it, man? There was this huge fucking flash of light and *bam!* There you were, this weird glow all around you. *No fucking way* you could miss it."

Daniel said, "I was squatting down when I heard you coming and stood up real sudden—might have been the headlights reflecting off the case here, lots of bright metal, might have caught the light perfect."

Slowly shaking his head, the blond man stared at Daniel and his belongings. He shrugged. "Maybe I was having a 'palm flashback. Looked like the true item to me, though. Fuck, who cares, huh? Why sweat the little shit when Death knows your address, that's my motto."

"It's a good one," Daniel said.

"So, what is it, you hitching here or what? I'm going west till dawn, then I turn around and head back."

"Thanks," Daniel said. He picked up the attaché case and bowling bag.

The blond man said, "What are you got up as there, anyway? You the Wandering Bowler or what?"

"I'm a professional bowler and a religious zealot," Daniel explained.

"Yeah, just about anything beats the fuck out of working." He opened the door for Daniel.

"How about you?" Daniel said, slipping inside. "You're out late for a nine-to-five man."

"I repair slot machines at the Shamrock. Swing shift, two to ten. Gives me the hard side of midnight and early morning to ride patrol."

"What are you patrolling for? Or *against,* if that's the case."

"My old employer," the man said. "Death. I used to be Death's Chauffeur."

"For true?" Daniel said. He didn't feel like listening to bullshit.

"Straight skinny, brother; mortal fact. Let's get it rolling here and I'll tell you how it is." He shut the door.

"Great." Daniel barely said it aloud, but he couldn't decide if he felt ironic. "Don't sweat the little shit," he reminded himself. "Ride on through."

The blond man's name was Kenny Copper. Shortly after his eighteenth birthday, a judge had presented him with a choice between two years on the county labor farm for disturbing the peace/resisting arrest/assault on a police officer—which the court saw as a cluster of offenses, not a logical progression of self-defense—and immediate enlistment in the marines. He landed in Saigon eight months later, a PFC rifleman with Baker Company. Within the week they were shipped to Khe Sanh.

He told Daniel as they rocketed northwest on 95, "I put my head up the Dragon's ass, man, and I saw the World of Shit. The Cong were shelling the holy fuck out of us. We sent out a couple of recon patrols just for drill; never saw the dudes again. Anything that touched the airstrip got blown away. No Med-Evac. No replacements. They air-dropped rations and ammo, but whatever came down outside our perimeter—which was about half the shit they dropped—that was Christmastime for Charlie. We owned Hell; Charlie owned everything else. But here's the twister, Herm, your basic cold fuck—we were just *bait* for the trap, dead and stinkin' meat, 'cause they *wanted* the Cong to mass for a siege, get 'em all heaped up on us, and then bring down the hammer. Real neat thinking, huh? Real swift. I mean, the gooks didn't whip our ass by being dummies, not that you needed a Ph.D. in chemistry to figure it out, right? The Cong kept the pressure tight enough to choke, but they didn't overcommit. So *we* went down, not any fucking hammer.

"It wasn't too bad at first. I'd brought a pound of Buddha weed in on the chop—fifty Yankee dollars on any street corner in Saigon—and that cut us some slack between the shit-rain and fire-fights. Everybody on base knew our bunker was Boogie City. Black dude I booted with, name was Donnell Foxworth—Arson, we called him, 'cause he said he specialized in burning pussies to the ground—Arson had two ammo boxes full of primo sounds. Motown, Hendrix, the Doors, Dylan, Stones, you name it. Between the Buddha weed and the music, the troops stayed loose.

"And man, we needed some *serious* morale boosting, because the gooks had the high ground, their mortars and light artillery locked down on us dead zero, like frogs in a tub. Whenever they took the notion, day or night, for two minutes or twenty hours, they sent down a shit-rain of fire. You never been there, man, you just *can't know* what it's like to hear incoming, incoming, incoming till that shrill death whine has your blood howling like a gut-shot dog; your whole fucking body peeled back to bare nerves; your asshole puckered so tight that when it finally relaxes you crap your chaps; Dylan turned up loud on the deck, screaming in your ear, 'Well *HOW* does it *FEEL!* to be on YOUR *OWN!*'—I tell you true, if a round didn't blow you away, the rest of it did. I don't give a fuck if you had all the weed in 'Nam and a sound system that'd cave in your skull—*all* the smack; *all* the pussy in the world. Just *no way* you could keep it from getting too real. Constant sickening fear.

"About the third week, they really started pounding it in, and the perimeter turned into Sapper City. Try sleeping when them mortars are walking the dog all over you, when you know there's someone outside who'd love to slit your throat. I was holding on to myself in a muddy trench, literally had my arms wrapped around me, curled against the dirt wall, down with some killer gook dysentery, gagging on the smell of my own fear, shit pants, powder, smoke, exploded earth and bodies, when we took one inside, about half a football field down from where I was hunkered. Concussion fucking near blew my brains out my ears. I pushed myself up on my knees and looked up into the rain and the night, stunned so fucking bad I was wondering if I could see *way up there* the *actual* point where the rain started to fall. I was looking hard when a white square came fluttering down beside me. The second I touched it I knew what it was. Though I would have given anything not to look, this was something I was supposed to see. A guy in our outfit, Billy Hines, young guy from Missouri, real quiet, kinda bashful, was married to some seventeen-year-old sweetheart named Ginnilee whose first letter to him in-country said she was pregnant from his last leave. She'd sent a picture her mother had taken of her standing on the front lawn, the small house in the background out of focus. Written on the back, written it said, 'Wife with child. Never forget I love you. Ginnilee.' And her face . . . oh man, so young and hopeful and brave, the sweetest little strawberry-blond with freckles, man, fucking *freckles*, and all you had to do was see the light around her face to know she was pregnant. Chester wore it on his helmet. One time I asked why he didn't tuck it away where a pretty lady like that wouldn't get so jungle-scuzzed and rained on, and he said"—Kenny's voice began to quaver—"he said, 'She's my good-luck charm. She's gonna shine me right on through all this shit, home to her and the baby.' And man, when I picked her picture up out of the mud and *saw* her, man, *saw* her all the way to my soul, I vanished somewhere inside myself. You know what I mean, man? *Left* the premises. Stepped *out.*"

In the headlight glare of an oncoming semi, Daniel caught the wet flash of tears on Kenny's cheeks. He wiped at his own. Nothing he could have said seemed adequate.

Kenny glanced at him, then back to the road. "The doctors told me I was gone about three weeks, but that don't count the one it took before they got me out of Khe Sanh on a chop that was crazy enough to come in. 'Shell shock,' some of the docs called it, or 'catatonic shock.' I didn't bother to tell 'em I'd been all right until I looked into her face. But I don't give a fuck what the doctors want to call it, I *know* what it was. It was a limbo trance. Until my spirit could get itself together again, heal itself, the rest of me was not real, and my ass was up for grabs.

"And that's when Death snagged me for his personal chauffeur, dressed me in a white satin suit and put me behind the wheel of his black, ultra-swank seventy Caddy limo." Kenny paused and glanced at Daniel again. "You following this shit?"

"So far," Daniel said.

"I don't *see* Death, right? He always rides in the back, behind a smoked-glass partition with this tiny little slot just over my right shoulder. He'd get in, I'd start the limo, he'd slip a stiff white card through the slot with a name on it—no address, just the name—and I'd go find the person. Don't ask me *how* 'cause I have *no* fucking idea. Just *knew*. I'd find the person, park, Death would get out and be gone a minute, then he'd get back in and slip another name through the slot. No food, water, sleep, piss, shit—one name after another.

"At first, when I was still on the fire base, I knew some of the names, guys in my outfit. And there were some Vietnamese names, too. After a while I didn't know any of the names. But I fucking always knew where to find them.

"Then one night driving along there's a huge flash of light behind us, like an ammo dump getting off, and when I glance back the light's just right somehow so I can see through the partition into the backseat, see Death. He's a skeleton all right, man, with this mad, hungry, lonely grin, but forget the Grim Reaper shit, 'cause he's wearing a business suit, one of them sharp, pinstriped jobs, and his finger bones, every one of them, is crusted with diamond rings.

"The next card comes through the slot, I don't even have to look to know my name's on it. When you see Death, Death looks back, and there's millions of fucked-up people to chauffeur him around.

"I didn't think twice—if I was going down, I was gonna take that mother-fucker with me. So I stood on the gas until we were howling through the dark and then I jerked the wheel hard right and hit the door rolling.

"But I didn't get him. He's got some kind of dual controls in the back-seat there, and I hear the brakes lock before I clear the car. Now feature this, man: I don't hit the road, the bushes, nothing—I'm just falling through space. All I can concentrate on is the image of Ginnilee's face. I look into it, into her eyes and her smile and her dreams and the life inside her, and I don't know whether I'm imagining, remembering, or actually seeing her, because when I stop falling and open my eyes, I'm looking at this ugly old nurse who growls, 'About time, soldier. There's a war on.' But they sent me home to the VA.

"Not many know what Death looks like, what kind of wheels he has. Those that do have a responsibility to ride patrol and waste the motherfucker on sight. No questions. No answers. I got my piece from 'Nam under the seat. When I see him, I'm gonna blast them diamonds off his fingers, blow him down to dust."

Daniel said, "You think you can kill Death?"

"I don't know. But I sure as fuck can try."

"Almost have to," Daniel said softly. He leaned back in the seat and shut his eyes. He tried to imagine Ginnilee's face but he was too weary. He opened his eyes only to be blinded by the high beams of an oncoming car. As it passed, Daniel, struggling to refocus, thought he caught a glimpse of a black limo. He wheeled to look out the rear window, telling Kenny, "I got an eyeful of headlight, but I think that might have been it, the black limousine."

"Fuck, man, are you on drugs? That was a red seventy-seven Toyota."

Daniel watched the taillights move closer together as they faded in the distance. From what he'd seen, the car was long, low-slung, black. "Are you sure?"

"Relax, man," Kenny reassured him. "It's a crazy story to get behind, I know. Hard news. Cut the spook loose in ya is all. Remember, I *drove* the fuckin' limo; I'd know it blind. *That* was a red seventy-seven Toyota—bank it."

Daniel turned back around on the seat. "No problem," he said. "It's your call, your patrol—only trying to help out."

"I roger that, bro', and much obliged. Fuck, man, you were crying with me there during the war stories—think I don't know you're on my frequency? I pick up every hitchhiker I see on patrol, and I tell 'em all about Ginnilee's face and that gone month driving Death around. Some of them say nothing, some tell me I'm full of shit, some humor me like I'm some sort of war-psycho-moron, and almost all of them decide that they'd rather stand on the empty desert highway than ride another mile with me. Maybe one out of a hundred has even a little fucking tiny tear to shed, has the *heart* to cry because it hurts. And you're one of them, man. You ever seen Death?"

The question, sudden and oblique, caught Daniel off balance. "What makes you ask that?"

Kenny shrugged. "A hunch. A feeling. I wasn't meaning to get in your shit about it. You don't have to tell me diddly."

"I almost died once," Daniel said. "From a bomb explosion. My heart stopped when they were loading me in the ambulance; they had to shock it to get it started. That's what the doctor told me, anyway—I don't remember. I was falling, that's the last thing I remember, falling till it seemed I'd fall forever, then right in front of me, out of nowhere, was a mirror, and I remember lifting my hands to protect my face but I don't know if I fell through it or it shattered or what. I guess the closest I've ever come to seeing Death was in that mirror, but I don't remember what I saw there, if I saw anything at all."

"That's Death, all right. He loves to fuck around with mirrors, mirrors and windows—two of his favorite toys."

"If you don't mind a personal question, something you said has got me curious."

Kenny glanced over at him. "Do it, man. Shoot."

"I'm not quite sure how to put it," Daniel replied. "You said when you looked at Ginnilee's picture, you vanished inside yourself. Do you mean your body actually disappeared, turned into air?"

"Negative. Just the fucking opposite. My body stayed and my mind vanished. You had the right track, though; just the wrong train."

Daniel thought about this. It actually seemed to make better sense than the way he was going about it. He tried to imagine his mind vanished, smiling when he realized he'd gotten ahead of himself, that first he'd have to imagine his mind. The thought cracked him up.

Kenny eyed him nervously. "What got you off, man?"

"I was trying to imagine my mind."

"Yeah, I know—it's weird, huh? Like a TV watching itself, or a slot machine playing itself, shit like that."

"Shit like that," Daniel repeated, still chuckling.

Kenny, eyes back on the road, seemed almost solemn. He nodded his head once, as if confirming a decision, and turned to Daniel. "I got a deal for you, Herman, a stone guarantee. Why don't you hook up with me for awhile, ride some patrol. I can get you decent work in the casino if you want some play money, but if you'd rather kick back I've got an extra bunk and lots of rations. I'm no fucking Julie Child, but I cook good enough I don't use nothing from cans."

Sobered by the offer, Daniel said, "I'm honored, but I have a mission of my own. Maybe when it's over, I'll take you up on it."

"What's your mission, man. This some of that 'religious zeal' stuff?"

"Some, I guess. You see, I found the Grail—"

"Say what?" Kenny cocked his ear. "The Grail?"

"Like the Holy Grail," Daniel said.

"You mean like in the Knights of the fucking Round Table? Some kind of trophy cup from God or something like that? I always dug those knights thundering off to lance some flipped-out dragon. Foxworth used to laugh at me about it. Said, 'Fuck dem knights and da round table. Thas a *lot* of hard riding fo' *not much* pussy.' I told him pussy wasn't the point. The point was the quest, fighting your way through. He said, 'Thas cool wi' me, Kenny. You *quest* it, I'll fuck it.' That was Foxworth, man, pussy and music. Fucking Foxworth. Ate a Claymore at Song Be. Heard about it from a guy in the VA, bed next to—" Kenny stopped, lifting his hands from the wheel in a helpless shrug. "Sorry, man," he apologized. "I shit all over your riff. I get spaced here at night. Get the diarrhea jaws."

Daniel said, "I understand. No problem."

"So anyway, before I went drifty, you were saying you're after this Grail, right?"

"Not exactly. I found the Grail—not the Holy Grail, but one like it. My mission is to figure out what to do with it."

"Fuck, man! *Hang on* to it."

"I thought of that first, too," Daniel said, "but now I'm convinced hanging on to it is the one thing I *can't* do."

"I know some people in Vegas who could move it for thirty percent, if what you mean is *too hot* to hang on to. Free introduction, just to help a brother get clear."

"Not necessary. It can't be sold or bought or stolen or kept. But maybe it can be opened."

"Got a torch in the shop," Kenny offered.

"No, wouldn't do it, but thanks for the thought. I'll find a way, I'm sure."

"Right on, brother. One way or another, blow the walls down. Soul belongs to Jesus but your ass belongs to the Corps. Any way I can help you, call the Shamrock and let me know. I'll ride in like the fucking cavalry, my iron flipped to rock'n'roll. Me and fucking Foxworth, man, we had this secret army, all the drug-suckers and wailing fools, the loonies and the lonely and the desperately fucked up, a secret army of us called The Brotherhood of the Hideous Truth. Foxworth was the supreme commander, and I was his field general, General Chaos he called me. Only had one rule for meetings. They couldn't begin until everyone was too stoned to stand up and salute the flag. Fucking Foxworth, man . . ."

Daniel listened till he could almost imagine Foxworth sitting between them, drinking Bacardi with beer chasers, grinning at his certain knowledge that of the five billion adult human beings on the planet, over half had pussies—and even if that wasn't the ultimate point, it surely offered reason to live.

At Daniel's insistence, Kenny let him off near dawn in the middle of nowhere, just road and sagebrush as far as you could see.

"Look me up any time, man; I'll be there," Kenny reminded him as Daniel got out.

"Shoot straight," Daniel said.

Kenny raised a clenched fist. "Now you got the spirit. Semper fi, bro'." Daniel smiled and started to close the door. "Whoa, mofo! You forgot your bowling ball. Get your shit squared away, son. There's a war on." He handed the bag out to Daniel with a wink. "How can you bowl 'em over without a fucking ball? That'd be like going questing without a lance."

"Indeed," Daniel said as he took the Diamond back. "Thanks again."

Kenny swung the Trans-Am across the center divider and headed back to Las Vegas. The loss of Daniel's company depressed him. In that vanished month as Death's Chauffeur, Kenny had developed an acute sensitivity to the thin musky odor released in the breath of those who would die soon. Kenny shook his head dolefully. "You stupid jaw-jacking shithead, he was the best bait you've had in fifteen years and you fucked it up just like you've fucked up everything. Get your shit squared away, boy; there's a war going down." He remembered saying the same thing to Daniel. When he thought about it, he realized those were the last words Foxworth had ever said to him. Fucking Foxworth. He started crying again.

Gurry Debritto smiled as he finished decoding the transmission. He put the message with the others his West Coast listeners had picked up. If the locations were accurate—his subcontractors were the best in the world—the Diamond had been flown to Seattle, driven by van to Coos Bay, Oregon, and was now on an unnamed ship seventy miles due west of the mouth of the Smith River, headed down the coast. He reread the last transmission:

> SAIL AWAY. PROBLEMA. FIRST NEST FOULED. BACKUP SHAKY. SAME
> BAY AND DAY BUT SHIFT STORAGE OKIE TURF 107772400. SHINE ON
> HARVEST MOON. BLT T GO.

Gurry Debritto nodded. They were good, these people, but always the little problems and changes required adjustments. Evidently the original destination had been somehow fouled and the backup couldn't be trusted, so they were shifting to a new place. He had a hunch where. The boat was headed south along the coast to the same bay as planned, and San Francisco Bay seemed a logical place to start, particularly in light of OKIE TURF—Oakland, if his hunch was right. He turned to the keyboard and punched up the Oakland Index, then the street directory. He assumed the time and address were contained in the numbers 107772400. He studied them for a moment, deciding to start with the obvious—2400 as the time. He tapped out 107 77 Street on keyboard and there it was: CARDINAL LIGHT IMPORTS, twenty-one-thousand-square-foot warehouse, owned by Tao-Hihe Chemical, leased to Cardinal Light Imports in January. He punched in the access code for Langley Central Records, then the security clearance sequence that was one of the perks he'd insisted upon as a condition for his services.

Not much on Harvey Moon, but enough. President of Cardinal Light Imports, a board member of Tao-Hihe Chemicals, and an elder of the Breaking Wave Temple, a Taoist church that drew their religious inspiration from

Lao-Tzu and their social analysis from Karl Marx. Suspected of smuggling arms for Mao (unconfirmed) and drugs for the Danish Provos (unconfirmed; perhaps disinformation). Lives aboard yacht [*Susy-Q;* Cayman Reg: LV967769] Married seven times; thirty-one children . . .

Debritto read on. *Thirty-one* fucking kids. Didn't these people understand that they had to quit breeding like dogs?

He repunched the Oakland street directory and jotted down the map file number for Seventy-seventh Street. If they were bringing the diamond down on Moon's yacht, it would be sweet to take it right there on the boat. But the yacht would be risky, too hard to secure. He'd have to hire help, and he'd always worked alone in close.

When he pulled the Seventy-seventh Street aerial from the map case and located the Cardinal Light warehouse, he dropped all consideration of hitting the yacht. The warehouse was perfect. One story, open ground all around it, a large skylight on the roof. He always appreciated skylights. He liked looking down. Perhaps Mr. Moon would show up in person. So far, they'd been more than accommodating. They were bringing it right to him. He was in Berkeley, right next door. He could take the Nimitz and be there in twenty minutes.

He went down to the basement and opened the weapons locker. He would have at least a day to set up the warehouse. It was just past midnight, a perfect time to go take a look. He decided he could afford the extra weight and bulk of four grenades, a drag on stealth but nice to have if even half the Moon kids showed. In a way, he wished they would.

"Thirty-one kids," he muttered, slipping the .380 in his ankle holster. "That's a crime against humanity. This has to stop. If the idiots keep breeding and the intelligent wisely don't, humans will devolve back to animals. Beasts. Goddamn cunts. Let's make a baby. If the fucking women weren't so weak we'd have a chance."

As soon as he had the diamond in his control, he'd brush up on his underwater demolition techniques and go slap a mine on Mr. Moon's floating pleasure dome.

Debritto rolled up over the roof gutter and came up in a crouch. The warehouse was just like in the picture: flat tar roof, skylight, three small vent pipes. He held himself motionless for a full minute, eyes scanning the roof, listening. Staying low, he moved to the edge of the skylight. He laid out flat and listened. He could hear muffled music inside, probably a radio. He slipped the silenced .357 from its shoulder holster and inched forward.

What he saw confused him. A man's face stared up into his. In the instant he realized the warehouse floor was covered with mirrors, the dart hit an inch below his left ear. He tried to roll and snap off a shot but instead flopped onto his back. His body went rigid, the gun slipping from his hand as the fingers stiffened and spread until they were almost bent backward. His lungs were filling with ice. Just before he lost consciousness he saw a tall figure in a black cape and black nurse's cap step from behind the closest ventilation pipe and raise the blowgun to his lips. The back of Debritto's right hand stung.

He heard footsteps, a rustle of cloth, a burning sensation in one of his arms. His eyes were open but he couldn't see. His body had turned to frozen glass. He was a fly in amber, paralyzed, senseless. But he could hear, he realized, had heard footsteps and a rustle of cloth.

A woman's voice whispered in his ear, "Dimethyl tubocaine chloride, a neuromuscular blocking agent. To slow you down enough to listen. I suggest you listen as if your life depended on it. The second dart was a mixture of curare and datura. I gave you two injections a moment ago, both containing synergistic combinations. Belladonna. Tetraclorothane. Methyl iodide. Sodium acid sulfate. Plus a few others I'd lost the labels for. Oh, and some hallucinogens for color. I won't bore you with the specific effects of each. You'll know soon enough. And I can't tell you the cumulative effects because I've never tried these combinations before. You'll be the first to know. Maybe the only one who ever will. And you do deserve to know, don't you, Mr. Debritto? I think so. Information is the root of understanding, and compassion is its flower. I'm an understanding and compassionate woman, Mr. Debritto. I am also a Raven, quicksilver's daughter, the moon's witness, a messenger between the dead and the living, and a dweller in both realms. I know you doubt my compassion as you lie here so pathetically trapped inside your senseless flesh. Doubt is a tribute to intelligence, as I'm sure you'd agree if you could. So let me prove my compassion, Mr. Debritto, prove it with a promise and a gift. I promise I will call you an ambulance within twenty minutes. And the gift is a critical piece of information that could mean the difference between life and death. I'm *not sure* whether I've given you a lethal dose or not. Lucky, lucky you. Yet another adventure in self-discovery. Poor baby. Poor, poor baby." She paused, and though he couldn't feel it, gently stroked his brow. When she spoke again, her voice seemed harsher and more intense: "He was able to steal the Diamond because he believed in the Diamond. Now we'll find out what you believe in."

Debritto heard the rustle of her skirt as she walked away. He tried to move his right hand to find the gun but it was impossible, his mind trapped in a block of ice. He pitted his rage at her against the terror of his own helplessness. He would not be beaten by a woman, by a weak, brainless cunt. She probably hadn't given him a fatal dose. Too soft to make irrevocable decisions, too sentimental to exercise full power. He tried to concentrate on remembering the poisons she'd said she used. How stupid to mention them. If the paralysis faded he could tell the doctors, who'd know the antidotes. But concentration was difficult lying there paralyzed on the roof. He tried to squeeze his attention back to the poisons she'd named. He heard a female voice whispering in his ear, but it was another woman speaking. His mother's voice told him, "You are evil. Corrupt with evil. Sick with evil. Mad with evil. Evil, evil, evil."

Debritto's rigid body barely twitched when he tried to scream. This couldn't be his mother. He had no memory of her. She'd died when he was five months old. That's what his father had told him. Why should he doubt his father? He'd always told him the hard truth. No, it had to be the poisons—some sort of auditory hallucination.

"You were *born* evil. Full of sickness and rot. Shame of my flesh. Shame of my heart. You know my voice from the womb. You have dreamed my dreams. I gave you life. I gave you life, and you defiled it. Now I've come to take it back."

Tape Transcript (partial):
Interrogation of Elwood and Emmett Tindell, brothers (ID Access
LCR 86755)
File: OPERATION NEST EGG
Tonopah Emergency Field Office, Nevada
April 10, 1987
Present: Reg. Sup. Keyes; agents Stanley, Dickerson, Peebe

PEEBE: Okay fellas, I want you to tell it to Supervisor Keyes. He's flown in after a hard day, so keep it short and to the point.

ELWOOD: We got the same deal still? No charges on us—nothing; half of any reward or business deals; you take brother Emmett to the hospital and get his nuts fixed up; we get us a new Camaro and two thousand bucks each? That what we talking?

EMMETT: El, you're fucking hopeless. Don't tell 'em shit.

ELWOOD: Don't fret on me, Em; your big brother knows what he's doing. We're in the big time here. This is CIA, not your sheriffs and highway troopers. This is *national* law. They can deal. So, Mr. Peebe, Mr. Keyes, how about it?

KEYES: That sounds reasonable to me. However, since we're overburdened with paperwork, would you take twenty thousand in cash to cover the car and the medical bills yourself? You still get half of any reward money, walk out of here clean.

ELWOOD: You got the money on you, I wouldn't mind looking it over.

KEYES: Dickerson? Show him. You can count it later. You don't walk till you pass the polygraph, though.

ELWOOD: The what?

KEYES: Lie detector. We pay for truth and punish bullshit.

ELWOOD: I got no problem with that. Brother Em, how about you?

EMMETT: Officers, he's been using drugs something fierce ever since he was a baby. There's lots of things he thinks are true that ain't even close.

ELWOOD: Why are you being like this, Em? We got outer-space invaders running around and you don't want to cash in. Your nuts still swoll and achy, that it? Getting whopped in the nuts always did get you strange. Remember when we were seven and that red-headed Simmons girl liked to kicked your nuts up your throat for waving your pee-pee at her? Remember? You got real fretted and grumpy, and—

KEYES: I'm sure you both had charming childhoods, but I'm much more interested in what happened this morning on Highway Ninety-five.

ELWOOD: Well sure. Okay. Me and Emmett was driving along, heading up to Reno to see if we could get us some jobs, and—

PEEBE: [to Keyes] Car was stolen in Phoenix yesterday. We just put the make and numbers out on the us-only line, Phoenix west, but it was already on a general APB.

ELWOOD: Hard to look for work without a car.

KEYES: Forget the car. Never happened. Go on.

ELWOOD: So we're driving along about an hour after sunup and we see this guy sitting alongside the road. Kinda got his head tucked down on his chest and his hands over his face. Looked like maybe he was feeling puny. So me and Em, we pull over, see if he's all right. But this guy—said his name was Herman—he wasn't even next door to right. We seen that straight off. One thing, he's wearing fucking *bowling shoes,* I mean right out there in the sage-brush and all. Bowling shirt, too. Name of some construction company on the back—Rice Construction, Price, something like that. He's packing his bowling ball with him, and he's got this backpack and real nice briefcase, too. Weird. Like he don't know if he's a bowler, forest ranger, or banker. What's weirder, he's *crying.* Not "boo-hoo," you know, but his eyes are 'bout as red as granddaddy's long johns and his cheeks are all wet and streaky. But what's—"

KEYES: What'd this guy look like? Age? Size? Eye color?

PEEBE: We got it in detail already; went out with the car descrip-tion on our line. I can run it by you quick.

KEYES: Quick.

ELWOOD: Hold on, dammit. It's just getting to the *really weird*—

PEEBE: [to Keyes] Mid-twenties, six feet, hundred sixty to eighty pounds, blue eyes, brown hair, scar on right temple, dressed as described.

KEYES: White man?

PEEBE: Yes sir. Sorry.

EMMETT: He's just jerking your chain. Ain't too many blue-eyed spades or spics I ever saw.

ELWOOD: You guys want to hear the weird part, or what?

KEYES: Okay, let's hear it. The guy was crying . . .

ELWOOD: So naturally I ask him what's wrong. And he says, "I think I was remembering a dream my mother had when I was in her womb." You got that? Guy fucking thinks he's remembering dreams from inside his mama? Me and Emmett weren't much for school, but you don't need no graduation papers to see this guy is bat-shit loony, maybe run off from a nuthouse or something. His eyes looked crazy, too, kinda glassy and far away, and he generally looked all grungy. So wasted, me and Em had to help him get in the backseat.

KEYES: How much help? I mean, did he voluntarily enter your vehicle?

ELWOOD: Pretty much, yeah. We said we'd take him on to Reno, wouldn't even make him pay for no gas. Me and Em was being nice.

PEEBE: Spare us. No charges, right? Just what happened.

ELWOOD: So we're driving along and talking with this guy—Brother Em's at the wheel, me riding shotgun, this Herman weirdo in the back—just getting acquainted, you know, and I ask him what he's got in his bags and briefcase, just out of being curious. And he says real matter-of-fact, real cool, that he's got extra clothes and shit in the little backpack, a grill in the bowling bag, and in the briefcase he's got about twenty thousand dollars, cash money. So—

EMMETT: El, you dumb shit, he said grail. *Grail,* not grill.

ELWOOD: Me and Em's been arguing over this all afternoon, but *grill*—like for cooking up meat—is what I heard. Struck me as kinda odd, too, that he'd be packing around some little grill in a bowling bag, 'specially since it looked like it already had a bowling ball in it. So I asked him if we could see this grill. He said seeing the grill was something you had to earn. So I said how 'bout seeing the money, and son of a bitch if he don't say "Sure" and open it right up. I took a *good* eyeful—never seen so much in my life—and then I looked at Em, and Em was looking at me. Me and Em been poor ever since we got orphaned off when we was pups. We—

PEEBE: Get *to* it, Elwood—save the shit. Your rap sheets are longer than your dicks.

ELWOOD: Okay. Sure. So we pull off on a nice little turnout a ways up the road—one of them history monuments—and Em gets this Herman guy out of the car to check out the marker, take a leak. Guy takes the fucking bowling bag *with* him. Now the way we work it, Brother Em's the holder and I'm the whopper. I use a sawed-off ax-handle, 'bout this long, top foot drilled out a quarter-inch wide and filled back up with lead. So I come up behind him real easy as he's standing there beside Em. Em nods he's ready, so I plant myself solid, and when Em grabs him around the shoulders, I swing down with the club, swing hard. And this is the *truth*—hook me up to the biggest lie detector you got—right in the middle of the swing, the guy fucking *disappears*. And Em's standing there with his legs braced, holding nothing but air, and the club smacks him right in the nuts. I'm sorry, Em. Fuck, what can I say?

EMMETT: *Nothing,* you dumb shit.

ELWOOD: He's an *alien,* Em. People are *into* aliens. We're gonna make a *ton* o' money just by warning people against him. Could get us on TV.

KEYES: Whoa, you two. Let's get back on track. Emmett, did you see this guy disappear like your brother claims?

EMMETT: That's what my eyes saw. The rest of me ain't believing it.

KEYES: Okay then. He disappeared. Then what happened?

ELWOOD: Well, Emmett screamed and went down. I was trying to figure out what the hell was going on—looking around kinda wild to see where the guy mighta went to, but he was nowhere. Emmett's sorta gurgling at my feet, so I bend down to see if I can help him, and the car starts up. Guy had snuck back to the car and was *stealing* it. Drove right off toward Reno, giving the horn a couple of big honks. Was another hour before your people happened by.

KEYES: I want you both to think hard: You said this guy got out of the car with the bowling bag, right? So when he disappeared, what happened to it?

EMMETT: No idea.

ELWOOD: Me either. I don't remember seeing it on the ground by Em. Didn't see him come back to get it. Figure it must have gone with him.

PEEBE: We searched the area. *Nada.*

ELWOOD: We're dealing with some kind of outer space alien, right? Some sorta critter from the stars that can take our shape but get back invisible when it wants?

KEYES: So it would seem. But whatever he is, we'll find him.

EMMETT: Hey, officer—don't you listen? The guy can *disappear.* Get it? Poof! If he can disappear, maybe he can do other things. Ask me, you'd have to be superstupid to fuck with him. *Super-* super.

Daniel fidgeted behind the wheel of the Tindell brothers' turquoise-and-pink Cutlass. Their alleged Cutlass, anyway, since he'd wisely checked the registration only to find it in the name of Mrs. Heidi Cohen. Daniel somehow doubted she knew Emmett and Elwood personally. He remembered Mott telling him that if you were going to drive what he called "blind loaners"—vehicles that the owners didn't know they'd lent—you should borrow a new one every twelve hours.

When he discovered the registration anomaly shortly after leaving the brothers in the dust, Daniel had decided to ditch the car. He'd pulled off on a spur road and gathered his stuff to walk away when he was taken with the notion to try vanishing with the Diamond in daylight again.

He vanished for three futile hours. He still couldn't see the Diamond's spiral flame in daylight, and without its axis to mark the center, he couldn't focus. He'd tried imagining the spiral flame but this split his attention. He gave up in a fit of frustration. He needed to step back. He was acting as if there were deadlines. He could take the rest of his life to work with the Diamond.

The time pressure he felt was actually the phantom pressure of pursuit, the sense that he had to enter the Diamond before he was caught. But objectively, they couldn't catch him or seize the Diamond as long as he could vanish and take it with him. In an oblique way, his urgency was a failure to be true to himself, a failure to trust his powers.

"I don't trust me. Me don't trust I. Is this a natural neural lag in accommodating change, or do we have a serious disagreement? And if it's a disagreement, how can it be harmoniously resolved?"

Daniel tried to think about this, more from duty than passion. One evening at Nameless Lake Wild Bill had said the trouble with self-analysis was the built-in human eagerness to accept all sorts of preposterous and absurd suppositions, not the least of which were both the possibility and desirability of knowing one's self. Bill had likened this to using a corkscrew to pull your image from a mirror. Daniel smiled. With mock sternness he told himself, "*You* have a problem with self-image. Admit it—I admit it." He came to his own defense. "But if you can vanish, you're *supposed* to have problems with self-image. You'd be insane if you *didn't.*"

Daniel started laughing. Knowing himself was no more improbable than a frog bringing him an armload of roses or falling petals turning into frogs.

The laughter relaxed him, collapsed the manic pressure to solve it *all right now.* He was a moth flinging itself at the sun. Volta was wrong. The Diamond wouldn't destroy him; the Diamond was simply a possible means for him to destroy himself.

He decided his best strategy was to give up for awhile. He'd offered himself to the Diamond and so far had been refused. Fine. No more vanishing with the Diamond except in defense. If he was patient, maybe the Diamond would come to him.

He also decided to keep the twice-swiped Cutlass. If he couldn't be captured, nothing could compromise his safety—or nothing except losing the power to vanish. Conserving his strength for emergencies was even more reason to quit vanishing with the Diamond.

His new approach, he thought, was adventurous yet eminently sane. Yet he was fidgeting behind the wheel because he kept imagining himself looking into the Diamond, pouring himself into the spiral-flamed furnace at its center, and he couldn't allow himself that anymore. He turned on the radio for distraction.

A half-hour later, with the first stars glimmering above and the lights of Reno a pale hollow on the horizon, a blast of static fried the local station and Denis Joyner took the air.

Transcription:
Denis Joyner, AMO Mobile Radio

Good evening, ladies and gentlemen, I'm David Janus, your host for this sundown program of ontological inquiry, "Moment of Truth," brought to you from the mobile studio of the Public Bullcast System on the frequency to which you're evidently tuned.

I trust you'll find this evening's program as compelling as I do, though its format is slightly different than our usual broadcast fare. That's right, Santa, there is no Virginia. And while it saddens me to disabuse you of such sweet beliefs, I can only echo my old friend Ludwig Wittgenstein's sweeping disclaimer that "the world is the case." Alas, dear listeners, we can only drink it by the glass.

Which brings me to the creative origins of tonight's presentation. This afternoon as I browsed my library, sipping a young but ambitious petite syrah, I realized my enlightenment, while total, has become slightly stale of late. I therefore resolved that I would henceforth seek to explore complexities worthy of my pretensions. Thus decided, I fortified myself with an ounce of Serbian caviar accompanied by a chilled liter of Thunderbird *(sic itur ad astra!)*, and began to search for neglected volumes from which I might glean information on topics which have traditionally bewildered less formidable brains than my own.

Quickly then—*tempus fugit,* as old Thoth said—tonight we'll examine that most intractable mystery of existence, the *sine qua non* of consciousness itself, the irreducible element of being, the gray jelly smeared on each cracker of thought, the meat and potatoes of knowledge, the very fire in the forge. I refer, of course, to the human mind.

The mind is a glass floor.
The mind is the spirit's tear.
The mind is our prior and subsequent ghost.
The mind is the Bullion Express and the blood on the tracks.
The mind is a stone door.
The silver on the backs of mirrors.
The wave that defines the coast.
It's what the drunk grave robbers couldn't stuff in their sacks.
The mind is the sum of all and more.
The spasm between one and zero in the Calendar of Black-Hole Years.
The contract between the lash and the whipping post.
A quilt of dreams stitched with facts.
A meaningless argument among the whores.
Rain that keeps falling when the sky clears.
A masquerade party, guest and host.
A candlelit landscape of puddled wax.
The mind is what thought is for.
The parking lot at the Mall of Fears.
The fire-pit for the piggy roast.
What the soul surrendered and won't take back.
The mind is neither either nor or.
The real center of an empty sphere.

This has been your man of the hour on "Moment of Truth." I trust your attention proved worthy of my intelligence, and that as you listened you cried out that ultimate Destructuralist accolade, "Tha's a big ten-four, good buddy!" And so, until next time, do keep in mind that *every* moment is a moment of truth. But for now: *Ciao,* baby, and *Adieu.*

Daniel snapped off the radio and stared down the road. He remembered Volta talking about an AMO-financed mobile pirate radio station and wondered if that's what he'd been listening to. It figured. He'd have to mention it to Volta the next time they talked, tell him that it had strengthened him while he was running with the Diamond. The reminder that he was part of an ancient alliance of magicians and outlaws cheered him up. But also, and perhaps more importantly, David Janus was hard evidence that he, Daniel, was relatively sane. He was impressed that the DJ could still function. This gave Daniel hope. He needed hope. Hope and rest and patience. And food. He needed to eat. He needed lots of things.

Thankful, Volta watched Red Freddie's plane lift from the Eel River airstrip and bank toward the mist-shrouded moon. Volta hadn't enjoyed the flight. From the moment they'd left El Paso, Red Freddie had lobbied him hard. Red Freddie wanted AMO to "strike more blows against the Empire, *real* blows instead of this candy-ass policy of gentle subversion." Red Freddie wanted to blow up dams and burn banks and bind and gag the president of Maxxam in the top of an old-growth redwood the company had marked for harvest. *Direct* action, that's what Red Freddie wanted.

Volta wanted to indulge the seeping melancholy that infused him the moment he'd understood the Diamond would destroy Daniel. He was tired of control. But Red Freddie was a member of the Alliance as well as a friend. His policy suggestions deserved a thoughtful response. So Volta had listened and answered with diplomacy and patience.

Volta was so glad to be alone that he drove three miles up the hill before he remembered he needed groceries. He took mental inventory of the Laurel Creek pantry as he drove. There was probably enough to get him through a week, but he wanted to stay home at least a month. He decided to go back to town and stock up so he wouldn't have to interrupt his retreat later.

Volta judged his decision sensible and efficient. No surprise there. He hadn't surprised himself in years. Solid, sensible, honorable Volta. He felt trapped inside his integrity, an integrity that had slowly turned arid. He had accepted the responsibilities of the Star, and he had honored them. They *were* responsibilities so serious that to accept them virtually forbade foolishness. No regrets. But now he needed to water his garden. Needed to be foolish.

As if to test his resolve, a golden opportunity for foolishness presented itself on the outskirts of town. This was the smallest carnival Volta had seen in all his wanderings—four games, a junior Ferris wheel, a House-Trailer of Horrors, and a booth the size of a one-hole outhouse selling clouds of cotton candy, soda water, and caramel apples. Skimpy, true, but it *was* a carnival.

Volta was taken first by the force of her concentration and not her long, lovely, reddish-blonde hair. She was ten or eleven, that strangely mercurial age of female prepubescence that actually ranges from three to thirty-five. She was fiercely focused on tossing ping-pong balls into a mass of small goldfish bowls arrayed on a plywood-sheet table. Volta quietly walked over and stood behind her. She tossed and missed, shaking her head angrily, her waist-length hair shimmering in the stark, bare-bulb light.

She dug into her pocket and finally produced a quarter. "Last chance," she told the man behind the plank.

He handed her three ping-pong balls from his apron, squinting at her through the smoke from his Marlboro. "Your last chance, huh? Well, good luck."

Volta watched her concentrate. She was a sweetheart, freckles and all. Volta foolishly allowed himself a pang of regret for his childlessness.

When her last toss bounced harmlessly off a bowl's rim and landed in the dust, the girl stamped her foot and said "Shit" quickly, as if velocity made it acceptable. Her shoulders slumped and she turned to walk away. Volta was ready.

"Miss," he said as he bent down to pick up something from the ground, "I believe you were standing on this." He held up the dollar bill he'd palmed.

She looked confused. "I don't think so. I spent both of mine."

Volta admired her honesty, but he relished the sudden glint of hope in her eyes. "Miss, you were *standing* on it. It must be yours. And if it's not, it's yours by right of good fortune."

She took the bill with a grin that made Volta happy in a foolishly uncomplicated way. "Thank you," she said.

"May I offer you some technical advice on tossing ping-pong balls into goldfish bowls?"

"What?" Her tone was a dead heat between wary and eager.

"The trajectory of your toss is too flat. While the bowls look close together, they're actually far enough apart that a ball seldom skitters into one. Also, the balls aren't that much smaller than the neck opening on the bowls. The outcurving edge makes the opening appear wider than it is. Appearances are the best deception. We *want* to believe our own eyes. But I trust you see the secret by now: *Loft* the ball high instead of tossing it low—that way you get a straight drop on the opening, the full circle to shoot at."

Her seventh ball dropped in so perfectly it almost bounced back out.

The sallow guy behind the plank raised his voice a few desultory decibels, "Awwwrighhht here. 'Nother winner."

She grinned up at Volta. The wrinkle in her nose was enough to fuel his melancholy for days. "My name's Gena Leland. What's yours?"

"The Great Volta," he bowed. He hadn't used his stage name in twenty years.

"Really? You in the carnival?"

"No. I'm a retired magician."

She was about to ask something else when a towheaded boy, clearly kin, ran up and grabbed her arm. "Come *on,* Gena. Mom's getting *pissed.*"

The man behind the plank tapped her other arm. "Here, kid; you won it." He handed her a goldfish bowl, but this one held water and a tiny goldfish.

Gena hissed, *"Okay,* Tommy, just a sec." She accepted the goldfish and handed it to Volta.

Surprised, he took it, but immediately tried to hand it back. "No, you won it; it's your prize."

She put her hands behind her back. "But you taught me how. Besides, I don't want it. I wasn't doing it to win a goldfish. I just wanted to *do* it, get one of those balls in."

"Oh," Volta said. "I thought you wanted the goldfish."

"No. My mom says it's a pretty big responsibility to take care of another living thing. Gotta go."

And she and her brother were gone on flashing sneakers.

The bowl cupped in his hands, Volta looked down at the goldfish. With a sudden and startling clarity, Volta felt Daniel open a door. "Shit," Volta said quickly. Then, with a freedom more befitting his age, he added a long anguished "Fuuuuuuuck!"

Daniel stopped at Jackrabbit Pizza in a mini-mall at the edge of Reno. The Cutlass wouldn't lock, so he took the Diamond, money, and day pack in with him. When he opened the pizzeria door, he was startled to see a large rabbit behind the counter. As his eyes adjusted to the light, the rabbit slowly turned into a tall, gangly, teenage boy with a small, pinched face and wispy mustache. The kid was wearing a pair of stiff, slender rabbit ears and a light-grey smock made of the same sheeny velveteen fabric, a material closer to carpet than cloth. The kitchen workers also wore rabbit ears and furry smocks. Clearly a uniform, Daniel decided, unless all three shared the same sartorial eccentricity.

The pizzeria had two long aisles of tables and benches, padded booths along the near wall, and a mini-arcade of computer games, pinball machines, and a mechanical pony ride along the back wall. It was noisy and warm, a fragrant braid of yeast, garlic, tomato, and sizzling pepperoni wafting from the kitchen. Daniel stepped up to the counter.

"Good evening." The tall rabbit-boy reached for a pad. "Ready to order?"

Daniel decided you could say anything you wanted to someone wearing jackrabbit ears, so he said, "The mind is a pizza with the works."

The kid's button nose twitched just like a rabbit's scenting danger on the air. "I'm sorry, sir," the kid said, "I missed that." He glanced timidly at Daniel and immediately shifted his gaze back to his order pad.

314

"Pardon *me,*" Daniel said, "I get mumbly alone on the road. I said 'I wouldn't mind a pizza with the works.'"

"Small? Medium?"

"Medium."

"Anything to drink?"

Daniel looked at the menu board. "A pitcher of beer."

The rabbit-eared kid said, "Comes to nine ninety-five."

Daniel set the bowling bag down and dug in his front pocket. He handed a hundred-dollar bill to the kid. "Keep the change."

The kid looked at the bill and then back at Daniel. "That's a hundred-dollar bill, sir. It's only nine ninety-five."

"That's right," Daniel said. "So, if my math doesn't fail me, that leaves you a tip of ninety dollars and five cents. Correct?"

The kid shook his head, his rabbit ears swaying slightly. "Gee, that's more than I make in a *week.*"

"Please," Daniel said with a dismissive flick of his hand, "I can afford it. Furthermore, I admire your courage."

"My courage?"

"In wearing that outlandish rabbit uniform."

The kid winced. "Don't remind me. I forget till someone reminds me. Owner makes us wear them. He catches you without your ears on, you're fired on the spot."

Daniel didn't respond. He was looking at the kid's ears.

Nervously, the kid went on, "Sometimes it's a real bummer. Girls from school come in once in a while, know what I mean. Pretty hard to look cool when you look stupid. This one girl, Cindy, thought I looked so silly she still cracks up giggling every time she sees me in the halls."

"Marry that woman," Daniel said, "she'll keep you honest."

"*Right,*" the kid said with a plaintive sarcasm, "she's really going to marry Mr. Rabbit Ears. It's not like I'm Paul Newman to start with."

Daniel advised him, "Tell her you are a master of the Nine Tantric Circles of Intimate Permissions."

The kid lowered his eyes. "I don't even know what a tantric is. Even if she'd be interested in knowing it, and I doubt she would. *That* would impress her, huh? 'What nine tantric circles, Carl?' 'Uh, well, Cindy, gee, duh.' Gotta tell her something, right?"

"Absolutely," Daniel agreed.

"So, you got any suggestions? You know about these tantric circles?"

Daniel winked. "That knowledge is the source of my wealth. Unfortunately, I'm bound not to reveal them, though in fact they're open secrets. I *can* point you to the right path, though. Use your imagination. That's what

I did. And if Cindy uses her imagination, perhaps you'll enter the First Circle together."

Carl looked at Daniel, clearly puzzled. Daniel was vaguely disappointed when he said, "Well, thanks for the tips, sir. Let me get your pitcher, and I'll call when the pizza's ready. You'll be number ninety-three."

Daniel's disappointment turned to an anger spawned more by the kid's sloth than the implicit slight. "What I can't decide," Daniel said, "is whether you should get down on your knees and thank your boss for forcing you into foolishness, or whether you should twist those rabbit ears together and tell him to stick 'em up his ass. If you're going to be foolish, at least have the sense to enjoy it. If you find it demeaning, quit. The bosses of the world can't do anything to you that you can't stop them from doing. We all deserve ourselves."

Carl was filling the pitcher from the counter tap. "You sound like a teacher," he said without enthusiasm.

Daniel considered this a moment. "I'm not sure I know enough to be a teacher, or could teach what I do know. I'm more of a romantic religious idiot trying to get his bearings in the Diamond-light of existence."

"Oh yeah?" the kid said, sliding the pitcher across the countertop. "You with some church, some Eastern religion?"

Daniel sensed the kid's eagerness to be rid of him, but rabbit-boy clearly hadn't learned that religious inquiries encouraged conversation. Daniel decided to spare him. "No, none of that mystic Eastern woo-woo for me. I'm a Judo-Christian. I flipped." He gave the kid the wildest grin he could summon.

It must have been good. Carl gulped and turned for the kitchen, mumbling over his shoulder, "Better get your order in . . . be ten, fifteen minutes."

Daniel sat at a table facing the mini-arcade. The machines flashed invitingly, but nobody wanted to play. Not the rabbit-eared kid at the counter, not a single patron. Daniel felt himself sliding toward depression and fought for equilibrium. He moved his left foot over and softly pressed it against the bowling bag. The feel of the curve against his foot gave him an immediate impulse to leap on the table, shout for attention, and vanish. That would wake them up. Instead, he concentrated on his beer, feeling the cool glass against his lips, tasting each drop.

Daniel was halfway through his pizza when a small boy tore by him, aiming straight for the pony ride—a fiberglass golden palomino cast in full gallop, ears laid back. The boy still had some baby fat in his cheeks and two front teeth were missing. He had brown eyes as lustrous as melting chocolate chips. Daniel sensed a delicacy about the boy, though there was nothing delicate about the way he swung into the saddle, twisted the plastic reins around his wrist, and shoved in his quarter; nothing delicate at all as he spurred the pony to full speed or whipped out his trusty six-gun—extended index-finger barrel, cocked-thumb hammer—and began blazing away, *"Blatch-ooee! Blatchooee!"* The loud, wet report cut through the noise from other patrons.

"Dad!" the boy yelled. "Look! I'm killing the bad guys!"

The boy's father was arguing in a low, tight voice with a woman Daniel assumed was the boy's mother. They continued the argument without looking up.

"Hey!" Daniel yelled at them. They and most of the other diners looked up, startled.

Daniel didn't care. He was going to be himself. He pointed at their son on the pony. "Your son is killing the bad guys."

The mother turned without really looking and called over her shoulder, "Good for you, Billy." The father, a stocky, crew-cut guy not much older than Daniel, turned and shot him a challenging stare.

Daniel almost said *Attention is the key to the vault, Dad,* but thought better of it. He didn't know anything about being a father. He shifted his gaze back to the cowpoke blasting away from the back of his swift steed, dropping one grubby bad guy after another until time ran out and the pony shimmied to a stop. The boy dismounted with panache. His father was saying, his voice tight and mean, "Read my lips, Mary: We don't *got* the fuckin' money for a new dryer."

As the little boy passed, Daniel said, "Looks like you rid the world of some pretty nasty guys."

"Yup," the boy said, slowing but not stopping. "That Snake sure is a good horse."

"Well, you handle him real fine, too."

The boy gave him a sidelong smile as he passed, a smile of deep and secret pleasure. "Thanks, pardner."

"Hey, you, pal," the kid's father called, "you got some kinda *problem* with my boy?"

"Not at all," Daniel smiled. "I was merely complimenting him on his imagination. You've got a fine son there." Daniel wasn't feigning his smile; he was wondering how the jerk would like getting his liver pulverized by a Reverse Heel-Whip out of the Drowsing Crane position.

The father let this go, sliding over on the bench for his boy to sit down.

By the time Daniel finished another slice, the golden palomino had a new rider. He wasn't as trigger-happy as the first, but he dropped his share.

And then a whole birthday party of children, accompanied by four harried mothers, came rabbling through the door. Carl-the-Counter-Rabbit already had a slice of pizza with a birthday candle ready for each of them, and one of the mothers produced a roll of quarters for the pony.

The boys, to a man, rode fast and hard with some fancy tricks thrown in, like hanging on the side and shooting across the saddle. The boys were full of bravado and purpose. Daniel loved them. But he loved the little girls even more. They rode with a quiet and stately abandon, eyes closed, the wind blowing their hair out behind them, taking on the power of the golden palomino but not confusing it with their own. He wondered what the little girls imagined as they rode, where they were going, how far away. He wanted to gather them all, boys and girls together, gather them all into his arms and carry them somewhere safe from the slaughter of time and change.

When the birthday party left, Daniel felt his depression ooze forward again. He wanted to vanish into the children's minds, into some moment he could barely remember, before you were cornered by the lines you drew or trapped by someone else's. He sat with his hands folded on the table, watching flecks of foam thin to scum and dry inside the empty pitcher. The pizza and beer, his first food since the Two Moons, left him feeling bloated and half-drunk. The last tatters of his energy fled to his stomach to aid digestion. Energy to make energy, and with each transformation a tiny bit lost to entropy. Running down to nothing. Those kids, so innocent. You couldn't truly appreciate innocence until it was lost, and then you couldn't get it back. Run down to nothing. The mind is a golden palomino. Hang on, children; it's the ride of your life. Don't be afraid. You're safe with me but I'm not with myself, that's our problem. There's time, time, time. All the time in the world. Eat when you're hungry, sleep when you're tired.

Carl-the-Counter-Rabbit's voice boomed over the loudspeaker, "Ladies and gentlemen, it's ten o'clock, Jackrabbit Pizza's closing time." Daniel, who wasn't aware he'd been drowsing, leaped wildly to his feet, spinning around to check the room. Carl was being tactful. Daniel was the only one left.

He left the Diamond and money under the table and walked up front, taking the empty pitcher and glass with him. Carl was in the kitchen wiping down a prep table. He came out immediately, looking nervous. "Hate to hurry you, sir, but the boss'll be here to cash out in about five minutes, and he gets *really* pissed if the place ain't cleared—you know, on account of robbers and all."

Daniel said, "Carl, you should explore the spiritual life. You must be a mind-reader, because I was *just* going to ask you if the boss was coming in tonight. When he gets here, would you inform him that I would like to see him for a moment at my table. My name is Nova Rajneesh. I have a business proposition for him."

Carl was backing away. "Oh no, now, come on, mister, please. I shouldn't of said nothing."

"I'm not a robber," Daniel assured him. "I want to do business."

"Well geez, do you think you could call him in the morning?"

"Unfortunately, I'm forced to leave town tonight. And let me assure you that he'll find my business proposition so enjoyable he'll likely give you a bonus that will make my recent tip seem meager. Now, if you'd be kind enough to lend me a pen and one of those empty pizza boxes, I'll let you return to your work."

Carl reluctantly unclipped the pen from his velveteen smock and handed it and a pizza box across the counter. "You sure this won't get me in trouble?"

"You're covered," Daniel said. "I promise."

Daniel began writing rapidly on the pizza box. When he had finished, he opened the briefcase and counted the money: nineteen thousand dollars. He doled out four grand and zipped it in the day pack. When he looked up, a red-faced man, forty pounds overweight and bald, was bearing down on him. Daniel rose to greet him.

Before he could, the man bellowed, "My name's Max Robbins, I *own* this place, and I'd like to know what the fuck you think you're doing here after closing time? Carl, one of my fucking cretin employees, said you want to talk business. I don't wanna talk business. I want your ass outa here."

Daniel lifted the case's lid and turned it so that Mr. Robbins received the full effect of the neatly bound sheaves. Daniel offered his hand. "Mr. Robbins, my name is Nova Rajneesh. I am what the media fondly refer to as an 'eccentric millionaire.' Actually, I'm an impulsive *multi*millionaire, but why quibble." They shook hands, then Daniel continued, "I haven't much time, so excuse me for jumping to the point. I'm the Supreme Chairman of the Nova Rajneesh Philanthropy Fund, a perfectly legal tax dodge, the intricacies of which need only concern my attorneys. The substance of my proposition is contained in this hastily drawn contract."

Daniel picked up the pizza box. "You'll note, Max, there are actually two contracts, but they're identical. One will be my copy. If you'll allow me to read:

> The owner of Jackrabbit Pizza herewith agrees to accept the sum of $15,000 to provide free mechanical pony rides for all children upon request until such time as the money (at 25¢ a ride) is exhausted. Administrative and bank fees may be subtracted from the original sum, but in no event may the total fees exceed $3000.
>
> In further consideration of this bequest, no employee of Jackrabbit Pizza will be forced to wear any type of uniform or costume as a condition of employment, effective on signature of this agreement.

A separate account shall be kept of this bequest, with books subject to audit at any time.

Dated and signed, etc.

Robbins said, "Don't see much there for me."

"Then you're either stupid or greedy. Not only do you get a customer attraction which will undoubtedly be reflected in increased revenues, you also get an undeserved reputation as a generous man—and, of course, most of the three-thousand-dollar administrative fee."

"All right, prick, you're on."

Daniel called Carl to witness the deal. Daniel tore the signed boxtop in half, giving Robbins his copy along with the briefcase of money. Robbins sat down to count as Carl and Daniel watched. Finally Robbins smiled. "All there," he said, starting to close the case.

Daniel cleared his throat. "I believe, Mr. Robbins, that the witness fee is properly an administrative expense. Two hundred dollars is standard."

Robbins glared. "Witness fee? What's this shit? You think you can just roll me over and fuck me?"

"Fair enough," Daniel said, "we'll split it." He gave Carl two fifties from the day pack.

As Robbins reluctantly handed Carl a matching hundred from the briefcase, Daniel said, "While this pizza-box contract may strike you as unusual, and while it's true my ways are unorthodox, I didn't become wealthy by accident. I am an excellent businessman. My contract and litigation departments are used to seeing contracts written on cocktail napkins, the upholstery of Rolls Royces, bicycle seats, lipstick on mirrors, paper bags; and in every court case we've undertaken—and there have been many—those contracts were found to be binding. My contract department also directs our teams of investigators, whose random visits will ensure that the provisions of the contract are being followed to the letter. *And* the penny." Daniel stowed his copy in the day pack.

Robbins was rereading his copy of the contract, his lips moving slightly. "Don't see nothing about investigators here. Where's it say investigators?"

"Auditors—same thing." Daniel put an arm through the day pack's strap and slung it over his shoulder. Carl was carefully securing the two hundred dollars in his billfold.

"So, all right," said Robbins, "these investo-auditors come, maybe somebody's spilled coffee on a ledger, numbers don't come out exactly even, stuff like that. What happens?"

"The investigators or auditors, as the case may be, report to the contract department. Contract calls litigation. Litigation assembles a battery of attorneys. We file suit. We own a little pizzeria in Reno, the whole business probably worth less than a tenth of our legal fees. You see, Mr. Robbins, with *me* it's a matter of principle, not money. How many more millions do I need?"

"I didn't hear none of this lawsuit shit when we were signing contracts. Forget it. I'm backing out. It smells like grief."

"Too late," Daniel chirped. He picked up the bowling bag.

Robbins started to rise, muttering, "Now wait here just a fu—"

"He's right," Carl cut him off. "I saw you sign it. You wanted to."

"Hey, Carl," Robbins turned on him, "who took the dick out of your mouth? You go do some of that work I pay you for. *Work?* Remember? And take off that silly, fucking rabbit costume—makes you look like some kinda *homo* Bugs Bunny or somethin'."

"Mr. Robbins," Carl said, his voice quavering, "I *am* a homo. That's why when I take off my bunny uniform, I'm going to roll it up neatly and stick it up your ass."

Robbins's head snapped up as if he'd been kicked in the chin. He stared at Carl; the intensity of his gaze matched the purplish-red flush seeping downward from his bald pate toward his trembling jowls. Daniel was ready to intervene, but Robbins, perhaps sensing Daniel's sentiments, smiled instead of erupting. He lifted his right hand up beside his ear and waggled his chubby fingers as he cooed, "Bye-bye, Carl. You're fired."

"Hey," Daniel said, "you *can't* fire Carl. He's our *witness.*"

"Fine." Robbins nodded his head rapidly. "He witnessed. He signed. Now his faggot-ass is out of here in two minutes or I call the cops."

Daniel said, "What is it with you, Robbins? You ever opened a law book in your life? There's three kinds of contract witnesses: there are *signatory* witnesses—that's what you thought Carl was, I guess; then there are *material* witnesses—they document the contracted *transfer of materials,* not the contract signing; and the third—Carl's category—are called *I-witnesses*—not *e-y-e* eye, but the personal pronoun, capital I—because they are appointed by one of the contracting parties—me—as a *lock sito* representative—that's Latin for "constantly there"—to keep tabs on the contractual compliance of the other party. If you fire *my witness,* you should plan on spending the next ten years of your life and every penny you have in court."

"Come on! What're you telling me? I can't fire the pansy? Ever? That's bullshit. S'pose he starts hanging his whang over the counter? Comes in wearing bra and panties and fucking prancing around, huh? Fuck *that.* Take me to court."

Daniel shook his head. "You're hopeless. Of course he can be dismissed— *if* he's convicted of a felony. But since the money would be gone by the time he even came to trial, the point is moot. Your only other option is a CWBO."

"Like I'm supposed to know what the fuck that is?"

"Actually, you *should*. It's the Contested Witness Buy-Out. If you can't get along with an I-witness, you can pay him a two-thousand-dollar buyout severance and replace him with a mutually agreed-upon substitute."

Robbins was incredulous. "You mean I gotta give this dork-snorkeler twenty yards to get him out of my face?"

"That's correct. It's deducted from the administrative costs, by the way, as our auditors will be informed."

"Fuck it," Robbins said, "I gotta think this is some kind of setup here, but it's your money. Sure."

Robbins counted out the two thousand and tossed it at Carl. "Bye, fuck-face."

Carl grinned at Daniel. "Oh, now I can buy a new dress. But you, Max, I'll always love you." He tried to put some smolder in his voice. "Ever since I met you I've known where you secretly want it. You're one of those poor, poor souls who can never admit it to themselves." He pivoted on his heel and headed for the employee exit, laughing wildly as he tossed away his rabbit ears.

Since Robbins was glaring at Carl's back, Daniel, for the fun of it, vanished, leaving by the front wall.

Four cars surrounded the Cutlass, the two with their flashers on imparting a strobed jerkiness to the movements of the men swarming the Cutlass. Invisible, Daniel walked over beside an unmarked car. A description of his bowling shirt was coming over the radio. That wasn't good news, but wasn't a major problem, either.

Two cops walked right through him as they headed toward the pizzeria. That was a major problem. They'd impound the money, fingerprint the case. He thought this over. No rides for the kids. No idea whose prints could be on the case, except his own. He went back through the wall just as the cops knocked on the door.

As Daniel entered, he almost lost his concentration in a fit of laughter. Max Robbins was going crazy looking for the briefcase—Daniel had forgotten it would vanish when he did. The case was right on the table where Robbins had left it, but he couldn't see it. He was down on his knees searching under the tables. His florid face turned fish-belly white when he heard the pounding from the front and the word "Police."

Daniel closed the case, picked up the contract on the table, and left through the back wall. Invisible, he walked about twenty blocks toward town, then turned right on Industrial Way. He walked north for awhile, then turned back east on a dark, quiet cul-de-sac. At the very end was a old, wooden-sided warehouse that was too perfect to be possible—*T. H. Hothman's Theatrical Supply*. Daniel walked through the closest wall to check it out. Eighty percent of the inside space was a single storage area, aisle after aisle of costumes and props. There was a modest office behind the partition, an adjoining bathroom with shower, and a bedroom. And though the bedroom was hardly the size of two decent closets, it had a firm bed, a narrow dresser, and, on top of the dresser, a thirteen-inch portable TV. Daniel snapped it on to see if he'd made the news.

Almost. The bodies of Elwood and Emmett Tindell, reputed international drug dealers, had been found by a rancher earlier that evening. They had been professionally executed at close range. Unnamed sources speculated that Colombia's Piscato cocaine cartel had ordered the execution over unpaid bills.

THE FIRST NOTEBOOK OF JENNIFER RAINE
APRIL ? (LOST TRACK)

I found the truth, and it is simple: Life is amazing. Me and Mia left the donut shop at midnight, seven hours ago, and now I'm rich, loaded, and just got laid. Better things could happen to a nicer girl, but I'll settle for these.

I owe it all to the DJ. (No, change that to Snake-eyes and Boxcars. Change it to Lady Luck and wonder drugs and a giant country-and-western outlaw gambler known as Longshot, who is now peacefully sleeping in the next room after having, as he sighed, "his brains fucked out and danced on." Change that to pranced on. Change it to blitzing.) Oh, them amazing changes. Roll on, river! Roll the dice.

I left the donut shop near midnight and walked downtown. I'd decided to buy a bus ticket to Jim Bridger's grave in eastern Wyoming with the money Billy had given me. If $50 wasn't far enough, I'd go as close as I could.

I'd looked up Greyhound's address in the donut shop phone book, but when I got there, it wasn't. It had been torn down to make room for a new casino. Funny, I can't remember the casino's name, but I remember that the neon outside seemed to pulse, pulse like a gaudy heart. Hypnotized by the rhythm, dazzled by the colors, I tried to decide what this meant. Was it a sign that I should gamble the money rather than play it safe, or was it a temptation that would prove the pain of folly should I succumb?

I was still thinking—hey, it's a tough choice—when a guy wearing this incredible burgundy greatcoat with gold piping and enormous epaulets grabbed me by the arm, hard, and hissed in my ear, "Hustle it somewhere else, Sugar Hump. There ain't no independents on the strip, and I don't know you. You want to push some pussy, that's your business; but don't hustle it here, take it across the tracks, 'cause if you don't, you must not like your face, 'cause I can just about promise if you stay here somebody will pull it off and fix it so that no one else will like it either."

He thought he was doing me a favor, explaining how it was. When he saw I was listening he let go of my arm.

When he finished, I let him have it: "Listen, you presumptuous jerk, I'm looking, *not hooking. I'm trying to decide if I want to gamble my fifty dollars or get down the line. You wouldn't know a whore from a horticulture handbook." (Girl, you do go on!)*

"What are you saying?" he snarled. "I'm dumb?*"*

I realized then he wasn't a pimp standing his turf, but a casino doorman. I said, "Not dumb, mistaken. *We all make mistakes."*

He started to say something but glanced over my shoulder and shut up. When I turned around I saw why: there was a man six foot seven and a trim 240 who looked just like Jesus if Jesus was a cowboy who'd got dressed up for the big city. He was wearing snakeskin boots that probably moved some exotic species from the rare *to* endangered *list, a western-cut sport coat with a beaverskin yoke, a white cowboy hat with a band of rattlesnake rattles strung on a gold wire, and a solid silver belt buckle in the shape of a gila monster.* Knocked me out.

Impressed the doorman, too, or at least drained the nasty from his tone. "Evening, Longshot. Still picking winners?"

"Enough to keep even," Longshot said, his voice like polished oak. He glanced at me—just for a second, but he really *looked—then back at the doorman. "Slow night, Lyle?" he said, sounding plumb puzzled that Lyle had nothing more interesting to do than hassle an absolutely provocative lady, even if she was a little rumpled and road-grubby.*

"Just telling the sister how it is," Lyle shrugged. "Spare some grief."

Longshot's nod said "Understood, appreciated, see ya later." He turned to me and said, "Ma'am, I couldn't help but overhear the decision you're struggling with, whether to put it on *the line or use it for gettin'* down *the line. That's a rough choice every time you've got to make it; I know, 'cause I'm forty-three years old and had to choose a bunch o' times. My name, by the way—'scuse my rough manners—is Longshot."*

"I'm Jennifer Raine," I said. (I felt that safe with him.)

He tipped his hat!

So I lifted the hem of my imaginary dress and curtsied.

When he grinned, light danced in his lonesome-prairie, sky-blue eyes. "Jenny Raine," he repeated softly, as it should be said. "Jenny Raine. Sounds close to 'gentle rain,' but I bet you can get stormy, too."

I smiled right at him. "Hurricane," I warned, but with what I hoped was an inviting smile.

"Have you made your decision, or are you still mulling it around?"

"Mulling," I said, trying to make it sound as if mulling was something I

did with my hips. "You said you were a man of experience. Have any advice for the young?"

"Matter o' fact, I do: Lay it on the line."

"Always?"

"Nope. But anyone in town can tell you that the best thing I have going is my ability to know when someone's about to break loose and go hog-wild lucky. Jenny, you're so ripe for a hot roll that I'll back you ten grand, right now tonight, for half the action."

"Nope," I said, imitating his flat inflection. "But if you'll match my fifty, anything either of us hits we'll split down the middle."

He offered his arm. Lyle, who'd faded back to his post, opened the door as we swept inside.

I know shit about gambling, so I let Longshot choose the game. He led me straight upstairs to a $10,000-limit crap table, took our pooled money, and bought one black chip. The guy who sold him the chip looked amazed. He said to Longshot, "Musta been a nightmare run to leave you short."

Longshot grinned his easy prairie-sky grin. "No bad dreams, Ed; more like good vision."

He asked what I wanted to bet it on—Come or Don't at even money, numbers from two to twelve, Snake-eyes to Boxcars—I stopped him right there. "Boxcars," I said. I could hear the roar and rattle of a train coming down the mountain, see newspaper-wrapped hoboes watching the stars hurtle by.

Longshot said, "Double sixes pays 30–1, but it's 36–1 against rolling it. Long odds."

He was explaining what I'd done, not challenging my choice. I batted my pretty blue eyes and said, "I like long shots, Longshot." (Jenny, you're so bad.)

A skinny guy in rimless glasses rolled the dice. Boxcars. Three thousand dollars.

Longshot smiled at me and said, "How much and on what?" God, does he have style.

I could still hear the train wailing lonely through the night. "All of it," I said. "Boxcars again."

The guy running the game lifted a brow at Longshot. Longshot told him, "The lady says let it ride."

When I heard "let it ride," I knew we were rich. We were. Boxcars. Ninety-three thousand dollars.

Longshot gave me the sweetest smile. "It's a $10,000-limit table." I loved that—not even asking if I wanted to stop, right, but regretting we couldn't bet more. Now that gave me confidence.

Good thing, because I didn't hear the train anymore. The train was gone. And in its place, as if its fading whistle had snagged her breath, Mia keened *softly in her sleep. For an instant I flashed through her dreams, and she was dreaming again of snakes falling on her in the darkness, their eyes like tiny beads of moonlight.*

"Snake-Eyes," I told Longshot. "Last roll." And then, because I wanted him to know me, I said, "I have an imaginary daughter I have to take care of."

That splendid man looked me right in the eye and said, "Whatever you say. Whoever you are."

As we girls say, I was swooning.

Hello, aces! Snake-Eyes! Yes. Three hundred thousand dollars. Three hundred and ninety-three thousand dollars total. One hundred and ninety-six thousand five hundred each. Minus tips. I gave Lyle $500 on our way out.

Me and Longshot (Mia, after that one cry, had fallen deeply asleep) celebrated our good fortune by assaulting his drug supply—cocaine, killer weed, and disco-biscuits (my first time with any of them except marijuana, and that was nothing like these crusty buds), and then by joining in those sweet little obliterations that keep us alive.

Life is great.

Nina Pleshette, an R.N. at Oakland's Kaiser Hospital, dialed the number she'd been given from a pay phone in front of the building. An answering machine picked up her call on the third ring. The message said, "Thank you for calling on TNT. At the tone, please punch in your code, followed by the code you seek."

The tone was a bugle blowing *Charge,* followed immediately by Red Freddie screaming, "Smash the State!"

Nina punched in RN43, paused, then punched R77. There were two clicks, then the sound of an autodialer.

The phone rang twice in a concrete bunker three hundred miles northeast before Charmaine put down the research paper she was reading and answered with a soft "Hello."

"This is RN43. The patient died at 11:45 P.M. without regaining consciousness."

"That's too bad," Charmaine said. "Did he have any visitors?"

"No."

"Has a cause of death been established?"

"No. No official diagnosis, either. The doctors were proceeding on the assumption it was a rare allergic reaction to an undetermined agent. His immune system just seemed to collapse."

"Thank you for calling," Charmaine said, and replaced the receiver.

She returned to the paper on ricin, a poison for which she'd been working

326

on an antidote for almost two weeks. She concentrated on the molecular diagram, trying to imagine how it interacted with various coenzymes, but after a few minutes she put the paper aside and thought about Gurry Debritto. She was surprised he'd given up so quickly. She must have released a terrible force inside him, some mirror image of his own murderous power. She knew it wasn't the drugs. The two darts had carried nonfatal doses of neuroblockers. The two injections she'd given him were harmless. In fact, since both had contained a balanced combination of vitamins and minerals, they should have given him strength against himself.

Daniel was exhausted and sickened by the televised news. If Elwood and Emmett were international drug dealers, he was the ghost of Elvis Presley. Their murders had been professional all right, and so was the "official speculation." But it didn't make sense that the CIA would put his description on an APB. Volta had predicted with virtual certainty and Daniel had seen the logic in his reasoning, that the CIA would fear the exposure of its incompetence and its secrets more than the loss of the Diamond.

He tried to remember the scene around the Cutlass. Four cars. Two city police with their flashers, one sheriff, and one more—an unmarked gray Ford, a little off to the side, whose radio described his bowling shirt. Two guys inside, coats and slacks. The spooks. He made a surmise he liked—the cops merely had the Cutlass on the hot-sheet from the Tindells' original theft, but the CIA, having somehow snagged the Tindell brothers, knew the car had been boosted again, and by whom. So they knew he had been crying over his mother's dream, that the Diamond was likely in the bowling bag, and that he could disappear—if they believed the Tindell brothers, which might have been difficult.

Daniel was disgusted with himself. He'd gotten cute and vanished when he could have as easily handled the Tindells with Tao Do Chaung. He'd had to show them what *real* power was all about. If he'd just kicked them senseless, they'd probably still be alive. The "unnamed sources" wanted to remain that way, and weren't likely to tolerate people like Elwood and Emmett swearing up and down in national media that they'd seen this disappearing bowler who claimed he had the Grail, and that even the CIA had questioned them. But who would have believed their proofless account of a hitchhiking bowler who vanished? Their deaths had been unnecessary.

He was so tired he almost missed the message: *We know who you are and we're not fucking around.* That's why the bodies had been dumped where they'd be discovered immediately. Pressure. *Every time you reveal yourself, someone will pay the consequences.*

He couldn't allow himself any more foolishness. No more fun. Frivolity was fatal. He winced recalling his righteousness with Volta: *The Diamond is my responsibility now.* Dumb. The only thing he could honestly claim responsibility for was the dangerous indulgence of mindless whims. He'd been acting as if all this was make-believe in Meta Land. This was the real world, even if he wasn't in it. Real terror the Tindells had felt. He wondered if they called out to each other as they knelt beside the road. He started to cry. He closed his eyes tightly against the tears, but his hands suddenly felt wet with blood and he had to open his eyes to check. His hands were dry. He pressed them hard to his face, pushing his head down into the pillow.

"That's right," he said aloud, "if you can't indulge your funny little whimsies, indulge the guilt."

And what about Bunny Boy Carl and Max Robbins, his boss? Daniel tried to concentrate. He assumed Carl had washed the pitcher and glass, but decided to check. Carl had left before he'd vanished with the money and contract—good, no prints there—but Carl would probably get questioned. Not as hard as Max, though, especially if he started babbling about a case full of money and a guy who just seemed to vanish. Daniel realized it had been stupid not to hang around invisible and listen to Max's conversation with the cops. Yet the worst Max could tell them was the crazy truth, and Max hadn't struck him as the sort to make himself look dumb. Whatever Max's story, it was out of Daniel's control.

That left the prints in the car. And maybe the pitcher and glass at the pizzeria. Daniel sagged, but he had to do it. He exchanged his bowling shirt for the first one that fit from one of the aisles of hangered costumes. It was white with muted ruffles down the front, a riverboat gambler's shirt. A cutaway black coat went with it. No hat. Oh well. He started to take the Diamond and decided that a riverboat gambler going bowling at two A.M. was too whimsical. He hid it in a costume box labeled SWISS MAID SIZE 12.

He walked back to the pizzeria, staying visible until he approached the empty parking lot. He walked through the Jackrabbit Pizza wall. The pitcher and glass had either been washed or taken by the cops. He called a cab to meet him on the corner. He told the cabbie his girlfriend had gotten busted for drunk driving and they'd impounded his car. The cabbie knew where to go.

Daniel loitered in front of the Stolen Car Impound till the cabbie was out of sight, then he vanished. He walked into the car, hunched down, and reappeared, quickly wiping it down. He'd just vanished when the fingerprint team arrived to start dusting.

Daniel reappeared in a phone booth down the block, called a cab to let him off a half mile from Hothman's Theatrical Supply, vanished, and walked the rest of the way. He reappeared in front of the box holding the Diamond, took it into the tiny bedroom with him, lay down, thought *responsibility is hard, serious work,* and fell asleep without a thought of vanishing.

He awoke late in the afternoon. After first checking the warehouse to be sure no one was working weekends, he showered in the small bathroom. Refreshed, he returned to the bedroom, shed his towel, and stretched out naked on the bed to think about what to do next. The possibilities overwhelmed him. As he took a deep breath, he saw the faint image of a young blond girl offering him a sphere with a gold center, saying something. He was not sure if this was memory or a desperate hallucinatory invention, but her face floated out of formlessness like an image rising in a darkroom tray. He strained to hear what she was saying, but she was too distant, the words wouldn't carry. He concentrated on her lips as she began to fade, tried to hear the shape of her sounds as she dissolved. He thought he heard, "It's a bead."

The mind is the shadow of the light it seeks.

The mind is a mess.

Daniel felt he understood. A bead. Yes, yes, yes. The Diamond was a bead on the Solar Necklace, strung on the golden spiral of flame through its center. The notion of a Necklace of Light, a circle of spherical diamonds, each reflecting all, containing all, emptying all the golden light back into the Infinite Dazzle, excited Daniel's imagination. He reached down and patted the bowling bag. "Now we're getting somewhere."

Where exactly, he wasn't sure, but he intended to make the journey one careful step at a time. First, he needed to understand if the Diamond was a bead out of its proper order, whether it needed to be returned to its place.

Daniel decided to head for the Rockies. He'd outfit himself for long hauls and hike the wild high country considering the Diamond until he was sure of his next move.

He had a sudden insight, as if in reward for his wisdom: he'd been heading west because that was the direction to Nameless Lake. Daniel cringed. Wild Bill, he felt certain, would know that, and would be waiting there, maybe with Volta. He felt a deep surge of admiration for the clarity and strength Volta brought to responsibility, and a new appreciation for the cost of that commitment. Daniel decided that if his time in the mountains proved futile, he would take the Diamond to Volta, combine forces with him and whoever else they agreed should join. He figured he'd be humbled enough by then to bless any help he could beg.

He needed a new identity for the trip.

He needed to head east. They wouldn't expect him to reverse directions.

He needed to decide how to travel. This time he wouldn't compromise anyone's safety by letting them see him vanish, or by revealing anything about the Diamond. He decided to keep hitching. Hitching provided him with instructive company. He'd felt lonely driving the Cutlass, self-enclosed.

He was impressed by the simplicity of his plan, and grateful for it. He swung off the bed and padded naked into the warehouse's high-shelved aisles of costume-box identities and five long racks of hangered selves.

His identity should provide comfort, warmth, and a natural way to carry the Diamond. An Italian Duke with a bowling-bag? Too much. He needed something with a certain symbolic congruence with his journey. He liked the idea of the Spanish Explorer—Cabeza de Vaca in the Rocky Mountain high— but he'd have to cut off the damn collar. The Riverboat Gambler, which he'd already mostly assembled, was as good a choice as any if he could find the beaver top hat to crown it and a way to pack the Diamond. He spent twenty minutes pawing through hatboxes but didn't find anything fitting.

The mind is the sum of the identities it assumes.

Frustrated, Daniel thought of randomly plucking from the racks and boxes. He ambled down the aisle marked Miscellaneous. Staggering under the armload he'd collected, he set it down on the floor to see what he'd snagged and how the pieces fit each other.

There were some arresting possibilities: a Coptic tunic of undyed linen inlaid with roundels of multihued wool; an Aegean helmet with boar tusks jutting from each side (it would be daring with the Riverboat Gambler outfit); two tasseled cloaks, one a brilliant cardinal, the other lapis-lazuli blue; another tunic, this one fur-lined, with a sleek taper to the sleeves; a Babylonian *kaunake*; a white turban.

Daniel was squatting there wondering if he could hide the Diamond under the turban when he saw, directly across the aisle, at eye level, exactly what he was looking for. The listed contents indicated a complete costume:

MOUNTAIN MAN / TRAPPER
AMERICAN CIRCA 1840–60
SIZE 46 (APPROX.)
BUCKSKIN SHIRT/PANTS
ELKSKIN MOCCASINS & LEGGINGS
FOXHEAD CAP (7¼–½)
CHEYENNE DYED-QUILL BELT W/ ANTELOPE SKIN POUCHES
LARGE POSSIBLES SACK: BUFFALO HIDE, BRAIDED OTTER-SKIN STRAP
POWDER HORN, BUCKSKIN THONG

The first two words—MOUNTAIN MAN—convinced him; the contents delightfully confirmed it. Perfect. Especially the possibles sack, which if he remembered correctly from his boyhood reading was a large pouch for the miscellany of the trapper's work as well as personal treasures, totems, and medicines. Johnny Seven Moons had told him the mountain men were about as close as whites ever came to being Indians.

Daniel, for a long moment, remembered walking naked in the spring rain between Seven Moons and his mother, each holding a hand, how safe he'd felt, how complete, as the warm rain streamed down his body. Seven Moons and his mother were both dead now, but he knew the memory would remain when there was no one left to remember, curving through space like light from a dead star, curving back to its origin in the Infinite Dazzle.

Daniel dressed slowly, savoring the assumption of another self. As he slipped on the buckskins, he imagined the odors of pinesap and smoke and grease dripping from buffalo steaks. The moccasins and foxhead cap fit like they'd been custom made, and the pouched belt decorated with dyed porcupine quills was a work of art. The rough-tanned possibles sack, however, looked worrisomely small.

He picked up the powder horn and returned to the bedroom. He lifted the Diamond from the bowling-bag. To his great satisfaction, the Diamond slipped right in the possibles sack. He cinched the thong around the elkhorn catch, knotting it securely. He put his few toilet items in the belt pouches, then carefully stuffed the powder horn with some of the money from the attaché case—around eight thousand dollars.

He hid his old clothes in various costume boxes, stashed the day pack and its four thousand dollars in the SWISS MILKMAID box. He slipped the case—with about five thousand left in it—onto a shelf with other luggage and hand grips. He returned all the costumes he'd strewn around to their proper boxes.

He smoothed out the bed and hung the damp towel behind the dresser after using it to wipe off prints.

He stood a few minutes, pondering what he might have missed. Granted, the mountain-man garb would attract attention, but, as Jean Bluer had taught him, the outlandishly improbable is often the best disguise. Besides, seriousness needn't necessarily compromise style.

Daniel loved the hang of his buckskins, the way the moccasins connected him to the floor, the slung weight of the Diamond under his left arm, the idea of a fox curled on top of his skull. Without the case and bowling bag, he felt lighter. Lighthearted, too, but not giddy.

He vanished and exited through a wall, heading north. A half mile later he reappeared, turning west toward town. He ignored the curious stares, waved back when someone yelled from a passing car. He tried to recall what he'd read on the mountain men, their stories, their names. He wanted a name that fit his journey. He chose Hugh Glass. He remembered the story of Hugh Glass, who had crawled two hundred and fifty miles to the nearest fort after

331

a grizzly had mauled him. Strength. Determination. Tenacity. He would be Hugh Glass.

A dusty old pickup waited in the gas bay of a Shell Station on the corner while a stooped gray-haired man watched it fill. On impulse, Daniel asked if he happened to be heading east. He was. But his wife and granddaughter were with him, just freshening up in the bathroom, and they were taking Highway 50, which he called the "loneliest road in the world," and their turnoff was only thirty miles out, and that would leave Daniel in the middle of goddamn nowhere in the dark. But hell, if it didn't make him no mind, hop on in the back.

Daniel felt lighter and lighter.

THE FIRST NOTEBOOK OF JENNIFER RAINE
APRIL/LEAVING RENO

Life is still great.

My name is Susanna Rapp. Says so right here on my driver's license, birth certificate, and passport. Rapp is an old Germanic word meaning "young raven" or "brilliant counselor," depending on the root. I do like to talk, and Rapp sounds tough. "Susanna" because I always liked that song, "Oh Susanna, don't you cry for me . . ." Hey sweetheart, I'll cry if I feel like it. Even though I'm not the sort of woman men serenade.

When Longshot got up this morning, I had to tell him that as much as I liked him—which is a lot—I'd have to be moving on. I told him about meeting the DJ at Jim Bridger's grave. Longshot understood. And because he did understand, because he honestly cared to, I told him the short version of my life.

When I had finished, he said, "I don't think you're crazy. You're kinda intense and slippery and taken with some fancies. I've gotten out there myself, more than once to tell the truth, and I always got back."

"How?" Imagine my eagerness.

"Well, I have a kind of unusual method. Works good for me, but it's on the order of fightin' fire with fire. I get an ounce of blow and a fast car and drive straight to Kansas City, then turn around without stoppin' and drive right back. Reams out the sludge."

I tell you, that man is charming. And since I'd hoped he'd beg me to stay, preferably forever, I was a little depressed. But let me tell you, a little depression is no problem *for a woman with nearly two hundred thousand dollars in her purse.*

First, with Longshot's help (he seems to know everybody), I spent five grand on a new identity. Clicked my picture and rolled my thumb, and an hour later I was Susanna Rapp.

I bought a brand-new cardinal Porsche. Seventy thousand. I was cheering up.

I felt good enough about myself then to buy clothes. Ten thousand dollars—but that includes luggage and shoes.

I bought Longshot a big silver belt buckle with two glazed plastic eyeballs glued to it. Engraved around the edges is the motto: "The eyes of Texas are upon you."

Longshot said, "The best thing about being crazy is you can do crazy things."

From Longshot I bought an ounce of cocaine and an ounce of weed and twenty Quaaludes—all for a grand. He claimed that since the drugs were for therapeutic purposes, not recreational, he was honor bound to sell at cost. When I asked point-blank if he was a drug dealer, he said with that easy grin, "Not really. I stock up for hard times when there's quality available. Long shots wouldn't be long shots if they always came in."

His farewell kiss had true affection. He said his arms would always be open. As we said in junior high, "Is that cool, or what?" He was wearing his "Eyes of Texas" belt buckle when he waved good-bye.

I decided I couldn't spend a thousand dollars on drugs without spending at least that much on Mia. She'd been sleeping ever since her nightmare in the barn. I tried to wake her up for a little mother-daughter shopping spree. When I couldn't wake her, I almost panicked. But I could hear her heartbeat, slow but strong.

I tried to imagine what she was dreaming, what she was doing, but I couldn't get inside her. I think she's in a trance, maybe trying to imagine something herself. We have to imagine each other to reach each other, so maybe that's why I feel blocked out. That's okay. I have to trust her to know what's best for herself.

But for that moment I thought she was dead, so scared my first instinct was to rush her to the hospital. That's what I've got to be careful about—acting as if she were real. That's when I get in trouble. Terror makes me forget. Pain makes me forget.

I bought Mia an amazingly soft, thick, pale-blue silk comforter big enough for a double bed. I wrapped it around her in the backseat, fluffed the two matching plush pillows to cushion her head.

I'm sitting in my Porsche at Uncle Bill's Bugle Burger Drive-In, where I've just finished half a Bugle Burger and both a large and a medium Pepsi. As Longshot warned, cocaine discourages gluttony for anything but cocaine. Sure makes you thirsty, though. Better buy a case of mineral water before I hit the road.

My new Easter outfit, a back-zippered sheath with a slit skirt, is made of raw silk, the color of buffed cream, the lines clean and supple. My Easter bonnet is a wide-brimmed straw hat, airy and light, with a rainbow of silks braided around the crown, the unraveled ends trailing down my shoulders like a waterfall of color. I'm wearing these crazy platform shoes with a four-leaf clover cast into each of the three-inch clear-plastic heels. Keep luck rolling. I also bought a sleek black suit with a black hat and veil for the meeting with the DJ on Jim Bridger's grave.

    Now for a few toots and the long highway to Wyoming. I'll have plenty of drugs left for the DJ. I'm already a little tired of them. That's how I've always been—I adore them for a while, but then I get tired of the same point of view all the time.

    On my road map, I-80 looks like the straightest shot to eastern Wyoming. But I'm intrigued by Highway 50, which is so barren on the map there's plenty of room to note: "Highway 50, the Loneliest Highway in the World." That sounded like a tourist attraction for explorers of the psyche, something of a lonesome highway itself. From 50 I can cut north to Wyoming. A difference of hours. If the DJ is serious, he'll wait. If he isn't there, I'll be so heartbroken crazy I'll give Longshot's cure a shot and fight fire with fire, wired to Kansas City and burning the return. I shall return. But now I've got to go.

Four: FIRE

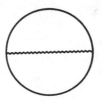

Double, double toil and trouble;
Fire burn and cauldron bubble.
—Shakespeare, *Macbeth* IV.i

THE MIND IS A FULL MOON RISING IN A WARM SPRING
rain.

Daniel felt lighter and lighter and lighter, despite the rain soaking his buckskins, despite the Diamond in his sack that seemed to be gaining an ounce every fifteen minutes, lighter and lighter until he thought he might actually rise with the moon. He stood where his ride from the Reno Shell Station had left him. The old guy had apologized for not being able to invite him for the night, but space was cramped what with the granddaughter and all, and Ma wasn't much on strangers.

Daniel had been sorry, too. The granddaughter was no toddler but a drop-you-to-your-knees smoldering redhead about nineteen years old. Daniel had gathered from the old guy's brief conversation while waiting for the women to return from the restroom that she had been sent to her grandparents' desolate ranch because she'd gone boy-crazy in Santa Rosa. Twice in the course of the ride he'd pressed his hand against the cab's rain-streaked rear window in an unconscious attempt to touch her hair. He'd been sorely tempted to vanish, go sit on the dashboard, and just watch her. He'd resisted, cursing his strength.

Now, as he watched the moon rise, he tried to imagine what she was feeling miles away, and he received a sensation of alien pleasure, the friction between pressed thighs as the old truck seat vibrated down the dirt road. The sensation made him feel lighter yet.

Blinking against the rain, he watched the blurred moon rise with a majestic inevitability so erotic he wanted to vanish. He sensed a powerful and mutual receptivity slowly opening in the warm, moonlit rain, a rain so warm for a Nevada April the old guy had said he damn near couldn't believe it. Daniel believed it. Daniel believed if he vanished he could rise with the moon, float up through the top of his skull and join the moon's constancy, its fastness, its light. He was gathering himself to vanish when a low sexual growl snapped his focus.

The cardinal Porsche shot past in a blink, but one blink was sufficient for a glimpse of the striking woman at the wheel. *Stop,* he thought, as the rain-smeared glow of taillights faded.

When the car was almost out of sight, he caught the sudden brightness of brake lights. Daniel ran toward the car, hoping his glimpse of her hadn't been some rain-blurred moonlight mirage.

The mind is a mirage with real water.

When he reached the passenger door and bent to look inside, her loveliness took his breath away. The door was locked.

She leaned across the seat—to unlock it, he hoped—but only rolled the window down a crack.

She examined him a moment then said, "Are you Jim Bridger?"

She might as well have said, *You're in love with me now.*

"No ma'am, I'm not," Daniel said with the drawl of an old beaver-trapper, "but I knew the Bridger boy when he was greener'n a mountain meadow. Fact is, he an' that worthless John Fitzpatrick left me in the mountains to die. I'd gotten chawed on somethin' pitiful by a she-grizzly. The Mountain Code is to stay till you're sure, but the Bridger boy and that Fitzpatrick fool was in a tizzy about some marauding Indians nearby, so they left me for dead. That wasn't so bad, but they took my rifle and my possibles with 'em. Had to live on what the wolves left on buffler carcasses, and had to fight the damn buzzards for that. Had a broken leg and back tore raw, so I had to go it on my hands and knees. Made pads out of dried buffler hide. Two hundred fifty miles to Fort Kiowa and the only thing that kept me going was revenge. You shoulda seen that Bridger boy's face when he spied me crawling through the gates, like I was nightmare turned real, come to collect."

The woman bent closer to the crack in the window. "Did you kill him?"

Daniel, bending close to hear the question, caught the scent of cinnamon on her breath. "No, ma'am, I didn't. Revenge is a powerful lure till it's time to pull the trigger. Then it's thin justice, weak murder. Don't get me wrong, now. I didn't kill 'em, but I didn't forgive 'em either. Well actually, I forgave the Bridger boy some. He was a tenderfoot, hadn't grasped the fine points of the Code. He went on to be a genuine mountain man. Ol' Gabe—that's what he come to be called. Fitzpatrick, though, he stayed worthless, and unforgiven."

The woman said, "When was this?"

Daniel squinted up at the moon. "Musta been eighteen forty-five, forty-six—sometime close."

"That was a hundred and forty years ago."

Daniel smiled at her. "Only if you keep track real close."

"But you couldn't have been alive then."

Daniel squatted so they were at eye level. He said, with careless conviction, "Ma'am, I can be whoever I want to be as long as I know who I am."

"Get in," Jenny said, unlocking the door.

Daniel obliged.

Jenny watched him as he slid in and settled, then asked, "Do you know the DJ? Guy on the radio?"

"Ain't much for this modern stuff, but I did hear a guy named David Janus on a program called "Moment of Truth," all about the mind, and this David Janus sounds like he lost his oars in some swift water, if you follow my drift."

"What did he say about the mind?"

Daniel, taken aback, was slow to reply. "Lots of things, but I guess the nut of it would be that the mind is everything you can think about it."

Jenny nodded. "The DJ. When did you hear him?"

"Let's see. Two nights back, comin' into Reno."

"I knew he was around," Jenny smiled. "I'm supposed to meet him at Jim Bridger's grave in eastern Wyoming."

"You might find a *Fort Bridger* there around the Green River, but they didn't bury ol' Gabe where he belonged. Shipped his body home to Saint Louie. I don't know, but I think it'd be hard to rest easy on city ground. All that bustle and traffic and chatter." This piece of information from his youthful reading had particularly moved him.

Jenny looked at him appraisingly. "Who are you?" she said.

"Name's Hugh Glass, ma'am."

"No, it isn't," Jenny said. "Take off your foxy cap."

Daniel removed it, turning to face her.

They looked at each other, both afraid they were going to start trembling.

Jenny said, "You're a kid like me, barely twenty."

"My name's Daniel Pearse." He felt light-headed speaking his own name.

"I'm Jennifer Raine," Jenny said. "Susanna Rapp if anyone should inquire."

"Am I to take it we share outlaw status in the culture at large?"

Jenny cocked her head, smiling, the rainbow tassel on her hat sliding across her left shoulder. "And am I to take this radical change in diction and voice as an indication of candor?"

"Please do," Daniel said.

Jenny said, "I'm not sure *what* I am. I escaped from a mental hospital in California and won about two hundred thousand dollars last night on three rolls of the dice and here I am, no longer sure where to go. But it's odd—just before I saw you staring at the moon, I was thinking about what I am. Not *who*—I'll be working on *that* one for a while—but what. What I *am*. For now I'm an apprentice poet and I'm a Lover of Fortune. Not a *Soldier* of Fortune. A lover. And I suppose that'd make me a borderline outlaw."

"You forgot something else you are," Daniel said.

Cautiously, Jenny said, "What?"

"A mother. Unless you've kidnapped that child bundled in back."

Jenny stared at him, stunned by terror and relief.

Afraid he'd offended her, Daniel said quickly, "If you're offering me a ride—and I *want* you to—let's agree to respect necessary secrets."

Jenny reached over and lifted his left hand into hers, pressing it softly between her palms. "She's my daughter," Jenny said huskily, "but Daniel— she's imaginary. She's my *imaginary* daughter. How can you see her?"

"I don't know," Daniel said. He thought he would faint. She squeezed his hand harder. "I saw her swaddled in that lovely blanket when I got in the car and I still see her now. Certainly I have a strong imagination, but I've never experienced anything like this before." Then he remembered that he could see a spiral flame inside the Diamond when he was invisible, and added, "Well, there is one similar."

"You can imagine my imaginary daughter? Is that what you're saying?"

"Yes. But probably only because you let me."

Jenny released his hand and reached for her door handle. As she opened the door, she glanced back at Daniel and said, "C'mere, sailor."

He followed her about twenty yards away from the car into the scrub-sage desert. She told him to stop. He did. She walked another ten yards then turned around to face him. She kicked off her four-leaf clover shoes. Took off her hat and shook her dark blond hair, the color of sugar just before it burns. She said, "Tell me what you see," and turned around, deftly unzipping her dress down the back, gracefully shedding it with a wiggle of her hips.

Over her shoulder Jenny said urgently, "Daniel, what do you *see?*"

"I see," Daniel began, his voice quavering, "a scar at the base of your spine, shaped like a lightning bolt, and I see a beautiful woman, her shoulders wet with rain, who I want to hold in my arms so bad I can't keep my voice from shaking."

Jenny turned around.

If it weren't for the Diamond's weight, which seemed to be gaining an ounce every five minutes now, Daniel would have lifted off the earth. He watched her delicately touch herself, the moonlit whiteness of her exposed inner thigh, rain dripping from her tight nipples. He saw the nakedness beyond her flesh. Her eyes promised what they might know together: fearless hunger, fearless trust. He wanted to meet the offer with all of himself, heartbeat to heartbeat, breath to breath. Though he felt his assent with a serene clarity, light without shadow, he was speechless.

Jenny wasn't. She nodded toward the Porsche and told him, "Bring Mia's blanket."

When Volta arrived home he cleared the living room of every stick of furniture except a long low maple-top table and a cushion to sit on while he worked. He put the goldfish's bowl directly in his line of sight on the far side of the table. He finished listening to various messages—nothing urgent—and turned off the tape deck. He gathered a pen and pad of paper and began to compose his letter of retirement from the Star. The tiny goldfish was darting wildly around the bowl.

On impulse, Volta leapt up and ran to his bedroom. He returned a few minutes later, wearing only his old magician's robe, indigo silk randomly patterned with small golden stars, the phases of the moon emblazoned on the back and up each sleeve. He sat cross-legged on the cushion and cupped the goldfish's bowl in his hands. The goldfish was circling around the glass edge of the bowl, but now less frantically. The fish kept slowing as Volta watched. With a flick of its tail, it swam to the center of the bowl and stopped, suspended, fins barely shimmering. Volta could feel the Diamond grow denser in Daniel's mind.

The mind is the light of the shadow it seeks.

When they finished making love, Daniel and Jenny rolled onto their backs on the blue silk comforter and let the light, warm rain fall on their bodies. Daniel had never felt so clean.

A half hour later, without a word, they began gathering their soaked clothes. Jenny shook the rainwater off her straw hat. The unraveled cascade of rainbow threads was plastered into a dull rope. She took the silk between her circled thumb and index finger and stripped it from soaked to damp with a smile that snared Daniel in its sweet contentment.

But Daniel didn't smile when he picked up his possibles sack. Something wasn't right. The Diamond had doubled in weight—either that or the buffalo-skin pouch had soaked up a gallon of water. He wanted to take the Diamond out and examine it, but he couldn't risk implicating her. He'd decided to ask her if she'd mind waiting for him in the car while he attended to some necessarily private business, when the moon vanished and the rain stopped.

Jenny had thrown the wet comforter over them both. She put her hand on his chest, right over his heart, a fingertip barely brushing his nipple, and whispered, "Let's pretend we're a double ghost, two spirits who have become each other—not become *one,* you understand, but two who have created a meeting point through which their forces join."

Daniel slipped his arm around her waist and held her closer. He asked softly, "You want to play for pretendsies or for keeps?"

Jenny murmured, "You don't know how happy it makes me to hear you say that. But Daniel, look at us: naked lovers whispering sweet nothings under a soaked silk blanket in scrub-sage, having met an hour ago under false identities and true hearts. We're fools, Daniel, fools trying to perfect their foolishness. We'd be unfaithful to ourselves if we didn't imagine something for our double ghost to do."

"I love the way you talk." Daniel nuzzled her wet hair.

"So what should we pretend?"

"Whatever your heart desires," Daniel whispered.

"No," she said, so sharply Daniel pulled away. "We have to imagine it together. That's the fun of it, the importance."

Daniel understood exactly what she meant, understood how the solitary imagination could not imagine itself. Maybe that was what Volta had been trying to tell him.

"Let's pretend," Daniel said, "that our double ghost has been temporarily blinded by pleasure. Without looking, it must find a red Porsche with Jenny and Daniel's imaginary daughter asleep in the back. They have to rely solely on their other four senses, their instincts, and their joined imaginations."

Jenny said, "And if they find the car and daughter, their joined ghosts will separate into their seats, but they'll remain naked, driving the lonely road as outlaw Lovers of Fortune until the moon sets. They'll only talk to each other if it's necessary to keep the junction open. Otherwise, they'll be silent, trying only to imagine each other and what the morning might bring."

"Free to imagine anything," Daniel added.

"Yes," Jenny said. "Anything."

"You *are* Fortune," Daniel told her.

Jenny said, "My name is Jennifer Raine, Susanna Rapp, Goldie Hart, Emily Dickinson, Malinche, Cabeza de Vaca, Cinderella, Lao-Tzu, Mia, Longshot, Daniel Pearse."

Daniel's laugh was muffled by the draped comforter. "Do you guys have all your clothes gathered up so this ghost can begin searching?"

"I've got my hat and shoes. I'm going to leave my dress where it fell."

Their mutual ghost floated silently back to the highway. Without speaking, Jenny folded the blanket while Daniel wrung his buckskins out and

342

stashed them under the Porsche's front seat with the powder horn. He kept the sack with the Diamond at his feet. Jenny slipped in behind the wheel and started the car. They were both naked, sheened with rain. Daniel glanced in the back at Mia. Her eyes were open, but locked on some distant point within herself.

"Jenny," Daniel said, "Mia's in a trance."

With her eyes on the road, Jenny nodded. "I know. I think she's out searching for something, something I don't understand. Even imaginary daughters have lives of their own."

Daniel said nothing.

Jenny turned to him. "Do *you* know what Mia's doing, what she's after?"

"No. I have no idea. But I can try to reach her if you want me to."

Jenny thought a moment. "Only if you want to."

Daniel tried to imagine himself entering Mia's mind. Instantly a sense of danger seized him. The danger was formless yet he could discern a shape, a vague configuration of a face. Daniel concentrated on drawing features from vague suggestion. Volta. Daniel was stunned.

"Tell me," Jenny said. "I want to know."

Daniel said, "I saw the face of a man named Volta. Do you know him?"

"No."

"I do, intimately. He retrieved me from a coma one time, entered my psyche. Maybe he's trying to again, and it's being magnified through Mia, because we've joined our imaginations. Or it may have been sheer projection on my part, a reflection off the wall of mirrors protecting Mia's trance. But my impression from Volta's image was danger, real danger. Do you see or feel anything like that?"

"No," Jenny said, "but I feel it in you."

"Probably with reason," Daniel agreed.

Jenny said evenly, "I have a feeling it might be a secret, but I'd like to know what's in your pouch."

"I can't tell you. If I did, it could put you in danger for no reason."

"I appreciate your regard," Jenny said, "but we're always in fatal danger. Life couldn't be great without it."

With all the directness he could muster, Daniel said, "Jenny, I love you."

"Ohhh." Jenny half giggled, half moaned. "You sweet-talking boy. But love *us,* too, Daniel, what we are together."

They were silent for seventy miles until Jenny, already braking, smiled and arched her brow. "Again?"

Daniel sighed. "Jenny, I have to tell you that in my past, my sexual past—which hasn't been extensive—I've never been able to have an orgasm with the same woman twice."

Jenny, pulling off the road, said, "You can't cross the same river twice."

"I'm not sure I understand," Daniel said.

"I change. You change. Change changes. Why be afraid it won't stay the same? It's not supposed to. Even if you have to be crazy to appreciate how great that is."

"A woman named Charmaine said I loved myself more than those women."

Jenny opened her door and stepped out naked. The warm rain had turned to a misty drizzle. She reached into the back for the folded comforter. "Come on, sailor," she said to Daniel, a playful sultriness in her tone. "Let's cross the river. I'll bet you love against fifty thousand dollars we can cross that mighty water again, me and you, together."

Love won going away. Far away.

So far away that Daniel realized he was in danger. When they floated back to the Porsche, Daniel hefted the pouch. The Diamond had almost quadrupled its weight without changing size.

They drove the next forty miles in silence. Daniel leaned back, trying to imagine what was happening with the Diamond. He was afraid to look, afraid to ask Jenny to pull over so he could take it out on the flats for a private glance. He sensed what he'd see: the Diamond preparing to open. Quickly, with a joy-shredding certainty, Daniel's choice was becoming a decision between Jenny and the Diamond.

The mind, Daniel remembered, is neither either nor or.

The mind is a box canyon.

Daniel squeezed Jenny's bare shoulder. She turned at his touch, smiling questioningly. Daniel pointed to the side of the road.

"Again?" she said, delight overwhelming her attempt at mock incredulity.

"I want to marry you," Daniel said. "Here and now."

Jenny was already pulling over.

As they coasted to a stop, Daniel said, "You bring the bridal suite, I'll get the ring."

They walked out naked in the sage desert, the folded comforter under Jenny's arm, the possibles sack slung over Daniel's shoulder, free arms around each other's waists, until they found a clearing in the brush. The mist that eddied in the moonlight was brighter now that the rain clouds had dissolved. Jenny spread the damp silk comforter in the clearing, smoothing it out with her hands. The lightning-bolt scar at the base of her spine gleamed in the moonlight. Daniel knelt behind her and kissed her scar, startled and aroused by its heat on his lips.

Jenny turned to face him, her eyes burning with tears. *"I don't care,"* she said passionately. "I *don't care* if you're real."

"Do you care if it's so dangerous it could kill us both?"

"Life is great."

"Well then, dearly beloved," Daniel intoned, slipping the Diamond from the possibles sack, "with this ring I do thee wed. May I now kiss the bride?"

Jenny, staring into the Diamond, muttered, "In a minute."

They both stared into the Diamond. Daniel saw immediately the glow was more brilliant—not brighter, really, but sharper. He needed to vanish to see inside.

Jenny put her hand on his thigh. "Tell me," she said.

Daniel looked at her and said as plainly and directly as he could, "I love you."

Jenny threw back her head and laughed at the moon.

Perplexed, Daniel said, "That's not what you wanted to know?"

Jenny stopped laughing, but couldn't help smiling as she shook her head. She lifted the Diamond from his hands and placed it gently at the head of the comforter, the Diamond's light and the light of the moon shimmering on the pale blue silk as if it were a pond in a high mountain meadow.

Jenny turned back to Daniel, on his knees facing her. She put her arms around him and pulled him close, whispering, "I do. I do. In sickness and in health. In life and death. Madness and folly. Till we part and after we part and right here and right now. I do."

"I have to tell you some things."

"No you don't," Jenny promised.

"I can vanish," Daniel told her, hoping she'd understand that he did have to tell her, that he owed her the honor.

"Don't vanish," she murmured against his shoulder, her tongue tracing his collarbone. "If you vanish, I won't be able to feel you inside me, I won't be able to feel those things we can only feel together."

Daniel said, "There's something there I need to know, something I'm meant to understand."

Jenny released her embrace and in the same motion eased backward on the comforter. Her eyes held a glint of playful challenge. "Daniel, I want you to seek whatever you think you need to find, see whatever you're meant to behold. That's what marriage is all about. But first, Daniel, before you ride off on your beautiful white charger, dragons to slay, maidens to save, grails galore, I want to be sure you understand the basics."

She turned on her side and patted the comforter. When Daniel lay down beside her, she touched his cheek. Her voice thick, Jenny said, "Do you understand that?"

"Yes," Daniel moaned, closing his eyes.

"Look at me, Daniel," Jenny said forcefully. "Look in my eyes. Do you see me?"

"I don't know," Daniel said. "I don't know who I see anymore."

"If you can't see me, Daniel, you'll never see yourself." Jenny slipped her arms around him. "Come on. We'll look for each other."

Daniel held her tightly. He smiled at her, and suddenly, finally, he relaxed. "Mrs. Pearse, it will be the joy of my life to consummate our marriage, but I must ask you first for another vow: If something should happen to me, if I vanish and don't make it back right away, I want you to take the Diamond—your wedding ring—and drop it in any large body of water you choose. Or anywhere it's unlikely to be found. It's stolen. They'll kill you to get it back. Don't show it to anybody."

Jenny whispered fiercely, *"Done.* Now let's imagine something real—each other."

Slowly at first, bathed in the light of Diamond and moon, blurred in the drifting tatters of mist swirled by their cries, they imagined each other, the forks of a river joining for the plunge to the sea.

When they'd quit laughing and trembling and crying and kissing, Jenny said, "I rest my case." She curled against him, head on his chest.

Daniel squeezed her close, but he wasn't there. Even with his eyes shut he sensed the Diamond's light intensifying. He had to trust her understanding, trust himself. He looked over his shoulder at the Diamond, focused on its center, and vanished.

The Diamond didn't.

But for a moment Daniel thought it had vanished with him. He could see the flame inside, but it wasn't the spiral flame he'd always seen before. As if compressed by the Diamond's growing density, the flame condensed toward the center, tightened to a single whirling point, the visible tip of a solar vortex, heat so intense it vaporized bone. But Daniel had no body to burn.

He hurled himself toward the spinning center. And as he was swept across the threshold, sucked through the vortex and into the solar furnace, spilled into the Diamond Forge, Daniel learned what he was meant to know.

He was a god. He was Hermes, Thoth, Mercury; the prophet Hermes Trismegistos. He had accepted birth to refresh his compassion for the human soul.

He felt joyously released. He'd made it back! The Diamond was his door out, love the key that opened the lock. Above as below. Stone junction. He blessed his mother for allowing him her womb, for letting him father himself. He heard her scream inside him, *"Run, Daniel!"* but there was nowhere left to go, no possible escape. He blessed his teachers, his friends, his lovers—Jenny especially, Jenny his wife. He heard Volta chanting deep within him, *"Life, life, life, life."* He blessed Volta for his wise help, though he knew Volta wouldn't understand. Roaring upward in the solar vortex, Daniel laughed. It was all life. No levels or dimensions. Not even the gods could escape. He crossed his arms on his chest, closed his eyes and let himself go, vanishing into the Diamond-Light forever.

Volta sat cross-legged on the floor, the goldfish's bowl cradled in his hands, his imagination locked on Daniel. He felt Daniel enter the Diamond, the joy of his surrender. Volta cried out softly, "No, Daniel. Oh no, poor Daniel." Another beautiful, deluded spirit consumed by powers mistaken for his own. Gently, Volta set the bowl on the table. The goldfish began languidly finning around the bowl.

"Ahhhhhhh," Volta sighed, "go." Daniel had made his choice, if it could be called a choice, if a raindrop chooses where to fall, a river to flow. Grant Daniel his choice and mourn his loss. Live by life and remember the dead. Volta stood up and walked briskly to the door. He needed the clean night air, the real moon and stars.

When Volta opened the door, Shamus pointed a pistol directly between Volta's eyes. They both froze. Shamus held the pistol in his good hand. A small automatic. Cocked. Shamus's scar-twisted hand was lifted to his ear, its tucked thumb forming a crude mouth.

His voice calm and even, Shamus said, "Walk slowly backward into the house, keeping your arms outstretched at shoulder level, fingers spread and palms facing me."

Volta stepped carefully backward to the center of the room. Shamus followed, keeping his distance, pistol steady on Volta's forehead. He kicked the door shut behind him.

Volta sagged when the scarred hand shrilled in Shamus's ear, the voice utterly different from Shamus's own, "Make him naked. *Naked.*"

"Take off your robe," Shamus ordered Volta.

"No," Volta said.

"Kill him," the hand urged. "Now. Not another word."

"Do it," Volta agreed. "Then you'll never know who betrayed you. I expected, given your work with Jacob Hind, you might decipher Alex Three. You were quicker than I anticipated."

"Watch him!" Shamus's hand warned.

"You admit you tipped the CIA?" Shamus said coldly.

"Yes. Reluctantly, by request."

Shamus hissed, "Fucking Daniel."

"I gave my honor that I wouldn't reveal my source."

"You did, huh?" Shamus sneered. "What honor could you possibly have, snitching us to the CIA?"

"I was forced to act on extremely short notice. The CIA was the best choice."

"Who told you?" The pistol shook in Shamus's hand. "You tell me or I'll shoot off little pieces of you until you do. All I want from you, Volta, is what I deserve—the truth."

Volta looked past the gun barrel into Shamus's eyes. "Annalee betrayed you."

Shamus went blank. His ravaged hand screamed in his ear, "Kill him, kill him, *kill him*—he's fucking with your head!"

Volta spoke directly to Shamus, who was staring at him, shocked. "I'm sorry, Shamus. I believe everyone deserves the truth, but I promised Annalee I would never tell anyone, *never,* unless my life depended on it. I told her I wouldn't die to protect her betrayal."

Shamus stared at Volta, ignoring the scarred hand muttering in his ear. Volta calmly met Shamus's gaze. Shamus blinked rapidly, his lips drawing back in a sickly grin. A muscle twitched sharply in his cheek, and again; then, as if the spasm had ignited his nervous system, his entire body began to jerk. Volta sensed Shamus knew this was the truth. Though Volta believed Shamus deserved the truth, he also understood that this was a truth Shamus couldn't survive. As Volta perfectly understood, that meant he wouldn't survive it either, not unless he could shock Shamus into paralysis or sense. But clearly, there were two Shamuses, the hand that held the gun, the other hand hideously disfigured by molten silver.

Shamus's face contorted. *"Never!"* he screamed. *"No!"*

Volta said softly, "The truth."

"It's a trick, a trick, a trick, a trick," the hand yammered in Shamus's ear.

"I *know it is,* goddammit!" Shamus yelled at his hand. Shamus began to pace tightly back and forth, keeping the gun trained on Volta. Shamus and his hand were muttering, but both were so low and garbled Volta couldn't make out a single word. He looked for a lapse in Shamus's awareness, a point of escape, a move to make. Failing that, he could try to strike one clean, shattering blow to Shamus's psyche that would make him accept the truth. The longer Shamus paced, growing more careless with the gun, the more Volta liked his chances.

He liked them a whole lot less when Shamus quit pacing and slowly raised the gun until the front bead locked solidly on Volta's forehead. Sneering, Shamus said, "You *cold* bastard. You *heartless* piece of shit. Do you think I'm stupid? I *know* Daniel was the traitor. He tipped you, you tipped the Feds—keep it tidy that way—and now, out of your legendary sense of honor, you are protecting Daniel. It's an excellent ploy, really. You admit you snitched us to the CIA, but claim it was at the request of a fine, brave woman who is—fortunately for you, heartbreakingly for me—dead. Dead by the treachery of her own son, and the corrupt accomplice of his future mentor who foresaw great possibilities for such a poisoned soul. If I'm interpreting the few whispers I've heard correctly, your prize graduate of the black arts has now betrayed you. I always sensed that in Daniel—a feeling that he would only find forgiveness in oblivion."

"He has," Volta said. "But he wasn't seeking forgiveness. He was seeking beyond sin and forgiveness, and he didn't return."

"Oh my," Shamus said derisively, "how convenient. Now the only two people who could have told you are—"

Volta cut in sharply, "Shamus, think clearly. Daniel is dead. Why wouldn't I tell you what you need to believe, that it was Daniel who betrayed you? Why?"

Shamus's hand babbled wildly in his ear, "Don't fall for it he's fucking your head he has moves and outs and smarts don't match him don't let him . . ."

Shamus, his puzzled gaze locked on Volta's face, said, "Why?"

Volta said, "Because the only way you'll heal is through the truth. And because I respect you, and because I'm now free to help. Annalee betrayed you. That's the truth."

Shamus held the bead on Volta's forehead. "You cruel son of a bitch. You know you're going to die, and even though it makes no difference anymore, you won't leave what I have left of her undefiled."

"I have proof," Volta said.

"Blow the fucking scum away!" the scarred hand squealed. *"Do it now! Don't listen. Don't. Don't."*

Volta continued, his voice calm, precise: "Annalee called me an hour after she'd left your apartment on the day of the planned attempt. Her call came in on a gold-access number, and every gold-access call is automatically taped. The tape is in this room, in a narrow vault behind the mirror to your right. There's a tape deck on the table behind me." He paused, then added, "If you want the truth. If you have the spirit to bear it, as I have, for years."

"Okay," Shamus said with confidence, "I'm going to call that bluff." He seemed oblivious to his hand's frenzied drone-chant in his ear, *"Nonowdoitnow-nonowdoitnownonowdoitnownonowdoitnow . . ."*

"My compliments," Volta said, "on an intelligent choice. Your only hope, Shamus, is to accept the truth."

"Hey," Shamus spit, "I'm calling your bluff, remember? And if I've caught you, you lose. One piece of your body at a time, or five clips—whichever comes first. So where is this tape?"

"In a vault behind that mirror. Lift off the mirror and press the nail it hangs on—three long, four short. The vault door will open. The tape is coded AGAPE. I'll get it myself if you prefer."

"Very slowly," Shamus murmured, indicating the mirror with a slight movement of the gun barrel.

Breathing deeply, Volta opened the vault as Shamus covered him from ten feet away, his disfigured hand still hovering at his ear, but silent now, as if it too were watching. As soon as the vault door sprang open, Shamus ordered, "Now step away from the vault, move ten feet to your right along the wall, and then I want you to assume the position against the wall. You die if you twitch."

Volta calmly spread his legs and stretched his hands over his head, supporting the weight of his leaning body.

He heard Shamus run the gun barrel down the boxed and stacked cassettes, scanning the codes. There was a sudden silence when he found it.

"I'd be glad to put it on the deck," Volta offered. He felt helpless leaning against the wall.

"Don't move," Shamus warned. "Don't even jiggle."

Volta listened as Shamus crossed to the desk and inserted the cassette.

"Don't do it, you stupid fucking sentimental fool. You weak-willed, self-pitying failure. Yellow, spineless whipping-boy idiot of such heroic, soaring dreams. Give me that gun. You make the decision; I'll execute it."

Shamus handed the gun to his ravaged hand and then punched the *play* button on the deck. He moved ten feet from Volta, his back inches from the open vault.

On the tape, a phone rang seven times before Volta answered, "Yes?"

ANNALEE: *A woman will plant a bomb at an alley between Livermore warehouses at Las Postas Avenue this evening. She must be stopped. She will have a child with her. The child must not be harmed. If the woman is arrested, the child must be cared for. No one—*

VOLTA: *[cutting in] Annalee, I can't pretend this is an anonymous call.*

ANNALEE: *Then I want you to promise me with all your soul that you'll never tell anyone who made it. Never. Even if you have to die.*

VOLTA: *Annalee, I can admire what you're trying to do, even if it's too late for safety; I admire your love for him that you would risk yourself to preserve its possibility; but it's nonetheless a betrayal of his trust, a necessity that might have been forestalled if you'd called when he first returned. I'll honor your secret as completely as I can, but I will not die for it.*

ANNALEE: *Fine, yes, as far as you can. But stop me from planting that bomb.*

VOLTA: *I assume it's diversionary. Livermore? Plutonium?*

ANNALEE: *Just stop me. And if anything happens, take care of Daniel.*

VOLTA: *I'll try, Annalee. That's all I can do.*

ANNALEE: *Do it.*

The tape clicked off.

Volta, face to the wall, couldn't see Shamus's reaction, so he said what he felt: "I'm sorry you had to hear it, Shamus. I know it's painful."

"Painful?" Shamus laughed wildly. "That *fake?* That cruel, cowardly, chickenshit *fake?* Who was it, one of the legendary AMO mimics? Maybe even this Jean Bluer I've been hearing about? Fuck, you can *hear* the splices! It isn't even *close* to her voice. I remember her voice. I remember her laughter and skin! Proof? *Bullshit!* Truth? Here, Volta, turn around here, I'll show you the fucking *truth.* "

Volta turned to face Shamus. When he saw the gun in Shamus's scarred hand, Volta knew he was about to die.

Shamus wailed, "You want the truth, huh, the *whole truth* and *nothing but,* and not any of your *bullshit* lies?" He grabbed the mirror leaning against the wall and thrust it toward Volta, holding it up for him to see his face. "There! That's *your* truth. Look at it! Look! Look at yourself! *Look at what you are!"*

Volta met himself on the surface of the mirror. He looked into his own eyes. No escape. He lifted his head and met Shamus's gaze. "I know who I am," Volta said.

The bullet hit Volta above the left eye, the impact snapping his head back as it blew away the back of his skull. He staggered for an instant, took a stumbling step forward, swayed as he gathered his last living breath, and then, just as Shamus lifted the mirror to shield himself, Volta drove his fist through it, shattering the glass. A splintered shard sliced the carotid artery an inch below Shamus's left ear, and another nearly severed his scarred hand at the wrist.

Volta wanted to stay on his feet, to walk outside and watch the moon and stars as he died, but Shamus—howling, blinded by glass slivers—shoved him backward. Volta collapsed against the table, sending the goldfish bowl smashing to the floor.

Shamus, his spurting wrist pressed against his shirt, his other hand clamped against his neck, staggered along the wall until he found the door, fumbled the knob open with his blood-slick hand, and lurched outside.

Volta lay dead face down alongside the table, his arms stretched out slightly above his head, the spreading pool of blood just touching his finger-tips.

Spilled free of its shattered bowl, the tiny goldfish flopped on the oak floor, trying to fling itself back into the lake, the spherical river. A last wild leap carried it to the edge of the pooling blood. The goldfish thrashed itself upright, then, its back shining above the shallow pool, half squirmed, half swam through Volta's blood, splashed up the shallows like a golden salmon battling upriver to spawning grounds, its movement mirrored in the sinuous waves spreading in its wake, fought on across the surface, to shimmy at last up the star-flecked, moon-spangled sleeve of Volta's magician robe.

Still naked, the silk comforter pulled snugly around her, Jenny stared into the Diamond. She hadn't seen him actually enter it—in fact, she'd been drowsing when she'd realized he had left—but she knew that's where he'd gone. She wasn't sad she'd helped him on his way. No difference between dream lovers and real lovers like Longshot or the mangled love of Clyde. Love was what you made, then what you could make of it. Abandoned on her wedding night. Widowed at consummation. She looked into the centerless, sourceless light of the Diamond and decided she'd wait for Daniel till dawn. If he'd rather vanish than settle down with a crazy woman and an imaginary daughter—fine and farewell. The love they'd made was real even if he wasn't. Any man who kissed her scar was always free to go. And so was she.

When the first sunlight touched the Diamond, Jenny slipped it carefully back in the possibles sack, slung the comforter around her, and walked back to the Porsche. She decided to believe Daniel's information: Jim Bridger's grave was in Saint Louis. Perfect. She could try Longshot's sludge-reaming cure, continue on to Saint Lou, fall in love with the faithful, fascinating DJ she hoped was real, and then, if Daniel hadn't showed up, get rid of the Diamond. After looking at it most of the night, Jenny decided she didn't like the Diamond. Too perfect. Lifeless. As she opened the car door, Jenny felt a strong suspicion that the Diamond wasn't real, another illusion, a mirror to hide behind.

When she opened the Porsche's door she immediately sensed what her eyes confirmed: Mia was gone. "That rotten son of a bitch!" Jenny said. "Fuck you and burn you and leave you alone in the Big Alone." Daniel had taken Mia with him, wherever the hell they'd gone.

Rage vented, Jenny considered two other possibilities: perhaps Mia had followed him freely; or maybe Mia had been his guide. Mia could have imagined him in her trance. Made him bring the Diamond. Get her mother lost in rapture and slip her mind for a different life. *Her own imaginary daughter running off with her dream lover!*

She laughed. She wished them happiness and good fortune.

When Smiling Jack's third straight-access call to Volta went unanswered, he caught a plane for the Coast. He could have asked a number of Alliance members closer to Laurel Creek to check on Volta, but he felt he should do it himself. Volta had never failed to return a straight-access call. If Volta was dead, Jack would know which secrets to protect.

As Smiling Jack stepped out of his rented Ford at Laurel Creek Hollow, he smelled amid the light fragrance of the blossoming apple and plums in the orchard the stench of rotting flesh drifting through the house's open door. Jack tried to steady himself, clearing his mind so he could discern what had happened and what needed to be done.

Despite the sprayed splatters of blood on the porch, he checked the house first. He had tried to prepare himself but was still shocked to see Volta's body face down in the gelatinous pool of blood, a whining swarm of flies clustered in the ragged cavity the bullet had blown in the back of his skull. He wanted to drag Volta from the coagulated mire of his blood to spare him the indignity of being seen like that. But Smiling Jack left him lying and methodically began to examine the room. The open wall-vault. The smashed mirror. The tape box next to the player. The heavy trail of blood leading out the door.

Jack wanted to hear the tape, but instead he followed the blood trail out to the porch, across the yard, then downhill toward the river. Smiling Jack would have bet his customized Kenworth against a sheet of one-ply toilet paper that he'd find Shamus Malloy dead within a quarter mile. He would have won by a hundred yards. Shamus's body, the slashed wrist of his deformed hand clamped to his sliced neck as if the blood could pass between the wounds, was curled at the base on a majestic Douglas fir. Jack carried Shamus's body up the hill, leaving it at the edge of the trees.

Jack listened to the tape three times before he erased it, then looked at Volta's body. To Jack's mind, once Volta had agreed to help her stop the theft, he had drawn his line in exactly the right place: He would honor her secret, but he wouldn't die to protect treachery, no matter how lofty its cause. Volta had drawn his line precisely, honored his promise to the point of exposing himself, then honored himself at the threat of death by giving Shamus the truth. And died for it. There are no lines you can draw against an unbearable truth.

Smiling Jack carried Volta's body to the kitchen and covered it with a sheet. Then he went down to the barn to make some calls.

He called Dolly Varden first. He wanted her there as quickly as possible to help with Volta's remains. He made the other calls, then took a shovel from the tool rack and began digging a grave for Shamus.

Dolly, exhausted from the all-night haul from Portland, arrived at dawn. They cut off Volta's blood-stiffened magician's robe and had silently begun bathing him when Dolly said, "Holy shit. This for real?"

Jack didn't see it. "What?"

"This." She lifted Volta's arm slightly, pointing to his wrist. "Unless old age is eating up my brain, it looks to me like a baby goldfish glued to his wrist here."

Jack came around for a closer look. "Yeah—a baby goldfish. Don't know about being glued, though. Its own slime or maybe some blood—that could make it stick."

Dolly looked at Jack. "So, what do think? Scrape it off or leave it on."

"Leave it, I reckon. Volta always said, 'Trust what's there.'"

"I'll go for that," Dolly said.

When they had finished bathing Volta's corpse, Smiling Jack slung him awkwardly over his shoulder. With Dolly leading the way, he carried him down to a shady alder flat along Laurel Creek, right above where it began its steep drop to the river. They left him face up in a clearing, arms folded on his chest, as Volta had requested years before.

Smiling Jack and Dolly continued on to the creek, stopping at a slow, deep pool. They stripped off their clothes and, with lung-cleansing whoops, plunged into the cold water.

THE SECOND NOTEBOOK OF JENNIFER RAINE
MAY DAY

My name is Jennifer Raine.

I have come to an end I recognize but haven't begun to understand. I left St. Louis this evening without a destination. For the last two weeks I waited faithfully at Jim Bridger's grave, entertaining myself with hopes, dreams, wishes, fantasies, yearnings, and the last of the drugs I brought from Reno. I'm glad they're gone.

The DJ never showed. Daniel never came back. I can't imagine Mia anymore.

I think Daniel may have been the DJ. I know he kissed my scar. I know what passed between us was us, *a warm-rain moon waltz, everything joined and hurled at the stars. I know I imagined Mia, but Daniel was real, real enough to imagine me.*

I kept the Diamond until today. I was convinced that Daniel was and is real and that the Diamond was not. I never looked at it once. But I did pick it up in its sack and caress it, because everything round invites caresses. Every day the Diamond seemed to lose weight, grow lighter but not smaller, and then I got scared that if I kept it, it would gradually exhaust itself, collapse into emptiness, and Daniel could never find his way back.

The Diamond, in an odd way, was all I had left of us, yet I didn't believe it was real. So this evening at sunset I carried the Diamond out to the center of a bridge over the Mississippi River. I married Daniel. I honor vows, keep my promises.

I slipped the Diamond from the sack and looked into it as deeply as I could. I wanted a sign, a vision in the crystal ball, something to keep. I saw nothing, felt nothing.

I opened my hands and let it go. I watched it fall, utterly certain it would hit the water and sink without a ripple, like a breath entering the air.

The Diamond hit the river like a comet, half the Mississippi erupting in a geyser, a magnificent fountain turned golden by the setting sun.

I don't know a fucking thing. That must mean I'm finally sane. And that's an excellent place to start going crazy again.

About the Author

Jim Dodge is the author of *Fup, Not Fade Away,* and three chapbooks of poetry. He lives in northern California.